DI...
PRIVATE HOUSE

'Now then, slave,' Max said. 'We're at the training room. You've probably realised that today you're a little puppy. You're going to be taught how to behave and be obedient. We'll turn you from an unruly puppy into a well-disciplined bitch.' He allowed himself a little smile.

'Therefore,' Ilsa continued, 'from the moment we lead you through that door we want to see you acting like a puppy. You will be boisterous. You will run and jump aimlessly – until such behaviour is beaten out of you, of course. You will be pathetically eager to please. The slightest failure to act in a puppyish manner will be regarded as a breach of your promise to remain submissive and obedient. And, as you are about to discover, today your adherence to your vow will be particularly closely monitored.'

A NEXUS CLASSIC

DISCIPLINE OF THE PRIVATE HOUSE

Esme Ombreux

'But nothing worth saying *is* proper!'
From *Candida* by George Bernard Shaw

This book is a work of fiction.
In real life, make sure you practise safe sex.

First published in 2000 by
Nexus
Thames Wharf Studios
Rainville Road
London W6 9HA

www.nexus-books.co.uk

ISBN 0 352 33709 5

Typeset by TW Typesetting, Plymouth, Devon
Printed and bound by
Mackays of Chatham plc, Chatham, Kent

One

The new girl – Ingrid, that was her name – was late. Julia stood in the darkness of the antechamber and tapped her riding-crop against the stiff leather of her boot. Flames flickered in niches along the corridor.

Julia heard a door open and close in the shadowy distance. Black-clad figures outlined in glimmering red approached. In their midst, a pale naked form.

'Blindfold her,' Julia whispered urgently as the guards drew near. 'Can't you remember simple instructions?'

Julia stepped from the doorway into the corridor and studied Ingrid as she struggled between two of the guards. Yes, this one would do: short, spiky blonde hair; wide cheekbones; a generous mouth, filled and held open by a ball gag; a slender body, pale as alabaster, with heavy breasts. Lustrous blue eyes that flashed defiance until concealed behind the black velvet blindfold. Despite the chains that pulled her wrist cuffs together behind her back and ran down to ankle restraints, the girl was fighting to be free. She tossed her head. The guard couldn't tighten the blindfold.

Julia lifted her crop. The flat tip touched the girl's left nipple, and she was abruptly still. 'Don't overdo it, Ingrid,' Julia said. 'A certain reluctance will be quite adequate. Charming, in fact. Understood?'

Ingrid nodded. She allowed the blindfold to be secured. Her breasts rose and fell. Reluctantly, Julia lowered her riding-crop. There would be plenty of time for that later, if Jem found Ingrid interesting.

1

Surely Jem would find this one interesting.

Julia hooked the crop's wrist-loop on to her belt and tugged the glove from her right hand. She flexed her fingers. Her hand was warm.

The girl was still now, but trembling. Bound and naked, she looked vulnerable among the stiffly uniformed guards.

'Are you cold?' Julia pressed the palm of her hand against the girl's cheek.

Ingrid shook her head, slowly, as if reluctant to lose contact with Julia's hand.

'My name's Julia. I'm the commander of the guards. The commander-in-chief.'

Ingrid sobbed through the gag and drew away, averting her face.

'You've already heard of me, then,' Julia whispered. 'I'm afraid all the rumours are true. But you needn't worry. As long as you perform well tonight. Just be a good girl.' Julia stroked her hand along the girl's jaw, down her throat, and cupped her left breast. 'Remember to keep your legs apart.'

Chains jingled as Ingrid shuffled her feet across the deep red carpet.

Julia squeezed her fingers into the soft mound of Ingrid's breast, and with her left hand pushed the empty leather glove between Ingrid's thighs and then upwards. The girl stretched her neck and sobbed again. Julia smiled briefly. This was taking up too much time. She didn't like to leave Jem's side, not this winter, not now the evenings were dark and long. But there was no alternative. The girl had to be made ready.

Julia rubbed the glove back and forth. She pinched the girl's nipple and was rewarded with a moan. She inspected the glistening glove by the ruddy light of a wall-torch, then pressed the damp leather into the hollow of the girl's neck.

'Feel that, little Ingrid? That's your wetness. I think you're ready to meet the Mistress of the Private House, don't you?'

From the room below came the sound of voices, male and female, raised in anger or excitement. Olena couldn't tell

2

which. Outside her window, closed and curtained against the cold night, were the noises of the street, still busy. So many people in the city; so many people with things to do, places to go. Other people to meet.

Olena turned on her back in the bed and stared at nothing in the darkened room. She was used to retiring soon after dusk and rising at dawn. Her rhythms were still those of her rural community. Yet she didn't feel tired this evening.

She envied Barat. He seemed to have adjusted easily to the ways of the city. She supposed he had been here previously. He was only a few years older than her, but he could find his way through the crowded streets. He rode the public omnibuses with ease. He understood the rapid, slurred diction of the people here: unlike Olena, he didn't have to ask meekly for simple questions to be repeated.

Without Barat, she wouldn't have been able to survive the first few days. The rushing traffic, the babble of voices, the insolent, curious stares. It was becoming more bearable: she knew the route from her tiny apartment to the University; she was no longer bewildered by the wickedly alluring abundance of wares in the shop on the corner of her street.

It was Barat who had persuaded her family that Olena should take up the opportunity of higher education: she was the first from the community to have earned the chance. And it was Barat who had volunteered to come with her to the city, to be her guardian and adviser. Only then had her family relented, reluctantly. So Olena felt and expressed over and over again to her family and to the elders – and, above all, to Barat – a gratitude that at times she thought would burst her heart. She was going to be able to study. It was her only passion.

And here she was, in this bustling, noisy, colourful, threatening place. She hugged herself and merely smiled, for it was unseemly for a young woman to laugh or cry out.

Now she had to rise and dress. Barat had asked her to come to his room. Nervously, she had asked him to

3

confirm the time of the meeting: he had specified an hour that she was sure was after nightfall. He had merely smiled his reassuring smile and insisted that the time would not be inappropriate; they were in the city now, and must learn to adopt those city customs that did not conflict absolutely with the ways of their rustic community.

Standing in the narrow space between the bed and the dressing table, Olena drew her nightdress over her head. It was dark in the room but she couldn't help catching a glimpse of her nakedness, reflected dimly in the mirror. She averted her eyes and groped for her bodice and pants.

She was shivering, and she knew that it was not entirely because of the cold. She had noticed on several occasions that the moments of nakedness as she changed made her think of Barat and his reassuring smile. So, too, did washing herself in the bath. Sometimes the scratchy texture of her underclothes made her think of him. And usually, when she thought of Barat, she felt shivery in a way that was not entirely unpleasant.

Olena sighed. Tears sprang into her eyes. She wasn't stupid; she could see the connections clearly enough. But she didn't understand why she felt the way she did, and she was almost certain that such feelings were sinful. After only a few days away, she was becoming a disgrace to her family and to the entire community.

She struggled with the heavy fabric of her dress. She tied the strings of her headdress under her chin. She knotted the laces of her shoes. She was ready. Perhaps Barat could explain things to her; if anyone could prevent her being tempted into transgressions, it was Barat.

The bed-sitting room was so tiny that Barat crossed it and reached the door in two strides. Two more brought him back to the bed; two more, and he was again at the door. He paced back and forth and tried not to think about Olena.

Great God, but he hated being poor. This room was scarcely bigger than Olena's. Neither was much bigger than one of the henhouses back home. The elders had tutted and sighed when he'd pointed out that he would need funds in order to keep himself and Olena in the city. They'd eventually agreed on a sum that they claimed to know was generous: brother Barat and the student girl would be able to live comfortably, well above the squalor and temptations that the elders knew, by repute, were to be found in the disreputable urban quarters.

What did the elders know? Nothing worth knowing, in Barat's opinion. More than half the money was already committed to these thin-walled cupboards that the landlord called 'studio accommodation'.

Barat sat on the bed. Olena would be here soon. He knew she would be punctual. There were advantages to small rooms, he thought. She would have to sit beside him on the bed; it would be perfectly natural if their knees were accidentally to touch. Her smell would fill the enclosed space: the dry-earth smell of her skin, and the sweet smell of the oil in her hair.

The room was illuminated by nothing but the weak bulb of the rickety bedside lamp. The half-light excited him. He had never before seen her after dark – except for the one vision of her that was engraved in his memory, even though it was three years ago that he had seen her naked. Newly adult, and now one of the brothers in the community, Barat had revelled in the freedom to wander through the village after dark. His nocturnal walks usually took him near the house of Olena's parents, as he had already noticed that Olena promised to grow into the prettiest maiden in the village. At the back of his mind was the desperate hope that one day, perhaps, the shutters of her room would be partly open and he might catch a glimpse of her hair, released from its headdress and spread across the pillow, or of her undergarments, drying before the fire.

And one evening he found that the shutter of the women's bedroom was indeed partly open. When he looked through the gap he could see nothing, as the room was in darkness. Olena, her mother and her sisters had all gone to bed at sunset and were no more than shapeless lumps stirring under heaps of blankets.

Then a sudden movement caught his eye; the coverings on one of the beds were thrown back; a slim, pale figure rose wraithlike in the darkness. It was Olena, naked, walking on tiptoe towards the window; Olena, far from shapeless, her swaying breasts already full despite her youth, her long legs converging in a mysterious delta of shadow that would haunt Barat's dreams for years to come; Olena, stepping towards the very window at which Barat stood transfixed.

She stopped only inches away from the opening between shutter and window frame. Barat saw her hair: long, dark and lustrous. He watched her dark eyes widen as she peered through the gloom. He saw her nipples stiffen in the chill draught; he saw her breasts tremble as she lifted her flawless arms to run her fingers through her hair. She leaned forwards; Barat could have reached through the gap and cupped one of her breasts in his hand. He was on the point of doing so when she found her nightdress and hurriedly turned away.

Olena had then covered herself quickly. Barat had stumbled away from the house, his movements made awkward because he was monstrously aroused.

From that evening Barat spared no effort in befriending Olena's family. He allowed no one to suspect that he was interested in, still less obsessed with, Olena. He studied hard, ingratiated himself with the elders, and was rewarded by being trusted to go on expeditions outside the community. The elders all agreed that he was the most promising of the younger brothers. But all he wanted was to have Olena to himself, away from the eyes and ears of the villagers. At first he had thought in terms of a few hours, or perhaps a day: time enough to find a private place – a cheap hotel or the heart of a deep wood – strip her naked, touch her soft body, and introduce her to the pleasures for which he had had to pay during his occasional trips to the outside world.

Barat laughed. The sound was loud in the tiny room. He still couldn't believe his luck. The old fools had given her to him. And not just for a day. Not even for a month. For

6

a whole academic year. Three years, if Olena didn't blab about him when they returned to the village next summer.

Barat looked again at the wristwatch he had bought that morning. She would be here in a few minutes. She was clever enough to come to the University, but she was hopelessly naive. Barat forced himself to remain calm. He willed his incipient erection to subside as he smoothed the rough cloth of his robe. He intended to debauch her thoroughly, but there was no need for haste. He would enjoy each lingering moment of her gradual descent into sin.

In the darkness behind the blindfold, Ingrid's imagination tried to conjure a picture of her surroundings. The carpet beneath her knees and shins – positioned well apart, as she had been instructed – was deep and soft. The guards had been dismissed and she could hear only two voices: one the cultured, modulated tones of the guards' commander, Julia, and the other – a husky voice with a slight drawl – obviously that of Jem Darke, the Mistress of the Private House, about whom Ingrid had heard so many rumours. The two women were speaking quietly but their voices echoed a little: Ingrid could easily imagine a high-ceilinged chamber, typical of the Gothic architecture of the rest of the House.

'She's not merely pretty,' Julia was saying, 'she's also very new. I had her brought to you as soon as I saw how delightfully she struggles under the lash. Would you like to see how quickly her bottom colours?'

Ingrid tossed her head in frustration. If only she could see the whip as it descended! Unable to see, she found herself imagining the swish of the lash's descent and, as if it were real, the sudden sting across her left buttock. Or would it be the right? Or both? The anticipation, in the black silence, was far worse than the harshest flogging.

The silence continued. Ingrid rattled her fetters and shook her hips. It would look as though she was struggling in her bonds, while all she wanted was for someone to touch her, with a hand or a whip, before it became evident that she was already becoming aroused. It would be difficult to maintain the pretence that she was an unwilling innocent if everyone could see that the very thought of her buttocks writhing as the lash rose and fell was enough to bring her on. Perhaps the room was full of spectators, after all; at that thought Ingrid felt again the warm tingling in her loins, and her labia beginning to part.

Julia was being less than entirely truthful. Ingrid was a recent arrival in the Private House, it was true, but she had come voluntarily and had already been in training for a week before she had been brought to the attention of the commander of the guards. She had herself told her Mentor, Anton, that since adolescence she had fantasised about being kidnapped, tied up and smacked, and Anton had wasted no time in putting Ingrid's fantasies into practice.

For a week Ingrid's bottom was punished once or twice a day. And each time the smacking stopped only when Ingrid had achieved a climax. The first time, laid comfortably across Anton's lap, with Anton's fingers stroking between her legs and his palm slapping softly on one cheek and then the other, she had taken almost ten minutes to come. By the second spanking of the third day, when Anton tied her legs apart and used a leather strap on her sore buttocks, Ingrid had started to come within seconds of his fingers sliding from her wet vagina towards her erect clitoris. After that she had been caned while being penetrated by one of the male guards; whipped while tied up with a buzzing vibrator secured inside her; made to hold her buttocks apart for a particularly painful caning while squatting astride the face of one of her fellow trainees; and, most humiliating and exciting of all, spanked while using her own fingers to bring on her climax, while being closely watched by a squad of Mentors and guards. Each time, the pain spurred her on to orgasm, at which point the punishment was stopped.

The daily smackings suddenly ceased. For three days no one had so much as touched Ingrid's bottom or clitoris; she had even had her hands tied to the bedhead at night, to prevent her playing with herself. Anton had merely told her that she was being prepared for something special. Now she understood: she was to be a present from Julia to the Mistress. And she had to appear new and unwilling, it seemed, because the Mistress's appetites had become jaded.

'Yes, Jules.' The Mistress's husky voice sounded tired but amused. 'You're right, of course. It will be entertaining to see her whipped, and she is certainly pretty. So carry on, by all means.'

Ingrid imagined the Mistress as a tall woman of ageless beauty and aristocratic languor. She sounded weary. Julia's voice was bright and animated but, with the sensitivity of the temporarily blind, Ingrid thought she could detect an undercurrent of anxiety, perhaps even desperation, beneath the commander's gaiety.

'Would you like to whip her yourself?' Julia asked. 'You really should keep in practice. Or she could kneel in front of your chair and you could hold her breasts while I whip her bottom.'

'She does have very tempting tits,' the Mistress said, and Ingrid shuddered as she felt slim fingers press against her left nipple. 'Take off the gag and the blindfold,' the Mistress added with sudden decisiveness. 'If she's lively and intelligent, this one could keep me occupied for tonight. Maybe longer.'

'Yes, Jem,' the commander said, with what Ingrid suspected was a sigh of relief.

Ingrid sensed Julia moving behind her; she felt fingers unbuckling the harness at the back of her head. She heard the whistle of leather through the air and, as the gag was pulled from her mouth, Julia's crop landed between her parted buttocks. She let out a howl of surprise and relief that, she realised, was indistinguishable from a cry of outrage.

The crop landed again as the blindfold fell away. She gasped, and blinked her eyes because she had expected to be dazzled by sudden light. In fact, the room was dimly lit, but she hoped that the spectators could see the bright tears she had managed to produce.

9

While tossing her head in order to look defiant, she glanced about the candlelit chamber and was disappointed to find that Julia and the Mistress constituted the entire audience.

The Mistress was in front of her, sitting in an armchair. Kneeling with her head bowed, Ingrid could see only the Mistress's feet, which were small and clad in pointed, black velvet ankle-boots, and her stockinged legs. Ingrid lifted her head and found herself gazing into huge, quizzical, violet eyes.

Jem Darke bore no resemblance to the Mistress Ingrid had imagined. She was slim, but petite and not remotely aristocratic or languorous. Her hair was a tumble of titian curls, her face was heart-shaped and elfin, and her lips were wide, kissable and curved into a mischievous smile. She was the prettiest woman Ingrid had seen in the Private House, which was full of beauties. And she looked like a lot of fun.

'What big blue eyes you have,' the Mistress said as she stood up and stepped towards Ingrid. 'It's against the rules to stare, little one.'

Ingrid knew the rules, but she couldn't take her eyes off Jem. The Mistress was dressed in a black velvet bodice that drew attention to the uncovered parts of her body: tightly cinched, long-sleeved and high-collared, it left her throat and breasts exposed. At the front of the collar there was a silver ring from which two taut silver chains ran to delicate clamps on her nipples. The skirt of the bodice, like those of Julia's guards, was cut away at the front to reveal the Mistress's pubic mound, which was shaved. Each black stocking was held up by a single silver chain; the chains ran up between the Mistress's thighs, and Ingrid could only imagine how they were held in place.

'You shouldn't be looking at me, slave,' the Mistress said, and sank to her knees so that her face was only a finger's length from Ingrid's. 'But as you insist, let's see how expressive those big blue eyes can be. Move your knees further apart. Dip your back, and push your bottom out.'

10

Ingrid remembered, too late, that she was supposed to appear reluctant. The Mistress's eyes held hers, and she could only stare imploringly. She wanted to be touched. She pulled at the chains that held her hands behind her back, hoping that the movement would draw Jem's attention to her pendant breasts.

'Give her ten, Julia. Not too hard.'

Ingrid tried to look shocked and hurt as the burning stripes were laid across her buttocks. Ten strokes were just enough to ignite the smouldering warmth throughout her lower body that she had come to expect and yearn for at Anton's hands.

'Now put your hand between her legs, Julia. Tell me whether she's getting excited. And no evasions!'

Ingrid felt Julia's gloved fingers suddenly and ungently thrust against her vulva. There was no resistance; her outer labia were already distended and open, and within she was sopping wet. She felt her face colour as the withdrawal of Julia's fingers caused a distinctly liquid sound.

'She is a little moist, Mistress,' Julia said.

Jem's eyebrows lifted sceptically. 'Is that so?' she said, toying idly with Ingrid's stiff nipples.

It was obvious that Julia's understatement was not going to deceive Jem. Ingrid bit her lower lip to stifle her moans of pleasure as the Mistress's skilful fingers plucked at her breasts, but she could feel her juices trickling from her sex and down her thighs.

The Mistress stood. She was so close that merely by extending her tongue Ingrid could have licked her depilated cunt. The Mistress smelt of musk and citrus.

'Come here, Julia,' the Mistress said. 'And give me your riding-crop.'

The commander's leather tunic gleamed in the candle-light and creaked as she kneeled beside Ingrid. She proffered the crop. 'Mistress,' she began, but Jem silenced her with a gesture.

The Mistress studied the kneeling women. Ingrid took the opportunity to look covertly at Julia.

The commander of the guard of the Private House, Jem

11

Darke's confidante and adviser and, it was rumoured, most frequent lover, was a striking woman. She was older than the Mistress, but had ageless, gypsy looks and a lithe body. Her curling black hair shielded her face from Ingrid's glances, but Ingrid remembered dark, troubled eyes and a mouth of vivid red. Her black leather uniform – skirted tunic, gloves and long boots – left exposed only her shoulders, her concave belly, and the tops of her thighs.

'What am I to do with you, Commander?' the Mistress said, clearly not requiring a reply. 'This pretty young thing would be a delight to play with, I'm sure. But then, the same could be said of the muscular guy you brought to me two nights ago, and the twins of whom you promised so much last week. And so on, since the beginning of the fall. I want to be entertained, Julia.'

Julia spoke in a low voice, without lifting her head. 'You would be less bored, Mistress, if you were to resume your interest in the running of the Private House. Since you delegated all authority to the Council –'

'Hush now,' the Mistress said. 'I've made my decision. The Private House can run itself. Why, I appointed and trained every single one of the Council members. They don't need me. But *you* need a lesson. Advance to the chair and present yourself for punishment.'

Julia sighed and shuffled on her knees to the chair. As she reached to sweep her hair over her right shoulder, Ingrid saw that she was smiling ruefully. She crossed her arms on the seat of the chair and leaned forwards until her head was resting on her arms. Her stiff skirt lifted to reveal slim, deeply separated buttocks.

The Mistress seemed suddenly playful. She tapped Ingrid's nipples with the tip of the crop, making them tingle and sway. She suddenly leaned forwards and greedily kissed Ingrid's open mouth. 'You must count the strokes I give Julia,' she said, pressing the plaited leather into Ingrid's bosom, 'and tell me when she's had enough. Then you'll get the same here, on your breasts.' Her lips descended again, and Ingrid responded eagerly. 'Would you like that?'

Ingrid nodded. Yes, she wanted to see the haughty commander whipped, and she wanted to feel the whip on her own tits. But how many lashes? The way she felt at that moment, Jem could have whipped her for ever. But she had never been punished that way. How many would she want?

'Remember to count, little one,' Jem said. She knelt beside Julia and started to whip Julia's buttocks.

The Mistress used the riding-crop almost coquettishly, seldom lifting her arm high but from time to time flicking her wrist to deliver a particularly telling blow. She spent more time caressing Julia than punishing her, stroking the reddening globes or dipping her hand between Julia's thighs and then tracing with a wet finger a fading crimson line on Julia's flesh.

Her left hand was busy, too, between her own thighs, and Ingrid thought that as the Mistress became more aroused she grew more intent on playing with Julia and kissing her bottom than with punishing her. Ingrid wondered whether she should count as whip-strokes the playful little flicks that the Mistress administered between kisses and the little pushes of the crop's end against Julia's anus and vulva. Both Julia and Jem were moving their hips in a gentle rhythm and giving little moans of pleasure. Ingrid could hardly prevent herself from moaning aloud, too, from sheer frustration.

Jem removed her hand at length from the wetness of her sex, and leaned forwards to push her fingers into Julia's mouth. 'See how wet you've made me,' she murmured. 'Open your legs wider, my darling, and push your bottom out more.'

Julia, sucking on her Mistress's fingers, obeyed. Ingrid gazed longingly at Julia's taut, red-striped buttocks, the mass of black curls between her thighs dripping with moisture, and the deep cavern of the cleft of her arse. 'I expect you'd like me to finger your anus,' Jem said, and barely waited for Julia's grunt of assent before dropping the crop and delving with her slim fingers into the dark crevice. Ingrid could see Jem's fingers circling, prising and pushing. Julia gave a delighted groan and suckled the

13

fingers of Jem's other hand. Jem rested her cheek against Julia's bottom, watched her fingers working at Julia's anus, and then closed her eyes contentedly.

The two women had obviously made love in this way many times before. Ingrid felt she would burst with impatience. When would the Mistress remember *her*?

'I don't know why you bother to bring me new slaves,' Jem said dreamily. 'I could easily spend every night with you.' She removed her fingers from Julia's cleft and instead pressed her face between Julia's buttocks.

Julia pulled her face away from Jem's left hand. 'That's almost unbearably pleasant,' she said. 'But you know,' she added sadly, 'that one of us, at least, has to attend to our duties. I have to work every day. Your withdrawal from affairs makes it harder for me to keep control out there. You can't expect me to keep you amused all night, too.'

Jem, her lipstick spread around her pretty mouth, had pulled away from Julia's anus. 'Still the same old refrain,' she said. 'Jules, you know I don't want to hear this. Lift yourself up on to your elbows and unbutton your tunic. I'm going to hurt your nipples.'

Julia gave a snort of rueful laughter and obeyed. Ingrid saw her body flinch as the fingers of Jem's left hand held and pinched her left nipple. Jem picked up the crop and delivered ten quick, hard lashes. Five vivid stripes appeared on each of Julia's reddened buttocks. Julia cried out and tossed her mane of black hair.

'And how many is that?' Jem asked, turning suddenly to Ingrid.

Ingrid swallowed. She had been counting, but now that she had to volunteer the total as the number of strokes her breasts would receive, the figure seemed insupportably large. 'Sixty-seven, Mistress,' she whispered.

'How very precise,' Jem said, and released her grip on Julia's nipple. Julia gasped and lowered her body back on to the seat of the chair.

A little while later Ingrid, her hands still bound behind her back and still kneeling with her knees wide apart, had counted up to thirty-three: thirty-three times the crop had

14

stroked her breasts. Julia was sitting behind her; through a mist of swarming sensations Ingrid was sure that at least one of Julia's fingers had some time ago penetrated into her arsehole, and from time to time Julia touched her elsewhere, with a caress close to her clitoris or a pinch of one of her distended labia. It was as if Julia knew that any more frequent contact would cause Ingrid to climax.

Ingrid's breasts were hot and tingling and felt as though they had expanded to twice their normal size. Jem, who had stepped back to admire the handiwork she had already wrought on Ingrid's breasts, leaned forwards and swung the riding-crop upwards so that the leather flap at its end slapped against the underside of Ingrid's right breast. Ingrid gasped as she felt the sting, and almost came as the trembling of her breast echoed the vibration that travelled along her body and into her loins. Her clitoris pulsed. This was even better than having her bottom spanked by Anton.

'Thirty-four, Mistress,' Ingrid said.

Jem laughed happily. 'She certainly does seem to be enjoying this,' she said. 'Jules, how many fingers have you got up her arse?'

Ingrid felt a circular movement in her anus, and blushed.

'Just the one, so far, Jem,' Julia said.

'Time to double up, then, I reckon,' Jem said. 'I guess there's no shortage of lubrication?'

Ingrid closed her eyes and felt her face flushing more hotly as Julia's fingers, with a slithering sound, explored her open vagina. She felt Jem's cool hand cupping and stroking the hot mass of her left breast; she felt Julia's fingers between her buttocks and the addition of cooling moisture there. There followed a pressure against her opening, a spasm of discomfort, the moment of yielding, and then the solid, stretching knowledge that two of Julia's digits were now embedded inside her.

'I find that having something up my bottom always makes my breasts feel more sensitive,' Jem said conversationally. Then she brought the crop swiftly sideways against Ingrid's right breast, catching the nipple. 'Do you agree, little one?'

15

It was no longer pain or pleasure; it was a jolt of pure sensation, sparking from Ingrid's nipple to her anus, and only then melting into a glow of hurting warmth in her breast and simmering heat in her sex.

'Ah. Oh, yes, Mistress,' Ingrid breathed. 'Thirty-five.'

Jem laughed again. 'How very cute,' she said, stroking Ingrid's burning face. 'Why, my breasts are beginning to feel jealous of yours. When this is finished, little one, I'll show you how to give me pleasure with my nipple clamps. I hope you're feeling cruel.'

Ten strokes, five to each breast, followed hard and fast before the Mistress paused again and allowed Ingrid to recover her composure.

'She almost came,' Julia murmured. 'I hardly touched her. Shall I let her come while you're whipping her?'

'Not yet, Jules. Maybe right at the end. We mustn't be too kind to newcomers. They have to learn the value of restraint. She wouldn't be permitted to come if she were being trained at the Chateau, for instance.'

'The Chatelaine runs an exemplary establishment,' Julia said drily. 'But it's not a regime that suits everyone. Still,' she added pensively, moving her two rigid fingers back and forth, 'perhaps this one would benefit from the experience.'

Jem leaned forwards and took Ingrid's right breast between her two hands. She squeezed the heated flesh, moulding it into a smooth bulb. 'At the Chateau,' she said to Ingrid, 'they would bind your breasts, after a certain amount of punishment, to keep them swollen and firm, like this. And then the Chatelaine would probably insist on the use of a cane, or a strap; not a toy like this ceremonial riding-crop. Would you learn to enjoy such severe pleasures, little one?'

Ingrid had no idea. The sensation of the Mistress's cool hands squeezing her punished breast while Julia's fingers moved gently inside her had brought her to the brink of orgasm. 'I don't know, Mistress,' she gasped. And then, perhaps because she had been thinking about how she would use the nipple clamps to pinch the crinkly skin of Jem's areolae, she blurted out, 'Would you? Oh, I'm sorry,

16

Mistress. But I thought, well, you obviously enjoy, you know, this sort of thing. But do you enjoy being on the receiving end? Maybe you'd like that as well. Or even more.'

There was a silence. Ingrid looked up, and was surprised to see Jem in a reverie, with a faraway look clouding her violet eyes and a curious smile on her lips.

'Maybe,' Jem said softly. 'Maybe that's –'

Julia interrupted. 'Maybe it's not a good idea to dredge up old memories,' she said firmly. 'The Private House needs you to be in control, Jem. And as for this little minx: I think she needs the gag again.'

'No, it's all right, Jules, honey. I'm not going soft on you. And you mustn't gag my little one: I have plans for that wide, luscious mouth of hers. She's mine for tonight, anyway,' the Mistress said. 'And I don't intend to let her forget who's in charge. Kneel up. Curve your back inwards. That's right.' Jem also knelt and prepared to resume the punishment of Ingrid's breasts.

'And that means I might get some sleep tonight,' Julia said, and placed a kiss on the small of Ingrid's back.

The far-reaching establishment called the Chateau, which was itself a part of the organisation known as the Private House, had at its centre a moated, conical-towered Renaissance palace. This luxuriously converted fortress was in a country separated by sea and many miles of land from the rambling mansion within which Jem was entertaining herself with Ingrid. But national boundaries and geographical distance were irrelevant to the Private House.

The Chatelaine was working late. Nicole was sitting at the end of the long leather-topped desk, outside the pool of light cast by the lamp. Only her hand, holding a pen, and the squared paper on which she was writing notes were illuminated. The Chatelaine was in the penumbra of the lamplight. Nicole could discern her slim, upright form, the sheen of her tightly fitting gown, and the precise movements of her hands as she picked through the papers arranged in neat piles on the desk.

'The report on the slave Gregor is incomplete,' the Chatelaine said. 'I'm sure he was due to be fitted with a larger anal plug today.' She sounded amused. 'Perhaps Trudi forgot about it. I've noticed that she's taken quite a liking to Gregor: once she's brought on his arousal she can't wait to sit astride his face and torment that large member of his while he pleasures her with his tongue.'

Nicole giggled. 'The poor fellow is almost continuously erect, madame,' she said. 'Trudi has only to walk close to him and he becomes hard. Even when he's wearing a control belt. It must be unbearably uncomfortable.'

'As it should be,' the Chatelaine stated. 'Make a note, Nicole, to have the report checked. If Trudi has allowed her own enjoyment of a slave to make her forgetful, then she will wear the plug tomorrow. That should act as a reminder.'

Nicole wrote, and shifted her naked buttocks: it was not many days since she had suffered a similar indignity.

'That's everything for this evening, Nicole, except for the matter of our two strays. Would you ring for Robert?'

Nicole stood. Her eyes were accustomed to the gloom, and she made her way easily across the wide chamber to the row of brass buttons next to the gaping stone fireplace. The orange embers were still radiating heat, but very little light.

As she threaded her way back between the black shapes of chaises longues, settees and armchairs, Nicole noticed that the Chatelaine was no longer seated at the desk. She looked around; a muted gleam caught her eye. The Chatelaine had moved to the leather-upholstered recliner; she was almost lying in it, rather than sitting, and her silvery gown had parted to reveal her long, slender, silk-clad legs. Nicole felt a thrill of anticipation.

'Bring two pairs of cuffs from the desk,' the Chatelaine said, without looking up. 'And take your clothes off.'

As usual when on duty in the Chatelaine's chamber, Nicole was wearing very little. As she removed her lace bra she felt her nipples harden. It nearly always fell to Nicole or to one of the other staff to amuse and arouse the

Chatelaine at least once a day, if none of the slaves or visitors had been selected for the purpose. But it had been some time since Nicole had been chained. And tonight, Nicole knew, Robert was on his way. By the time he was summoned into the room, Nicole would be naked and on her knees in front of the reclining chair – with her face pressed against the Chatelaine's sex.

Nicole removed her shoes and stockings. As she leaned forwards she felt the insides of her thighs squeeze her labia. She was already excited.

'Come along, Nicole. Let me look at you.' The Chatelaine's eyes gleamed in the darkness. She could have formed only a general impression of Nicole, her form outlined by the distant half-light from the lamp and the fading fire: a slim, pale body; short dark hair; white teeth in a broad slash of a mouth; pert breasts.

'Kneel,' the Chatelaine said. 'Give me the cuffs. Place your wrists here, on the arms of the chair.' The cuffs clicked. Nicole was secured. 'Move your legs wider apart, Nicole. Start just above my knees. Kisses only, at first. I'll tell you when you may begin licking.'

Nicole lowered her head between the Chatelaine's parted thighs. She didn't need to be reminded to curve her back downwards and to push up her bottom; such displays had become part of her nature. She breathed in the Chatelaine's clean smell, with the merest hint of subtle perfume. She brushed her lips against the silk of a stocking-top, and kissed the cool, flawless skin above it.

There was a loud knock at the door. Nicole knew better than to allow herself to be distracted. She continued to press her lips against the insides of the Chatelaine's thighs.

'Enter,' the Chatelaine said. The door opened and then closed again. Nicole heard footsteps, loud on the flagstones, muffled on the Persian rugs.

'Robert, I need to talk to you about the couple who have gone missing. I know it's late, but I'd like to formulate a plan as soon as possible.'

'Of course, madame,' said the Chatelaine's deputy.

'I don't believe Nicole has been punished today,' the

Chatelaine went on. 'She's been perfectly well behaved, of course, but I believe she relishes a touch of the whip while she's servicing me. Or perhaps you'd like to penetrate her in some way?'

Nicole pressed her mouth against the hood of the Chatelaine's clitoris and lifted her bottom higher. She didn't like Robert, but she was in the mood for having her bottom smacked, and she was feeling so aroused that she would enjoy being fucked or sodomised by a man – even by the Chatelaine's hateful deputy.

'As you wish, madame,' Robert said. Nicole could hear the gloating in his voice. 'Perhaps I could suggest that I should apply my belt in the first instance, while we talk. Then, with the help of a dildo, I could penetrate Nicole twice, simultaneously, while she attends to your pleasure.'

Nicole could imagine Robert's sinister smile. The Chatelaine rarely found his suggestions other than acceptable. Nicole heard his heavy leather belt sliding through his fingers. She kissed the Chatelaine's smooth labia. She felt a bubble of excitement expand inside her. This was going to be painful, exhausting and very enjoyable.

'A good idea, Robert,' the Chatelaine said. 'Don't be gentle with her.'

Barat heard slow footsteps on the bare floor of the hall. After a while, there was a tap on the door. Olena had arrived.

Barat adjusted the bedside lamp one more time, tilting the shade to ensure that he would be in shadow while what little illumination the lamp provided would fall on the farther end of the single bed. He had covered the chair with books; Olena would have nowhere to sit but beside him, in the pale pool of light.

He waited. Olena knocked again, two tentative taps.

'Come in,' he said, keeping his voice low and controlled.

The door opened. Olena stood in the doorway, silhouetted against the harsh yellow light in the hallway. In spite of the swathes of rough cloth that the ridiculous

20

customs of their community condemned women to be cocooned in, he saw – or craved, or imagined – the bountiful curves of her body.

'Brother Barat?' she whispered.

'Come in,' he repeated. 'Close the door. And you may address me as "Barat",' he added. He thought that he might as well continue to take even the smallest of opportunities to undermine her faith in the community's ways. She closed the door and stood uncertainly in the shadows.

'These rooms are so small,' he continued conversationally. 'And the landlords don't provide much in the way of lighting. You can sit here, next to me.'

'On the bed?' she said.

He allowed himself a smile. Even if she could see it, she would interpret it as reassuring. He found her voice delightfully timid.

'Where else?'

She lowered herself on to the bed. The mattress was old and soft. She couldn't help leaning towards him, and jerked upright when her shoulder touched his.

'Sorry, brother,' she said.

'It's nothing,' Barat said. 'It's not like our country village here. So many people, so little space. We will have to learn not to mind touching occasionally.'

She turned to look at him. Heavens, but she was lovely. Her skin was lighter than his: the colour of milky coffee, and without a blemish. Such huge, dark eyes. Such full lips.

'Lean on my shoulder again. Just to demonstrate that there's no harm in it.'

She looked shocked. 'Again? But –'

He placed his hand on her back and pulled her towards him. She hardly resisted. He had to restrain an exclamation of joy. She wanted him. It was obvious.

Her shoulder came to rest against his. She was close enough to kiss.

'There,' he said. 'That's not so bad, is it? There's so little room in here. The commandments permit us to make allowances for the situations we find ourselves in.'

21

'Do they?' she asked. She smelt of soap and perfumed oil. 'So this isn't sinful?'

'Of course not,' Barat assured her. 'After all, I'm your guardian here. The elders appointed me to look after you. You can trust me.'

He heard her sigh. 'That's all right, then,' she said.

They sat in silence for a while, and then both started talking at once. Olena giggled.

'What is it?' Barat said.

'That's what I was going to ask you,' she said, laughing and displaying little white teeth. 'What is it you asked me here for?'

'Oh, all the usual things,' Barat said, taking the opportunity to lay a hand casually on her knee. Two pats, and remove the hand: mustn't make her anxious. 'How are you finding the work at college, are you managing to sleep in that tiny room. That sort of thing.'

He didn't wait for a reply. He knew that she found the college course straightforward, and that she didn't like her room. 'Don't you find the omnibuses oppressive? And do you think that people stare at you in the streets?'

'Perhaps,' Olena replied. 'Yes, I think they look at me. I don't like it.'

'I think it's because of our robes,' Barat said sadly. 'And, in your case, the headdress, of course. That must look very strange to the city people.'

Unlike Olena, Barat had spent some considerable time walking through the streets of the city, particularly in the seamier quarters, and he was aware that in this cosmopolitan environment even the most outlandish costume would pass unremarked. But he guessed that Olena felt self-conscious.

'You can take the headdress off,' Barat announced, and added, to allay her fears before she could state them: 'We're alone. I'm your guardian, I'm here in place of your mother and father. You would let your mother see you with your hair loose. It's all right.'

Olena was already reaching for the pins and the ties that held the ornate structure in place on her head. The thing

22

must be intolerably uncomfortable, Barat thought; I'll have no difficulty persuading her that she need not wear it very often. Perhaps not at all, while we're in the city.

And she had such lustrous hair. Barat found himself reaching to touch it, and as Olena gazed at him he managed to turn the gesture into a wave of approval. Her locks, dark and wavy as the night-time ocean, fell to her shoulders and halfway down her back. She shook her head, and her tresses shimmered.

'That's better,' Barat said. 'If you would prefer it, you can go without the headdress. Perhaps not when out in public, but certainly in your own room and when you're with me.'

'Thank you, Barat,' she said.

He noticed that this time she had addressed him by name alone, without his formal title. Her cheeks were flushed and, although her head was lowered, she was continually looking up at him.

He smiled at her. She had to rely on him; she knew no one else in the entire city. She would do whatever he instructed her to do, as long as he could convince her that the community's rules could be interpreted sufficiently widely. And he sensed that she wanted to be convinced.

'Let me put my arm around you,' he said, 'to symbolise my protection of you.'

Olena didn't protest. He held her. He could feel her heart beating. Silently he cursed the layers of cloth between their bodies.

'Tomorrow,' he said, 'after your morning lecture, would you like to visit some shops? You know that I have been entrusted with a small sum with which to keep you clothed. I don't think the elders could object if we were to find you some clothing that made you a little less conspicuous in the street. And perhaps some more comfortable, simple clothes for you to wear when you're in your room and when you're with me. What do you think?'

'I'd like that, Barat. If you're sure it's all right.'

'Of course it is. Now, kneel in front of me. We'll say our prayers.'

23

Olena kneeled and lowered her head over her hands, which were clasped together only a finger's length in front of Barat's knees. Barat prayed devoutly: he prayed for the day when the two of them would be like this, but naked, with Olena's slim fingers curled around the shaft of his erection. He knew he could make his prayers come true.

'So it's decided,' the Chatelaine said. 'You'll send Stefan and Itomi to find and bring back our wandering twosome. It's that tall, dark-haired fellow Heinrich, isn't it? And who is with him?'

The steady rhythm of Robert's lashes seemed to Nicole to slow a little as he considered his reply. 'Leila,' he said. 'A young girl. Much admired. It's difficult, madame, to prevent some of the trainees from forming attachments to each other.'

'No doubt. And you're sure this won't be a case of sending out two incompetents to round up two miscreants?'

Robert delivered a quick, stinging lash to Nicole's sore bottom. He seemed reluctant to bring the discussion to a close. 'Stefan and Itomi aren't incompetent,' he said. 'Merely inexperienced.'

His belt landed again, on Nicole's left buttock. The tip caught the sensitive skin of her perineum. Her yelp was muffled because she was in the middle of kissing along the length of the Chatelaine's labia.

'And the missing couple should be easy to find,' Robert went on. 'They are never apart. They can't bear to wear anything but the leather harnesses they became accustomed to wearing here, and so during the day, when outside, they shroud themselves in very distinctive long robes. They look like a mendicant monk and nun. Even Stefan and Itomi should be able to track them down. We know which part of the city they were sent to live in.'

'They're probably just having too much fun to report in,' the Chatelaine said. 'They're young and headstrong. And they will have to be chastised most severely.'

'Talking of fun, madame,' Robert said, 'may I point out

that Nicole's posterior is now bright red, and she's quite obviously ready for penetration. In fact, she's almost dripping.'

'Not so fast, Robert,' the Chatelaine said. 'Nicole is here for *my* benefit, not yours. Press your mouth hard against me, Nicole. That's right. Now push your tongue inside. That's lovely. Now, Robert, give her ten more strokes. Very hard. I want to feel Nicole being pushed into me with each one.'

Somewhere in the midst of the ensuing blaze of pain that engulfed her rear end, Nicole felt the Chatelaine's hands grasping her head, and the Chatelaine's thighs clasping her face, and the Chatelaine's voice urging Robert to strike harder. Nicole's mouth was running with the Chatelaine's sharp juices. Her world had been reduced to the taste and smell of the Chatelaine's hot vulva; the burning, throbbing pain of her arse; and the equally insistent throbbing of her clitoris and nipples, demanding attention.

Nicole dimly heard Robert's voice. 'With your permission, madame, I'll insert the large ivory phallus into Nicole's vagina, and for her anus I'll use this.'

'Very impressive, Robert, as ever. Lubricate her well, first.'

'Of course, madame,' Robert said. Nicole thought he sounded thwarted. She felt his fingers delving into her sex and smearing her wetness around and into her anus. 'I'll ride her hard, madame, so that you can feel the thrusts.'

'How very considerate,' the Chatelaine said. 'Nicole, you can start licking now.'

It felt to Olena curiously wicked to leave on a light – even the dim illumination of the bedside lamp – as she undressed. Vanity was a sin, but she couldn't resist the idea of looking at her body reflected in the mirror. For the first few days she had kept the small mirror turned to face the wall, but Barat had told her that it was all right to use it, in order to check her appearance before leaving for college, for instance. It still felt wicked to pick it up and use it to inspect her own naked body. And even if that wasn't a sin, she was sure that there was something wicked and shameful about the feelings that she had when she thought about Barat, or her body: the warmth between the tops of her thighs, and the sinking sensation, like being scared but much nicer, in the pit of her stomach.

Her breasts – she said the word to herself, in a whisper, and shuddered – seemed to have grown each time she looked at them. She was sure they were larger than those of any of the other young women on her course. Olena liked her breasts. She knew it was naughty to touch them other than when strictly necessary, of course, but when she was washing herself, or dressing, she sometimes found herself stroking them. It felt very pleasant. The skin of her breasts was soft, yet she found that as she caressed them her breasts became firmer. She liked the fact that they were now so large and round that they looked almost too big for her girlish chest and shoulders; when she lay on her back in bed, her breasts would overlap her armpits; standing, she could create a deep valley between them by moving her arms together only slightly.

When she heard her fellow students talking about the necessity of padded underwear and low-cut dresses for making the most of their busts, Olena felt smug – which was a sin – and, even worse, she felt envious of their freedom to display such charms as they had.

But Barat had said that she could have some different clothes. Perhaps, while they were shopping, she would dare to suggest that she should have some new underclothes, too. She knew the kinds of things that young women wore here in the city; she averted her eyes but she couldn't help catching glimpses of advertisements for lingerie and swimming costumes. In fact, some of the clothes that the students wore were so sheer that she could see the underwear beneath.

She imagined her breasts no longer compressed within the stiff bodices that she had brought with her from home, but instead supported in cups of coloured lace. She imagined wearing a diaphanous dress, with nothing underneath but a tiny pair of panties. It was so pleasurable

26

to have such imaginings; surely they couldn't be sinful? But she knew they were.

She moved the mirror lower and found herself looking at the reflection of the deeply shadowed triangle of dark curls below her belly. She looked away quickly; this area seemed to her to be the centre and source of the wicked feelings she was having.

Instead, she held the mirror at her hip and twisted her head in an attempt to see her bottom. This was, she knew, a part of her body almost as forbidden as the area between her legs, but she had heard the other girls on her course talking quite openly about their own bottoms – usually complaining that they were too big – and also, to Olena's amazement, discussing the bottoms of some of the male students.

Olena was as pleased with her bottom as she was with her breasts. It, too, seemed to have become rounder and fuller in recent months, while her waist and legs had remained slim. It had occurred to Olena that she had a secret: everyone thought that her body was as shapeless as the heavy robes she wore, but in fact she had a figure that was both trimmer and fuller than those of the lingerie and swimwear models she had glimpsed in pictures.

Suddenly she realised that she had been admiring her own body for at least ten minutes. Her behaviour was becoming worse and worse. It was so difficult, in the crowded city, to keep to the rules of the community. She was so glad that Barat was with her.

What would Barat say if he found her naked, looking at her own bottom in a mirror? The thought of being discovered by Barat didn't seem to dismay her as much as she had expected it to. In fact, it made her feel warmer, and shivery, in that forbidden place between her legs. Barat would see every part of her body. He would admire her breasts. Perhaps he would decide that such wickedness deserved to be punished. Many of the children in the community had been spanked by their parents, with the elders' permission, when they had been naughty. Would Barat insist on spanking her – on her naked bottom?

Olena shuddered. She realised that her daydreaming had taken her into depths of sinful carnality. She moved her hand, the fingers of which had been sliding down the inward curve of her stomach as if possessed of a will of their own.

She threw the mirror on to the chair. Thank goodness Barat was with her. He would prevent her from going astray.

Two

The meeting was interminable. Jem, at the head of the table, had gazed over the heads of her councillors, through the mullioned windows and out into the wild parkland where the dismal day had darkened gradually into dusk and then night. Silently, servants had lit lamps.

And still they talked. Every item on the agenda was discussed and dissected, and each debate led into a maze of corollaries and codicils, until no one could remember what the original item had been. They make it seem such hard work, Jem thought. She was able to follow the ebb and flow of the conversation with barely half her mind and when, as frequently happened, one or other of the disputants appealed to her for guidance, she was able to dispense advice that seemed temporarily to quell the strife. But she found the whole thing very dull.

I'm not bored just with this, Jem thought as the discussion moved on to the topic of the arrangements for a meeting of the full High Council of the Private House; I'm bored with myself. In fact, that's probably the root of the whole problem. I need to change myself somehow. The Private House doesn't need me any more, except as a figurehead.

Julia had insisted that at a meeting such as this Jem should be seen in her official costume: the ornate version of the black uniform worn by Julia and her corps of guards. Jem had therefore insisted on dressing otherwise, and had arrayed herself in a confection of white lace and pink ribbons: pink high-heeled pumps, white lace

29

stockings, a pink suspender belt, a very short skirt of flouncy white tulle, and pink ribbons binding her torso and breasts in the eastern bondage style. And, because she was the Supreme Mistress, her managers had expertly concealed their initial surprise. Each one, on entering the council chamber, had complimented her on the prettiness of her outfit.

But not one of them put a hand up my skirt, or offered to bed me or to spank me, Jem thought. I suppose it's my own fault. I know they're whispering that I'm moody. I prefer to call it capricious. And it's just how I am. Or how I wish I could be, again.

They need shaking up.

Jem pushed her chair back and lifted her feet on to the council table. The councillors glanced at her. She moved her feet apart, slowly. They all glanced at her again; looked away; looked back. She brought her right hand to her face and placed two fingers into her mouth. She licked her fingers. Although she was sitting in shadow, they could all see what she was doing.

She withdrew her fingers from her mouth and trailed them down her body, lingering for a moment to toy with her nipples before letting her hand drop into her lap. She cupped the bulge of her sex. The managers were pretending not to notice her movements, but she knew they were watching her, and that knowledge was making her wet.

With her left hand she gestured to one of the servants. He was a tall man, no longer young but slender and, Jem knew, possessed of an impressive manhood. He approached her chair and leaned towards her.

'Yes, Mistress?' he whispered.

'I want to play with your cock, Philip,' Jem said, in a less quiet voice.

Philip straightened, moved closer to Jem, and unbuttoned the flap at the front of his breeches. Jem took his member in her hand and felt it begin to harden and swell. She caught the odour of male sex emanating from his genitals, and slipped one of her fingers into the moist opening of her own sex. This, she thought, was the way to cope with long meetings.

'Carry on,' she said to the room at large. She shrugged, and enjoyed the tightening of the ribbons around her breasts. 'This is the Private House, after all. And I am your Mistress.'

Itomi had been born and brought up in a city in the Orient, but she still found Western cities exciting. She knew that, with her long straight hair, almond eyes and girlish body, she looked exotic to these people. Since she had undergone training, first at the hands of an employer and then, much more thoroughly, within the Private House, at the Chateau, she also knew she was desirable.

She knew now how to dress to emphasise her desirability. She wore a long black coat and high boots partly to keep out the cold. When she opened the coat, however, her outdoor garments contrasted with the minimal clothing underneath: a white cut-off singlet that left bare her midriff and the lower curves of her high, round breasts, and a white skirt so short that whenever she moved she displayed her skimpy white knickers.

As Itomi strode along the crowded streets, trying to keep up with Stefan, she pulled open her coat from time to time in order to shock the passers-by.

It was dusk and the street lamps were alight, creating pools of orange illumination within which Itomi and Stefan could perform for the passing crowds.

They kissed, because public displays of affection seemed to offend some of the bustling throng and also because they enjoyed kissing each other. They had made love together several times since they had met at the Chateau, but liaisons of any permanence were frowned upon, and were punishable, by the Chatelaine. Now that they had been thrown together on this trip to the foreign city, they had spent the entire night on the ferry and most of the following day in bed together.

'How is your poor little cunt?' Stefan asked loudly, in the hope of alarming someone nearby, as he and Itomi danced under another lamp. He pulled her to him, drew apart her coat, and thrust his thigh between her legs.

31

Itomi rode his thigh, rubbing the taut gusset of her knickers against the heavy cloth of his trousers. 'My cunt is hungry,' she said. 'She needs to be filled up.' Stefan's gloved hands were under her singlet, clutching at her breasts and catching on her nipples which felt as hard as pebbles. Already she wanted him again; she wanted him to hold her down and do all the things to her that he had done last time, only more and harder.

'That's very naughty,' Stefan said, and kissed her eagerly. 'You'll have to be punished again. How is your poor little bottom?'

'Still quite sore, thank you,' Itomi said. 'But I hope you intend to make sure it stays that way.'

During the recent months of her tutelage Itomi had discovered many routes to pleasure, but her chief delight was still to receive corporal punishment on her bottom. The merest touch on her buttocks was enough to awaken her clitoris. A prolonged whipping, when administered with care and skill, would not only make her so wet that the juice would drip freely from her sex-lips but would, if the final strokes were delivered hard to the lower inner curves of her buttocks, bring her to orgasm.

Punishment was an essential element of the regime at the Chateau, but chastising Itomi's bottom, no matter how severely, had no disciplinary effect on the girl. When the Chatelaine had realised this she had devised different, more inventive punishments for Itomi; the thought of the things that had been done to her brought a blush of shame to Itomi's cheeks. Itomi was one of the few trainees for whom a whipping was a reward for good behaviour.

Stefan was not yet as skilful as the Chatelaine's servants with the strap, the cane and his hands, but what he lacked in finesse he made up for in enthusiasm. Itomi found that she felt melancholy and listless unless her bottom was stinging from a recent smacking; it seemed that on this expedition with Stefan there was little likelihood of melancholia.

Stefan pulled her coat together. 'Turn round,' he said. 'Lift up the coat and let me see.'

Itomi turned away from him, buttoning her coat. Hand over hand she tugged the coat-tails upwards – slowly, so as to tease Stefan. She made sure she pulled up her skirt with the coat, so that when the material was bunched in the small of her back he was able to see every part of her oval buttocks, with the white thong of her knickers threaded between them. The cold air thrilled the sensitised nerve endings.

'Is my bottom still bright red?' she asked, looking over her shoulder.

'Pink,' Stefan said. He slapped a hand on her right buttock and squeezed hard.

Itomi gasped as she felt a thrill of pleasure: humming-bird's wings at the entrance of her sex. 'It's cold,' she said.

'Some of the stripes are still visible,' Stefan said, 'even in this light. Still, perhaps it's time to warm your little bottom again. Do you think so, Itomi, my dear?'

'Oh, yes,' Itomi murmured.

'But perhaps we'd better get a second opinion.' Stefan moved quickly; he grasped her wrists and held them, below the bunched coat and skirt, behind her back. Then he span her round to face him. Her bottom, pink and striped and naked but for the string between her buttocks, was exposed to anyone who might walk past.

Itomi could hear footsteps approaching. She buried her face in Stefan's jacket.

'Excuse me,' Stefan said, exaggerating his foreign accent. 'Could I ask your opinion, please?'

The footsteps stopped.

'My girlfriend says it's time to whip her bottom again. What do you think?'

There was no reply. Itomi wriggled her hips and pushed out her rear.

'Come, you can feel her if you like. She says she's cold and wants to be warmed up. Would you smack her? Would you like to try a smack? She won't mind.'

But the footsteps had started again, and receded quickly. Stefan held Itomi as she was and stroked her buttocks. From time to time he gave one or other of them a hefty slap. Itomi was getting very excited. She heard several more people pass them, but from the sound of the footsteps they gave the couple a wide berth.

'She likes to be smacked,' Stefan called out. 'Look, her knickers are getting damp – just here, where they cover her cunt.'

Stefan's fingers were between her thighs, stretching and pushing at the strip of white cotton. Itomi felt the cotton band slide between her parted labia, and her knees buckled as a particularly strong wave of pleasure flooded her.

'That's enough,' Stefan announced, and released her. He was becoming practised at bringing her to the brink and leaving her there. She wanted more pleasure now, immediately, but she knew that he was right to allow the tension in her to subside. He would wind it up again, perhaps several times, before allowing her the release she craved. Like Itomi, he had learned many lessons in the Chateau.

'We must at least try to find our quarry,' he told her. He picked up his pack of equipment and slung it across his shoulders. 'We'll go back to the cab, I'll use my belt on your bottom, and then we'll continue to the street where we know they have an apartment.'

Barat would arrive at any moment, Olena was sure, but she couldn't bring herself to cover the pretty things he had bought for her.

She had been only too pleased that he had volunteered to make the purchases himself: being measured by the severe-looking sales assistant had been so embarrassing that Olena had thought she would expire with blushing. Olena still shuddered at the recollection of the look of disdain on the woman's face as Olena had reluctantly shuffled off her robe to reveal the coarse undergarments beneath.

However, Olena thought she had detected surprise and perhaps even admiration in the woman's eyes when she had, after calling out to Barat one final time to ensure that it was permissible, unbuttoned and removed her bodice.

Olena had heard the woman's indrawn breath as she had had to stretch to make the tape measure reach round Olena's chest. Olena had found herself thinking triumphantly to herself: Yes, I was right – I'm as shapely as the best of the girls in the advertisements.

The sales assistant had held Olena's breasts firmly, one in each hand, and squeezed them with her fingers. This was, she had told Olena, an important part of the measuring exercise.

'You won't find this size in all the ranges of lingerie,' the assistant had said, writing down Olena's bust measurement. She hadn't been able to keep her eyes off Olena's body. 'And you're still so young. And so slender round the waist,' she had added wistfully.

Barat's eyes had widened, too, when Olena had shown him the paper on which her measurements were written. But he had said nothing, except to ask casually whether Olena wanted to start with skirts and blouses or with underwear.

But when Olena had seen the lingerie department of the store, with scandalously frivolous clothing displayed as far as the eye could see, she had been overwhelmed with shyness and had insisted on being allowed to leave. Barat had chosen clothes for her and had brought them to her room some hours later.

It had taken Olena a long time to pluck up the courage to open the shiny bags and gift-wrapped boxes. Each garment that she had unwrapped had been a surprise and a delight: the wedge-heeled sandals that Barat had already mentioned as being more feminine than slippers, for wearing indoors; a skirt that was so short that it would reveal her knees, and another that would have been more modest but for the split at the back; T-shirts and blouses; and a dress of light cotton. The bright colours and soft fabrics were themselves so sinful that merely looking at them and touching them made Olena's head swim.

But the underwear that Barat had bought was even more wonderful and strange. Olena had only ever glimpsed such things in magazines, on those pages from which she had

35

always averted her eyes. To have them here, in her little room, ready for her to wear, was wicked – and very, very thrilling. These were the kinds of underclothes that all the young women in the city must, she supposed, wear every day: stockings, in white and in black, with lace tops; knickers that appeared to be made of almost no material, and what little there was almost transparent; and matching bras with supported cups that Olena could tell would make her breasts look very prominent under even the loosest of outer clothes. The lace and satin were a glimmering temptation in the dim light from the bedside lamp.

After she had taken off all her everyday clothes, Olena had stood looking at the underwear strewn across her bed. The scanty things seemed more of an affront to decency than did her own nakedness. But, she told herself, Barat had assured her that it was not sinful to wear these clothes. He was her guardian, after all, and he had bought the clothes himself. He had even hinted that it might be permissible for her to wear such things not only in private but when actually going out. The very thought made Olena blush, but she was secretly thrilled at the idea of walking into a lecture wearing her new city clothes. The other young women would look, and pretend not to be impressed; the young men would stare.

Eventually Olena, with trembling fingers, had pulled on a pair of the knickers. Sometimes, in her bed in her parents' house in the community, she had pulled the sheets tight between her thighs, even though she knew it was naughty, because the pressure felt warm and exciting. But she had never worn clothes that were tight between her thighs, tight against the secret places down there. Never any clothing that almost disappeared between the cheeks of her bottom, drawing attention to the prominent twin globes.

She wanted to touch herself there, even though she knew that she must never do such a thing except when washing herself. And she had no such excuse. Instead she squirmed, gasping as the material seemed to hold her even more tightly.

How did city women manage to wear such underclothes

all through the day? Surely at every moment they would be aware of the soft fabric touching their most secret parts?

Putting on the bra was even more confusing. The feeling of the lacy cups enveloping her breasts took Olena's breath away and, as she struggled with her hands behind her back to hook up the unfamiliar catches, she was aware of her breasts jiggling within their comfortable imprisonment. She had to slide her hands into the cups to make sure that her breasts were sitting properly; her flesh felt hot and sensitive.

She stood in her room, half in shadow, hardly daring to move.

Footsteps in the hall. A knock at the door. Barat's voice: 'Olena? Are you there?'

She started, and reached for the dress. 'Just wait a moment, please,' she called, and pulled the garment over her head. No time for stockings; no time for shoes. Without thinking, she tightened the dress's belt. Then, as she made for the door, she caught a glimpse of herself in the little mirror: her hips and breasts, emphasised by the cinching of her waist, appeared almost unnaturally swollen.

There was no helping it. Barat was calling again. She opened the door.

Barat appraised her calmly. There was a smile on his lips, so she assumed he was not displeased. Nonetheless, she felt she had to be sure.

'It must be wrong to wear these things, Barat,' she blurted out. 'Surely –'

He stopped her by raising his hand. It was almost a gesture of blessing. 'Do you like your new clothes, Olena?'

Olena considered the question. Of course she liked her new clothes; the problem was to protest enough to convince Barat of her righteousness, but not enough to make him agree that she should return to wearing the robe and headdress.

'Yes,' she replied cautiously. 'I suppose so.'

'There you are, then. You must learn to follow your feelings. That's the sure way to avoid temptation.'

'Is it?' This sounded paradoxical to Olena, but if Barat said it was so then she was prepared to agree. And she was feeling so strangely excited that she was in no mood to consider points of theology.

'Of course,' Barat said. 'Now come closer. Let me look at you properly.'

Olena stepped closer to Barat. There was something in that last word of his, in 'properly', that made her shiver and brought a rush of disturbing and disgraceful images into her mind.

She was close to him now. So close that he could touch her. For a breathless instant she imagined his hands touching her breasts, then she banished the thought.

'Your breasts,' he murmured.

'What?'

'You have a very nice figure,' he went on. 'I confess I don't know what women in our community wear as underclothes, but I imagine that your new things feel more comfortable. Is that so?'

'Comfortable,' Olena repeated. Her breasts seemed to be reaching towards him. 'Yes, Barat,' she said, 'but the ends of my, my breasts,' she stammered, faltering as she realised what she was about to say, 'they feel very strange.'

'Strange? In what way? Not painful?' His voice was full of concern. He was so good and thoughtful, and she was so wanton.

'Not exactly,' she said, her voice firmer now. 'But tingly and the very ends feel swollen.'

'The ends? You mean your nipples?

Olena nodded.

'Then say the word,' Barat chided, with a smile.

'My nipples,' Olena whispered. 'They feel swollen.'

'You mean they feel hard,' Barat said, in a tone that was noticeably harsher. 'Hard and stiff. Is that right?'

'Yes, brother Barat.'

His hands pressed against the front of her dress. 'Why, I can feel your nipples through your clothing. Look, you can see how hard they are. This isn't good, Olena.'

'Is it wrong to have stiff nipples?' Olena asked.

'Not always.' Barat was judicious. 'There is a much surer sign of impure thoughts in a woman.'

'And what is that?' Olena said, although she felt her stomach sink and a perverse wave of pleasure run through her, because she was sure that she already knew.

'The elders tell us that impure thoughts cause a woman to become wet in her private places. Although I cannot imagine how such a thing could be.'

Olena bowed her head. She wanted his hands on her breasts again. 'I'm very wicked,' she said.

His fingertips under her chin lifted her face. He is like a brother to me, she thought. But I want him to kiss me. I am truly wicked.

'I find it hard to believe this of you,' he said. 'But don't worry; impure thoughts do not constitute the worst of sins. Far from it. The elders make much of it, to instil goodness in the children, but for adults impure thoughts are not uncommon. Particularly in young women.'

Olena blushed.

'A little punishment is all that needed. A brief penance.'

'Punishment?' Olena's mind was in a whirl; she didn't know whether to be delighted or distressed. 'What sort of punishment?'

'Oh, I don't know,' Barat said with a shrug. 'I don't think it really matters. What kind of punishments did you receive from your parents?'

Olena recalled the hungry nights, the peeling of vegetables, the hours spent digging the family plot in freezing darkness. 'Nothing special,' she said. She hesitated. Then she added, 'But some of my friends were spanked when they were naughty. On their bottoms.'

She couldn't look at Barat. What must he be thinking? She imagined lifting her skirt so that Barat could place his hands on the swelling spheres of her backside. She realised – she had realised all along – that the punishment would be futile. Worse: a spanking would only engender more impure thoughts in her.

'All right,' Barat said, with a strange catch in his voice, 'I'll spank your bottom. But later; before you go to sleep

39

tonight. I'll come here at your bedtime. Before then, however, I think we should go out.'

'Out? But Barat, it's dark outside.'

'We're in the city now, Olena. There are street lamps. Many people go out after dark. It will be all right, I assure you. And anyway, I want you to try on one more new garment. I've brought you a present.'

From one of the pockets of his robe Barat produced a small packet. He offered it to Olena. She took it.

'Open it,' he said.

Carefully she peeled off the paper. Inside was a small roll of cloth: shiny, smooth, pale blue. There were slender straps of the same material. Flustered, she pushed the crumpled paper into Barat's hands. The garment unrolled, and Olena recognised it as a swimming costume.

She didn't know what to say. The implications were too numerous for her to consider any of them for more than a moment: a swimming pool; a public place; crowded changing rooms; men and women in the same pool. Olena had seen pictures of such places. Everyone almost naked. She would have to appear wearing nothing but this costume.

She was on the point of weeping. 'But Barat,' she said. 'I can't swim.'

'Don't worry,' Barat said. 'I've thought of everything. It's quite late now. There is an establishment nearby with a pool; at this time in the evening it is nearly always empty. There will be no one to see you.'

Olena felt strangely disappointed. 'But you will see me, won't you? And you're a man.' She hoped her voice indicated proper indignation rather than the anticipation she felt.

'I'm your guardian,' Barat said. 'My duty is to look after you as your parents would. Of course I'll be there. I'll be watching over you.'

Jem's display had swiftly brought the meeting to a close, and she and her closest advisers had retired to a room in her private apartments. She had called for champagne. The half a dozen men and women – the people who ran the Private House for Jem, and who were therefore among the most influential people in the world – had sunk gratefully into leather armchairs before a blazing fire. There was no other light in the oak-panelled chamber. Servants in revealing costumes stood silently in the shadows.

Now, Jem thought, we can have some fun at last.

She summoned her chief of guards. Julia approached Jem's chair and bowed her head.

'Take off your tunic,' Jem said.

Julia looked up. Anger flashed in her dark eyes. Jem understood Julia's irritation, but was not prepared to be thwarted.

'Do it,' she said. 'If you won't obey my orders, who will?'

Julia's belt, with her crop and her strap hanging from it, dropped to the floor. She unhooked the fastenings of the shiny black leather tunic.

'I know why you don't want to,' Jem said. 'You're concerned that your authority will be lessened in front of the others. And that it will reflect badly on me, because you are my right hand. But you needn't worry. They will all be jealous of you. And afterwards I'll make them do much more humiliating things with each other.'

By now, Julia was naked but for her collar, her boots and her long gloves. In the orange glow of the firelight Jem could see little more of Julia than the slim outline of her body. It didn't matter: Jem knew every part of Julia, intimately. She had suckled at Julia's small brown nipples; she had licked the length of Julia's slim, muscular legs; many times she had whipped Julia's small round buttocks; she had plunged her tongue into Julia's prominent, deeply split pudenda and into the dark, deep cave of Julia's anus.

'Sit in my lap,' Jem said. In a moment Julia's lithe body was pressed against her. Each woman held the other; their lips met. Jem felt at peace.

'I love you, Jules,' she breathed.

Julia nibbled her ear. 'And I you,' she whispered. 'You can trust me. Always.'

41

Jem giggled. 'I can trust you to be lecherous,' she said. 'Move your legs apart.'

Jem's fingers were already pushing into the gap between the tops of Julia's slim thighs. As Julia parted her legs, Jem slid her hand down to cup Julia's dark mound. The women kissed passionately; Jem's fingers parted Julia's outer lips and invaded the wet interior.

'Ask me,' Jem said.

Julia sighed, and tossed her mane of dark curls. 'Please, Mistress,' she said. 'Play with it.'

The piercing had been Jem's idea. A small gold bar had been inserted horizontally in the hood of Julia's clitoris. It was small enough to be invisible most of the time, although Jem liked to try to spot the glint of gold in the midst of Julia's black pubic hair.

When Julia was aroused, the bar rested on her tumescent clitoris. There was nothing Jem enjoyed more than playing with the little gold rod and watching Julia's face as desire overwhelmed her, softening her features, and made her mew like a kitten.

Jem's fingers teased Julia's pubic curls. 'Wider,' she said. 'I want you wide open.'

Julia pouted, and moved her right foot to rest towards the back of the arm of the chair. She drew up her left leg and placed her foot on the chair's seat.

'That's better,' Jem said. Her fingers explored. 'Now your wet little cunt is open and I can easily put my fingers inside. And if I reach a little further down – Ah! Here's my favourite secret place.'

Even after all this time, Jem thought, Jules still blushes and wriggles when I touch her anus. But then, I never tire of touching her there. Such soft skin in the channel between her buttocks. Such a deep, dark cleft, with the sensitive little hole almost out of reach.

Jem had long since tired of trying to find a way satisfactorily to whip Julia's anus: the guard commander's buttocks were so firm and round, and the valley between them so deep, that even with Julia's thighs stretched and bound far apart it was difficult to land blows accurately with anything wider than the flimsiest cane. Instead, Jem had devised more intricate punishments, and Julia carried always at her belt a leather drawstring purse containing, for Jem's sole use, a selection of small brushes, plugs and probes.

Now, however, Jem wanted the most intimate contact possible. Pushing her hand firmly between Julia's buttocks she began to rub and pinch between her fingertips the silk-soft crinkled skin.

Julia had slid from sitting on Jem's knees to a position almost lying across Jem's lap. Julia was the taller and stronger of the two women, but she was devoted to her Mistress; Jem's touches and kisses and whispered commands reduced her to childlike helplessness. Now Jem leaned over her friend and grinned in a predatory fashion as she placed cushions under Julia's head and shoulders. 'Kiss me, Jules,' she said, and lowered her lips on to Julia's. For several minutes she inhaled Julia's gasps and exclamations as her fingertips pinched and twisted Julia's most delicate tissues.

Jem looked up. The room was silent but for the crackling of the fire. The others were sitting or standing where they had been when Jem had summoned Julia but were no longer talking. In the dim light they must have been unable to see what Jem and Julia were doing. But they all knew Jem's predilections.

Jem felt Julia's lips nuzzling her left breast. She leaned forwards slightly and freed her hand momentarily from between Julia's buttocks in order to slide her thumb into the hot, wet tunnel of Julia's vagina. Jem laughed as she heard Julia groan, and then felt Julia's lips close about her nipple. Julia began to suck to the rhythm of the movements of Jem's thumb.

Jem shivered. She could feel her own juices leaking from between her shaved labia. She pushed her thumb harder and faster into Julia, making liquid noises that must have been audible throughout the room, while two of her fingers violated Julia's smaller opening.

'Use your teeth a little, and your tongue,' Jem

whispered. 'Let's come together. And let's make a lot of noise.'

The idea of being heard in the throes of orgasm evidently excited Julia, as she began to pant and writhe on Jem's lap, thrusting her hips to meet Jem's invading thumb and fingers. At times Jem's nipple escaped Julia's mouth altogether; at other times Julia gripped the bud between her teeth and flicked it hard with her tongue.

Jem could bring herself off by caressing her own breasts; therefore being licked by her adored friend Julia, while she was thumb-fucking and finger-buggering Julia to orgasm, was more than enough to bring Jem to a climax. Her sensations became narrowed but very intense: the hot, tingling feeling that arced from her nipple to her loins; the sound of Julia's gasping breaths and indistinct vocalisations; the heavy, musky smell that Julia's body exuded when she was highly aroused; the rhythmic thrusts of her hand into Julia's sopping orifices.

The voices of the two women rose together in a confusion of stifled shrieks and guttural cries. And then silence reigned again, but for the panting of Jem and Julia and the hiss and crackle of the fire.

Jem shook her titian locks about her head, took a deep breath, and decided that the evening had improved yet more. She leaned forwards, cradling Julia's head, and kissed her friend's swollen lips. 'Don't stop, Jules,' she said, sufficiently loudly for the others to hear. 'Suck the other one. But first: ask me again.'

'Oh, Jem,' Julia groaned. 'Now?'

Jem merely smiled and stroked Julia's cheek. Her other hand moved, just slightly, just enough to remind Julia that it was still embedded in her. Jem waited. She knew that Julia didn't like being excited immediately after coming, but she knew also that the resulting second orgasm was never less than spectacular.

'Please play with it, Mistress,' Julia said.

Jem pulled her thumb from Julia's vagina and, pressing the ball of the thumb along the length of Julia's vulva, she allowed the pad to come to rest barely touching one of the little metal spheres that were the finials of the gold bar in Julia's prepuce. Julia shuddered. Jem began to move her thumb, very gently; she felt Julia's warm lips around her right nipple.

Jem allowed herself to enjoy dominating Julia for a little longer, pushing her fingers deeper to stretch Julia's sphincter while flicking the gold bar with her thumbnail, making Julia suck ever more desperately at her nipple.

Already Jem could feel a second orgasm building. She needed a distraction. She pulled her gaze from Julia's face and looked up.

'Rhoda,' Jem called out. 'Would you please suck Sebastian's cock? Don't let him come, though.'

Sebastian, tall and hook-nosed, folded his lean frame into an armchair. Rhoda, red-haired and buxom, promptly knelt between his legs and applied her mouth to his genitals. Jem could see the movement of Rhoda's head; the lower half of the woman's buttocks, beneath the hem of her short skirt, reflected the ruddy glow of the flames.

'Is that Lucy, standing in the corner?' Jem said. A tall blonde emerged from the shadows. 'Come and join in, Lucy. Take off that silly little dress and kneel next to Rhoda. Turn to face me; that's right. Now lift up Rhoda's skirt and give her a spanking.'

Just before the first crash of palm against buttock sounded loudly in the still room, Jem heard Rhoda's muffled cry of protest. Jem smiled. Rhoda preferred administering punishments to receiving them, and Lucy had a strong arm.

For a few moments Jem watched Lucy's hand lift and swoop, lift and swoop. Her thumb nudged Julia's piercing to the rhythm of Lucy's spanking. Julia shivered at each touch.

'You're hardly trying, Lucy,' Jem called out. 'Put your whole body into it. I want to see those big tits of yours really bouncing.' In the semi-darkness Jem could in truth see little of Lucy but for her silhouette. It was clear from the loudness of the reports, however, that she was now smacking Rhoda with considerable energy. Other people

45

had drifted from the edges of the chamber and were now standing, in twos and threes, in a loose circle around the chair in which Sebastian was slowly writhing and before which Rhoda and Lucy were kneeling. Even the servants had moved stealthily in from the shadowy corners, and were watching in awe as Rhoda the disciplinarian submitted to a blistering chastisement.

Jem's right nipple felt suddenly cold: Julia's face was no longer pressed against it. 'Would you like to spank me, Mistress?' Julia said. Her voice quivered; her body was trembling continuously as each slight movement of Jem's thumb induced a minor convulsion. Her unfocused eyes were hardly visible beneath her fluttering, lowered lids.

'No, darling. Not yet,' Jem replied. 'But turn to face the others. You can watch. I'll play with your bottom for a while.'

Julia smiled dreamily and turned slowly away from Jem, who allowed her fingers to slide from Julia's anus as Julia shifted on her lap. Jem leaned forwards and pressed her nipples into Julia's back. She teased Julia's dark tresses and nibbled and kissed her ear. Her right hand explored the familiar curves of Julia's rear, stroking, slapping and pinching the warm, firm flesh.

A tall figure was standing behind Lucy. Jem recognised Terence Headman, and was surprised to feel a shiver of apprehension. Headman had been her predecessor: the Master of the Private House. A peculiarly wilful Master.

I defeated him, Jem thought. Easily. Years ago. Most of these people helped me. Especially my dear Jules. Terence is as loyal as the rest of them now. He merely needed to be house-trained.

'Terence,' Jem said. 'Lean over and hold Lucy's breasts, please. Just a few more smacks, Lucy. I can't believe your arm's tired yet.'

And then she added, 'Terence, take Lucy's nipples between your fingers. Pinch them hard. I don't want her slacking.'

Why did I say that? Jem wondered. Lucy won't thank me, and it's no longer in Terence's nature to be cruel.

But it used to be, she reminded herself. She had been Terence Headman's plaything: at his mercy. He had treated her cruelly: careful doses of pain, pleasure and humiliation that were calculated to seduce her and bend her to his will. She had almost succumbed. She had been on the point of surrendering to a life of base subservience when Julia had come to the rescue.

She had never looked back. She had taken control, and she had been in control ever since. Even when she offered her buttocks or breasts to the whip, as she did from time to time because the sensations aroused her, she stipulated the conditions. But now, for the first time since she became Mistress, as she watched Lucy squirm with Headman towering over her, she remembered what it was like to be in his power.

She shook her head. 'That's enough, Lucy,' she said. 'And you, too, Terence. And Rhoda, you can remove your lips from Sebastian's cock. I imagine it's quite hard enough now.'

Jem allowed her performers only a brief respite before she rearranged them. Soon Sebastian was on his back on a couch, with Rhoda kneeling astride his face. Jem was enjoying herself hugely. She used her fingers to extract moans of pain from Julia as she gave instructions. 'Lean forward, Rhoda, until his nose is just touching your clitoris. Now ride him very gently.'

Next Jem ordered one of the servants to bring certain items. 'Lucy,' she said, 'use the cords to tie Rhoda's elbows to Sebastian's knees – separately, not together. The idea is to keep Rhoda in her position and to keep Sebastian's legs up and apart and out of the way – while you use the leather strap on his scrotum and his anus. Touch his penis from time to time; I want you to keep him ready to come.'

It was soon arranged. Rhoda's legs were splayed as she lowered and rotated her hips just above Sebastian's head, so that his aquiline nose brushed time and again against her most sensitive nerves. Her reddened buttocks were rounded; her back was arched inwards as she was obliged by her bindings to lean forward. Lucy wielded the leather strap with leisurely precision; her upward flicks between Sebastian's buttocks were applied apparently at random, but Jem knew that Lucy was clever enough to add to Sebastian's pleasure by not allowing him to guess where the next blow would fall.

Now Jem stirred in the final ingredient. 'The lotion is for you, Terence. Apply it to Rhoda's anus and then sodomise her. I seem to remember you enjoy that.'

Headman looked towards her. Jem couldn't see the expression on his face, but she imagined him to be surprised. She was surprised herself.

Rhoda, oblivious to almost everything as she rode on Sebastian's face towards the summit of her ecstasy, started to protest only when she felt the warm bulb of Headman's erection pushing against her sphincter. Her exclamations were futile: her arms were tied, her climax was rolling towards her like a juggernaut, and Headman's long penis slipped into her easily.

'Terence,' Jem called out, 'do try not to come until Rhoda starts to come. Be a gentleman. And Lucy: I think you should stop whipping Sebastian now. Kneel and put your tongue up his arse. I find he can't resist that. But keep hold of his cock until he comes. I think that it would be a nice touch if you could direct his semen on to Rhoda's face. After all, she's made use of his.'

Jem watched for a while, and then returned her attention to her darling Julia. But every now and then, as the panting and moaning of the performers continued in a crescendo, she glanced up to watch Headman as he thrust himself into Rhoda's rectum, his lips pulled back in a snarling grin.

The gymnasium was almost deserted. One attendant, sitting behind a desk at the entrance, idly addressing envelopes to while away the final hour of her shift; one middle-aged man struggling to lift weights. There was no one in or near the swimming pool; the changing rooms were empty.

It had occurred to Barat that he could have instructed Olena to come with him into the men's changing room; he

48

could have invented a plausible pretext – something to do with having a duty to protect her. She would have believed him. But he had decided to restrain his burning urge to see her naked. He would have that pleasure soon enough: tonight, in her little room, when he would have her strip, expose herself, and bend willingly to let him touch and smack her round bottom.

Barat was glad that he had decided to remain in his robe. Swimming shorts would have been inadequate to conceal the stiff member jutting upwards from his loins.

Reflected light rippled dimly on the dark glass vault of the ceiling. The air was warm and moist. The silence seemed to murmur with the soft susurration of the liquid stirring in the pool.

There was a click: the sound of a door opening. He forced himself to turn casually.

He saw her. He smiled. He beckoned her to approach.

Inside he was shouting with elation. She was more beautiful even than his imaginings. The blood pounded in his ears. She was perfect, and she was his.

Attempting to maintain an air of detached consideration, he inspected her as she stepped hesitantly towards him across the white tiles. The swimming costume was not immodestly cut, compared with the most fashionable styles, but it clung to her curves and barely contained the swelling mounds of her breasts. Her waist seemed impossibly slim. Her hips swayed as she walked; she was naturally sensual, even when trying her utmost to be reserved.

'Don't be nervous,' he called softly to her. 'There's no one else here to see you. Walk round the pool; get used to this place. I'll just sit here and make sure we're not disturbed. When you're ready, try the water.'

He sank on to a bench, arranging the folds of his robe to conceal his erection. Olena's stroll around the pool was for his benefit, not hers: he wanted to watch her without her being aware of his attention.

Her long dark tresses were piled loosely on her head, showing off the graceful curve of her neck. Her large, dark eyes darted from side to side as she stepped nervously past him. The flawless light brown skin was glowing across her wide cheekbones, and beneath her broad nose her wide, full lips had a slight, shy smile. Under his robe he touched the hot, hard flesh, and he imagined those lips opening reluctantly to admit his cock. He imagined her tongue emerging to lick the last drops of semen from those lips – and from the tip of his penis.

Or maybe he would come between her breasts. They were magnificent. He had bought for her a swimming costume that would support her bust, and he had bought the largest size he could find, yet the two perfect hemispheres of flesh were barely contained, swelling at the tops of the cups and at the sides. The blue material was stretched thin, and the contours of Olena's nipples and her large areolae were distinct. Her nipples appeared to be very hard: was she feeling cold, or could she possibly be excited by the situation? Barat could hardly wait to feel the soft heaviness of those heavenly globes in his hands.

But apart from her breasts, her body was not fleshy. Her arms and shoulders were thin; her ribs could be discerned through her costume. Her waist was tiny. Her legs were long and slender. And between her waist and her legs was a second abundance of smooth and bounteous curves: round thighs, with a bulging 'V' between them; swelling hips promised much about her backside.

'Do you like it here?' Barat said as Olena paused in her progress round the pool to stand next to him. She was close enough to touch; the blue material stretched with her every breath.

'Yes, Barat,' she said. 'Thank you for bringing me here. And for giving me this costume. But –'

'Yes, Olena?'

'Well, it is a little small for me, I think.'

He peered at her as if noticing the costume for the first time. 'Nonsense,' he said. 'The material is designed to stretch. Continue with your walk.'

'As you say, Barat,' Olena said, lowering her head and with a quirky smile on her luscious lips.

She walked past him. Barat's gasp was almost audible, he was sure. Olena's arse was even more generous then her bosom, though no less perfectly shaped, and the swimming costume, cut high at the hips, had given up attempting to cover the undulating spheres. The blue material had gathered itself into the deep valley between her buttocks and could no longer be seen between the two smooth, coffee-coloured hills that rolled against each other with every slow pace that Olena took.

And Olena, he reminded himself, had agreed that she needed to be punished. Tonight her naked body would lie across his lap; at his instruction she would lift her perfect buttocks to meet the chastisement of his hand.

Olena was climbing down the short ladder at the side of the pool, into the lapping water. Barat stood, waved to her encouragingly, and went to find a large towel in which to wrap her when she emerged. He wouldn't let her stay long in the pool: just long enough to ensure that the swimming costume was thoroughly soaked. The material would be almost transparent when wet. He would dry her a little with the towel; it would seem considerate of him. And then he would hurry her back to her room to begin her education in the ways to please him.

The dark streets were empty now. There were no pedestrians. Vehicles could be heard rumbling along the wide boulevards, but these narrow alleys were deserted.

Itomi had come twice: once almost as soon as Stefan had started to bring his belt down on her bottom, and later, when her buttocks were burning with pain and Stefan had inserted his hand between her thighs and into her knickers to massage her copious juices round her clitoris. Now, feeling alive and excited and daring, she was walking the streets with her coat and skirt pulled up to her waist. Stefan was half a step behind her. She revelled in the sensitivity of her buttocks; she felt every draught of the cold night air and rolled her hips to encourage the caresses and slaps of Stefan's hand.

'Itomi, my angel,' Stefan said. 'This is the place.'

51

'They are hiding here? On this road?'

'It is a poor area,' Stefan said. 'But it's quiet. That's better for our purposes.'

'Look!' Itomi whispered urgently. 'Coming out of that big, low building. Two people.'

'Where? Yes, I see. A man and a woman. I'm sure of it. And wearing cloaks! They must be Heinrich and Leila.' Stefan swung the pack from his back. 'They're coming this way. I'll hide in this doorway. I have the tranquilisers and the nets. Itomi, go and bring the cab. Do you remember where we left it?'

Itomi touched her backside, and winced. 'How could I forget? I'll be back in a moment. We'll have those two back at the Chateau by morning.'

Three

'They are idiots, madame.' Itomi felt Robert tug spitefully on her chains as he spoke. 'Idiots. They do not deserve your mercy.'

Itomi and Stefan, naked and in chains, were kneeling in a circle of light in the centre of the Chatelaine's study. Itomi didn't dare to lift her face to look towards the shadowy bulk of the desk behind which the Chatelaine was sitting. Instead, she turned her head in the hope of exchanging a glance with Stefan. He was staring at the carpet, however, and Itomi caught the eye of the Chatelaine's servant Nicole, who was watching the scene with serene amusement, as pert and pretty as ever in her maid's uniform.

Itomi heard a swish and out of habit leaned forwards slightly to receive the lash. Robert's whip-stroke landed like a line of fire across both of her buttocks. She shivered, and held the position in the hope of a second stroke. There was a slender chance that the Chatelaine might prescribe a whipping as the punishment for Stefan's and Itomi's failure.

'Lift your head,' Robert said. 'Look at your mistress while you are being chastised.'

Itomi looked shyly at the tall, elegant figure sitting straight-backed behind the desk. She tried to look contrite, but one stroke of the whip had, as usual, been enough to ignite the warmth in her loins. She hollowed her back in expectation: already she wanted to feel the whip on the lowest parts of her buttocks and on the insides of the tops of her thighs. She had been punished by Robert many times, and she knew she could rely on him to be thorough and to seek out the most sensitive places.

'That's enough, Robert,' the Chatelaine said. 'The effort is wasted on little Itomi. You will have no punitive effect.'

Itomi was surprised to see the Chatelaine's icy expression thaw into a smile. Her voice, too, was pensive rather than severe.

'Stefan and Itomi must be punished, of course. A week of enforced abstinence should be adequate. Nicole, make a note of this. The two of them will wear control belts for a week; at night the belts will be removed, but they are to be chained so they cannot touch themselves. Each of them will sleep alone, of course.'

Nicole looked mischievously at Itomi. 'And should there be a dildo fitted in each belt, madame?'

'No, Nicole. But note that they are to wear the belts with the metal frames. They must not be able to enjoy any stimulation. They are to be watched when washing and bathing: note that. And make it known that under no circumstances is either of them to undergo even the mildest of corporal punishment.' The Chatelaine smiled again at Itomi as she said this.

Tears welled in Itomi's eyes. It was the cruellest sentence imaginable!

The Chatelaine had not quite finished pronouncing her judgement. 'And I suppose that, during this week of punishment, they might as well refine some of the skills they have been taught. Nicole, let it be known also that the mouths, lips and tongues of Stefan and Itomi will be available for all to use. While they are wearing the control belts they will not be permitted to refuse anyone. That, I think, will teach them to pay attention next time we give them a task to carry out. Robert, take them away. And remember to keep your hands off Itomi's bottom.'

Itomi stood and bowed, in the manner of her native land, to the Chatelaine and turned to allow Robert to lead her from the room. She could hardly bear to think of the next seven days. She wouldn't mind having to use her mouth to pleasure a succession of men and women: in fact, under normal circumstances she would enjoy tasting the liquid secretions and swallowing the ejaculations, and moulding her lips to a variety of penises, nipples and vulvas. But in normal circumstances she could expect to be smacked, at the very least, for such wanton behaviour. And she was going to have to survive for a week without even a slight tingle across her backside. It would seem like an eternity.

As she was trudging from the room, Itomi heard Nicole's voice. 'And what about the prisoners, madame? The ones we have upstairs instead of Heinrich and Leila? They will wake soon.'

'Well, Nicole,' the Chatelaine said. 'That's why I haven't been too hard on Itomi and Stefan. It seems they've brought home a couple of prize specimens. The girl, in particular, is said to be quite extraordinarily attractive. It would be a shame not to show them some hospitality. I sense they might have some potential.'

The room was small and sparsely furnished, but comfortable. The walls were of plastered stone and there were age-darkened beams across the ceiling, which suggested that this prison was old. It was certainly a prison: the door to the tiny bathroom was open, but the other door was locked. Olena had tried it three times.

The view from the window told Olena a little more about her situation: she was in the countryside, or else in a vast park, for as far as she could see there were trees; and she was in a castle, for far below her room there was a moat of dark water and to her left she could see turrets and circular, cone-roofed towers. The evening sky was dark with clouds, and raindrops struck the glass of the window.

The room was warm, however, which was as well, because Olena's cloak was nowhere to be found.

She could remember little of how she had come to this isolated fairy-tale castle. She had felt very sleepy, and her memories were confused: a vehicle of some kind, driven fast through the night; Barat, asleep opposite her, and a man and a woman talking; the smell of the sea, and the rolling motion of the waves.

She had woken in this room: her first sight had been of the white walls reddened by the setting sun. Had she been asleep one day? Two? She had no way of knowing. She had been hungry and she had found on the table by the window a tray with a simple meal of bread, cheese, meat and fruit. She had eaten ravenously, even before she had thought to search for clothes or try the doors. She had found the bathroom and had showered, dried herself and brushed her hair. She felt well, but very nervous. The place was utterly silent. She had put on all the clothes she had been able to find: the bra and the pair of briefs she had donned at the swimming pool. Pathetically small scraps of lace. Underwear that Barat had provided for her. She had wished for his calm presence, and had wept a little. She had told herself that there was no point in crying, and had set out to explore the small confines of the room. Now she sat on the bed, and waited.

The door opened without warning. Olena jumped up and tried to pull the covers from the bed around her body. Two people entered the room, which seemed suddenly crowded.

The man was stocky and muscular. His trousers and waistcoat were of black leather. He had deeply set dark eyes and a neatly trimmed beard. Olena thought he looked sinister. The woman was wearing a maid's uniform, although it was too brief and flimsy to be practical; rather, it seemed designed to show off her slender legs and the tops of her stockings. She had short, straight, dark hair and a bright expression.

They spoke to Olena and to each other. They were clearly doing their best to sound reassuring and friendly, but Olena understood not a word. They were speaking in a foreign language, and Olena knew only her native tongue. Other languages had not been taught in the community's schools: the elders tried to hold at bay all outside influences, and what could be more alien than another tongue? Olena realised that she was in a foreign land, an unknowable distance from her home, in a place where she was even more of a stranger than she had been in the bustling city.

Only the dim memory that Barat had been brought here with her gave her the resolve to stem a flood of desperate tears.

The woman tugged gently at the sheet Olena was clutching. Olena thought of bolting through the open door but realised that she had no idea where she could run to. She loosened her grip on the sheet and the woman dropped it on to the bed.

Olena curled her arms around her bosom as the couple inspected her in silence. She couldn't meet their appraising gazes; she felt her face reddening. She wished the stone floor would open and let her drop out of sight; when the man whispered to the woman in the strange sibilant language she was sure he was passing comments about Olena's body.

She would not let them intimidate her. From somewhere within her she found the strength to lift her head and address her captors.

'There was a man with me. In the city. I think he is here. His name is Barat. I must see him.'

The man looked at the woman. Olena's heart leapt. They seemed to have understood her.

'Nicole,' said the woman, pointing at herself. She indicated the man. 'Robert.'

'Master Robert,' the man growled.

'Do you understand this language?' Nicole asked. Her words were clear, but spoken with a curious accent.

'Yes, of course,' Olena said.

'Barat is here,' Nicole said. 'We will take you to him.'

Olena could almost have cried out with relief. Barat was her guardian; he would protect her.

'May I have my clothes?' Olena said. 'My dress, and my shoes, and my robe?'

'No,' Robert said. 'They are not necessary. Follow me.'

The Chatelaine stood still and silent, with her nose and forehead touching the fretworked pattern of the screen that separated her study from the inspection room. She found the position undignified, but consoled herself with the thought that she was alone in her study and no one could see her.

She, on the other hand, would be able to see anyone in the inspection room. Although small, the room was lined with gilt-framed mirrors that reflected the glow of the wall lamps and gave an illusion of space.

The door of the room was opened, and a young woman stepped nervously into the doorway. She glanced over her shoulder, as if seeking assurance that she was to enter this deserted, disorienting chamber of reflections. The Chatelaine saw Nicole waving her on, smiling.

The girl stepped over the threshold, the door closed behind her, and she was alone with her many reflections.

The Chatelaine felt her heart beating faster as she studied the form of the woman called Olena. Stefan and Itomi had brought to the Chateau an unexpected prize.

The young woman was perfect. The Chatelaine, accustomed to scrutinising each newcomer, whether guest, servant, or slave, had rarely seen such potential, even in those seconded from other Private House establishments or selected for recruitment by her undercover operatives. And this one had arrived by accident – by mistake.

She first studied Olena's body. It was a study in sensuality, blessed with generous curves. The Chatelaine went through her usual list, starting with the most basic features.

Olena was of medium height. Her skin was light brown, and apparently flawless. Her build was slim: her waist, neck, shoulders and arms were slender. However, the exuberant bounty of her feminine contours was so pronounced that it was impossible to consider her thin. The inadequate covering of the lacy underwear she was wearing served only to draw attention to the abundant globes of her breasts. As she walked tentatively into the centre of the room her ample, round buttocks, reflected in the mirrors, rolled against each other. She was naturally graceful; her hips swayed with each step. Her thighs were plump, but between them at their tops there was an inviting gap, above which the lace-covered mound swelled.

The Chatelaine found her mind wandering from the task of inspection. She couldn't help wondering how the girl would respond to the lash. Her buttocks could accommodate plenty of stripes, and would dance and darken prettily under a heavy strap. Her breasts, if they were as firm as they appeared, would be perfect for prolonged whipping. The insides of her thighs; those ample curves between her legs.

The Chatelaine permitted herself a rueful smile. While she administered discipline even-handedly she had to admit that she had a preference for punishing young women. It was, she told herself, purely a matter of aesthetics and practicality: a woman's hairless, curvaceous body was a more attractive canvas on which to practice the art of chastisement; a woman could be whipped, and made to squirm prettily, and brought to a climax, and would soon be ready for more punishment and pleasure, while a man, once spent, provided little further entertainment.

This young woman had a body that the Chatelaine vowed she would put to the most stringent tests. The Chatelaine unbuttoned the front of her dress, carefully so as to avoid rustling the heavy silk, and curved her long fingers against her sex. She was wet, as she had known she would be. Perhaps, she thought, I will allow myself to come, just this once, during an inspection.

With her fingers moving gently between her labia she turned her attention to Olena's face. The girl's dark hair hung in lustrous waves whose final wayward curls reached almost to the small of her back. Her tresses had clearly never enjoyed the attentions of a fashionable coiffeur, and equally clearly did not require them. Her face, which the Chatelaine could merely glimpse between curtains of curls whenever the girl darted an inquisitive glance at her surroundings, was strong but pretty. Her cheekbones were high and broad, her eyes large and dark, her nose straight, and her lips – her lips were wide and full, and looked like miniature plump cushions of scarlet velvet. The Chatelaine noted with fascination that she parted them from time to time to reveal even white teeth and a pointed pink tongue that would emerge nervously to moisten the Cupid's bow of the upper lip.

It was obvious that the blatant sensuality of Olena's body was not reflected in her demeanour. She appeared wary and withdrawn; she kept her head bowed at first, and her arms across her breasts, although once she was sure she was alone she became more animated, examining the furniture and inspecting her many reflections. The Chatelaine was gratified to see that, after a little while, Olena began to relax and to move more freely. She watched herself in the mirrors as she prowled around the small room; she stopped to pose, stretching her arms above her head, turning to look at herself over her shoulder. The Chatelaine pressed her fingers into her sex and stifled a moan of desire. It was all she could have wished for: Olena was enjoying the sight of her own body, and was even touching herself and grinning lasciviously at her reflection.

There is a wanton heart, the Chatelaine thought, within that reserved and timid young woman. I will reach it, and educate her.

Olena started, turned to the door, and covered her breasts with her arms. The door opened. The Chatelaine cursed silently; she could have enjoyed watching Olena on her own for hours. A young man stumbled into the room. The door closed behind him.

'Barat!' Olena exclaimed. This, then, was the man whom Stefan and Itomi had recovered the previous night.

'Olena,' Barat said. 'Are you well? Have you been treated kindly?'

'Yes, Barat. I am quite all right.' Olena giggled suddenly. 'You look funny without your robe.'

The Chatelaine was struck by the stilted formality of their speech. And why did Olena think Barat looked odd? He was, the Chatelaine judged, a perfectly normal specimen of manhood: tall, well-built and somewhat swarthy, with regular features and only a hint of fleshiness. He was wearing a pair of shorts, but nonetheless kept his hands protectively over his groin. Olena, too, continued to attempt the impossible task of concealing her breasts and her pubes, even though she wasn't naked. The Chatelaine began to form some ideas about the kind of background from which this unlikely pair had come. And they had arrived by accident at the Chateau, of all places. The Chatelaine stifled a snort of laughter. She was going to enjoy her latest visitors.

Both Olena and Barat were trying to conceal the fact that they were stealing glances at each other's body.

Barat at length moved his hands to his sides and stepped towards Olena. 'Don't be alarmed,' he said. 'Remember, I'm your guardian. I'm here to protect you. I'll keep you safe.'

He placed his arm protectively about her shoulders. Olena, with her head lowered, did not see the predatory grin on his face. The Chatelaine noted it, however, and began to consider how best to bend to her own purposes the strange relationship between the two captives.

Olena's voice was so low that the Chatelaine could hardly hear it. 'I shouldn't see you like this. Without our robes. We shouldn't be touching.' But she made no attempt to move away; instead, she turned slightly towards him so that her head was tucked into his neck and her arm and hip pressed against him.

Barat closed his eyes and gasped. 'But it seems we have no choice, Olena,' he said. 'As long as our minds are pure and clear, our bodies can withstand a few indignities. At the moment your body is displayed brazenly and provocatively. Are you ashamed?'

'Yes, Barat. Of course. Very ashamed.'

'That's good.' He took her hand and placed it on the front of his shorts. She tried half-heartedly to pull away, but he held her tightly. 'Do you feel the hardness there?'

'Yes, Barat. What is it?'

'It is the result of your unchaste attire. It also shows you have been thinking unclean thoughts. It happens whenever you behave or think improperly. Until now I have always been able to conceal beneath my robe this evidence of your impropriety.'

61

'Poor Barat. Does it hurt?'

'A little,' Barat replied, and the Chatelaine found she could believe him. His shorts were tight fitting, and the bulge in them was alarmingly large. 'It would help if you would stroke it,' he said.

'Will that reduce the swelling?' Olena asked. The Chatelaine was beginning to suspect that Olena was not quite as naive as she appeared.

'It is very firm,' Olena said. 'I think it's getting bigger and harder than ever.'

Barat seemed to find it difficult to reply. 'It is your fault,' he said, 'for failing to abide by our customs. You must try harder to be dutiful. But don't stop,' he added. 'The firmer you make me, the firmer is my resolve to guide you and guard you.'

'Thank you, Barat,' Olena said, and she cuddled him, pressing her breasts against his chest and continuing to let her hand stray against the bulge in his shorts. 'I feel safe now you're with me.'

The Chatelaine rebuttoned her dress and moved away from the screen. She pressed a button on the wall next to her desk. It was time to separate the two newcomers. And time to make Barat aware of the realities of life in the Chateau.

Barat's awakening after his abduction in the city had been similar to Olena's. He had found himself locked in a small but comfortable bedroom, with food, drink and a well-equipped bathroom, but with nothing to wear except his undershorts. After what had seemed an endless wait he had been escorted from his room by a wordless, leather-clad man who had led him along lamplit corridors and then pushed him through a doorway – beyond which, in a mirrored chamber, he had found Olena.

And now he found himself stumbling in the man's wake again, along more dim corridors. His progress was impeded because his erection was slow to subside, and because his hands had been tied behind his back. He could only imagine what might befall him next; his sense of

62

helplessness, being bound and almost naked, served only to make his imaginings more lurid and fearsome. He had almost convinced himself that he was to be executed, and that he had been allowed to see Olena one final time before his doom was sealed. He couldn't forget the hard-tipped warmth of her breasts pressing against his bare chest.

The leather-clad man came to a halt in front of a pair of ornately carved wooden doors. Lost in his fears and fantasies, Barat almost collided with him. The man knocked on the door, and a woman's voice replied in a strange language. Barat had suspected that he and Olena had been taken to a land distant from their own, and now he was sure of it. However, the man now addressed him in words he understood.

'Kneel in front of her. Keep your eyes lowered. Don't speak unless you're spoken to. And if you do speak, address her as "madame".'

With that, the man opened one of the doors and thrust Barat through the doorway.

Barat staggered into a large room and almost tripped on the edge of a rug. He heard the door close behind him. He took a few steps forwards and lowered himself to his knees. During this stumbling entrance he did his best to gain an impression of the room and its occupants.

To judge from the shelves of books and the heavy furniture, he was in a study or library. The windows were concealed behind heavy curtains; inadequate illumination was provided by lamps set in the walls. A circle of yellow light radiated from a lamp on the corner of the monumental desk that dominated the room. In the shadows beyond the circle sat a tall figure; Barat thought it was a woman. The only other person in the room was definitely female: a dark-haired young woman, wearing a scanty parody of a maid's uniform, who was standing beside the desk. Barat would have liked to spend more time looking at her, but he remembered the instructions he had been given and lowered his head.

He stared at the dark red carpet and waited. He could sense that he was being examined by both women. The thought was unnerving and yet somehow exciting. In the silence he could hear his own breathing; the sound of a stiletto heel on the floor as the maid shifted her stance; from somewhere, the rustle of silk. He was aware that his manhood, which had not entirely unstiffened, was beginning to throb again. The fact that he could not hide the shameful swelling, because his hands were tied behind him, seemed only to exacerbate the problem.

'Your name is Barat?' It was a woman's voice: heavily accented, but crisp and clear. The voice came from the far side of the desk; the figure seated there was definitely female, then. She sounded like a person who was used to being obeyed.

'Yes, madame,' Barat said. This was, he thought, no time for flippancy or defiance. He would be acquiescent, for a while, and learn as much as he could about his captors. He would bide his time.

'Approach,' the woman said. 'Come into the light. Remain on your knees.'

Barat shuffled forward.

'Look at me.'

Barat lifted his head and met the unwavering gaze of the woman behind the desk. Even seated, she seemed tall. She was wearing a gown of dark green silk that was tailored to fit tightly the willowy contours of her body. The material shimmered where it caught the light; her breasts jutted proudly. Her blonde hair was tied back to reveal a face that was agelessly and coldly beautiful.

'I am the Chatelaine,' the woman told him. 'I am the mistress of this place, which is known as the Chateau. It is an establishment devoted to education and discipline. You have arrived here by chance, but you will nevertheless be assessed. If you are deemed suitable, you will remain here until you have been trained. While you are here, you will be obedient to my instructions and to those of my servants. Do you understand?'

'Yes, madame.' Barat could think of nothing else to say.

'When you kneel, Barat, you must keep your knees wide apart.'

Barat felt his penis flex. It was uncomfortably restricted in his shorts. He couldn't marshal his thoughts. He felt frightened and yet, curiously, elated. The Chatelaine and her maid were strikingly sexual; he had never encountered women like them. He desired them both, and it irked him to be bound and on his knees in their presence. Why should he pose for them as if he were a woman offering herself to a man?

'Nicole, fetch a narrow cane. Stand behind him.'

The maid moved out of Barat's view, and then returned and approached him. As she passed he smelled her perfume. Her short skirt was stiff and flared; he could see the pale skin above the tops of her black stockings. He saw the slender ferule that she carried nonchalantly at her side.

'I will give you one more chance to obey,' the Chatelaine said. 'Part your legs.'

Barat knew what would happen if he failed to comply. But he guessed that, whatever he did, he could not for long escape some sort of punishment. And although he hated the idea of being subservient to these women, he thought he was beginning to understand the nature of the place in which he had found himself. In the Chateau, it seemed, authority and submission, punishment and pleasure were all part of the regime. It was becoming perfectly clear; it was a place where Barat sensed he would feel at home, at last.

And I already know, Barat protested inwardly. I don't need to be told. I should be a teacher here, the strict mentor of young women: not a slave.

The Chatelaine lifted one thin finger. Barat heard a swish as the cane cut through the air, and yelped as the rod inscribed a line of fire across his buttocks.

The pain was bearable. The indignity was intolerable. Better to obey than to be whipped like a dog. He moved his knees apart.

'That's better, Barat,' the Chatelaine said. 'Now prostrate yourself before me. Lower your forehead to the ground.'

Barat opened his mouth to object, to try to explain that

this was all unnecessary, but the Chatelaine glared at him until he dropped his eyes from her gaze. Almost without willing it, he found himself bending forwards until he felt his hair brushing the thick pile of the carpet. He was acutely aware that with his legs wide apart, his hands tied behind his back, and his bottom thrust into the air he was presenting himself in a most humiliating posture. Only the thin material of his shorts, stretched taut across his rounded buttocks, gave any sort of protection to his dignity and manhood.

'Barat, you have been obstinate. You must learn to follow instructions without hesitation.' The Chatelaine's voice sounded almost friendly. 'You will receive ten strokes of the cane. More, if you dare to move during the punishment. Nicole, begin. Go slowly. Stop after five.'

Ten strokes. Barat was sure he could withstand the pain. He gritted his teeth as he heard the song of the cane swinging through the air.

Each stroke burnt a stinging line across Barat's flexed buttocks. Each stroke made him wince and flinch, but he was determined not to cry out and not to move. He would give the Chatelaine no excuse to prolong his ordeal. In fact, he found himself welcoming the stinging stripes, and wishing that Nicole would ply the rod faster; each lash served only to harden his resolve. He was a man, and he would not be defeated by mere women.

As instructed, Nicole paused after the fifth stroke.

The stinging sensation subsided. In its place Barat felt a general heat; his bottom felt sore and prominent.

'Has he moved, Nicole?' the Chatelaine asked.

'Not at all, madame. He is trembling slightly. Perhaps I should check that I have not struck him too hard.'

'Yes, Nicole. That's a good idea.'

Suddenly Barat felt cool fingers stroking across the tight material of his shorts. Nicole was kneeling behind him, trying to detect through the cloth the welts caused by her cane. He gasped when her fingers encountered one of the stripes. He felt her fingertips follow the line across one buttock, then the other. She pressed her palm against the hot flesh and massaged gently.

Barat pictured her hands roaming over his sore bottom. He pictured her stocking-clad legs; her sharp heels; the pale skin glimpsed under the short skirt. His balls felt tight; he was getting hard. He couldn't help himself.

Nicole's fingers continued to explore. She ran a fingernail down the crease between his buttocks; the back of her fingers brushed against the cloth where it covered his testicles. Her hands moved away; she was not touching him at all. Then, suddenly, she cupped his balls in one hand while the other danced across his buttocks, re-igniting the embers of the pain. His manhood swelled; he was fully erect – or would have been, had he not been constricted by his shorts.

Nicole moved closer. She was kneeling beside him now. He felt her leg press against his thigh and her skirt brush harshly across his hip. She released his testicles and started to pat his backside gently; her other hand reached under him and gripped his cock.

'Madame,' Nicole said, and Barat knew that he was about to be shamed. 'Madame, he has a very big, hard penis. I think he likes to be punished with the cane.'

Barat could have wept with humiliation and anger. It wasn't true. He *didn't* like to be punished; well, perhaps he did when his tormentor was as pretty as Nicole, and when the beautiful Chatelaine was watching, but what man wouldn't? That didn't mean he enjoyed being caned.

Without releasing her grip on him, Nicole resumed the punishment. The remaining strokes were delivered with less force than the first five, but Barat found them much more difficult to bear. Between each stroke Nicole paused to squeeze his manhood, to report to the Chatelaine on its size and firmness and to slap his testicles through the material of his shorts.

During his short time in the city Barat had sought women of easy virtue whom he had charmed, cajoled or even paid to initiate him into the carnal mysteries that the community forbade to young men. None, however, had held him and toyed with him as teasingly as Nicole. With her fingers curled around his shaft he was almost unaware of the cane landing smartly on his backside; all sensation was concentrated in his prick, and the only coherent thought that penetrated the fog of intense pleasure was the urgent fear that he might come at any moment.

To lose control in front of the Chatelaine; to writhe, and groan, and feel the release of jets of hot fluid soiling his shorts – it was unthinkable. And yet, the more Barat tried to suppress the idea the more he was aware of the movements of Nicole's deft fingers, and the more nearly inevitable his climax became.

Nicole's hand released his manhood. He had received five more strokes. He heard Nicole stand and walk away to resume her position beside the Chatelaine's desk.

'Straighten up,' the Chatelaine said. 'You may look at me, and thank me for disciplining you.'

Barat lifted his head and torso. He stretched his shoulders. His bottom felt sore; his prick was so hard that it threatened to tear through the tented material of the front of his shorts.

He could hardly believe his ears. He was supposed to *thank* the Chatelaine for humiliating him? He would rather undergo ten such punishments. 'Thank you, madame?' he enquired with heavy sarcasm.

'That's perfectly all right, Barat,' the Chatelaine said warmly. 'I'm sure you realise now that not only is it necessary for you to be punished frequently, but it is also a source of gratification.' She looked down at his bulging shorts. 'Nicole, untie his hands. I must find out a little more about our new recruit.'

Barat had to speak. Even as Nicole freed his hands, he struggled out of his fetters and dared to address the Chatelaine.

'Madame,' he said. 'May I speak? Am I to understand that you intend to keep me here?'

The Chatelaine looked at him with an amused smile until his outburst was over. 'Oh dear, Barat,' she said. 'That will be another ten strokes. But we'll save them for later. I will answer your question – just this once. Yes, I have decided that you will do very well here. You obviously require a great deal of training, but I think you have potential. Ah! Don't even think of interrupting me. There is also the question of your companion, Olena.'

Barat stifled the protestations and complaints that he had been on the point of uttering. He had forgotten Olena. For the first time in years, half an hour had elapsed without her appearing in his thoughts. Now his mind was full of her again: her hesitant voice, her soft lips, her dark eyes, her luxuriant breasts. Was she too to be kept here in the Chateau? Would she too be trained in the ways of discipline and desire? If so, he would endure the place. His possession of Olena would be delayed, but he would have her eventually. Or perhaps he could gain her sooner, under the strange rules of the Chateau.

'Madame,' he ventured, 'Olena is not my companion. She is my ward. She is under my protection.'

The Chatelaine lifted an eyebrow. 'It is quite clear to me what Olena means to you, Barat. I can read you. I can see into your scheming heart.'

Barat slumped. There seemed to be no hope. He would be kept here, at the Chateau, at the mercy of the Chatelaine and her minions, and Olena would escape from his influence.

'Don't be so easily defeated, Barat,' the Chatelaine chided him. 'I have no intention of releasing Olena. She shows more potential than any new arrival I have received here for years. I would rather lose you than her. I intend to educate her slowly and very thoroughly. The question is, would you like to help me?'

Barat's heart was racing. Could it be true? Was the Chatelaine really proposing that he would be allowed to participate in the undoing and re-education of Olena? He was overjoyed, but also suspicious.

'What do I have to do?' he asked, forgetting in his anxiety the correct way to address the Chatelaine.

'It's very simple. First, you must do exactly as I say. No more resistance, no more rebellion. It's futile, anyway, as you will learn to love my discipline sooner or later. But if you want Olena, you must be compliant in all things. Immediately. Do you think you can manage that?'

Barat took a few moments to consider. The Chatelaine was clearly no longer teasing. And this, Barat thought, was not the usual kind of arrangement that she offered to new recruits. She had recognised that Olena was special – an opinion with which Barat heartily concurred – and she intended to provide some sort of special treatment for Olena. And in some way she needed Barat's help. Suddenly he and the Chatelaine were deep in negotiations, and Barat needed to keep his wits about him.

He would clearly get nowhere unless he agreed to the Chatelaine's opening demand. He would have to swallow his pride and submit eagerly to the discipline of the Chateau. The thought of Nicole's fingers on his cock flashed into his mind. It would perhaps not be too difficult to surrender.

'Yes, madame,' he said. 'You can rely on my obedience.'

'Good,' the Chatelaine said. 'And there is little else I need from you. Except for your disapproval.'

'Madame?' Barat had no idea what the Chatelaine meant.

'Your disapproval of immorality, Barat. Your stern, unyielding adherence to the tenets of whatever bizarre sect you and that poor girl have fled from. She looks to you for guidance, for authority. I want you to continue in your role as her guardian. Be firm with her, and tell her the error of her ways whenever she strays from the path of righteous behaviour – and you can be sure that under these battlements she will be tempted very often, and very often will stray. We will introduce her, slowly and gently, to the pleasures of the flesh. You will be shocked and appalled by her new appetites, and you will feed her guilt. We will punish her for her wicked desires. You will discover, to her shame, that she can take pleasure even in chastisement. You will instruct her to beg for ever stricter discipline. We will happily administer it, while ensuring that she enjoys every minute.'

The Chatelaine paused, as if aware that she was in danger of becoming carried away by her enthusiasm. 'I have a young woman here,' she went on, 'by the name of

70

Itomi. It was she and her partner who captured you. Itomi finds her greatest pleasure in the application of punishment to her bottom. She feels miserable if she is not spanked at least once a day; during a prolonged punishment she usually comes several times. My intention is that Olena will be taught to surpass Itomi. With your help I will ensure that not a thought will cross Olena's mind without it reminding her that she is sinful and deserving of chastisement. We will devise dozens of ways in which to torment her lovely body, and we will teach her to take pleasure in every one. Indeed, she will learn that pleasure comes only through the application of discipline. I assume that you will be happy to join this enterprise?'

Barat was dumbfounded. His intention had originally been simply to seduce Olena. Then, when he was appointed to be her guardian in the city, he had seen the opportunity to prolong the seduction, and to debauch Olena thoroughly – over a period of weeks, perhaps. The Chatelaine's ambitions took his breath away.

'Will I be able to see her?' Barat asked.

'Of course,' the Chatelaine replied. 'It will be necessary for you to be on hand to reprove her, to condemn her lechery. You will no doubt be obliged to witness certain of her punishments, as this will substantially increase her sense of shame. You will be able to shake your head sadly as the evidence of her arousal indicates that yet again, and even while being punished for her licentiousness, she has failed to live up to your expectations of her. As I have said, all you have to do is to obey me, and to remain resolutely disapproving of Olena.'

'I will do as you say, madame. And will I be allowed to have her?'

'You are incorrigible, Barat. You need to know your place. Nicole, stand in front of Barat. Face me. Lift your skirt and push your bottom out. Barat, you will lick Nicole's anus while I think about your request.'

Barat had barely time to think. In a second Nicole was standing in front of where he was kneeling. Her skirt was lifted, and Barat found his face almost touching the smooth skin of her slim buttocks. He registered that she was wearing no knickers. He had never been this close to a woman's bottom, still less had he been required to lick one. Nicole had placed her legs apart and had arched her back inwards, so that her buttocks were parted and were pushed towards his face. He could see the furry split purse of her sex and the crinkled pinky-brown hole of her anus. He could smell her excitement mingling with the scent of her perfume.

He couldn't resist touching. He lifted his hands and stroked the slim columns of Nicole's thighs, gliding his fingers up the sheer stockings and marvelling at the silkier, smoother sensation of touching the delicate skin above the stocking-tops.

'Don't touch,' Nicole snapped, and brushed away his hands with hers.

'Is he licking you, Nicole?' the Chatelaine said.

'Not yet, madame.'

'Really, Barat. Is this how you mean to obey me? Put your face between Nicole's buttocks now, and put your tongue up her arsehole. Or you can forget about Olena.'

Barat took a deep breath and plunged his face into the crack between the perfect ovals. Nicole responded by pushing her hips back to meet him. He was engulfed by her warmth, her smell, and the softness of her skin. He opened his mouth and pushed out his tongue. He tasted slippery, salty muskiness, and started to move his tongue in a circle.

'Too low,' Nicole said in a bored voice. 'Wrong hole.'

Barat pushed his face upwards. He could hardly breathe. His tongue encountered skin that was as delicate as moist silk voile; he pushed further, and his tongue was in a scalloped funnel that led to a tiny hole.

'That's better,' Nicole said. 'In fact, that feels very nice. Now start licking. Try to get your tongue right into the hole. That's what I like.'

'That's very good, Barat.' The Chatelaine's voice sounded very distant. 'Now, about Olena. Yes, I think you will be allowed to have her. Once she is sufficiently well trained. And as long as your behaviour remains

72

satisfactory. In fact, I think it would be amusing if she were to be persuaded that she has to seduce you. You must maintain your grim and forbidding demeanour right to the end, so that she has to beg you to punish her and to let her pleasure you, so that you can see how sinful she is. That will be sweet, will it not, Barat?'

Barat could only nod his agreement, thereby eliciting a moan of pleasure from Nicole.

The naked woman looked just like Olena herself. She was lying on a sea of rumpled satin, luminous curves and mysterious shadows emerging from the surrounding darkness. She was staring up at Olena. Her arms were raised around her head; her hair was spilt wildly across the pillows; her breasts swelled lazily on either side of her ribcage; her legs were parted wantonly. Olena had awoken from a barely remembered but pleasurable dream to find herself looking down on her double.

No, that couldn't be right. Olena was in a bed; she was lying on her back. So the other woman must be above her, looking down at her. But that was impossible.

Drowsy and comfortable, Olena liked the idea of being stared at by a naked woman who looked just like her. But as she shook off the veils of sleep she realised that she should behave more modestly. She moved her arms to cover her breasts – as, at the same moment, did her double.

It was, of course, her own reflection. The ceiling above Olena's bed consisted of mirrored panels; Olena had been watching herself. With an 'Oh!' of exasperation and shame, Olena closed her legs and curled into a ball.

The bed was very comfortable. Olena supposed that the elders would have decreed it sinful. Which is ridiculous, Olena thought. How can furniture be sinful? The sheets and pillows were so soft. She could lie here forever in the semi-darkness, enjoying the warmth and softness.

She lifted her head to look about her, and remembered that after her meeting with Barat she had been taken by the maid, Nicole, not to her simple cell but to this more sumptuous bedchamber. She couldn't tell what time it was or how long she had slept; the shutters at the tall windows allowed in only a little daylight. She was sure she was still in the strange castle, though.

She stole another glance at the mirror above the bed and guiltily admired herself. She admonished herself for being immodest. It was wrong to take pride in her appearance. It had certainly been wrong to let Barat hold her. And as for allowing him to press her hand against his erect penis – well, it was simply wicked, and she knew that she needed correction. She smiled as she remembered Barat's embarrassment at appearing unclothed before her. He must have been so concerned at giving offence, when in fact she had found it difficult to avoid staring longingly at his naked limbs and torso. It had been all she could do to prevent herself leaping to embrace him and cover him with kisses. And she had stroked the hardness under his shorts. What would Barat say if he knew that, far from finding such things repulsive, Olena was eager to learn everything she could about Barat's body? She would have liked to extract his manhood from his shorts; to fondle it; to kiss it.

It was impossible. If Barat even suspected that she harboured such wicked thoughts, he would reject her. And that would be insupportable. But, she thought, he might simply punish her. He had threatened to give her a spanking, after all. Olena clenched her thighs together; the warm, tickly feeling was beginning again, down there between her legs. She had a sudden vision of lying across Barat's lap, his hand smacking hard on her bottom. And she would kneel in front of him, and thank him for punishing her, and promise to try harder to banish all her immoral thoughts. And she would show her gratitude by giving him a kiss, right on the end of his hard member.

Oh, it was all so hopeless! She didn't even know what a penis looked like. Her fantasy was ruined. And, in any case, it was absurd to think that Barat would remain her guardian once he had a suspicion of the depths of her wickedness. He was an upright man, favoured by the elders. He would find her disgusting.

She *was* disgusting. You can't tell by looking at me, she

thought, staring up at her reflection, but inside I'm corrupt and evil. I have wicked feelings – more and more often, I'm sure – and I can't stop them. Sometimes I don't even want to stop them. What's wrong with me? I was always a dutiful daughter to my parents. I obeyed the elders. How can I have become so sinful?

'Olena! Breakfast!' It was Nicole's voice. The door opened and Nicole, bearing a tray, walked into the room.

Olena scrambled from the bed and, when she could find in the gloom nothing with which to cover herself, she stood in the corner furthest from the door with her legs pressed together and her arms cradling her breasts.

Nicole smiled widely and set the tray down on the dressing table. 'It's all right, Olena. Don't be shy. Come and eat. Orange juice, croissants, butter – all fresh.'

Olena moved cautiously into the room. 'Can I have some clothes?' she said. 'Just a robe, or something?'

Nicole shook her head. 'That's not allowed here in the Chateau. Perhaps later, when you've been here for a while. But no one wears very much. Look at me.'

It was true: Nicole's pinafore dress had a skirt that revealed the tops of her stockings, and a bodice that was so skimpy that it didn't entirely cover her breasts. As Olena approached, Nicole laughed and plucked up the hem of the skirt to reveal that she was wearing no knickers. Olena gasped, and felt her face reddening.

She looked away, and instinctively her hands flew to cover her own pubes.

'You must be a very naughty person,' Olena blurted.

Nicole giggled. 'Yes, I know,' she said.

Olena didn't think Nicole seemed at all contrite. She decided to change the subject. 'Is Barat still here? Is he all right?'

'Yes, he's here and he's very well. You will see him soon. Now, come and sit beside me on the bed. Let's have some breakfast together, and I'll tell you a little about this place and its rules. Then you can have a bath and make yourself ready for seeing Barat again. And some other people.'

Olena came to stand by the bed. Nicole brought the tray,

placed it on the bed, and sat next to it. 'Come and sit next to me,' Nicole said. 'I'll feed you. We're going to be friends.'

Nicole, with her short dark hair, sharp features and ready smile was definitely attractive. Olena thought that perhaps she and Nicole could be friends. She saw that Nicole made no attempt to conceal the fact that she was studying Olena's face and her body. Olena blushed again, but she also felt again the warmth growing between her thighs. She sat down on the bed, making sure that she was close enough to brush against Nicole accidentally.

I am becoming thoroughly wicked, she thought.

Robert was alone in the Chatelaine's study. He felt a little nervous, even though he was there on the Chatelaine's explicit instruction, because the study was one of the few rooms in the Chateau to which he did not have right of access.

Her scent was in the air: the delicate, floral perfume that once he had been privileged to watch her dab under her ears, between her breasts and at the tops of her thighs. He shook his head to clear the memories from his mind, marched to the windows, and pulled aside one of the heavy curtains to admit a dim shaft of daylight. He returned to the desk. He touched the handle of the three-tongued martinet that was lying on the dark wood; her fingers had gripped this instrument many times. Impulsively he picked up the martinet and kissed the handle. He felt his cock harden; he pressed the martinet against the soft leather of his trousers. With his other hand he touched the back of her chair. The leather-covered seat bore the impression of her slim buttocks. He lowered himself to his knees and pressed his forehead against the cool hide. He was as still as the books on their towering shelves; as silent as the dust motes drifting in the pale light.

Very few of the male staff at the Chateau had ever seen their mistress naked. Robert had been privileged indeed. Although the Chatelaine frequently amused herself with Nicole, Isabelle and any number of other women among the servants and guests, and although she had been known to have male slaves brought to her bedchamber, Robert was the only male servant she had invited to her bed.

She had instructed him to undress her. She had then applied perfume, and had allowed him to kiss her scented fingers. She had told him to remove all of his clothes but for his leather trousers, and then to fasten chains around her ankles and wrists. He had watched her buttocks sway as she had walked to the bedside cabinet; he had watched her breasts tremble as she had returned carrying the whip.

She had wanted to be whipped while standing, chained in an embrace with one of the stone pillars. He had flogged her buttocks until her cries for more had become raucous and unintelligible. When he had released her, she had turned, thanked him, and pressed her striped arse against the cold stone. 'Now do my tits,' she had said, lifting her arms above her head. He had obeyed.

When he had carried her to the bed, and entered her roughly, she had cried out again, and raked her nails across his back as they came together, suddenly and fiercely.

That had been the only time. The next day, and ever afterwards, she had treated him as she had before: as her loyal servant.

'Your loyal servant,' he said, and kissed the leather seat where she sat and from which she controlled the Chateau. 'Your most loyal servant.'

Someone was coming. It must be the Chatelaine. He stood up, replaced the martinet on the desk, and waited.

There was a knock on the door. Not the Chatelaine, then.

'Enter,' he called.

Nicole and Isabelle came into the room. 'Robert,' they said, almost in unison. 'What are you doing in here on your own?'

'The same as you, I expect. Waiting to be given more instructions about our two new arrivals.'

'Madame seems very taken with them,' Isabelle said. 'Are they as promising as the rumours say?'

The Chatelaine strode through the open door. 'You will see for yourself in a few moments, Isabelle,' she announced.

No matter how many times he saw her, Robert was always dazzled anew by her beauty, her poise, her elegance, and her air of authority. Today she was wearing a gown of bias-cut grey silk that clung to her slender body. It covered her from neck to wrists to ankles, and yet was so sheer and precisely tailored that every contour was visible. He could discern through the material not only her nipples but also the areolae around them. He was so enthralled that he almost failed to hear her address him.

'Yes, madame?' he said.

'It would appear, Robert, that you are a little overexcited.' The Chatelaine pointed with a slim finger at the protrusion at the front of Robert's trousers. 'Would you care to be relieved of that before we proceed with the day's business?'

Robert was pleased to note that he felt not a twinge of embarrassment; instead he was proud and grateful that she had noticed his state of arousal. He lifted his gaze to meet hers; her perfect lips bestowed on him the hint of a smile. Did he dare to suggest that she might like to touch his swelling manhood? Just the thought of her cool fingers around his shaft made him harder. But no; she would not favour him so publicly. He and she understood each other. 'I am at your disposal, madame,' he said.

'Then go and take one of the slaves,' the Chatelaine said. 'But don't take long about it. The Canadian girl, Ailsa, is being trained today in the cellar of the Square Tower. You can have her in any way you choose, I believe. Her attendants will keep her aroused.'

'May I have Isabelle, madame?' he asked. With trepidation he added, 'Here, across your desk?'

The Chatelaine thought for a moment. She looked at Isabelle. The other woman looked back, her blue eyes sparkling with anticipation. Isabelle was almost as tall as the Chatelaine, and as slender. Although she was dark, while the Chatelaine was blonde, Robert had found that whenever he had occasion to fuck Isabelle he could imagine that he was fucking his mistress.

'Yes, Robert, of course you may have her. You will have no objection if Nicole and I watch. And be quick; we have things to do today. Isabelle, position yourself at the desk.'

Isabelle removed her skirt. She was wearing nothing else but stockings, shoes, and a cropped, halter-necked top of sheer muslin. She stood in front of the desk, moved her stiletto-heeled feet apart, and bent forwards from the waist until her breasts were pressed against the polished wood. She curved her back downwards so that her hips were pushed back and her bottom was raised invitingly.

Robert unbuttoned the flap at the front of his trousers; his erection sprang free. He clutched the shaft and stroked it as he surveyed Isabelle: her dark curls were spread around her head where she was resting it on the desk, but he could see the blue glint of her eyes and the edge of her smile. She was expecting to enjoy a quick fuck. He could see that her shaven labia were already glistening and slightly parted. The absence of dark pubic hair made her sex reminiscent of the Chatelaine's, the pale hairs of which were kept closely trimmed. Isabelle's buttocks, too, resembled the Chatelaine's in their slim whiteness.

'She needs to be punished, first.' Robert's voice was thick. He cleared his throat. 'You will remember, madame, that she failed to address me by my correct title when she spoke to me a few moments ago.'

'If you wish, Robert.' The Chatelaine sounded as though she thought this would be a tiresome delay, but Robert had noticed her eyes had widened at his suggestion. He knew that the Chatelaine always enjoyed watching him administer discipline. It occurred to him that perhaps she, too, had realised that Isabelle's resemblance to her would make this punishment a reminder of the night they had spent together.

Emboldened by this thought, Robert made one more request. 'And, madame,' he said, 'may I use your martinet? It's just here.'

Isabelle lifted her head from the desk and exclaimed in

protest. The Chatelaine's martinet, with its three leather straps each as heavy as a belt, was a feared implement even among the well-disciplined staff of the Chateau.

'Isabelle has work to do today, Robert,' the Chatelaine said. 'It will be difficult to avoid marking her if you use the martinet.'

Robert was about to yield; his hand was moving to the short strap which he kept at his side when he realised that the Chatelaine hadn't precisely denied his request.

'I believe the martinet is appropriate, madame. It will be entertaining to watch Isabelle's buttocks turn bright pink and then dark red as I thrash them.' Robert knew how to appeal to the Chatelaine's desires. 'And she and I will both derive greater pleasure from my penetration of her if her bottom is made very tender before I thrust against it. I can achieve quickly with the martinet a level of sensitivity that would take much longer with a lesser instrument. And if Isabelle is marked, what of it? She will, I'm sure, wear the stripes and bruises with pride.'

'Very well,' the Chatelaine said. 'You've persuaded me. You are my right hand, Robert. I can't refuse you these little rewards. Nicole, you had better stand on the other side of the desk and hold Isabelle down. She is certain to struggle once she feels the martinet. Robert, would you like to tie Isabelle's ankles to the feet of the desk, to keep her legs apart?'

'I will do so only if it becomes necessary, madame,' Robert replied. 'I have disciplined Isabelle several times and I think she can be relied on to maintain her position.'

He took the martinet from the desk, weighed it in his grip, and flicked it experimentally a couple of times. He turned to see that the Chatelaine, with a pensive expression on her face, was stroking Isabelle's rounded bottom. Robert stared at the calm beauty of her features; the perfection of her body. She looked up, and their gazes locked together for a few long moments.

The Chatelaine looked away. 'Isabelle is quite wet,' she said. 'Ignore her protests. I think she's in the mood for this. You may start now.'

Robert took up a position behind Isabelle. I love you, my Chatelaine, he thought; the strength of my arm and the vigour of my manhood will demonstrate my love for you. I know you understand that I am doing this for you.

He lifted his arm, and then the martinet whipped through the air.

The harness was a complicated network of leather straps and metal buckles and rings.

'You must wear it, Barat,' Isabelle said, 'if you wish to be present when we start Olena's education. The Chatelaine wishes it. And I know you have promised to obey the Chatelaine.'

Barat stood, naked, in the centre of the small room which he was becoming familiar with as his bedchamber. With his hands cupped over his groin he was trying to preserve a last shred of modesty and to conceal the fact that his manhood was stiffening.

He told himself that it was the presence of a stranger, the young woman Isabelle, in her provocatively diaphanous costume, that was arousing him. It was true that as she moved about the room he couldn't fail to notice that she was wearing nothing under her gauzy skirt; the undulations of her slender buttocks; her slim thighs, glimpsed whenever the crossover skirt fell open; her small breasts, bouncing under the filmy material of her abbreviated blouse. The idea of seeing Olena again was also exciting, and the vagueness of Isabelle's descriptions of the programme of teaching that the Chatelaine had devised for Olena made the prospect even more enticing.

But to be made to wear a harness . . . He felt his penis twitch upwards a little more as he stole a glance at the contraption on the bed.

'Move your hands, Barat,' Isabelle said teasingly. 'Let me see what you're hiding.'

Barat closed his eyes, disengaged his fingers and allowed his hands to fall to his sides. He could feel the heat of the blushing on his cheeks. Only his penis, which continued to swell and rise, seemed oblivious to his embarrassment.

Isabelle touched him. He felt her fingers at his shoulder, on his chest, then on his hip.

'You're not a bad-looking young man,' she whispered. 'Tall. Strong. And big.'

Her fingers had closed around his shaft. He opened his eyes to find her face in front of his. She was smiling. Her tongue appeared briefly, to touch her lower lip. He stared into her bright eyes.

'Did you enjoy licking Nicole?' she said, and started to move her hand slowly up and down his rigid column.

He nodded.

'If you let me put the harness on you, I'll let you lick me, too, before we go to join the others. That would be a fair exchange, wouldn't it?'

'Yes, I think so,' he said. Even the overwhelming sensations caused by Isabelle's hand had not robbed him of all his cunning. He had remembered that he was in a place inhabited by people who thought as he did. 'I need to come, however. I fear I may not be able to control myself later unless my urgent need is addressed now.'

Isabelle's fingers circled his glans. Her thumb tapped the narrow slit as she considered his request. 'No, that will not be possible,' she concluded. Her nose was almost touching his as she stared into his eyes. 'The harness will help to restrain your urges. However, if you carry yourself well while we interview Olena, then perhaps I will reward you afterwards.'

Barat managed to keep his voice level, even though he was aware that his legs were trembling and he could concentrate on almost nothing but the movements of Isabelle's clever fingers. 'I accept your offer,' he said. 'It will be sufficient, I think, for you merely to repeat what you are doing now. But I also think that you are being a little too strict with me, and therefore I should correct you. I will spank your bottom before you touch me and make me come.'

Isabelle's eyes widened, and then half shut as she smiled wryly. 'I fear that will be inconvenient,' she said. 'My poor little bottom is already very sore. But you can pinch my nipples and smack my breasts, as long as you are quite

82

gentle and use your fingers to make me wet and make me come.'

'Yes, I'd like to do that.'

'Very well,' she whispered. 'Now,' she said briskly as she released his penis, 'lift your arms slightly and I'll put the harness on you.'

The thickest leather strap was a belt, which Isabelle buckled tightly around Barat's waist. Metal rings were set into the leather at regular intervals around the circumference. Isabelle then knelt in front of Barat and took care to fondle and kiss his straining erection as she clipped to the front ring a thinner strap attached to which were other loops of thin leather.

Barat soon discovered that the loops were designed to contain and restrain his testicles and the stem of his cock. Isabelle tugged fiercely on the buckles as she imprisoned Barat's genitalia, causing him to cry out as the thongs gripped his most delicate parts. Isabelle laughed.

She stood to admire her handiwork. Barat's testicles were separated by a thin strap; another circled behind them, making them protrude like shiny plums. Another strap was fastened around the base of his penis, which seemed to Barat harder and larger than he had ever seen it. Like his testicles, it looked swollen and was an angry red.

Isabelle had not finished. A tail of leather still hung from behind Barat's scrotum, and Isabelle went behind him to pull it up between the cheeks of his bottom and clip it to the back of the waist-strap. Barat gasped as the pressure on his testicles increased.

'One final thing,' Isabelle said, and picked up a small collar that Barat had not even noticed. 'You'll be wearing your robe when you see Olena, of course, and you wouldn't want her to see any curious swelling, would you?'

Barat gasped again as Isabelle fastened the collar around the neck of his penis, just under the flanged head. It felt cruelly tight. Then she attached a clip to the buckle of the collar and, pulling his erection into a vertical position, she clipped the collar to the front of the waist-strap.

'There. When you're wearing your robe, your cock will be completely under control now, no matter how excited you become. No one will know. But *you* won't be able to forget for a moment.'

Barat stared helplessly down at his tightly trussed cock and balls. He took an experimental step. The straps were certainly uncomfortable but threatened to be actually painful only if he moved quickly.

'I can hardly walk,' Barat complained.

'Don't be a baby,' Isabelle scolded him. 'Sometimes the Chatelaine uses a harness like this when she's training the male slaves,' she added thoughtfully, 'or when punishing one of the servants. Some of the guests volunteer for it, of course. She uses a small many-tailed whip, a very thin, light cane, or a narrow strap. I'm told it's excruciatingly painful. But the men are always very ready to come afterwards.' She ran her fingernails lightly down the length of his hardness and across the taut skin of his divided scrotal sac. 'And just be grateful that I wasn't instructed to put anything up your arsehole before strapping you in.'

Barat shuddered. He wanted to see Olena, rather than hear any more about the ways in which the harness could be made even more uncomfortable. 'Where is my robe?' he said. 'I must wear it if I am to exert authority in Olena's eyes.'

'I have it in the corridor,' Isabelle said. 'You will be permitted to put it on before Olena enters the training room. But haven't you forgotten something?' She climbed on to the bed, pulled a pile of pillows into the centre of it, and arranged herself face down with her legs apart and her bottom at the apex of the mound. As she pulled open her skirt Barat saw that her buttocks had a dull red glow and were criss-crossed with wide stripes. She had been whipped, and recently. Barat felt his engorged member twitch in its bondage. She looked over her shoulder at him. 'Come and lick me,' she said. 'Both holes, until I come.'

The cape should have made Olena feel less naked, but she found it made her even more aware of her body. Olena thought the garment would have been a good fit for a shorter woman with a much smaller bust.

Nicole led her along dark flagstoned corridors and through shadow-filled pillared halls. Olena found that, if she pulled the cape together in front of her, the material touched her breasts and the hem was pulled up at the back so that she feared that her bottom was on display; if she let the cape hang so that it covered her bottom and hips, it was open at the front and anyone walking towards her could glimpse her naked body. The two women did not meet many other people as they walked, but Olena was sure that each one they passed looked closely at her, and she felt very flustered as she tried to adjust the cape.

Olena was disturbed, too, by the muffled noises that emanated from beyond the closed doors that she passed. She heard voices speaking several different languages, including her own. She heard voices issuing commands, voices pleading, voices reciting – almost everything, in fact, except ordinary conversation. She heard wordless exclamations: cries, yelps, laughter, weeping, gasping.

The sounds were puzzling, and seemed to conjure the most unwholesome images into her mind. She couldn't rid herself of increasingly impure thoughts; she found herself listening for footsteps approaching, so that she could artfully let the cape fly open just enough to intrigue the passer-by; she would slow her pace and tarry behind Nicole at each doorway as she strained to hear the disquieting noises from within.

The air in the draughty corridors swept round her thighs and between her legs, making her aware of the damp heat there. She had noticed that whenever she had these strange sensations in her secret parts her nipples would harden and her breasts would feel more sensitive. It was all very confusing; the only thing that she was sure of was that the feelings were wrong and wicked.

'What are those noises?' she asked Nicole. 'What is happening in all the rooms we pass? What is this place?'

Nicole, looking alarmed, put a finger to her lips. 'I told you the rules,' she whispered. 'Don't speak unless you are spoken to. You will be told what you need to know in just a few minutes. We are coming to the training room now.'

They had arrived at a pair of polished wooden doors. Nicole knocked on one of them, and Olena heard a reply from within. Nicole pushed open the door and gestured for Olena to precede her through the doorway.

Olena found herself in a long, high-ceilinged room. Along one side there were tall, shuttered windows through which cracks of daylight could be seen. The light in the room came from lamps concentrated at the far end, where there was a long table. Olena formed a fleeting impression of furniture and other more unusual and complicated items occupying the shadowed edges and corners. But her attention was concentrated on the people she saw behind the table.

Sitting at the central point of the table was the sinister-looking man who had insisted on being addressed as Master Robert. On one side of him stood Barat, properly dressed in his robe and looking sombre. Next to Barat stood a young woman with almost transparent clothing and piercingly bright blue eyes.

'Approach the table,' Nicole whispered.

Olena walked forwards. She tried to catch Barat's eye, but although he looked back at her his face remained impassive. She stopped in front of the table.

Master Robert's deep-set eyes surveyed her. At last he spoke. 'Nicole. Isabelle. Bring a chair for our guest. And bring lamps so we can see her.'

There was silence again while the two women dragged an armchair to where Olena was standing, and brought standard lamps to place one on each side of the chair. Olena found herself illuminated from both sides with pale yellow light. The rest of the room seemed more than ever full of shadows. She clutched the cape together to preserve her modesty; then she thought that the gesture would appear nervous, and she let go of the cape and tried to relax; then she realised that the man Robert could see her breasts, and she clutched the cape together again.

Master Robert spoke again. 'Olena, welcome to the

Chateau. You are a guest here by chance but, having spoken with your guardian, Barat, it seems that your presence could hardly be more timely and appropriate. Therefore we have decided to allow you to stay.'

There was a silence. Olena thought she had to say something. 'Thank you, Master Robert,' she said.

Master Robert inclined his head and gave her a thin smile. 'You are an intelligent young woman,' he said. 'A scholar, I'm told. You will therefore already have become aware that the customs of the Chateau are different from those of the community from which you and your guardian have strayed so far.'

That, Olena thought, was a considerable understatement. 'Yes, Master Robert,' she said.

'That very difference will, I think, prove to be your salvation,' Master Robert went on. 'I understand that in your community you are expected to resist certain temptations. You are required to be clean and pure, in your thoughts as well as in your behaviour. Here at the Chateau we know all about those temptations. We can detect impure thoughts. We are connoisseurs of impropriety.'

His hooded eyes seemed to Olena to be capable of seeing into her mind and her heart. No one but she knew the extent of her sinfulness. But if anyone else could find it out, she feared that Master Robert could. She looked away and blushed. She could think of nothing to say.

'We have been watching you since you arrived here,' Master Robert said, and Olena felt her heart fill her throat; she could not fail to be found out. 'And my mistress, the Chatelaine, and I have concluded that we detect in you tendencies towards pride, self-love and unwholesome desires. Your guardian will have none of it.' He looked towards Barat.

Barat gave her an encouraging smile. 'My faith in you is absolute, Olena' he said. 'You are a model member of the community. I will not believe that you could shame your parents or deviate from the purity of our customs, even in your most secret thoughts. I know you will prove to be entirely righteous and chaste.'

Olena managed to return his smile. If her disturbing fantasies and feelings had not become apparent to Barat, then perhaps it would be a simple matter to conceal them from Master Robert.

'And?' Master Robert prompted Barat.

'Oh yes,' Barat said. 'I have therefore agreed, Olena, that Master Robert and his staff, on behalf of the Chatelaine, will put you to the test. I'm sure that you have no guilty secrets. Or, if you do occasionally have wayward urges – as it is understandable a young woman might – then I have agreed that you will submit to sufficient mild discipline as will restore you to the rightful path. I will, of course, stay with you at all times.'

Olena's mind was reeling. She was to be tested. She would be disciplined. Barat would be watching. She didn't have any clear idea of what would happen to her, but the very phrases seemed to resonate through her body. Her nipples felt hard again, and she suddenly felt an almost uncontrollable impulse to touch the warm place between her legs. She wished that she had been allowed to sit in the chair that had been provided for her.

'Thank you, Barat,' she stammered.

There was a long silence, during which Olena felt the eyes of everyone in the room on her.

'Olena,' Master Robert said. 'I will begin testing you immediately. Remove your cape and give it to Nicole.'

Olena was unable to move. If someone had taken the cape from her, had torn it from shoulders, then she would not have resisted. But to volunteer to expose her nakedness, with so many watching – it was impossible.

'Olena!' Barat whispered hoarsely. 'Be obedient. You know it is virtuous to obey. I gave my assurance that you would follow instructions. Take off your cape. Remember: your body is a shrine that only you can defile. There is no evil in being naked, as long as your heart is pure.'

Olena closed her eyes and took a deep breath. Barat was relying on her. She would behave and think properly, for his sake. She would use all her strength and intelligence to prevent Master Robert from discovering anything that would incriminate her. She lifted the cape from her shoulders, turned to give it to Nicole, and turned back to face her inquisitor. She remembered to suppress the smile that came to her lips when she found that Master Robert and Barat were both staring at her breasts.

'Stand with your legs apart,' Master Robert told her.

Olena was aghast; not just because the instruction was obscene, she realised, but also because she was horrified to discover that she found the brutally brief command somehow exhilarating. In desperation she looked towards Barat.

He smiled at her again, and nodded.

Well, Olena thought, if Barat thinks there's no harm in it, I'll stand however they want me to.

She placed her feet apart, and her hands together in front of her private parts.

She looked at Master Robert. He gave her another of his parsimonious smiles. 'Come now, Olena,' he said. 'When you present yourself for testing in the Chateau, you must stand, or kneel, or sit, as required, always with your thighs sufficiently parted to permit examination of your vulva, both visually and manually. And your hands are in the way; cross them behind your back.'

Olena bowed her head. She knew she had to obey; if she had had no hidden desires, and if she had been truly innocent, then she would have had nothing to fear. She had to act as though she were pure. To protest would merely make Master Robert suspicious. She moved her feet further apart. When she crossed her arms behind her back she had to push her chest forward and her bottom back in order to keep her balance. She felt the heat of her blushing suffuse her face and throat, and was uncomfortably conscious that the private place between her open thighs was also feeling hotter.

'Barat,' Master Robert said, 'let us go and start the inspection.'

Olena heard his chair scrape the floor as he stood; she heard his footsteps, and Barat's, as they approached.

'Nicole, Isabelle,' Master Robert said. His voice was

little more than a whisper; he was standing in front of Olena, close enough to touch her. 'Would you come a little closer? Stand beside Olena; make sure she doesn't move.'

Olena shivered as the hem of Nicole's skirt touched the back of her left thigh. She leaned slightly to her right, and her arm pressed against the softness of Isabelle's breast. She could smell Nicole's perfume, and the muskier scent that emanated from Isabelle.

'She has very well-developed breasts,' Master Robert said. 'I wonder if perhaps they are slightly enlarged. One can almost feel the warmth of them. What do you think, Barat?'

'I'm afraid I don't know, Master Robert. I mean, I've never —'

'Of course. Look at the nipples, too. Quite definitely erect, and the areolae also appear to be hard. I suppose you don't know whether this is their usual state?'

'No, Master Robert. My duties as Olena's guardian do not require me to know such things.'

'I suppose not. You see, Barat, this hardness of the nipples is often an indication of sexual arousal. And in order for there to be arousal, there must first be desire. But you think that this is unlikely in this case?'

'Very unlikely, Master Robert. Olena knows her duty is to tell her guardian everything. And she has never spoken of any such desires.'

Olena had not dared to lift her eyes during this exchange. It was bad enough merely to imagine the two men with their gazes fixed on her out-thrust breasts. Sexual desire — that must be the source of the titillating sensations that were afflicting her nipples and her secret parts. She sniffed back a sob. It was so unfair! She had never intended to have sexual desires. She knew that to do so was unutterably wicked. How was it possible that she could have sunk into such sinfulness?

'Nicole,' Master Robert said, 'come and kneel in front of Olena. Yes, that will do. Now, can you see any visible signs of arousal?'

There was a long silence. Olena could see Nicole

90

kneeling between her feet; she could feel Nicole's breath on the insides of her thighs. Isabelle's breast pressed more insistently against her upper arm. She glanced up: Barat had his eyes fixed on her breasts, but Master Robert was looking from under hooded lids straight into her face. Olena closed her eyes.

In the pit of her stomach she felt a slow, sinking sensation; it was like the feeling of fear, but with none of fear's urgency. It was a weight descending slowly, inexorably, within her. As it reached her belly the feeling expanded and began to merge with the warm tingling between her thighs. It became a delicious heat within her, and her head was swimming with the pleasure of it. She caught her lower lip between her teeth and felt her eyelids fluttering. In the back of her mind she hoped that Master Robert would not understand the significance of the expressions on her face. But such mundane considerations were overwhelmed by the wonderful, sinking warmth inside her.

'Well, Nicole?' Master Robert said.

Olena gasped as his voice brought her to her senses. She wanted suddenly to close her legs, but dared not.

Nicole was judiciously cautious. 'Her labia are parted, that's certain. And they look rather swollen. Ah! There, I can see she's wet. In fact, I think she's almost dripping.'

'Let me see,' Master Robert said. 'Make your fingers wet with her juices.'

Olena couldn't hold back her sobs now. She felt the sting of tears in her eyes.

'It's all right, Olena,' Barat said. 'I know you must be unaware of any wrongdoing; you are not responsible for the responses of your body. But don't be alarmed by them. Master Robert is an expert in these matters.'

Barat has no idea, Olena thought; I know these things only too well. I'm crying because I'm about to be exposed as wicked and filthy.

Nicole's fingers touched her. It was the merest brush against the damp membranes that she had on a few recent occasions explored cautiously herself, but it felt like an

91

invasion of the centre of her being. She cried out, but kept her legs apart and her arms behind her back. Until that moment only Olena herself had touched that mysterious, fleshy, slippery crevice; now, as she recovered from the shock, she was appalled to find herself wishing that Nicole would touch her there again. Perhaps Barat would touch her; that would be heavenly.

'She's obviously wet,' Master Robert said. He was inspecting Nicole's proffered hand. 'Incontrovertible evidence of sexual arousal.'

'If you say so, Master Robert,' Barat said. 'But is it not possible that this is a purely physical response? That it indicates no sinful thought or intention?'

Master Robert snorted. 'Why, Barat, surely you must see that this test proves absolutely that the sexual urges are entirely Olena's? Until Nicole gathered the final evidence a moment ago Olena had not been touched. "Purely physical" is the one thing these reactions cannot be. No, Olena has excited herself; her own desires are to blame.'

So, Olena thought, I am discovered. Without even knowing it, I have become a cesspit of lewd thoughts. Barat must be revolted. I'll never see him again. He'll have to make a report to the elders. What will they then say to my parents? This will break their hearts. I can never go home again.

She started sobbing again, and felt hot tears roll down her face.

Barat was beside her. 'Don't be afraid,' he said. 'I believe in you. I know you are innocent at heart. I won't desert you. I will stay with you, however long you need to stay in the Chateau and whatever Master Robert's tests reveal about you. I promise.'

Olena looked at him with brimming eyes. She caught her breath and managed to smile at him. As long as Barat was with her she would be able to cope with anything. She knew she could trust him.

Barat turned to Master Robert. 'I know very little about these matters,' he said, 'but I would have thought that a woman of Olena's age would naturally be prey to certain, um, bodily desires. From time to time. The question, surely, is whether Olena can be educated to suppress such urges.'

'You may be right,' Master Robert admitted. 'What, then, do you propose?'

Barat's voice seemed tight and high-pitched. 'Discipline,' he said. 'If we discipline her, and her arousal subsides, then it will be a simple matter thereafter to teach her the error of thinking lubricious thoughts.'

Master Robert chuckled. 'There is another possibility, of course,' he said. 'However, I agree that we should try the swift application of punishment, and then assess the result. Olena, would you please turn round and kneel on the seat of the chair?'

Olena turned and groped for the chair. As she lifted one knee and then the other on to the seat, she remembered how much she had been looking forward to the spanking that Barat had promised her. That prospect had produced in her secret place the same delightful sensations that Master Robert said were symptoms of sexual desire; how, she wondered, could rightful chastisement have the same effects as wicked, lewd thoughts? She guessed, with a recurrence of the sinking feeling inside her, that if they spanked her now the punishment would do nothing to banish the shameful wet evidence of her sinfulness.

'Remember to keep your legs apart,' Barat whispered to her.

As she moved her knees as far apart as the arms of the chair would permit, Master Robert added, 'And lean forwards so that your breasts rest on the back of the chair. Hands behind your back, as before.'

The chair had a low, softly upholstered back, and as Olena leant her ribcage against it she felt her bottom pushing backwards and opening. She was more exposed than ever now. Master Robert and Barat would be able to see her private parts – even the little hole that no one had ever seen before. And the worst of it was that, although she was close to weeping with embarrassment, she could not deny that the idea of showing off her most secret places was making her feel warmer and wetter than ever. Her breasts, too, were on display, bulging over the back of the chair. Her nipples were hard and tingling. She folded her arms in the small of her back and couldn't resist the impulse to push her bottom out a little further.

'Isabelle,' Master Robert said, 'stand behind the chair. Nicole, kneel in front of it.'

From the corner of her eye Olena saw him come to stand beside the chair. She looked up and met Isabelle's bright blue gaze. Isabelle smiled at her.

'We'll start with a spanking,' Master Robert said. 'Six smacks to start with; three on each buttock. Then you, Isabelle, will test Olena's nipples for erection and responsiveness, while you, Nicole, will test again for lubrication of the vagina.'

Olena waited. There was almost no warning of the first smack: a brief sense of sudden movement beside her, and then a loud report and a hard stinging pain on her right buttock. She gasped.

Isabelle was still smiling at her. The pain melted away immediately, leaving only the sensation of heat and the memory of the sting. It was a lovely feeling. And Barat was there, and even though he was not spanking her himself he was watching her bottom and could see her intimate parts. One of Olena's most improper fantasies was coming true, and it was even more wickedly pleasurable than she had imagined it.

The second smack landed on her left buttock. This one was a little harder; she felt the flesh quiver in the warming aftermath of the pain.

Olena moaned, and hoped that Master Robert would interpret the sound as complaint or distress.

Only four more, and then Isabelle and Nicole would touch the places that were already pulsing with a warm rhythm. Olena silently urged Master Robert on.

I am wanton, she told herself; utterly wicked. I deserve to be punished. I hope I will be punished enough.

The light that seeped through the cracks between the shutters was fading. Robert ordered Isabelle to bring another lamp, and before he resumed his work he considered the young woman whose bountiful curves were delineated in the yellow light.

Olena had been put to the chair four times during the afternoon. There had been intervals to allow her to rest, and to be more closely inspected by Nicole; there had been a longer interval during which they had all taken coffee and brioches.

During the first three punishments Olena had been spanked: thirty smacks from Robert, then another thirty-six, and then twenty-four from Barat who, Master Robert had to admit, was playing his part with a subtlety that had to be admired. The admonishments with which Barat had punctuated his spanking seemed to have made Olena even more excited; Nicole reported that the young woman's juices were flowing so freely that drops of liquid were dripping on to the velvet seat of the chair.

After such a display of wantonness it had, of course, been clear to Robert and, after some feigned reluctance, to Barat too that Olena needed stricter discipline. So it had been decided that they would end the day's proceedings by caning her.

Olena had protested when she had seen the thin, flexible lath of hazel, but Robert had detected the gleam of excitement in her wide, dark eyes. She had mounted the chair, for the fourth time that afternoon, with barely disguised enthusiasm.

He had delivered eight strokes; there would be four more.

Robert flexed the cane in his hands. He tried to recall whether he had ever had the pleasure of chastising a woman as sensually provocative as Olena.

Her body was, of course, a delight to look upon. It seemed almost impossible that such a slender frame could support breasts and buttocks so generously rounded. Her skin was uniformly the colour of white coffee and was without a flaw; this perfection served only to emphasise the dark pink blush that suffused the two soft spheres of her buttocks and the eight thin, parallel stripes that marked them. Robert was sure that her breasts, which were as round and clearly as firm as her buttocks, would colour and mark as prettily; but, he told himself, there was no need to hurry. He had already concluded that Olena could be induced to take pleasure in every form of punishment, no matter how extreme or humiliating.

And Barat could be relied on to accompany her on that journey into depravity. He would be at her side at all times, reminding her of her wickedness, advising her to submit to further chastisement for her own good, and reassuring her that the staff of the Chateau would always know what was best for her.

Four more strokes. Robert tried to retain his professional detachment as Olena dreamily wiggled the two perfect globes he was about to strike. He would place one stripe low down on each cheek, he thought, where the top of the thigh joined the innermost curve of the buttock. The final two he would deliver vertically, one on each side of the valley between her buttocks; it had become clear that she was particularly embarrassed about revealing her arsehole so it would mortify her and therefore no doubt excite her were he to remind her in the most punitive way that her little hole was visible – and unprotected.

Robert saw the door opening. The Chatelaine entered the room. Robert experienced a wave of guilt: he had hardly spared a thought for his mistress all afternoon, so enchanted had he been by the innocent sexuality of Olena.

The Chatelaine put a finger to her lips as she approached the chair on which Olena was kneeling and around which Robert, Barat, Isabelle and Nicole were gathered. As she drew near she gestured for Robert to continue.

'How many more strokes are you to receive, Olena?' Robert asked.

Olena tossed her head once, slowly. Her eyes were closed. She was still in the trancelike state of near-ecstasy she had entered almost as soon as the first spanking had begun. 'Four more,' she said. 'But then I expect I'll deserve some more.'

'Push your bottom right out,' Robert said.

'More than that, Olena,' Barat added. 'Remember that we suspect that you have started to take an improper pride in your body. It is important that you feel the shame of displaying yourself.'

Olena sighed, and curved her spine inwards and bent her knees more until her buttocks were as taut and round as coffee-coloured balloons and the valley between them was completely revealed. Robert concluded that he had never seen an arse so fitted for the whip; he whisked the cane down hard.

The final two strokes made Olena mewl like a kitten. Robert saw that the Chatelaine's eyes were fixed on Olena, sparkling as Olena writhed on the chair.

The inspections carried out by Isabelle and Nicole revealed that despite the application of four separate punishments, Olena was still producing fluid evidence of lecherous thoughts. Barat professed himself disappointed and mystified. Olena drowsily promised that she would do her very best to be good in future, and it was decided that she would be tested again the next day.

'Remain where you are on the chair, Olena,' Robert said. 'Displaying the marks of the cane is part of the punishment. And Nicole will examine you from time to time until we are satisfied that there is no more to be done today.'

With that he obeyed the Chatelaine's wordless summons and followed her to the doorway.

'I get the impression that we have indeed found a rare jewel,' the Chatelaine whispered. 'What is your impression, Robert?'

He kept his voice as low as hers. 'You are quite right, of course, madame,' he said. 'If she is as tractable as she appears, I think it will be possible to train her to take pleasure only as a result of punishment.'

'She is a virgin?'

'In every respect, madame. I do not believe that she has ever had an orgasm, although I suspect that she came close on occasion this afternoon. She does not understand that the feelings she enjoys are to do with sex. She has no idea of what sex is.'

'So: you intend that she should be tested for a few more days?'

'Yes, madame. With gradually increasing rigour. Then, at the right moment, we will let her experience a climax.'

'And thereafter she will not be permitted to come, except when feeling intense shame?'

'Just so, madame. Then she will be punished for coming, and then she will be made to come again during the punishment. She will learn that pleasure comes from humiliation and the lash, and that pleasure condemns her to more punishment. And, madame . . .'

'Yes, Robert?'

'I propose to protect her virginity, madame. At least in the most literal meaning of the term. We will teach her how to use her mouth, her breasts and her anus to give pleasure to others, and we'll encourage her to take her own guilty enjoyment in the same ways. But we will not penetrate her vagina; not fully. And I suggest that we should make her understand that, no matter how much she may come to realise that she is defiled and debauched, she is still, in the most important sense, intact and undefiled.'

The Chatelaine smiled. 'I understand, Robert. You intend to keep alive in her a spark of hope of salvation. In this way you will ensure that her fund of shame and indignity can never be exhausted. She will strive always to be good, and will seek to be punished when, inevitably, she fails. You are a truly inventive disciplinarian.'

Robert bowed his head so that his mistress would not see him blushing with pride.

'But I fear, Robert,' the Chatelaine went on, 'that we shall have to leave the training of the delightful Olena in the hands of others for a few days. You and I have been summoned to a council meeting at the main House. We must leave tonight.'

Robert was incensed. 'The Mistress of the Private House shows you too little respect, madame,' he hissed. 'Why should you be at the beck and call of those soft-living part-timers at the main House? Their standards are lax. You, madame, are the true embodiment of the principles of the Private House. If I may say so.'

The Chatelaine hushed him. 'Your loyalty is praise-worthy, Robert. But perhaps misplaced. In any case, if we do not attend council meetings then we will have even less influence on the way our organisation is run. There is no alternative. We must go. Banish Olena from your mind for a few days. Nicole and Isabelle, with Barat's assistance, will train her well.'

Jem, at the head of the table, watched as if from a great distance the arguments among her councillors. At first the wrangling had seemed entertaining, but it was becoming tiresome.

It had been Julia's idea to summon a meeting of the full Council; she had told Jem that it would be an opportunity for Jem to confirm her authority over the sprawling spider's web of fiefdoms that made up the Private House. Jem had agreed, on a whim, but now felt insufficiently involved to do more than watch as personalities clashed and petty rivalries swamped the formulation of policy.

Robert, the Chatelaine's deputy, was upbraiding Sebastian for alleged shortcomings in the organisation of the main house. Jem recognised the attack as an encoded criticism of her, but felt unmoved by Robert's vehemence.

'At the Chateau,' Robert was stating, 'the rules are rigidly enforced. There is no laxity in the Chatelaine's domain. Why, I doubt if a single one of you –' and here he pointed directly at Sebastian '– could undergo the training that our slaves learn to love. Not one of you has the dedication to discipline of the Chatelaine. Not one of you would dare to go through the trials that we, at the Chateau, expect our slaves and volunteers to suffer.'

There was a chorus of refutation from around the table. Sebastian glanced imploringly at Jem. She smiled at him brightly. He turned away with a look of despair on his face.

Jem began to realise that she would have to do something. Julia was right, as always: in the absence of Jem's attention, the Private House was disintegrating. The House needed the firm hand of its Mistress. The problem was that Jem could not summon any reserves of desire to rule. Quite the opposite, she admitted to herself.

She held up a hand, and the squabbling gradually ceased.

'Chatelaine,' she said, 'are you in agreement with Robert's assessment?'

The Chatelaine, sitting as straight and as sombre as an undertaker, and suitably dressed for the part in a gown of shimmering black, pondered her reply. 'Robert is, I fear, Mistress, merely voicing – too enthusiastically, perhaps – what many of us are thinking. There can be no doubting the Private House's commitment to the pursuit of power and to the enjoyment of all forms of sexuality. However, I think that many of the councillors have forgotten the prime duty of all in the Private House. At the Chateau we have not forgotten that the first and only duty is to obey.'

This was, Jem realised, another subtle criticism of her leadership. The councillors had understood the hidden meaning, too, and were visibly shocked that it had come from the Chatelaine, who was the mistress of the most important site other than the main house and almost as close to Jem as Julia and Sebastian.

Jem closed her eyes as the arguments recommenced and rose in volume around her. The Chatelaine was right, of course. The only duty was to obey. Once, when Jem had first entered the Private House, Terence Headman had almost made her obey him; since then, however, she had been the Mistress, and had only had to require others to obey her. And now she felt drained of all desire to impose her will.

She stood up. The shouting ceased.

Jem unclasped the brooch at the collar of her robe and let the heavy material slide from her shoulders. Now she was revealed in her ornate version of the guards' uniform; she knew that the shining black leather, which drew attention to her naked breasts and crotch, never failed to impress.

'Chatelaine,' she said, 'do you – or does anyone here – suggest that the Private House would benefit if I were no longer its Mistress?'

No one spoke. Jem looked from one to another of her councillors. Which of them, she wondered, would prove to be disloyal? And did she care?

The Chatelaine smiled contentedly. Her deputy, Robert, was flushed and excited. Sebastian appeared to be speechless with outrage. Rhoda's face was inscrutable. Terence, like most around the table, looked puzzled. And Julia – dear, beloved Julia – was simply frowning.

'Well, it doesn't matter,' Jem said. 'I'm resigning, anyway.'

She waited until the hubbub died away.

'There is just one condition,' she said. 'I intend to take up the Chatelaine's challenge. I will become a slave at the Chateau for five days. If, during that time, I am once disobedient, then I will remain at the Chateau in whatever position the Chatelaine places me. But if I can, during five days of what I am confident will be very rigorous discipline, adhere to the duty to obey, then I will require all of you to renew your oaths of loyalty to me and never again to question my authority. Is that clear?'

Julia was staring at her with a look of unbearable sadness. The others were shouting at each other again.

Jem looked at the Chatelaine, and cocked her head. The Chatelaine nodded, and rose to her commanding height. She paced along the table and, with a final swish of her black gown, came to stand beside Jem. Robert hurried to catch up with her.

'Remove your clothes, slave,' the Chatelaine said.

Jem tugged at the fingers of her long gloves, rolled them from her arms, and dropped them on the conference table. She began to unclasp her tunic.

Julia arrived at the head of the table. 'Jem, Mistress, you mustn't do this. They won't let you come back.' Jem could see that she was almost weeping with anxiety as she implored Jem to reconsider.

'It will be all right, Jules. I promise you. I can do this. I want to do it. Just help me take off my boots, would you?'

'No talking,' the Chatelaine said into Jem's ear, and pushed her whip under Jem's short skirt to touch it against

101

Jem's buttocks. However, she didn't prevent Jem from accepting Julia's help.

As Jem undressed, the noise in the council chamber subsided until the night wind could be heard whistling through the trees in the park.

When Jem was completely naked, the Chatelaine's voice broke the silence. 'Stand away from the table. Let them all see you. Remember, you're a slave now.'

Jem bowed her head and backed away from the table into a clear space. All the councillors could see that she was naked from head to foot. Jem felt a great sense of anticipation, as though she were about to embark on an expedition into unknown territory.

'Robert,' the Chatelaine said. 'Collar her.'

Robert was behind Jem. She heard him approach. She felt the leather collar as he passed it round her throat.

She reached up and grasped it. It stopped moving.

This, she realised, is the moment of decision. I can pull the collar off, announce that this whole idea was a prank, a test of loyalty, a moment of madness – anything. I am the Mistress of the Private House; they will all do as I say. I don't have to be a slave. I don't have to do anything I don't want to do.

She released the collar, and let her hand fall to her side. The collar was round her neck now.

'Six lashes for that little exhibition,' the Chatelaine said, as Jem felt Robert fasten the buckle at the back of her neck. Jem shuddered; a jolt of yearning lust, as fast and as shocking as a bolt of lightning, sparked from her nipples to her loins. She was a slave.

'Shall we whip her now, madame?' she heard Robert suggest. 'It would be instructive for our fellow councillors.'

The Chatelaine spoke like an indulgent mother. 'No, Robert,' she said. 'I want to get this little slut into the Chateau as quickly as possible. We have only five days in which to break her. You can give her the six lashes while we're travelling. And don't worry: I'll make sure you have plenty of opportunities to discipline her.'

Four

The conical roofs of the Chateau's towers were burnished by the dawn sunlight. No morning light reached the courtyard below, closed round with stone walls. Instead, the flames of torches danced in chill gusts of wind, throwing curious shadows against the limestone blocks of the walls and across the cobbled ground.

The torches were held by more than a hundred men and women: the staff, guards, servants, slaves and guests at the Chateau, all of whom had been woken at dawn and told to assemble to witness the arrival of a most unexpected and prestigious visitor.

The Chatelaine had sent Robert ahead to make the arrangements. As she strode beneath the twin towers of the gatehouse and into the centre of the courtyard, the throng called out in unison, 'Good day, madame.' Robert had done well: the slaves were almost naked, and shivering; the staff and guests had been told to wear their most outrageous costumes; and all were standing in straight rows and looking wide awake, no doubt in fear of Robert's whip.

While Robert had been organising the welcome at the Chateau, the Chatelaine had remained in the carriage with Jem. She had used the time to give the erstwhile Supreme Mistress of the Private House a first taste of the trials she would undergo beneath the Chateau's battlements. The six stripes created by Robert's whip had already almost faded from Jem's pretty little backside, so the Chatelaine had held Jem across her lap while one of the coachmen gave her a spanking.

Then the Chatelaine had instructed Jem to thank the coachman, and to ask her for permission to lick madame's cunt. When Jem was on her hands and knees before her she had slapped Jem's face a few times and had grabbed two handfuls of Jem's titian locks in order to pull Jem's reddened face against her vulva.

'Coachman,' she had said, 'kneel behind this slave and fuck her. Put a couple of fingers up her arse at the same time.'

Jem was extraordinarily pretty and delicate; the Chatelaine had always thought so, and had for a long time harboured a desire to have the Mistress of the Private House at her command and once again licking between her thighs, and to see those elfin features smeared with the juices of her sex.

As the Chatelaine had reached her climax, gripping the leather armrests of her luxurious carriage seat and watching the coachman's cock and fingers plunging into her lovely new slave, she had concluded that the reality was even better than the fantasy had been. The casually proud Jem Darke was hers to humble; for a mere five days, in theory, but the Chatelaine was confident that no one could willingly submit to certain of the torments that she had conceived. And so Jem would be hers for ever.

She would have both Jem and Olena. Once they were both trained, she would hardly need any other diversion.

The Chatelaine's confidence had been temporarily disturbed when she had noticed that Jem, pulling back from between her new mistress's trembling thighs and with her new mistress's juices glistening on her face, had been grinning mischievously and licking her lips. Worse still, on being released from between the Chatelaine's thighs Jem had started to rock back and forth, meeting the coachman's thrusts, to the evident enjoyment of both parties. The Chatelaine was sure that if she had not ordered the coachman to withdraw Jem would have achieved a climax of her own.

Now, however, as she saw gathered in the courtyard the ranks before whom Jem was about to be humiliated, she once again felt sure that she would be able to transform her former mistress into the most abject slave. Jem was alone, and far from any friends or allies; the Chatelaine had at her disposal all the resources, staff and specialised training equipment of the Chateau. There was no hope for Jem.

The Chatelaine marched back and forth in front of the crowd. Her high heels cracked like gunshots as they struck the cobbles; the sounds echoed against the towers in the still, cold morning air. This morning she was in leather: a one-piece costume of tight-fitting burgundy kid that gleamed in the torchlight. She had had Jem dress her. Her boots were of the same material, as were her gloves, and the whip and the leash that she was carrying. Her blonde hair was tightly plaited and pinned in a coil on her head; her heels made her even taller. She knew she looked magnificent, and she paraded in front of her followers in order to impress on them her indisputable authority, and to emphasise the distinction between her and the slave they were about to see.

As she cast her gaze along the rows of expectant faces she searched for Olena's, and was satisfied when she was sure that the girl was not in the courtyard. Robert had, as instructed, kept her locked in her room; the Chatelaine had not wanted her to be disturbed by witnessing a scene that she might have found upsetting. It was important that Olena's innocence should be eroded only with great care and patience.

'Good day, everyone,' she announced at last. 'I have gathered you here at this unsocial hour so that all of you can witness the arrival of a new visitor.'

Cold feet shuffled; clouds, barely perceptible in the grey sky, raced over the roofs; in the courtyard the shadows still danced.

'The visitor has been here before, on several occasions. Some of you will recognise her, from her previous visits or perhaps from seeing her at other establishments belonging to the Private House. She is memorable, at least in part because of her beauty. And, of course, because she was

105

Supreme Mistress.' The Chatelaine raised her voice and shouted harshly. 'Enter the Chateau, slave. Let them all see you.'

Everyone in the courtyard, including the Chatelaine, stared into the darkness beneath the gatehouse. From the shadows a figure emerged: a young woman, naked but for a black collar, her form small and slender, crawling on hands and knees. Her wavy titian hair touched the cobblestones as, with head bowed, she made her way slowly and painfully towards the Chatelaine.

Whispers flew about the crowd. 'Is it her?' 'It can't be her.' 'No, it is, it's Jem Darke.' 'Yes, I saw her here in the summer.' 'It's definitely the Mistress.'

The Chatelaine did nothing – yet – to silence the murmurs. She wanted everyone to be sure that the pathetic naked waif crawling towards her booted feet was, indeed, Jem Darke. And so only when Jem had reached her, and had waited on all fours beside her for several minutes, did she hold up a gloved hand for silence.

'Master Robert, come forward,' she called out.

Robert pushed his way through the crowd and stood, smiling tightly, next to his mistress. She handed him her whip of burgundy leather. It was light and short, but its song would be audible in the enclosed space of the courtyard. And it would sting.

'The new slave will kiss my boots to demonstrate her subservience,' she announced. 'During the demonstration she will be whipped.'

She took a few steps so that she was in the very centre of the courtyard. 'Approach, slave,' she said.

As Jem crawled towards her the Chatelaine wondered, not for the first time, whether she should not take the responsibility for ending Jem's foolish behaviour. In the informal hierarchy of the Private House only the Chatelaine, and perhaps Julia as chief of the guards, had the authority to step in and call a halt to what could easily be seen as an aberration on Jem's part, a momentary whim that might well consign the former Supreme Mistress to a life of perpetual slavery.

The Chatelaine and Jem had never been close friends, but they had worked well together. It had been Julia, acting on Jem's behalf, who had recruited the Chatelaine and her disciplinary establishment into the Private House organisation. And, although Jem and the Chatelaine had not frequently been lovers, there had been a summer afternoon here at the Chateau, and a long night in the cellars below the main House, that the Chatelaine remembered fondly.

Those memories – Jem's slim body bound and writhing in chains, her pert buttocks wriggling and reddening as the Chatelaine plied her riding-crop, her pretty face suffused with joy as she came – were among the reasons why the Chatelaine was delighted to have Jem at her mercy in the Chateau. But the Chatelaine remembered also, with a shock of pleasure, that she herself had experienced the surprising strength in Jem's slender arms, and the skill with which Jem wielded a whip. In the candlelit cellar, locked into a wooden frame that permitted no movement, the Chatelaine had been able to do nothing but moan, and plead, and come over and over again as Jem had used on her exposed breasts, bottom, anus and vulva a whip, a strap, a cane, her tongue, her fingers, and a large artificial phallus. Jem had been pitiless: the punishments and the pleasurings had gone on for hour after hour, with interruptions long enough only to allow the Chatelaine a drink of water and for her limp body to be repositioned in the frame so that a different target was presented for Jem's remorseless attentions.

What concerned the Chatelaine now was that she remembered that Jem had enjoyed the Chatelaine's ordeal almost as much as the Chatelaine had, and had come almost as frequently, using the Chatelaine's face, or her own fingers, or the handle of the whip between strokes, or the phallus as she worked it into the Chatelaine's vagina or anus. Surely Jem would find it unthinkable to devote herself entirely to submission?

The Chatelaine looked down at the woman on all fours before her. Jem had parted her legs and hollowed her back,

107

like a well-trained slave, and her bottom was invitingly open and uplifted. I can't resist this temptation, the Chatelaine thought; or the challenge of breaking her spirit within five days. I will be firm, and very cruel.

She reached down and touched Jem's tumbling hair. 'My dear Mistress,' she whispered, 'I will do my best to make you suffer beautifully.' She stood straight. 'Now get your face pressed against my boots, you slut,' she ordered loudly, for the benefit of the crowd, 'and get your arse up for the whip. Robert: twenty lashes, delivered with long gaps. I want this moment to last. And I want all of you here today to remember it.'

Jem swept her hair from one side of her face as she lowered herself to rest on her elbows, with her lips pressed against the toe of the Chatelaine's right boot. The Chatelaine realised that Jem had revealed her face for the benefit of the audience: those who were not in a position to see the whip landing on her parted buttocks would instead be able to witness her devoted kissing of her new mistress's boots.

Robert lifted the whip into the air and brought it down with a ferocity that wrung a cry from Jem and a collective gasp from the crowd. The Chatelaine glared at him until it was clear that he understood he was to use the whip moderately. 'There will be a time for that, Robert,' the Chatelaine said quietly, in the pause between the first and the second of the lashes. 'But don't let your enthusiasm overrule your experience. As usual, we will proceed by degrees.'

'Yes, madame,' Robert said, and delivered the second stroke, eliciting from Jem no more than a grunt and a brief interruption in the kissing and licking that she was lavishing on the Chatelaine's boots.

After the tenth stroke the Chatelaine began to address the ranks again, pausing at intervals whenever the whip descended. 'You all know, now, the identity of the new slave,' she said. 'However, her previous identity and position are now erased. She is here of her own volition, and does not wish to be addressed by her name or by any of the titles she once held.'

108

The Chatelaine leaned forwards to look at Jem's buttocks. Robert's first stroke had left an angry weal, but the other stripes, while visible, were more decorative than damaging. Nonetheless, the Chatelaine was sure that Jem's bottom was beginning to feel very sore, particularly as it had already received a whipping during the night and a spanking that morning. She smiled at the thought as Robert administered the fifteenth stroke.

'This new slave,' she went on, 'enters the Chateau for intensive training and for a regime of hard discipline. She is, from this moment, the lowliest of the slaves. I expect all of you to assist me in ensuring that she infringes none of our rules, and that she is severely punished should she do so. You will report at once to any member of the staff if she is disrespectful, if she speaks without invitation, if she covers her breasts, her buttocks, or her sex, if she masturbates, or if she fails to be polite or to make her body available. As I have devised a thorough training schedule for her she will have little time at large in the public rooms and grounds of the Chateau; however, should you meet her, remember that she is the most subordinate slave, and therefore is at the disposal of any one of you.'

The Chatelaine wondered how her words, and the whipping while in such a humiliating position, were affecting Jem. Was she fearful, and beginning to realise the mistake she had made in volunteering to submit? Did she not care – was her decision to come here the result of some nihilistic despair? Or was she excited – were her juices even now starting to seep from between the shaven labia that she was displaying to the crowd as the stripes were laid across her bottom?

In the end, it didn't matter. The Chatelaine had no doubt that, whatever Jem's frame of mind, the erstwhile Supreme Mistress would sooner or later quail at one of the torments the Chatelaine had planned, and would be unable willingly to submit. And then Jem would belong to the Chatelaine for ever.

The whip descended for the eighteenth time. The Chatelaine looked down and saw Jem's body shudder.

'Finally,' the Chatelaine pronounced, 'remember that this new slave has no name. She will obey you if you address her simply as "slave", but you can use any description that suits her status: slut, whore, whipping girl. She will be punished if she fails to answer to any such description. Stop kissing my feet now,' she added, and stepped back.

The Chatelaine held up her hand to delay the application of the final stroke of the whip.

'Lift your face, whore-slave,' she said. It felt strange but very satisfying to address Jem in such demeaning terms. 'Look at your new mistress. Let us all see you enjoy the last taste of the lash – for the time being.'

Jem lifted her face. Her cheeks were flushed, her lips were swollen, and her violet eyes were bright with tears.

'Now, Robert,' the Chatelaine said, and smiled; Jem gasped as the blow landed, and then grimaced.

'Straighten up, pretty little slut,' the Chatelaine said. 'Kneel with your hands behind your back. That's right. Look at her, everybody; isn't she the very picture of a chastised slave? She looks very contrite now. Perhaps you're thinking that she's been punished enough? That now we should pardon her?'

The Chatelaine noticed a puzzled frown appear briefly on Jem's face. Did she expect to be reprieved? Did she hope for it, or fear it?

'You would be wrong,' the Chatelaine stated. 'I cannot tell you what offence this slave has committed; all I can say is that her behaviour has been such that no amount of punishment, and no amount of repentance, can possibly be adequate. She is cunning and manipulative; she will try to persuade you that she is sorry, and that she deserves to be forgiven. We must all be on our guard. We must show her no mercy.'

Grabbing a handful of Jem's hair, the Chatelaine showed her new slave's face to the crowd. 'She looks contrite,' the Chatelaine said. 'She will pretend that she is sorry. But we must ignore her. What she requires – what she knows she needs – is a strict regime of discipline. What do you want, little slut?'

'I want to be punished again,' Jem whispered.

The Chatelaine pulled her hair. 'Say "please", you despicable wretch. Address me properly. And this time, speak up.'

The hint of a smile appeared on Jem's face. 'I want to be punished again,' she said in a clear, firm voice. 'Oh, madame, please do have me whipped all over again.'

'Precocious slut,' the Chatelaine whispered, and released Jem's hair. 'I can see you're going to bring out the worst in me. And,' she added in a louder voice, 'do you bind yourself to obey me, and the rules of the Chateau, and the instructions of all within the Chateau?'

'I do, madame,' Jem replied, as loudly. 'And thank you for allowing me to kiss your boots.'

'Very good,' the Chatelaine said. It thrilled her to hear Jem speaking so subserviently; suddenly she wanted nothing more than to take her new slave to her chamber and hold that pretty, tearful, disconsolate face between her thighs.

'You are all dismissed,' the Chatelaine said. The lines of staff, guests and slaves began to troop from the courtyard into the surrounding ranges of the Chateau. 'Robert, have you arranged a room for the whore-slave?'

'I'm sorry, madame,' Robert replied. 'I didn't know what arrangements you would think best.'

'That's all right, Robert. I hadn't considered the question until now, and it does present certain difficulties.'

'Given her lowly position,' Robert suggested, 'the only place for her is surely the common slaves' dormitory. We have no accommodation less comfortable or more crowded.'

The Chatelaine took a few steps away from Jem, and beckoned Robert to follow her. The pretty little slut was still kneeling, with her head bowed, and looked entirely passive. The Chatelaine distrusted appearances, however. 'The problem with putting her with the other slaves,' she said quietly, 'or indeed with any of the staff, is that, as I have just decreed, she is to be available for general use at all times.'

111

'Are you concerned that she will be become exhausted, madame?'

'To some extent, Robert. But it would be wise never to underestimate the stamina of this particular slave. No, I'm more concerned that she might find the experience far too enjoyable. And more than that, I don't want her mixing with any others here. I want to know where she is and what she's doing at all times. I'm sure you've heard the stories of how she organised the staff at the main House to overturn the rule of Headman, when he started to become too autocratic. I don't want to give her any opportunity for exercising her political skills here.'

'A solitary room, then,' Robert said. 'A cell in the dungeon, perhaps.'

'Yes,' the Chatelaine said. An idea had come to her. 'The big cell. It has spyholes, and a listening chamber above. It's the best place to keep her under observation. And place Olena in the same cell.'

Robert was surprised. 'Olena? But only a few days ago we moved her to one of the guest chambers. I don't understand, madame.'

The Chatelaine laughed, and turned to see that Jem, left kneeling in the centre of the courtyard, was covertly scanning the four stone walls and watching the comings and goings of the few staff and slaves who were beginning their morning chores. The nipples on her proud breasts were stiff with the cold; her titian hair was swept by the wind; the stripes on her slim, pale buttocks were more pronounced than when Robert had created them. She looked more desirable than ever.

'Perhaps it's just a whim, Robert,' she admitted. 'I like the conceit of having my two most interesting slaves locked up together. And, as we need to keep a close watch on both of them, putting them both in the observation cell in the dungeon seems sensible. And isn't Olena ready for the dungeon? I would have thought that by now Barat and Nicole between them must have convinced her that Hades itself would be too virtuous a place for one as wicked as her.'

'You are right, madame. As always. Olena will find the dungeon a fearsome place, and will realise that being imprisoned there is yet another manifestation of her inner wickedness. And she is so innocent that she cannot possibly be of any help to the Mis–, I mean, to the filthy whore-slave.'

The bristles of the brush caressed the hard, vertical underside of Barat's penis. Isabelle's fingers cupped his left testicle, squeezed it gently, and then squeezed again more firmly as she used the tip of the brush to flick his frenum, the tautly stretched membrane that connected the helmet of his member to the skin of his shaft.

Barat took a deep breath. He felt perspiration break out again on his face and chest. By now, he thought, my dark skin must be glistening in the lamplight. There was hardly a breath of air circulating in the heavily curtained room. He could smell the sweat of his excitement, mingling with Isabelle's womanly scents.

He had been kept aroused for what seemed like an hour, although he knew it must be less than half that, and he could only just prevent himself from coming; it was almost impossible to keep still and silent. He tried to concentrate on maintaining his position and on staring straight ahead with no expression on his face.

His wrists had been crossed behind his back; each was cuffed, and each cuff was individually tethered to the harness that he was becoming used to wearing on his balls and cock. If he were to move his hands he would not fail to feel the movement, and Isabelle could not fail to see it.

'Did you say something, Barat?' Isabelle said. 'When I did this?'

She squeezed his bound scrotum again, and then deliberately pinched the skin of the stretched, bulbous sac.

Barat gasped. His right hand moved instinctively to try to protect his manhood, and before he could control the impulse he felt a thrill of pain as his erection was tugged sideways.

Isabelle tutted.

'Well,' she said, 'that was better than last time. You've earned only ten strokes.'

Ten strokes. That meant he had lasted for twenty minutes without reacting in any way. His target today was half an hour; whenever he failed to achieve his target he received one stroke for each minute of failure. The previous session had ended with fifteen strokes. He was improving, and he felt ridiculously proud.

'I'll punish you now,' Isabelle said. 'Then I'll remove the harness and allow you a short break. Then we'll start again: arousal, insertion of the anal plug and fitting the harness. You're getting very good at managing to keep quiet and still through all that. All you have to do is to continue to be stoical while I torment you. Next time I'll use my mouth: my lips, my tongue, and my sharp little teeth. Your poor penis! Will you be able to keep still, do you think?' She pressed her palm against the hard, hot, imprisoned length of his erection.

'I might be able to,' Barat said thoughtfully, 'if I were given an incentive.'

Isabelle laughed. 'Is the prospect of helping to educate Olena not enough for you?' she said. 'You have to learn how to show no emotion, no matter how great the stimulus. You know what Robert has planned next for Olena. I would have thought you would be looking forward to it.'

Thinking of Olena was not helping Barat's erection to subside. Nor was the insistent pressure of Isabelle's hand. His hard flesh was still sorely stiff within its leather bondage. 'That's all very well,' he said, 'but you know I won't be allowed to have Olena until Robert is satisfied with her progress. It could be weeks. I need some encouragement now.'

'Oh, I'll let you lick me,' Isabelle said carelessly. 'If you pass today's test – thirty minutes without moving or making a noise – I'll sit on your face and, if you lick me properly, I'll play with your penis. We can come together.'

Barat, surprised by Isabelle's untypical generosity and suddenly overwhelmed by the flood of images it conjured in his mind, had to clench all his muscles in order to prevent himself coming there and then. 'I look forward to it,' he said through gritted teeth.

'Ah yes,' Isabelle said, 'and so do I. You will lick all over my bottom, and inside my anus. Then I will sit down hard, and make you lick me for a long time while I ride on your face. But first you must succeed in remaining motionless for thirty minutes. And before that you have to be punished for failing just now.'

Ten strokes. Barat had become almost contemptuous of such minor chastisements. However, it was difficult to bend forwards – his erection, tethered upright against his stomach, prevented him leaning very far – and as he moved his legs apart, as he had learned to, he became more aware of the discomfort caused by the ivory phallus in his anus.

Isabelle, flexing the cane, came to stand behind him. 'Are you ready?' she said. He felt her finger press against the strap that ran between his buttocks. She toyed with the base of the phallus where it protruded through the strap. 'Do you find this more comfortable today? It helps to keep you hard, I think.'

Barat decided that the question was rhetorical, and merely grunted. It was true that he found the phallus less uncomfortable than he had on the previous day, and he had to admit that the constant sense of fullness in his fundament seemed to act almost physically to keep his penis pushed forwards and his testicles tingling.

The door opened and someone stepped into the room, creating a draught of cool air. The light from the corridor seemed unnaturally bright for a moment, and then the door was closed again.

Barat knew better than to look up but he recognised the polished black boots: Master Robert had come to assess his progress. Barat cursed under his breath; he had been beginning to enjoy being trained by Isabelle, but he didn't want Robert to observe his torments and punishments, and he particularly didn't want Robert to see that he was starting to enjoy them.

'Well?' Robert said impatiently.

'We've just finished the second session, Master Robert,' Isabelle said. 'Barat is improving. He received fifteen strokes after the first session; he's about to receive another ten.'

'Very good,' Robert said, although he sounded far from satisfied.

Robert's boots disappeared from Barat's view. The Master had gone to stand beside Isabelle. Suddenly Barat felt Robert's gloved hands mauling his buttocks.

'Has he taken to the plug?' Robert said, pulling on the base of the phallus.

'Yes, Master Robert,' Isabelle replied. 'I think so. Although, of course, he hasn't yet worn it for an extended period.'

'He's got a pretty arse on him,' Robert commented. 'A bit plump for some tastes, but very smooth and round. I must remember to give him a good buggering before he leaves the Chateau.'

Barat was about to turn and protest loudly, but instead was almost thrown off balance when a hefty swipe of Robert's hand landed on his left buttock.

'But look here, girl,' Robert said. 'There's hardly a mark on him. I thought you said he's had fifteen?'

'Yes, Master Robert.' Isabelle sounded worried and very anxious to please. 'With the cane. With this cane.'

There was a pause. Barat assumed that Robert was inspecting the cane. He could imagine Robert's dismissive expression. There was a shuffling of feet; a whistle in the air; the smack of wood against flesh; and a sharp cry from Isabelle.

'That's how to use a cane,' Robert said. 'But in any case a cane isn't appropriate for this type of training. Fetch a strap: not too broad, medium weight, and with two or three lighter tails at the end. You'll find one just like that in the equipment drawer of the desk.'

Barat heard Isabelle's footsteps recede and return.

'That's the correct implement,' Robert said. 'Now: stand well back from the target, use an upswing, and try to make sure that, as the strap lands on his arse, those tails catch him between his legs – that harness lifts his balls out of the way, so to catch them you need the upward motion and the extra length provided by the tails. Well, get on with it. Or I'll demonstrate on your pretty little backside.'

Isabelle hurried to reply. 'Yes, Master Robert.'

Barat closed his eyes and waited. He would endure the punishment. He just hoped that Robert would then leave, so that Isabelle and he could resume the intimate training and then enjoy the rewards of his success.

It was all relatively familiar and surprisingly enjoyable. Jem had to admit that even being addressed as 'slut' and 'slave' gave her a frisson of pleasure.

It seemed that on this first day of Jem's trial the Chatelaine had determined that her new slave was to be paraded in front of as many of the inmates of the Chateau as possible. Therefore Jem had found herself ordered to be the model or victim in a series of the day-to-day lessons and demonstrations that constituted a large part of the activities of the Chateau.

From the courtyard where she had been publicly whipped, Jem had been led, still on hands and knees, to the Chatelaine's bedchamber.

In the doorway, the Chatelaine took the leash from Robert's hand. 'You can leave us alone now, Robert,' she said. 'I'll ring for you when I've finished with her, and you can take her to her first lesson.'

The Chatelaine pulled on the leash and Jem crawled forwards into the curtained darkness of the room as the door closed behind her. The room smelled of the Chatelaine's perfume. Jem glanced up at the four-poster bed, and remembered vividly the hot afternoon that she and the Chatelaine had spent on it, giggling like schoolgirls as they had taken turns to instigate games of mastery and submission.

The first kiss had been tentative; both women had been accustomed to being obeyed, and neither was eager to compromise her authority. But after a few minutes of kissing, which became ever more intense, there had been no mistaking the mutual desire that had shone in both pairs of eyes. As they undressed each other, each recognised the other's beauty: the Chatelaine tall, slender and elegant, Jem shorter and, as the Chatelaine put it, as pretty as a doll.

They had not bothered to have brought to the room any of the equipment and costumes with which the Chateau was so well supplied. They had used their lips, tongues and fingers to tease and torment each other, and when punishments were called for they had used their hands or the belt that Jem had been wearing.

Jem recalled that she had returned again and again to the Chatelaine's proud breasts, using her fingers or the belt to draw cries of protest that Jem had captured in her own mouth with rapacious kisses. She had made the Chatelaine beg Jem to torture her nipples, and had made her come over and over again as Jem sat astride her, meting out cruel pinches with one hand while reaching behind to dabble in their mingled juices with the other.

And, Jem remembered, her own most intense orgasms had come while she had been draped face down across a heap of pillows in the centre of the bed, writhing languidly as the Chatelaine, whispering endearments, had whipped her bottom, and caressed her and opened her, and penetrated her vagina and anus with various numbers of fingers.

Now, as she waited patiently on all fours in the Chatelaine's bedroom, Jem realised that she was becoming very aroused. Her bottom was warm from the courtyard whipping; her breasts felt heavy; and she knew she was getting wet again.

The Chatelaine released the leash from Jem's collar. 'Well, slave,' she said, 'I'm going to enjoy you before I turn you over to my staff for the start of your ordeal. Crawl towards me – on your elbows and knees, as I want to see your pretty bottom on display.'

Jem crawled in the direction from which the Chatelaine's voice had come. She hollowed her back as much as she could: she always enjoyed showing off her bottom, and being under the Chatelaine's instruction was doing nothing to decrease her excitement.

'Turn around,' the Chatelaine said. 'Let me see the stripes. Ah, yes. Very good. I need hardly tell you that during your stay here your buttocks will at all times carry the marks of discipline.'

Jem was aware of the Chatelaine at her side, and stopped moving. The Chatelaine stroked her hair, her neck and then her buttocks.

'You stupid little bitch,' the Chatelaine said, very softly. 'Do you really believe that you have any hope of passing the test you have set yourself? I have certain tortures and indignities planned for you that it will be impossible for a woman of your spirit willingly to endure. And at the first sign of protest, you will become mine for ever. Don't expect any mercy; don't expect a reprieve. I'm sure you remember what it feels like when you submit to me. I remember, too. The most acute pleasure; the most treasured memories. I will do anything to keep you; therefore I will torment you until you rebel, and I will adhere rigidly to the rules that you have set for yourself. I'm sure you expect nothing less.'

'No, madame,' Jem said, trembling with fear as much as with excitement. 'Thank you, madame.'

The Chatelaine slapped Jem's backside. 'Now undress me, slave,' she said. 'Then climb on to the bed.'

Giving pleasure to the Chatelaine was no punishment. Jem adored the Chatelaine's high, conical breasts and their long nipples; she always enjoyed tasting another woman's sexual excitement, and using her tongue to penetrate and titillate. The fact that the Chatelaine required her to keep her bottom raised, and made her ask formally for permission to proceed with each act, and called her by the most degrading and obscene names, seemed to Jem to add to rather than detract from the experience.

Under Jem's expert tongue the Chatelaine came quickly and ground her vulva against Jem's face as, between the gulping breaths of her climax, she promised again to keep her new slave in chains for ever.

They ate a light meal: the Chatelaine had Jem feed her with her fingers, and Jem was then permitted to ask for the scraps, which she ate, sitting naked on the floor, while the Chatelaine ran a bath.

While she took small bites from the last piece of bread, Jem reflected that, so far, being the lowliest slave in the Chateau was far from disagreeable. Hunger, she thought, might be the most trying aspect of the place; that, and being continually aroused but not permitted to come.

She licked her fingers, and breathed in again the sharp, slightly lemony smell of the Chatelaine's sex. She felt a shiver of desire, and allowed her hand to fall into her lap, her fingers to curl around her shaven mound. It would take only a few slight movements to bring her to the edge. But she was a slave, and slaves were not to touch themselves without permission. She would have to ask; the thought of doing so caused another stab of desire. If permission were granted, the Chatelaine would watch her. And the pleasure, Jem realised, would be much more intense.

She got up, stretched, and strolled to the bathroom. In the doorway she sank to her knees. The Chatelaine was in the bath. The room was hot with steam, and smelled of the perfumed bubbles that rose in foaming piles around the Chatelaine's body.

'Madame,' Jem said, 'I apologise for interrupting. May I have permission to masturbate?'

The Chatelaine smiled. 'Certainly not,' she said. 'You are not here for your own entertainment. However, you may wash me.'

Once the Chatelaine had been covered in bubbles and then rinsed, and had had her breasts and her sex sponged until she had come again, Jem was allowed to reuse the tepid bath water for a few minutes in order to clean herself.

The Chatelaine also told Jem that, as long as she was quick about it, she could use the contents of the Chatelaine's dressing table so that she would look presentable for the rest of the day.

'Cosmetics are the only luxuries that you will be allowed,' the Chatelaine said. 'Not for your own benefit, of course. It's simply one of your duties as a slave to make yourself pleasing to everyone in the Chateau.'

Jem merely thanked her mistress very politely, and proceeded to help herself to perfume, powder, oils and rouge. She had succeeded in sampling all of the most expensive items in the Chatelaine's armoury when there was a knock at the door.

'I'm sorry to interrupt, madame.' It was Robert's voice. 'But the deportment class is about to begin, and I thought it best to check whether you had finished with the new slave.'

'One moment, Robert,' the Chatelaine called out. She almost ran to the dressing table, pulled Jem up, and kissed her. Then she held her at arm's length, nodded approvingly, and clipped the leash on to Jem's collar. 'On your knees, you pretty little whore,' she whispered. 'Now we'll see how long you can submit to real discipline.' She raised her voice. 'Come in, Robert. Take away this dirty little girl. And remember, don't spare her.'

The shutters at the windows kept Olena's room in half-darkness even when it was daylight outside. Nicole, on arriving with breakfast, had opened only one shutter, and then only slightly.

'It's late,' Nicole had said. 'But it doesn't matter: your next session is not until this afternoon. The Chatelaine and Master Robert have returned with a new slave. She's very special. It's all rather exciting.'

Olena had felt a sudden pang that she recognised as envy; she was already accustomed to being the centre of attention at the Chateau. The jealousy had been followed immediately by a wave of shame, as she had realised how self-obsessed she had become.

'And don't try to cover yourself,' Nicole had continued. 'You know that you must try not to think about your breasts and your pudenda. Put your hands behind your back. Come and sit next to me; I'll feed you your breakfast.'

Olena had submitted to being fed as if she were a baby.

During the meal Nicole had caressed Olena's breasts and the insides of her thighs, in order, Nicole had said, that Olena could become accustomed to finding such attentions normal and not particularly exciting.

After the last mouthful of croissant and hot chocolate, Nicole had wiped Olena's lips and had congratulated her on managing to remain unaware of her breasts and her private parts throughout the meal. Olena had blushed and stammered, but had been too ashamed to admit that Nicole's gentle touches had left her in a turmoil of emotions, and that she had felt the tell-tale signs of her wickedness from the moment that Nicole had told her to reveal her body.

She had known that she should have told Nicole that her breasts felt warm, that her nipples felt hard and tense, and that between her parted legs she could feel the hot tickling that indicated that she was getting wet inside. And she had known that she should have immediately asked to be punished. As Nicole had cleared the plates and cups on to the tray, Olena had tried to raise the subject of discipline.

'Yesterday,' she had begun, 'I did badly in the tests. And Barat said I needed to be smacked again. Well, Nicole, the thing is that I think today –'

'Don't concern yourself with yesterday,' Nicole had interrupted with a smile. 'You'll learn how to be good. It may take some time, but we'll all do our best to help you. Forget about yesterday. We'll give you more tests today, and you'll have another chance to show us how well you can behave.'

Olena had almost burst into tears of frustration. She didn't understand why she found herself looking forward to the testing and the examinations, even though she knew that she was doomed to fail and to suffer the humiliation of disappointing Barat. And she had wished that she could make Nicole, at least, understand that the punishments were doing no good. At the end of the previous day's examination Barat had held her gently in his arms and had whispered encouraging words from the holy texts while Nicole and Isabelle, each concentrating on one buttock, had spanked her soundly with their bare hands and then with strips of wood. And although she was filled with remorse, Olena had found herself floating on clouds of inexpressible pleasure, anticipating each smack with a guilty thrill and revelling in the pressure of Barat's coarse robe against her naked breasts.

'But today,' Olena had insisted, 'I've already had some of those sinful feelings today. Dozing in bed, I was thinking about Barat.'

'And what exactly were you thinking about, Olena?' Nicole had asked with a knowing smile.

Olena had blushed fiercely, and had had to make several attempts to start her confession. 'I was thinking about touching his thing – you know, his penis. I was holding it against my face.'

'That's a very wicked thought, Olena.'

'But that's not all. You were there, too, in my daydream. You were sitting next to Barat. I was across the knees of both of you. And you were smacking my bottom, as you did yesterday.'

'Oh, but that's much better,' Nicole had cried. 'You see? You are already beginning to associate sinful imaginings with punishments. That's the way to banish those wicked thoughts. I expect you felt very pure and virtuous after your daydream.'

Olena had once again had to choke back a sob of despair. No: she had not felt pure and virtuous. She had touched her breasts, and had wanted to touch the places between her legs which she had known were sticky with the wetness that she seemed to produce so readily.

'Perhaps Barat and I will try the test that you have dreamed up,' Nicole said. 'Today, though, you can rest until it's time for your examination. I'll take you to the library now. I know you're used to studying, and it must seem like an age since you last had the chance to do some reading.'

Nicole had told Olena that she would be allowed to wear her robe in the public areas of the Chateau. The prospect of being permitted to cover her nakedness and to browse in a well-stocked library had pulled Olena from her pit of self-criticism.

123

As she followed Nicole through dimly lit corridors full of baroque decoration, however, and as they silently passed and met other inhabitants of the vast mansion, Olena became increasingly conscious that she must be the only person in the Chateau who was not displaying her body. Several men and women, who hurried along the passageways as if on urgent errands, wore nothing more than arrangements of leather or rubber belts. Olena noticed with a shiver that all of these scurrying people displayed naked bottoms, and that some of the bottoms bore scarlet stripes. Other, more languid men and women were slightly more fully dressed, but in costumes that, like Nicole's, seemed only to draw attention to their bodies.

And, as ever in the Chateau, from behind the closed doors issued sounds that Olena was beginning to be able to decipher.

A few of the men and women in the corridors greeted Nicole with a smile, a word, or a kiss on both cheeks; all of them, however, stared at Olena. She imagined that they could see through her robe and were inspecting her naked body; that they could see into her heart and discover the extent of her sin. She told herself that she was being silly, and that they were looking at her simply because she was covered from neck to feet. She was flustered and blushing, however, and very relieved when Nicole announced that they had arrived at the library.

Behind the tall, ornately carved doors was a long, high-ceilinged room that smelled pleasantly of leather and dust. Halfway along one wall logs blazed in a vast stone fireplace; on either side there were only shelves laden with books. The yellow light from lamps mounted on wrought-iron pedestals picked out the gold embossing on book spines that were tall, short, wide and thin. The other side of the room was divided into small alcoves, each of which contained more shelves, a solid wooden table, fitted seats upholstered with red leather, and a high, square window of bottle glass through which could be seen only the dim daylight and the overhang of the battlements. The library was empty and, apart from the crackle of the burning wood, silent.

'It's warm in here,' Nicole said. 'If you take the alcove opposite the fire, you'll be very cosy. You can hang your robe on one of the hooks behind the door.'

'My robe?' Olena asked, even as she began to undo the buttons. 'Am I to be naked?'

'Yes, you silly thing,' Nicole said, laughing. 'There's no one else here. You won't be disturbed. You must wear your robe when walking through the Chateau, of course. It's a question of modesty. But when you are alone, or with others who are helping to train you, you must be completely naked.'

As Olena struggled, with some assistance from Nicole, to pull the heavy garment up to her shoulders and over her head, she realised that, although it was an alarming prospect to be naked and alone in such a grand chamber, she felt happier without the robe. As the hem reached her waist she felt the heat from the fire on her thighs and buttocks, and wondered momentarily how she would be punished later in the day after her inevitable failure in the tests. Nicole tugged on the robe and Olena's breasts fell free; she felt a stab of sensation that was too exciting to be painful.

Olena saw that Nicole, returning from hanging the robe on a hook, was appraising her bared body. She knew that she should cover herself, that she should demand the return of the robe. But Nicole and the others seemed to like looking at her breasts and her bottom, and she could not deny that she enjoyed the attention. It seemed that there was no end to her wickedness. In the city she had been prey to thoughts that she had feared were not strictly in accordance with the correct behaviour required by the community; here in the Chateau she was discovering that she was more vile than she had ever imagined.

With her heart thudding in her bosom and her inner voice, accusing her of deliberate wrongdoing, echoing in her head, she folded her arms behind her back and thrust her breasts forward as Nicole drew near.

Nicole smiled, caressed Olena's left breast, and lowered her head to place a kiss on the nipple. 'Very good, Olena,' she said. 'If you offer yourself up to temptation, it will become easier to resist.'

'Thank you,' was all Olena could say. But she was thinking: Please touch my breasts again, because I know you desire them, and I'm proud of them being big and smooth and firm, and I'd love you to squeeze them and kiss them so that they feel heated and tingling and give me those sticky, itching feelings in my secret place. Another voice in her mind was telling her that she was becoming more and more wicked and defiled, and that she deserved to be punished severely. And beyond that voice, in the centre of her being, lay the thrilling fear that no amount of punishment would be enough to drive her from sin.

'I have to go now,' Nicole said. 'The Chatelaine has other duties for me. I'll return later. You'll be all right here, won't you?' She touched Olena's breast again, briefly.

Olena shivered. 'Yes, thank you,' she said. 'I'll be quite happy sitting and reading. I'm sure I'll find something worthwhile to study.'

Nicole's dark eyes sparkled and her broad, red lips formed a grin. 'I'm sure you will,' she said. 'The volumes in the alcove opposite the fire are particularly noteworthy. Let me kiss you, my darling.'

Olena leaned forwards and offered her cheek, but Nicole lifted her hand and delicately adjusted Olena's face so that Olena's mouth met her lips. Olena was too shocked to move, and found her own lips softening and opening against Nicole's. And then Nicole turned, her heels clicked across the dark, varnished floor, and she was gone.

Perturbed and fearfully excited, Olena wandered along the towering shelves of books. She inspected the spines. She found works of philosophy and natural history; she found biographies and diaries of generals and statesmen. There were many books written in languages unknown to her; some she recognised as works in Latin and Greek.

She suspected that Nicole's knowing smile intimated that the books in the warmest alcove were dedicated to much less wholesome subjects, and would be all too easy to comprehend. She knew that she should select an

126

educational tome from one of the long shelves and devote her time to self-improvement. Above all, she should resist the temptation to sit in the seductive warmth opposite the fire and look at the books that came readily to hand there. She knew what she should do, but it was impossible.

She put her fingers to her lips. Nicole's kiss had been gentle and full of kindness. She touched her breast, where Nicole had caressed it, and felt again the thrill of wicked pleasure. Everyone she had met in the Chateau was kind to her; Barat was devoted to educating her correctly; and all she could do was to respond with thoughts and feelings of the basest sort.

She stood in front of the fire, stared into the glowing embers, and let the heat pulse against her body until she began to feel faint. She made her decision. If she failed the tests that afternoon she would be punished again anyway; if she exposed herself to temptation and resisted, then she would be better prepared for the tests, and if she could not resist, then the punishment would be merited.

She turned and stood for a moment with her back to the fire. She parted her legs and mischievously pushed her bottom out, so that her buttocks and her secret places were heated by the glow. Then she went to sit in the alcove.

It was a warm, comfortable, hidden place. The ridges of thickly upholstered leather creaked as she sat down, and seemed to insinuate themselves between her buttocks. She reached behind her, pulled a book at random from a shelf, and placed it on the table in front of her. The thick, yellowing pages fell open. She leaned forwards and began to read.

'Still upright, eh?' the Viscount remarked. He grasped Henri's stiff member in his gloved hand and wrung a groan from the bound youth. 'Even so hard a flogging does not quench your vicious ardour. Milady, would you care to milk the lad while I introduce him to the pleasures of Sodom?'

Lady Marguerite exclaimed, and held her fan before her blushing face. 'Husband,' she said, 'would you have

127

me suck the seed from a stable boy? Although I do declare this one is a pretty fellow, and has carried himself well under the whip.'

'Use your hand, for all I care,' retorted the Viscount. 'I will purchase a new pair of lace gloves, if those you are wearing become soiled. But I will bugger the man, and I will have him spend as I take him.' He beckoned two of the servants who had been summoned to witness the punishment of one of their number. 'Cut him down from the beam,' the Viscount commanded. 'Clear the tack from that table, and bend him over it.'

Angelique, who had been rendered dumb at the surprise of being discovered with Henri, and had failed to recover her voice while her clothes had been torn from her and while she had been obliged to watch the cruel indignities that the Viscount had visited upon the *fesses* and manhood of her beloved swain, spoke up at last. 'My lord,' she cried, 'spare him further disgrace. The fault is mine as much as it is his.'

The Viscount and his graceful lady turned their cool gaze upon her. 'I had not supposed that you were innocent,' the Viscount said, 'and I had intended that your chastisement would certainly follow, albeit in a less public setting. But, as you seem intent on advertising your degradation, please tell the assembled company your part in this wicked deed.'

It was apparent to Angelique that the Viscount would not be diverted from administering his cruel justice to both Henri and herself. In spite of her lowly station she was a young woman of noble mind, however, and she could not permit Henri to suffer inequitably, when she knew the fault was hers.

'It was I who invited Henri to meet me here in the stables,' she stated proudly. 'He had spoken complimentary words upon my bosom, and I proposed to him that if he were to meet me here, I would unlace and let him see.'

The Viscount came to stand before Angelique as she struggled in the grip of two of the kitchen maids. He favoured her with a leering smile and used his riding-whip to agitate her breasts. 'And whose conceit was it that young Henri should produce his manhood and rub it between these two bountiful globes of beauty?' he enquired.

Angelique's face became as red as the Viscount's coat. 'Mine, my lord,' she confessed. 'I thought he might like it.'

The Viscount laughed. 'And so he did, my dear, or so it would seem. He's been as stiff as a pikestaff since I came through the door and found him ploughing that sweet furrow of yours.' He stared for several moments at Angelique's bosom, creating in the young woman a ferment of lust and trepidation.

'As it was those pretty, well-formed globes that lured Henri to his bestial act,' the Viscount pronounced, 'so shall the punishment fall on them. Before I submit Henri to a well-deserved rogering he shall see your tempting bubbies dance under my whip. Bring ropes!'

Olena had reached the end of a page. Her nipples felt as hard as the table against whose edge they were resting. The library had become oppressively warm, but still she found herself trembling. As she leaned back the leather of the seat creaked loudly, and seemed to be adhering to the most intimate parts of her. She leaned forwards again, and deliberately pressed her nipples against the table. She turned the page.

For several seconds Olena could not comprehend what she was seeing. The left-hand page of the two that were open in front of her contained text – the continuation of the narrative. But on the opposite page was a picture. The original had been skilfully drawn in pen and ink, and the reproduction in the book was a triumph of the printer's craft. Every detail of the many lewd acts that were depicted could be discerned.

When Olena realised what was in the picture she gasped and looked away. Her eyes were drawn back, inexorably, and she was constrained to inspect every part of the illustration. It was as thoroughly depraved as she had suspected. A young man – presumably the stable boy, Henri – was leaning over a bench. As he looked over his shoulder with wide-eyed anguish, his gaze seemed to be fixed on Olena. He was naked but for a waistcoat, which seemed to make him look even more vulnerable. His arms were held by two poorly dressed servants; his ankles were tied, far apart, to the legs of the bench. His buttocks, thrust into round prominence by his position, were criss-crossed with fine lines. A lady, dressed in voluminous, richly decorated skirts, was sitting jauntily on the bench and was reaching with one gloved hand between Henri's legs.

Olena felt a momentary pang of disappointment, which she guiltily suppressed, that the young man's penis, surely the object of the fine lady's attentions, was not visible in the picture.

Nearby, a young woman with tumbling locks of hair was tied to a post. This, Olena assumed, was Angelique, and her breasts, pushed forwards because her arms were tied behind the post, were almost as large as Olena's. She was wearing nothing but the ragged remains of a skirt that barely concealed her private parts but did not cover her long, shapely legs, one of which she had raised in a futile attempt to protect herself. A man with a moustache, a riding coat and a short, slender whip was standing beside her. The whip was raised; he was smiling benignly; she looked expectant.

Olena imagined the whip cutting through the air and landing on those perfect white half-spheres. She tried to imagine the pain. It was impossible: all she felt was a tingling tightness across the surface of her breasts, and tremors inside her that intensified as she wondered whether Barat would ever find it necessary to punish her by chastising her breasts.

She closed the book. She picked it up – it seemed heavier than when she had chosen it – and replaced it on the shelf behind her. To do this she had to stand, and she closed her eyes and blushed with shame as she felt her secret parts peel from the leather seat. She was wet again, and she knew now that such wetness was the most certain indication that she was being particularly wicked.

Nonetheless, she pulled down another book. This was a smaller volume, bound in black leather, and unlikely, she thought, to contain any shocking illustrations. As she sat down she parted her thighs, and felt her buttocks and her sex opened by a ridge of cool leather. She began to read.

Tuesday, 19 May

Lisa is getting more submissive by the day. This morning she brought coffee to my room, and asked very meekly if she could play with her favourite thing while I drank it. I had to drink quickly, or I would have come! She is learning very quickly how to please me with her fingers – and her mouth, for that matter.

As soon as I set the cup down she was on her knees at the bedside asking for her morning spanking. She looked so pretty, and so anxious to please, that I would have granted her request even if spanking Lisa wasn't the thing I like doing most in the world. She jumped on to the bed like an eager puppy, and laid her naked body across my lap. Today I didn't need to remind her to move her legs apart, and to push up that sweet, petite rump of hers. The stripes from last night had faded almost completely, but, even so, as she was being so good I didn't smack hard enough to mark her.

In fact, I was very gentle, and I gave her as much fingering as spanking. The juice was dribbling out of her! When I stopped spanking, she didn't need to be prompted to ask for more, and so when I took up whacking her again, in earnest this time, I diddled her until she climaxed. Then she scrambled off the bed, and she remembered to kneel and thank me for the spanking.

I'm writing this in bed, round about lunchtime, as I thought Lisa and I needed a siesta today, and anyway I wanted to relax and have a climax in her mouth. She's lying curled up with her head on my thigh and my dick between her lips, trying to take my mind off my writing. And she's succeeding. She's got her legs drawn up so I

131

can give her a smack whenever she starts licking too fast. Also I break off from writing every now and then to play with her asshole.

(This morning I took Lisa into the utility room and tried out a few new bondage routines. Towards the end, when she was trussed up especially tight, I gave her an enema, and then set her on the pan and sat and watched her until the inevitable happened. Lisa hates having an enema more than anything, but it makes her really hot afterwards, and she especially likes having her asshole played with. So my pen's spending more time inside her than it is being written with, just now.)

Late this afternoon the Druizzi boys are coming over to pick Lisa up. The mood she's in, I'm sure she'll put on a good show for them. They're bringing over a girl named Michelle; Joe wants to find out whether she'll get a kick out of being screwed while she's tied up. I'm happy to oblige.

Got to stop for a while. Lisa's getting too good at this.

Olena realised that she had started rubbing her nipples against the table, and sat up abruptly. She had not understood some of the language in the text she had just read, but what she thought she comprehended made her head swim.

She knew that she should stop reading books from these shelves. She should go elsewhere in the library, and concentrate on an academic work about linguistics, or physical geography, or anything at all except wickedness and punishment. But she couldn't resist peeking into just one more forbidden volume; then one more, and then another.

Nipple rings are less decorative than jewellery or bells, but have many practical uses, most of which entail the clipping on of chains. This can be done quickly and easily using spring clips of the sort used to attach a lead to a dog's collar.

One chain, running from nipple to nipple, either by

way of the back of the neck or through a ring set into the front of a collar, provides decoration as well as a continuous slight upward pull on the nipples. A chain running from nipple to nipple round a post or through a wall ring is enough to constitute very effective bondage.

Olena touched her nipples again. In the corridors of the Château she had seen that some of the men and women had been wearing shiny, metallic decorations at their nipples. Were these the 'nipple rings' mentioned in the text? She tried another book.

She lay on her back, staring up at the canopy of leaves, and tried to calm her breathing. She was already feeling hot and sticky in the clinging costume. The bed of dry leaves tickled her naked buttocks, and the forest air cooled her naked breasts. Every other part of her, from head to toe, was encased in rubber. The goggles that were built into the ornate helmet restricted her peripheral vision, which put her at a disadvantage compared with the hunters, but she knew they were essential to protect her eyes.

She heard the sound of hooves. She was still too close to the edge. She needed to make her way quickly into the interior, where the undergrowth was thickest. A few scratches were a small price to pay to avoid being discovered.

She heard the Marshal's voice ringing out. 'Remember, ladies and gentlemen,' he said, 'only hits on the naked flesh of the prey will count towards your score. Make sure you're close enough to aim clearly for her arse or her tits. Markings on her costume will count against you, and if none of you achieves a clear hit on the target areas then the one with most hits off target will be tomorrow's prey.'

She would have laughed, if the helmet had not been so tight. She had played this game before, and she had always ended the day as someone's prize. The hunters never lost. But she would make them run a good chase. There was always a chance that she could evade them all.

'Each of you has a limited number of paint pellets,' the Marshal went on, 'and the pistols have a short range. That's two more good reasons to stalk quietly, and to get up close before trying a shot. You'll probably get only one shot in at a time: the pellets sting like crazy when they hit, particularly on the exposed target areas, and the prey will be off like a rocket. Finally, remember that the dye isn't permanent, so once she's been hit the prey will try to head for a stream or a pool to wash it off. You'll win her for the night only if she's still bearing your colour at the end of the hunt.'

The hoofbeats were receding now. She rolled over, and crouched on all fours. She knew she looked like an exotic beast: the helmet was shaped to resemble a panther's head, and the black rubber suit gave her the sleek lines of a large cat. Only her breasts, pendant through the two circular openings in the front of the suit, and her buttocks, divided by a strip of rubber and protruding from the surrounding blackness like pale balloons, revealed that she was human. Looking to right and left, she padded into the depths of the woodland.

'If you manage to corner the prey,' the Marshal's voice said from a distance, 'it's good strategy to get in very close and fire several rounds. Make sure she's peppered with your colour. Then all you have to do is to keep her away from water until you hear the sound of the horn that signals the end of the day's hunting. If she turns on you, which has been known to happen, or if you're close enough to herd her, you'll find your riding-crop is invaluable. So keep it with you when you dismount. You can tether your horse at any point on the perimeter of the forest. And remember, if you mark her on the target areas with your colour, she's yours for the night once she's been displayed at dinner. Good hunting!'

* * *

134

'Olena?'

Olena slammed shut the book. Barat was standing at the mouth of the alcove, his robes almost eclipsing the glow of the fire.

'Barat,' she stammered. 'I was just reading.' She couldn't help covering her breasts with her arms; she tried to move her thighs together without making the leather creak beneath her. She knew she was blushing.

'Of course,' Barat said. He smiled briefly, but his demeanour was serious. 'Nicole is here with me. She has your robe ready. It's time for a little lunch, and then we'll start testing you again. Master Robert has returned today, and he wants to see how you are progressing. So please, Olena,' Barat added, looking very earnest, 'do try to think pure thoughts today. I very much want to show him that you can be good. What have you been reading?'

'Oh, nothing much,' Olena said, hurrying to stand and escape from the booth. 'Several varied texts.'

Barat stood aside to allow Olena to pass. She found Nicole waiting, and struggled into the familiar protective cocoon of the robe. She turned, hoping to find that Barat had joined them and that they could leave the library quickly. But Barat was not in sight; he had entered the alcove in which Olena had been sitting.

During the ensuing silence Olena's heart sank. Barat would find the books she had been reading.

As she feared, Barat spoke from inside the cosy book-lined booth. His voice sounded strained. 'Nicole,' he called, 'I think you had better come here.'

Nicole pouted, gave Olena a conspiratorial look, and went to join Barat.

There was another silence. Olena was trembling with guilt. She heard Barat and Nicole speaking in low voices. She took a few steps towards the alcove, so that she could hear what they were saying.

'They're all like this,' Barat said. 'She's spent hours in here and she's read nothing but depravity and filth.'

'It's not just that,' Nicole replied. 'I am sorry to have to draw your attention to such a thing, but look at the

135

condition of the seat. This was where she was sitting; you can see that plainly. The leather is still warm. And look – just here – you'll see it's darker. And it's still wet.'

Olena gasped, and started to sob silently. She felt bitter tears pooling in her eyes. She had guessed what mark of her sin Nicole had found on the seat. She felt as though she could shrivel into nothing, so complete was her shame. She wanted the floor to open beneath her feet and swallow her.

'I don't know what to do,' Barat said, and the despair in his voice almost broke Olena's heart. 'I had no idea her sinfulness was this ingrained. She will have to be punished again before we can take the chance of testing her in the presence of Master Robert.'

'Of course,' Nicole said. 'We can see to that immediately. But don't worry, Barat. I am sure that Olena's heart is not entirely black. We may have to spend a very long time teaching her, but everyone in the Chateau will help you. Come; let's undress her again and spank her here. If we sit beside each other on one of these leather seats, you can hold her head in your lap and comfort her while I smack her bottom.'

'Very well,' Barat said.

The deportment class was one of the most basic taught in the Chateau. Those attending were newcomers: guests, staff and slaves who had been at the Chateau for less than a month. Nothing that was taught was new to Jem; however, she approved of the dedication of the instructor, and it was something of a novelty for her to find herself demonstrating the simple principles of carriage and behaviour.

The room was a barrel-vaulted cellar, hung with huge mirrors that left room on the walls only for lamps casting a red glow. The instructor was a tall, thin woman with bleached, cropped hair, a tightly fitting leather costume, and a long, flexible dowel that Jem assumed could be used both as a pointer and as an instrument of correction.

'Yes? What is it?' the woman barked as Robert pushed

136

Jem into the room and on to her knees. 'Ah, Master Robert. This must be the slave you promised me. You may unleash her. I'll take good care of her, I assure you.'

Jem felt Robert unclip the leash from her collar. 'She's all yours, instructor,' he said. 'Don't forget to pass her on to Kadif when your lesson is ended. And Teresa,' he added, 'don't forget this little slut is as cunning as a weasel. Don't make any allowances.'

Robert left. Jem was suddenly, and for the first time that day, acutely aware of her nudity. Everyone else in the room was wearing something; some of the guests were even fully dressed. She had only her collar, the Chatelaine's make-up, and the stripes on her buttocks. Nonetheless, she kept her arms crossed behind her back, her knees apart, her chest out and her head lowered. This was, after all, a deportment class, and Jem knew how to present herself.

'You're late,' the instructor said. 'We've been waiting for you. Stand, come to me, and prepare yourself in the position for an unsupported punishment.'

Now this, Jem thought as she rose to her feet, is doubly unfair. It's not my fault that I'm late, and I don't know precisely what position it is I'm expected to adopt, given that I haven't attended this class at the Chateau. It's a safe bet the Chatelaine does things slightly differently here from the systems I set up at the House.

It was, however, gratifying and exciting to feel all eyes on her as she went to stand beside the instructor. She positioned her feet well apart, crossed her arms behind her back and, with her legs straight, bent forwards from the waist until her torso was almost horizontal. She remembered to lift her head and look straight forwards, as she had seen the Chateau-trained hold themselves.

It was a difficult stance to maintain. Her bottom was perforce thrust back, in order for her to keep her balance, and thus made a perfect target for the purposes of punishment. Her vulva was exposed, her labia parted, and Jem knew that even a glance would disclose that she was aroused. She was leaning forwards enough to let her breasts hang unsupported; the continuous slight tug of their weight meant that she couldn't forget how vulnerable they were.

She was facing the dozen or so students in the class. They were of all ages and both sexes, although Jem knew that they were very far from a representative sample of the population of the world beyond the Private House. The Chatelaine's standards were high, and every person in the room was at the very least physically attractive, whatever other talents he or she might have. And every one of them deserved or desired the particularly strict brand of discipline that was the speciality of the Chateau.

They were all staring at Jem, and she stared back. She selected a young man, blond and tall, who was wearing only a singlet and a pair of tight shorts, and who was standing straight in front of her. She caught his eye, smiled, and then looked down at his crotch. She saw the bulge in his shorts begin to swell and become more clearly defined. She looked up at his face again, and pouted her lips at him.

Jem felt cool hands on her back, and then touching the insides of her thighs. 'Not bad,' the instructor said grudgingly. 'Remain in that position, and I'll give you three for being late. I want the rest of you to watch closely. If she moves, she'll get another three. As I'm sure you're all aware by now, this level of discipline is the custom at the Chateau.'

Jem heard the song of the instructor's rod as it sliced through the air, steadying herself just in time to receive a stinging stroke across both buttocks.

'When ordered to stand in this manner,' the instructor told the class, 'you can expect to be punished on your rear, as this position is rarely used for any other purpose. Its advantages are, first, that it requires no furniture, fixings or framework: you can be punished anywhere. Second, it is uncomfortable to maintain for any length of time, and thus allows you to demonstrate your discipline and fortitude. Third, in keeping your balance you are required to keep your rear end thrust well back, so that you cannot avoid presenting yourself well for the punishment.'

The second stroke landed unexpectedly, and Jem almost jumped up as she felt the sudden line of fire on her bottom.

'There are disadvantages, however. As you can see, although this slave has clearly been trained well to keep her back arched downwards when presenting herself, her rear is nevertheless not as uplifted as is the case with most of the punishment positions. Therefore I have a less than perfect view of the area I am punishing, and I am obliged to ensure that I aim my strokes low and slightly upwards. Second, this position is not suitable for punishments using heavy implements or the bare hand, as the force of the stroke can cause the slave to lose her balance. Therefore, when in this position, you can expect to be punished with a thin-edged instrument such as a cane or a whip.'

This time Jem was ready for the blow and felt a glow of satisfaction as the stinging pain appeared exactly where she had expected it, across the tops of the backs of her thighs.

'Stand,' the instructor said. 'Turn. Adopt the position again.'

Jem did as she was told, taking the opportunity to stretch her muscles before bending over again.

'You can see the marks of the rod,' the instructor said to the class, 'here, here, and here, appearing on both buttocks.'

Jem felt the tip of the wooden dowel pressing into her flesh, six times, and suddenly felt a wave of embarrassment. She remembered, for the first time in what seemed like hours, that she was – she had been – the Supreme Mistress of the Private House. As she was poked and prodded, as if she were an inanimate model, she realised the distance that she had allowed herself to fall.

'A pretty little rear end,' the instructor commented. 'Kadif will enjoy it. Notice, everyone, the difference between the marks of a whip and those of a thin wooden rod. The whip marks are beginning to fade, but even when fresh they are less distinct. I imagine that a thin leather strap was used to produce these results.'

To Jem's relief the tip of the dowel ceased to nudge her sore buttocks. But then, to her horror, she felt it touch the inside of her thigh; then it was between her labia, parting them and probing upwards.

'Although it's not germane to this lesson,' the instructor said, 'it is worth noting that this slave is in a state of sexual arousal. I've been told that this one is helplessly sluttish. She's as promiscuous as she is incorrigible, I believe. You probably can't tell, from where you're standing, but she's dripping wet. I'll collect some of her disgusting slime on my rod so you can all see.'

This will stop now, Jem told herself, and she took a deep breath in readiness to turn and vent her anger on the instructor and everyone in the room.

Then she remembered, and let her anger escape as a sigh. She had to take this. She had to bear it for five days, or she would remain here as a slave for ever. Not only that, but she had to submit willingly, without any show of resistance.

Oh well, she thought. It's not that bad. My bottom's warm and tingling again, which I like. And it's true that I'm excited. I can't deny it. I feel like having every person in this room, one after the other, with a spanking between each one.

'Stand.' The instructor's command interrupted Jem's pleasant reverie. 'I will now use the slave to demonstrate the standard postures for standing, sitting and kneeling in the Chateau, and then go on to place her in several more punishment positions.'

An hour later Jem was seething with a confusing combination of lust and indignation. Not a part of her body had not been exposed, prodded with the rod, pointed out to the class and, more often than not, manhandled by the instructor or one or more of the students.

The instructor had repeatedly remarked on the physical evidence of the filthy little slave's insatiable sexual appetite and, while Jem dutifully adopted and held a series of increasingly revealing poses, had encouraged the students to stick their fingers into her and to test the hardness of her nipples.

Now she was squatting, with her feet on tiptoes on the tops of two desks. The gap between the desks was, as the instructor demonstrated, wide enough for a person to stand in, either in front of Jem or behind her.

'You will find this position difficult to maintain for long,' she told the class. 'It is less of a strain on the calf muscles if you place your feet flat, but it is also less pleasing for others to look at. There are few positions that stretch the sexual areas as widely open as this; you can see that the slave's outer and, indeed, inner labia are parted. And you can see more clearly than ever that she is still producing copious amounts of lubrication.'

It's your fault, Jem wanted to shout at her. If you persist in sliding that rod into me, what do you expect?

'This is a good position for punishment or sex,' the instructor went on, 'or indeed both, serially or simultaneously.'

'Simultaneously, miss?' one of the students asked.

'Of course,' the instructor said. 'Once you have been trained to hold this position for some time, you will find that it is very adaptable. For instance, this slave can be penetrated from the front – would you use your finger, please, to simulate genital congress – while she is whipped from behind. The buttocks are widely separated, and thus very easy to punish with upward strokes. Perhaps more interestingly, in this position the slave's anus is very exposed – you see that I can place three fingers flat across it – and is therefore available for the more specialist punishments that you will be told of in other lessons.'

I'm going to come, Jem thought. This is so humiliating. If they don't stop touching me, I know I'll come.

Jem remembered, with a shock of anxiety that caused butterflies to flutter in her stomach, that if she were to enjoy a climax without having been given permission she could be reported to the Chatelaine. It could be enough to lose Jem her wager and condemn her to a life of slavery in the Chateau. Somehow the danger did nothing to damp the fire that was burning inside her.

'Alternatively, the slave can be penetrated anally and, simultaneously, punished from the front. Once again, you will be taught in other lessons about these particular techniques. Suffice to say for the moment that when punishing the genital area – of a man or a woman – it is

141

necessary to use modest instruments and to be very careful about the vigour of the strokes. This, however, is an excellent position for such punishments because, as you can see, the folds of skin are held open. If one of you would be so kind as to use a finger again, this time to penetrate the slave's anus, I'll just give her a few light strokes with the rod for demonstration purposes.'

Jem felt the finger slide into her. She rocked back on her heels to meet the gentle pressure, and then remembered that she had to maintain her posture. She went back on to her toes, and gasped as the rod, swung lightly upwards, landed between her open labia. She shuddered, sank backwards on to the finger, and waited for the next stroke.

Just a little higher, please, she thought; touch me anywhere near my clitoris and I'll be there. I am ready to come at any moment, and I don't care how many of you are watching. In fact, I want you all to see.

'Miss,' one of the students said, 'is the slave actually dripping?'

'I do believe you're right,' the instructor said. 'She has no self-control. Take your finger out of her. I can't bear to use her any more.'

Jem felt the finger being pulled abruptly from her anus. She heard the students' feet as they shuffled away. It was suddenly over: she wasn't going to be allowed to come; she wasn't even going to remain the centre of attention.

'Disgusting slave,' the instructor called out, 'the lesson's almost over. You're to stay in that position until the end. If there's any mess on the floor underneath you, you will lick it up before I escort you to your next class, where I will make a point of asking Kadif to be particularly severe with you.'

But Jem was hardly listening. She was berating herself for her lack of will-power. This was only the first day; she had to submit for five days to everything the Chatelaine had planned for her, and she was sure that this deportment class was a negligible test compared with those that were to come. Twice she had almost succumbed to the temptation to resist: once through anger, and once through sheer lust.

As the discomfort in her calves and thighs started to develop into cramping pains, she began to despair. She had set herself an impossible task. She had thought it would be easy – a relaxing interlude from the problems of running the Private House – to turn herself over to the disciplinary regime of the Chateau. She had expected it to be a matter simply of allowing herself to be whipped and sexually used – more frequently than was her habit, certainly, but there was no reason why she shouldn't enjoy every moment.

But she had reckoned without her own awkward character: her bursts of humour, of temper, of desire. In order to submit, willingly, for five days, she needed to discover reserves of equanimity that she was sure she did not possess. That, or find some other strategy by which to survive.

Another gloomy chamber, another instructor. Kadif, a burly dark-skinned man, was presenting a lesson in discipline.

'Usually,' he explained to the class as Jem kneeled beside him, 'it is my routine to demonstrate the various disciplinary techniques using students from the class. Today, however, I have been granted the use of the new slave whose arrival you saw this morning. She will receive all the demonstration punishments. Therefore we will begin by inspecting the slave.' Jem felt a pull on her collar as Kadif tugged the leash. 'Get up on the desk, you little trollop.'

Jem stood, and flashed a cheerful grin at the class as she climbed on to the desk. Most of them, she saw, were almost as naked as she was: they were wearing the leather harnesses usually worn in the Chateau by the most junior staff and the slaves. She knew, however, that among them could be temporary guests whose desire was to experience enthralment, or senior staff for whom this lesson was remedial – or simply entertainment.

Jem remembered also to smile at Kadif as she knelt on the cushions that were strewn on the top of the desk. She was determined to appear confident; however, she felt close to defeat. She had almost fallen at one of the earliest, lowest hurdles: a basic lesson in deportment. An hour or more of being used to demonstrate Kadif's skills with instruments of correction would surely be even more difficult to bear.

'Well, now,' Kadif said, in a friendlier tone than Jem had expected. His big hand stroked her face. 'It seems everything they said about you is true. You really are a pretty little thing. Give me another smile with that cocksucking mouth of yours.'

Jem obliged, and as Kadif gave her a huge grin in return she felt a little spark of optimism and defiance reignite within her. An hour or two of corporal punishment – not a problem. She had happily endured far more at the hands of Julia and some of her guards, on several occasions when she been feeling particularly submissive.

'Would you like me to suck your cock, sir?' Jem said, glancing down at the prodigious bulge of his crotch and then up to his eyes.

His grin broadened. 'It would be an honour as well as a pleasure, you pretty little whore,' he said. 'But I think we had better postpone that delight until after you have shown these people just how much you love to feel the whip on your worthless hide.'

He spoke slowly, and continued gently to caress Jem as he addressed her in terms that were so demeaning that she found herself blushing. She was becoming aroused; she found Kadif very attractive, and was looking forward to unbuttoning the flap at the front of his breeches and taking his big, dark manhood into her mouth. Before then, she would be punished several times, but she knew now that she could trust Kadif. This lesson was going to be very enjoyable.

And so it proved. Kadif was instructing the class in the uses of one of the less well-known corrective implements. With Jem kneeling, he showed how a small whip with a multitude of thin leather lashes could be used to bring a rosy glow to her breasts; then, once she had lowered her head on to the cushions, he produced the same effect on her buttocks. Finally he had her lie on her back, holding her knees to her chest, while he whipped the backs of her thighs. Then, with great care, he alternated downward and upward flicks of the lashes to her vulva and anus.

Throughout the demonstration he referred to Jem in the most insulting and degrading terms. He repeatedly pointed out to the students that 'the filthy cocksucking piece of garbage' was quite obviously enjoying every moment of the punishment; this was undeniable, as he used his large, surprisingly gentle hands, and the handle of the whip, to keep Jem in a state of panting need.

'Look at the disgusting little tramp,' he said indulgently, as Jem lay on her back, exposing her most intimate parts which were burning from Kadif's expertly applied strokes. 'It's right to call her no better than a piece of shit, because she loves to take it up her shit-hole.' Jem felt the cool tip of the whip-handle touch the hot ring of her anus. 'You see? The little piece of excrement wants the whip up her arse. See how her shit-hole opens like a little mouth? Like it's begging for me to push this inside?' He placed a hand on the burning membranes of Jem's sex. 'And if I start to push it in, and press down at the same time – yes, as you can see, the little tramp starts leaking her juice all over my fingers. Even her arsehole is whorish.'

And it was true. Every sexual part of Jem – her breasts, her buttocks, her vulva – felt hot and tingling, and alive with sensation. She was so close to coming that she almost forgot to clasp her knees to her chest, so when Kadif pressed his hand on to her labia and ground the heel of his thumb against the hood of her clitoris, she felt the waves of a climax begin to pulse more and more insistently.

Kadif moved his hand away.

'For the remainder of the lesson,' he said, 'I'll use the whore-slave to show you a variety of clips and clamps that can be used on nipples. I'll also show you how some of them can be used on other sensitive parts of the slave's body, such as the outer and inner labia, the prepuce of the clitoris, and the skin around the anus. Get up, piece of garbage, and adopt the kneeling position.'

Kadif was a thorough instructor. For half an hour he

toyed with the most delicate parts of Jem's anatomy. At times Jem felt as though her entire body must be decorated with glittering metal attachments, each of which was at least a little painful. Kadif was inventive: he pointed out that the skin of the areolae and indeed of any point on the surface of Jem's breasts could be gathered and pinched with either a simple peg or a complex, screw-tightened clasp. Using Jem's nipples, and then her outer labia, he demonstrated that a clip with a weak spring but with serrated edges could support weights as well as could a tightly fastened clamp or a clip with a strong spring. Referring in the crudest terms to Jem's alleged love of anal sex, he fastened tiny, jewelled clips on both sides of her anus, along the sides of the valley between her buttocks; although Jem was wincing with the pain, and tears were squeezing from the corners of her eyes, he merely had to touch the handle of his whip to her jewel-encircled ring to produce evidence that she was once again very aroused.

And all the time, as he encouraged the class to follow his example and call Jem by the lowest, most loathsome epithets they could devise, his hands touched her in ways that made her tremble with longing.

After he dismissed the class, he stood back and admired his handiwork. Jem, breathing deeply and with her eyes shut, tried to master both the sharp twinges of pain all over the surface of her body and the spasms of desire within it.

'How many, sir?' she asked. 'May I know how many I am wearing?'

Kadif laughed softly. 'I will count them as I remove them. This one will come off last, and I'll touch it from time to time. I think it's my favourite. You must keep still now, little dung-beetle.'

Jem felt a thrill of sensation so sharp that she couldn't decide whether it was pain or pleasure. Kadif had touched something between her legs; she felt something brush her thigh as it swung.

'What is it, sir?' she gasped.

'I attached a clip to the skin just above your clitoris,' he said. 'And I've hung a pendulum from it: a weight, hanging

146

on a chain, that is pulling the gathered skin down and over the tip of your clitoris. When I swing the pendulum – well, you know what it feels like, don't you, whore-slave?'

'Yes, sir,' Jem said. 'Thank you. May I suck your cock now?'

'In a moment, you sex-hungry bitch,' Kadif replied with a laugh. 'I must detach all of these decorations first.'

Kadif was slow and methodical. He removed the clips and clamps one at a time, allowing Jem to experience each release of pressure and the ensuing pain of returning circulation. From time to time he amused himself by flicking the pendulum that hung between Jem's thighs, and watching as she gasped and moaned until the weight stopped swinging.

'Forty-two,' he said as he removed yet another clip, this time from the underside of Jem's left breast. He cupped the tender globe in his hand as Jem quivered. 'That's the last. Except for this one.' He reached down and touched the hanging weight. This time he didn't leave it to swing, but pushed it back and forth until Jem was shuddering continuously and sobbing for breath.

Just when she was on the brink of a precipitous climax, he stopped.

'Now,' he said, 'you verminous shit-eating whore, wasn't there something you wanted to do for me? Get off the table and kneel in front of me.'

No matter how carefully Jem moved as she climbed from the desk, she couldn't prevent the pendulum swinging between her thighs and pulling on the sensitive morsel of skin that was pinched between the jaws of the clip. It would have been agonising if it hadn't been so insistently exciting. Shivers of simmering lust racked her body as she lowered herself to kneel at Kadif's feet.

'Unbutton the flap, slave,' he said. 'Take out my penis and my testicles. Be very careful. Then lick my balls.'

Jem's fingers were shaking. She could hardly remember when she had last been so aroused. The need for an orgasm was a dull ache in her loins: yet another sensation to add to the throbbing heat of her breasts and buttocks and the

147

sharp pull of the weight that swung tantalisingly close to her clitoris.

She managed to unfasten the flap of Kadif's breeches and his erect penis sprang free. Jem inhaled the scent of maleness, the salty, musky smell that never failed to put her in the mood for fellatio – not that she needed any further inducement on this occasion. Kadif's member was big: long, and broad at the base. Jem had a momentary vision of sliding herself on to it, and feeling her vagina filled more and more as she accommodated the widening girth. The head was of a more normal size, however, and Jem looked forward to taking all of it into her mouth.

First, however, she was to lick his balls. She put her hand into his opened breeches and cupped it beneath the warm, heavy sac. She used her other hand to fold back the loose material of the breeches as she carefully lifted Kadif's testicles. His erection was now very hard, so that his penis stood almost vertically, and it was easy for Jem to press her nose and mouth against the hanging sac. She breathed in the warm smell. The coarse hairs tickled her face. His testicles felt like stone eggs in a purse full of scented oil. She started to lick, and stopped briefly to smile when she heard him groan with pleasure.

'Now lick my cock,' he said. 'Go straight for the head, slave. I can't wait any longer.'

I've been waiting all morning, Jem thought; no one could be more desperate to come than I am. But she found that concentrating on Kadif's genitalia had diverted her attention slightly from the yearnings of her own body, and she had to admit that it was a pleasure to feel the velvety hardness and hot, rounded contours of his penis against her tongue and her lips. She circled the flanged rim of his helmet; she flicked his frenum, and the smooth, highly sensitive ridges on either side of it; she pressed her tongue against the slit of his urethra. It occurred to her, in a lucid moment, that it had been a very long time since she had taken so much pleasure from serving a man in this way. She kept her hand cupped under his balls, waiting for the sudden tension there that would signal the onset of his climax.

148

'You certainly know how to do this,' she heard Kadif say. 'But I'm going to take control of things now. Put your hands behind your back.'

Jem let out a moan of frustrated desire, but obeyed. Kadif pulled his erection out of reach of her questing tongue. 'Open your mouth,' he said.

She watched as he took his magnificent hardness in his right hand and began to stroke it, pulling the skin back and forth over the ridge of the helmet. The slit was open and leaking clear fluid; it seemed to stare at her like a single eye.

With his left hand he stroked her hair. 'Such a pretty little slave,' he said. 'And such a filthy trollop. Are you ready to drink my come?'

With her mouth open, and almost touching the glistening purple tip of his penis, she could only nod.

'Don't swallow a drop until I give you permission,' Kadif said, and Jem felt his hand tighten in her hair, holding her head in the position he required.

His right hand pumped faster as he inserted the head of his penis into her mouth. The underside of the helmet rubbed against her tongue; his hand bumped against her lips harder and faster as he masturbated more vigorously.

She heard him cry out wordlessly. He pulled back a little, so that the tip of his penis was just outside her open mouth. His hand moved even faster, and suddenly she felt a jet of hot liquid spurt on to her tongue. Another struck her palate. Another came, and another, until her mouth was filled with hot, viscous fluid.

He wiped the tip of his penis on her lips. He stroked her hair. She felt a dribble escape from the corner of her mouth and trickle down towards her chin.

'Look at me,' he said.

She lifted her head. He was smiling down at her.

'Cocksucker,' he said. 'Spunk-drinker. Pretty little whore-slave. You can swallow it now.'

Jem swallowed. As ever, it reminded her of eating oysters. She licked her lips and smiled up at him.

'Thank you, sir,' she said. 'I enjoyed that. May I ask a question?'

Kadif looked doubtful. 'What is it?'

'I'd like to come, too, sir. Can I, please?'

Kadif sighed, and pushed his manhood, still swollen, into his breeches. 'You should know better than to ask, slave. Why, I shall have to punish you now.' He leaned forwards until his face was almost touching hers, looked from side to side, and then whispered to her. 'But I suppose I might forget that you still have that weight hanging from the skin right next to your clitoris. And I could hardly be blamed, could I, Mistress, if you were to come while I was spanking you?'

Jem couldn't help grinning. He had addressed her by her former title; he was going to spank her; she was sure she would come; and she was sure Kadif would not report the incident to the Chatelaine. The day, she thought, just can't get any brighter.

'You'd better spank me, then,' she said. 'Please, sir.'

He moved behind her. She felt his hands on the insides of her thighs. 'Place your knees further apart,' he said. 'Keep your hands behind your back. Remember to roll with the smacks; get into the rhythm of the movement.'

Jem moved her hips forwards experimentally; she felt the tug of the weighted chain as it pulled at the pinched skin above her clitoris. She moved back and felt a keener twinge of pain – and then Kadif's large hand slapped against her left buttock, already sore from his whip, and she was propelled forwards again. The swing of the chain came back to meet her, and for a tantalising, electrifying moment the metal links were held against the exposed tip of her clitoris.

She almost forgot to rock back into the swing of Kadif's next smack, which resounded in the room as it landed on her right buttock. She was thrust forwards, and once again was rewarded with the touch of the chain on her most sensitive spot.

After a few more smacks, her bottom was feeling big and hot, her nipples were tingling, and she was thrusting her hips back and forth in a steady rhythm, urged on by Kadif's crude comments.

She became unaware of everything except the regular smack of smarting pain on her bottom and the kiss of the chain between her legs. She did not realise that she was exhaling an 'Oh!' of pain with each slap and gulping in a gasp of pleasure at each touch of the chain. She knew, however, that inside she felt as hot and liquid as lava: as she rocked back and forth, between the smacks and the pull of the weight and the caress of the chain, she was riding waves of pleasure that seemed to be lifting her higher and higher.

And then the waves overwhelmed her. She fell forwards, thrusting her bottom upwards, and Kadif seemed to realise that she needed him to increase the tempo of his spanking. He aimed low, and struck gently but very fast. The chain was no longer swinging, but Jem had passed the point of needing to be touched directly on her clitoris. The weight bobbed between her widely parted thighs, dancing as her body vibrated under the rain of smacks and pulling on the clip.

Jem shuddered as the first spasm of her orgasm flooded through her. She hardly noticed that Kadif had stopped spanking her. She scarcely felt him reaching between her thighs and deftly releasing the clip from which the pendulum hung. But, as the next wave of the orgasm crashed over her, she felt a great pulse of sensation begin to throb, as fast as her heartbeat, in the depths of her loins. The circulation of blood, and with it the return of feeling, was rushing into the morsel of tender flesh that had been gripped between the jaws of the clip.

Jem was dimly conscious that she was screaming, huge hoarse gulping shouts of ecstasy, as the most powerful orgasm she had ever experienced seemed to last for ever.

She collapsed sideways on to the cushions. After a few moments, she felt able to talk.

'Thank you, sir,' she said.

'My pleasure,' Kadif replied. 'But you have no time for resting, my girl. You're already late for the next lesson.'

The next lesson was a demonstration of corsetry, arranged for some of the more discerning of the Chateau's temporary guests. Jem, already feeling light-headed, found that being constricted in various ornate constructions of whalebone, lace, satin, leather and rubber gave her the sensation of floating through the day. Everything seemed very pleasant: the corsets were beautiful; the guests were appreciative, both of the costumes and of her as a model; and Jem always enjoyed wearing well-made, tightly fitting garments. She protested vaguely each time the laces were tightened; she posed languorously, and offered her body for inspection; she smiled smugly when the guests noticed and remarked on the redness of her breasts and the marks on her buttocks.

Jem's role as a demonstrator was interrupted for a late lunch. Jem was taken to a barely lit scullery, where she was told she could take whatever she wanted from the dishes containing food left over from the meals that had been served to the guests and staff.

I'm glad the Chatelaine regards cuisine in the Chateau as a priority, Jem reflected as she piled a plate with potted and sliced meats, stuffed vegetables, hunks of bread and a large slice of *tarte tatin*. And, she thought, I'm particularly pleased that her guests can't eat everything she provides.

Jem was tethered by her collar to the leg of a table and had to eat while sitting on the flagstones. Nonetheless, she ate ravenously and as she licked the plate clean she considered that the day was improving by the hour. She felt refreshed and ready for more lessons. At the back of her mind, however, was the knowledge that the trials she had been put through up to this point had clearly been designed merely to display her, as ignominiously as possible, to a large number of the people in the Chateau. This was the calm before the storm. The exacting ordeals were still to come. And Jem still feared that she would be unable to submit.

However, the remainder of the afternoon passed pleasingly enough. Jem was led from the kitchens through dingy corridors to the stable block, where a group of the Chateau's slaves had been assembled under the tutelage of a slave-master and a slave-mistress. Jem's role was to demonstrate how to don the various harnesses and accoutrements that slaves could be instructed to wear.

The slaves watched her closely as she was strapped into a pony harness and metal-shod boots and then, encouraged by flicks of the slave-master's whip, as she performed the prancing and trotting steps that the costume demanded. Soon she was feeling hot and breathless as well as humiliated and very aroused. The slave-mistress demonstrated how a pony-girl's speed, direction and deportment could be controlled by pulling on the reins and by applying brisk touches of the whip to the buttocks, the backs of the thighs and, with skill, to the sides of the breasts.

At last Jem was given a few moments in which to catch her breath and, as she stood panting, surrounded by the intense and admiring gazes of the slaves, she lifted her head and looked back at them.

The Chatelaine's slaves were drawn in large part from other institutions within the Private House organisation. One of the Chateau's purposes was to provide intensive training for those individuals who were found to have a penchant for corporal punishment or who it was deemed would benefit from a regime of strict discipline. A few of the slaves, Jem knew, must be men and women who had been invited to visit the Chateau as guests, and who had proved to be sufficiently servile to be brought back to serve in the lowliest positions. Once fully trained and disciplined, a few of the slaves would come to develop a taste for administering as well as receiving punishment, and might be brought on to the Chatelaine's staff; others would return, now fully aware of their needs and desires, to the parts of the Private House from which they had been recruited, or would be sent into the world beyond the Private House to further the organisation's aims there. Others would remain as slaves in the Chateau.

Jem recognised several of the group gathered around her. Some of them had come from the main House. With a shock she realised that the tall, dark-haired young man with pierced nipples was Bernard; less than three weeks previously, in what seemed now like a different existence, she had taken a liking to him and had summoned him to her chambers at the main House. He had proved to have remarkable stamina: he had kept Jem entertained for the whole of a rainy afternoon. He had a long, strong tongue, Jem remembered. He had come three times, but on each occasion not until Jem had pretended to become annoyed with him and had been obliged to put him over her lap for chastisement. Jem now recalled that it had been she who had recommended that he would benefit from a stay in the Chateau. His nipples had been pierced since Jem had last seen him.

The pretty little oriental girl – Itomi, that was her name – was also in the group. Jem had thought Itomi would be on the Chatelaine's staff, as Jem knew she was a spirited and clever young woman, even though she could always be distracted by the promise of a spanking. Perhaps, Jem thought, she's been made a slave again as a punishment.

Jem started as the whip-mistress's lash flicked across the front of her thighs. 'Don't slouch,' the whip-mistress said. 'You're rested now. Let's get you into another harness. Bernard, fetch me the phalluses and plugs.'

By the end of this lesson, Jem thought, there will be no doubt – in my mind or among the slaves – that I am the least of all the slaves in the Chateau. A few weeks ago I had Bernard in my power; I used him for my pleasure, and punished him at my whim. Now he's going to see me ask politely to be penetrated and held open; he'll watch me as I'm whipped, not as part of a pleasure ritual but casually.

But it's too late to protest, Jem realised; I have been given opportunities to withdraw from this subjugation, and I failed to take them. If I protest now, I will become the Chatelaine's plaything for ever. I must submit.

As the lesson passed, Jem began to appreciate the little ways in which the Chatelaine's regime was stricter than those in other parts of the Private House. The harnesses that the slaves wore every day were cruelly tight, especially the thin strap that passed between the legs and was drawn up between the buttocks to buckle on to the waist-strap.

It was, it seemed, a commonplace for the strap to hold in place a flanged plug in the slave's anus, or a phallus in the vagina, or both. Jem demonstrated how to put on the harness and how to carry oneself while wearing it. She was made to undo the strap between her legs and, kneeling on a bale of straw with her back to the slaves, show how to insert various objects into herself and secure them in place with the strap.

She was smacked while wearing the harness, an anal plug, a phallus, and nipple chains. She was made to show the slaves that the smacking had made her excited. She was instructed to walk, sit, kneel and squat while wearing the harness and the entire range of paraphernalia. She was obliged to ask the slaves to touch her: to feel for the base of the plug through the strap, to pull on the nipple chains to prove that they were securely clamped, and to move the phallus inside her.

It was all intensely arousing, and Jem soon found that she was yearning to be permitted another climax.

Instead, she was brought to the brink again and again as she modelled one of the less quotidian outfits that the slaves might be expected to exhibit themselves in.

She found the ball-gag the most oppressive restraint, until she was made to pull on a pair of rubber shorts that had two stems of solid, oiled rubber rising like slender, glistening mushrooms from the inside of the crotch. Struggling into the shorts, which were very tight, was infuriatingly difficult and demeaning; Jem could imagine how pathetic she must have looked as, grunting behind the gag, she danced from one foot to the other as she hauled the resisting material up around her hips. And there was nothing she could do to prevent her cheeks colouring and her eyes widening as she felt the two rubber phalluses begin to penetrate her. She heard the murmured comments of the slaves, overlaid with the voice of the slave-mistress reminding them that, as the awkward little slut was the lowliest slave in the Chateau, all of the slaves would be permitted to touch her, once the slave-master had demonstrated that a slave in rubber shorts could be caned on the buttocks and between the legs without leaving unsightly marks.

At this point Jem came close to protesting, but she realised that each time she tugged the recalcitrant shorts upwards the two stems lodged themselves deeper inside her, and the sensation was becoming far from unpleasant. And, although she had enjoyed many a sound caning, particularly at the hands of her beloved friend Julia, she could not remember ever having been caned while her bottom was encased in rubber.

Before she was punished, however, Jem was ordered to fasten around her head a black rubber helmet. It covered her completely from the neck upwards, apart from an open seam at the back through which she pulled her hair, and a space around her nose and mouth. She could see nothing, and could hear only muted sounds. She was suddenly more conscious than ever of the ball lodged in her mouth, and the rubber erections filling her vagina and rectum.

Hands grabbed her, held her arms behind her back, and bent her forwards. Her breasts swung as she leaned from the waist and suddenly they seemed very vulnerable. They were flattened against something soft and yet prickly, and Jem realised that she had been bent over a bale of straw.

Jem had no warning of the first stroke; the cane landed across both rubber-clad buttocks with a vicious sting. The pain was excruciating – Jem could remember few occasions when she'd experienced such keen sensations from a mere flogging – and she couldn't prevent herself making absurd, muffled cries with each unexpected stroke. She wriggled, ignoring the pricking of straws into her breasts.

The caning of her buttocks seemed to go on for ever, and when it ended she was given no respite. Her writhing body was picked up and she was placed on her back on the bale, with her bottom protruding over one side. Her ankles were pulled up and back, above her head, and then were abruptly pulled apart. The caning began again immediately: swift, sharp strokes aimed directly at Jem's anus and vulva.

The bases of the rubber stalks took most of the force of the cane-strokes. Blinded, gagged and almost deafened,

156

utterly helpless, Jem could concentrate only on the sensations of her body. Her bottom felt as hot as a furnace and was still stinging; as ever, Jem found that in the aftermath of a *fessée* she was acutely aware that she was aroused, and she knew that she was clenching her muscles around the two rubber intruders. Someone was touching her nipples, rolling them, pinching them and, Jem thought, pulling them to create upward-pointing cones of her breasts. Some of the cane-strokes landed awry and she was suddenly overwhelmed with the pain and the feeling of curling up inside; but most struck the rubber stalks and served only to make Jem convulse with pleasure as the stems were driven into her.

The spasms of pain and pleasure became indistinguishable. In her enclosed world, Jem was only half aware that she was pushing her hips up to meet the strokes of the cane, and that the guttural noises she was making behind the gag were becoming louder and more frantic. She knew only that she was riding a torrent of sensation towards a cataract over which nothing could prevent her from falling. And then she was at the edge, and over it, and crying out, her ecstatic shrieks muffled by the gag, as the flood swept over her and through her and carried her away.

A little later, as the slave-master and the slave-mistress wound ropes about her body to show the slaves how they could expect to be placed in bondage, Jem tried to order her thoughts. The slave-mistress, in particular, seemed outraged that Jem had achieved a climax while being punished, and took every opportunity to ridicule the idiotic grin that Jem could not remove from her face. Luckily the slave-mistress seemed to regard Jem's orgasm as a breach of etiquette rather than of discipline, and gave no indication that the Chatelaine would be informed.

Although she felt used, sore and thoroughly satisfied, Jem knew that her day of being paraded as a demonstration model in front of the denizens of the Chateau was drawing to a close, and that tomorrow she would face much sterner trials.

* * *

157

Olena sat on the bed and gazed round at the bare, windowless stone walls. The cell – two wide, vaulted aisles divided by a line of three carved pillars – was larger than the bedchamber that she had begun to think of as her home. The furnishings were, if anything, even more decadently luxurious than those to which she had become accustomed. And the bathroom, found by ducking through a narrow archway, was opulent with marble and gilt.

Yet it was still a cell. Olena, weeping in her distress at having failed the day's test in the most abject manner, had been brought here by Master Robert and Barat, and despite her tears and her distraction she had been able to see that she was being taken underground, into the bowels of the Chateau. These were the dungeons, and she was a prisoner in them. The cell had only one small door, and she had heard it being bolted and locked behind her after Barat had tried to console her and had then abandoned her here.

She knew it was no less than she deserved. Her case was hopeless. She was rotten to her core, a devious sinner whom no amount of chastisement could restore to wholesomeness. She wondered how Barat could bring himself even to look at her. He was so patient with her, so hopeful for her, so full of goodness and wisdom. And time after time she had proved herself unworthy of his trust.

Today they had concentrated on her breasts. Tears sprang again to Olena's eyes as she remembered the humiliation. The spanking in the library had done nothing to quell the sinful feelings that she had been experiencing since waking that morning; with a comfortably warm bottom, and the memory of the books she had found in the library, Olena had known that it would be futile to expect that she could exhibit purity of thought and behaviour while being tested.

Nonetheless, she had tried. As she had toyed with her lunch she had tried to banish from her mind every image that the books had summoned, every memory of her recent punishments, every thought about Barat's body. Instead she gave herself over to recollections from her childhood:

acts of worship with her family; games played at school; the countryside around her rural home.

By the time Master Robert had summoned them for the day's test, Olena had felt calm and secure. She had followed Barat willingly to the small, polygonal chamber in which the test was to be conducted.

Her confidence had lasted no longer than it took Master Robert to say the words, 'Disrobe, please, Olena.' She was about to be naked again, in a small room with two men.

As she had started to pull off her robe she had tried to analyse her feelings. It was surely right to feel shame: no respectable, worthy woman would feel any other emotion on undressing. But it was wrong – wickedly, heinously wrong – to feel a tremor of excitement at the thought of Barat casting his eyes over her nakedness; and the hot vibration in her secret place when Master Robert announced that today he would carry out the inspection for evidence of lewd thoughts – that was unpardonably worse.

Yet Olena had undressed and had lain, as instructed, on her back on the couch with her legs drawn up and widely parted. Master Robert had sat on the end of the couch, almost between her upraised knees. Olena had been able to sense his gaze, like fingers pressing against her skin, as he surveyed her secret parts.

'We have perhaps been trying to move too quickly,' Master Robert had said. 'I suggest that today we submit Olena to the very mildest of tests. A test,' he had added with a laugh, 'that even the most hardened whore might be able to pass.'

Barat had readily agreed, and had sat at the other end of the couch to stroke Olena's hair.

'Olena,' Master Robert had said, 'you should, if you have followed the teachings of your community as I understand them, be aware of your breasts only as inconvenient bulbs of flesh. Is that not so, Barat?'

'Entirely,' Barat had agreed. 'Their function is only to provide sustenance for your babies, should you be so blessed.'

'You should therefore be entirely unaware,' Master Robert had continued, 'that your breasts can inflame the desires of men, or that your breasts might be regarded as particularly admirable, or attractive, or especially well endowed in terms of size or shape. Do you understand?'

'Not really, Master Robert,' Olena had replied distractedly. She had been trying desperately to cling to thoughts of her parents' home, but she could feel the prickling at the tips of her breasts that indicated that her nipples were stiffening, and she was trapped between Master Robert staring between her legs and Barat gazing at her bosom.

'No matter,' Master Robert had said. 'This will prove a simple test to succeed in. Barat will touch your breasts, and I will watch vigilantly to ensure that you exhibit no signs of shameful excitement.'

But the very words 'shameful excitement' had been enough to stimulate Olena's secret parts. She had been getting wet there since she had been instructed to disrobe, and having the eyes of the two men on her naked body had filled her with precisely the feelings of perverse embarrassment that summoned sinful imaginings and engendered the tickly, trickling feeling inside her.

As Barat's hands had descended on to her breasts she had arched her back from the table, and when his fingers had brushed her right nipple she had been unable to restrain a gasp, which she had transformed immediately into a cry of despair: she had realised that at Barat's touch her body had shuddered, and she had felt her secret place opening. Master Robert, she had realised in that moment, would see at once that she had become aroused. And the thought of Master Robert watching the unfurling of her shame had caused another tremor of excitement.

Master Robert had hardly attempted to disguise the disgust in her voice. 'She's as wet as a swamp already,' he had announced. 'Barat, remove your hand from her flesh. At once, I say!'

Barat had then joined Master Robert, and while Olena had sobbed quietly the two men had stared in silence at her pudenda.

'I begin to think her case is hopeless,' Master Robert had said at last. 'She is surely blemished beyond redemption. She thinks of little but the stimulation of her desires, and she clearly enjoys flaunting her considerable charms in order to tempt others into lascivious thoughts. I believe that the mere act of removing her robe excites her.'

Olena had heard Master Robert's verdict with despair. She knew his judgement was accurate.

'I'll send her back to the community,' Barat had said, and she had cried out, partly with guilt as she heard the sadness in his voice, but mainly at the thought of being parted from Barat.

She had pleaded with the men to let her stay. She had promised that she would try harder to be good; that she would submit to any course of training, no matter how strict, that might restore her to the path of righteousness.

Master Robert and Barat had looked at each other. 'I am her appointed guardian,' Barat had said. 'I will remain with her for as long as is necessary.' Olena had almost swooned with relief at his words.

Master Robert had merely shrugged. 'Very well,' he had said. 'But from now on we will conduct ourselves in the manner prescribed here in the Chateau. She will be punished regularly, to remind her that she has still to prove herself. And we will begin to explore, rather than attempt to repress, her lewd thoughts and behaviour. We will plumb the depths of her depravity.'

Olena had acquiesced. She wanted to be with Barat, and she knew she deserved to be punished. But she knew also that there was no hope for her: they would find, she feared, that there was no limit to her wickedness.

Master Robert had told her to ask for an immediate chastisement. She had begged them to whip her. Master Robert had produced two short, leather straps.

'Kneel on the couch,' he had said. 'Lift your bottom as high as you can. Barat, you will work on the right buttock. I'll deal with the left. Up to now this young woman has had the mildest of spankings. She is about to begin to discover the true meaning of discipline in the Chateau.'

And as she had hollowed her back and pressed her breasts flat against the velvet seat, Olena had been horrified to realise that she felt only vain pride in exhibiting the plump roundness of her bottom, and a thrilling anticipation of the stinging heat that was about to suffuse it.

They had smacked her with hard, rapid strokes. Olena had begun to drift into an ocean of diffuse sensations when Master Robert had called on Barat to stop.

'As you see, Barat,' Master Robert had said, 'this is, as we feared, merely making her more aroused than ever. See how she's trembling? And look at the sheen of liquid on the insides of her thighs. I'll have her put in the dungeon. We'll continue with this tomorrow.'

And so she had been taken underground, down spiralling stone stairways and along grim tunnels, and had been locked into this cell.

She had wept for a while, and then upbraided herself for her weakness. She had slept, for she knew not how long, on the huge, soft bed.

And now, as she cast her eyes about her sumptuous prison, she heard the sound of the key turning in the lock of the door. The bolt was drawn. The door opened, and a young woman as naked as Olena herself stumbled into the cell. The door closed and was locked.

Olena instinctively moved her hands to cover herself. The other woman made no such move, but instead tilted her head to one side and smiled crookedly. Olena realised that the woman was not quite naked: around her neck was a black collar, and around each wrist was a black cuff. Each cuff was connected to the back of the collar by a length of chain.

The two women looked at each other. Olena felt that it was wrong to conceal her own body while the stranger was unable to cover hers, and lowered her hands. The stranger smiled again, and nodded as if she approved of what Olena was showing her.

'You're gorgeous,' the stranger said. 'What's your name?'

'I'm Olena.' She felt flustered; she hadn't intended to

sound so proud. 'I've been here only a few days. I've just been sent here. To the dungeon. I keep failing to be good, you see.'

The other woman laughed, but in a friendly way, as if she understood and sympathised. She was, Olena thought, quite the prettiest woman she had ever seen. She looked tired, but her blue eyes were sparkling and her lips looked as though they were permanently about to smile or laugh. Olena liked her instinctively and, although she knew it was probably wrong to have fun while she was being punished for her sinfulness, she could not help but be glad that the stranger had arrived to lift her mood.

'Well, you know who I am,' the stranger said with a rueful twist of her lips. 'It looks as though we're sharing this delightful accommodation, Olena.'

'I'm sorry,' Olena said. She wondered whether this woman was part of another of Master Robert's tests. 'I don't know who you are. And why are you in chains?'

The stranger stared at Olena. 'You didn't see me arrive here this morning? The dawn performance in the courtyard?'

'I was in my room,' Olena said, and could not suppress a sob. 'Not here. My nice bedroom.'

'Well, well,' was all the stranger said. With a jingling of chains, she started to walk round the cell, peering into all the corners and darting quizzical glances at Olena. The woman, Olena saw, had been punished: her pretty bottom was bright red, and criss-crossed with marks and lines.

'The chains,' the woman said, 'are to prevent me touching myself.'

'Touching yourself?' Olena asked, but as she said the words she suddenly realised to what the stranger must be referring. Olena had herself several times had to defeat an urge to put her hands between her thighs and seek out the source of the pleasurable sensations that crept through her when she thought of Barat, or when she was made to display herself lewdly, or when she was punished.

'I'm not allowed to masturbate,' the woman stated. 'Are you?'

Olena was at a loss for words. The stranger's speech was unusually direct. 'I don't know,' she stammered. 'It would be a sin, surely?'

The woman started laughing; the tips of her breasts jiggled and her chains jangled. She stopped when she saw Olena's mortified expression. 'I'm sorry,' she said, still trying to control her mirth. 'Perhaps they've put me in here with you so that you can cheer me up. Although I think that's unlikely.'

She came to the bed and sat beside Olena. She rested her head on Olena's shoulder, and began to whisper so quietly that Olena could hardly hear the words.

'My name is Jem,' she said, 'but don't call me by name unless we can be sure we're not being overheard. I like you. You're very attractive. I hope we can be friends.' She moved her head and placed the lightest of kisses on Olena's neck.

'Overheard?' Olena whispered.

'Hush,' the stranger said. 'Let's get under the covers. We can talk there, if we whisper. And I'll tell you all about how wonderful it is to touch yourself.'

Five

Olena, half awake, was dreaming of being spanked. She recalled the two punishments she had received the previous day: lying across Nicole's lap and feeling Nicole's hand slapping her bottom, and then later parting her legs and pushing up her buttocks so that they could be whipped by Barat and Master Robert. She knew she had deserved both punishments, and more. She began to imagine what it would be like to be spanked by Jem, who was asleep beside her.

But as she surfaced from sleep a little more, and realised that the lamps in the dungeon cell were dimly alight, she became aware that Jem wasn't asleep. Hidden under the covers, the elfin-faced slave was lying with one leg across Olena's, and with one hand in the gap between Olena's thighs. Her head was resting on Olena's arm, and she was kissing Olena's breast.

Olena remembered that she and Jem had gone to sleep kissing and cuddling each other. It had seemed to Olena a comparatively minor sin, and she had welcomed the attention and the gentle comfort of Jem's caresses. They had talked in whispers, between kisses, for what seemed like hours, exchanging confidences and secrets.

After a momentary pang of guilt – she knew she should not enjoy being touched and kissed in the way that Jem touched her and kissed her – Olena surrendered to her feelings of pleasure and comfort. She parted her legs a little, and sighed happily as she felt Jem's fingers slip further into the gap and begin to move gently but insistently there. She knew she was already wet, and that therefore she would have to be punished. She remembered again the cruel rhythm of two straps striking her buttocks, and moved her thighs even further apart.

'It must be morning,' she said softly, lifting the bedclothes and looking down at Jem. 'The lamps are alight.'

Jem stopped nuzzling Olena's breast and looked up at her. Jem's tousled titian curls surrounded her pretty, heart-shaped face. Her blue eyes were alive with mischief. Olena felt a wave of affection for Jem – and she knew that it was utterly, irredeemably wrong to have such feelings for another woman.

'Good morning,' Jem whispered. 'You have such lovely big breasts, Olena. I could kiss them for ever. Would you like that?'

Olena blushed and nodded. 'But I'm afraid I'm very wet again. Already.'

'I know,' Jem said with a grin, and pressed her fingers into Olena's secret place.

Olena felt a wave of longing that almost made her panic. 'But that's wrong,' she protested. 'I ought to be punished. Are you going to spank my bottom?'

'You are quite amazing and wonderful,' Jem said. 'I'd love to spank you. But I'm supposed to be chained up, remember? I can't be seen with my hands free; I'd lose my wager immediately. But I'll play with you a little longer, instead.'

Olena was about to protest, but the movements of Jem's fingers rendered her speechless. She could only gasp as Jem's insistent digits wriggled further into her and Jem's lips encircled the nipple of her left breast. It was becoming very difficult for Olena to differentiate between the sensations that were beginning to bubble through her body; the way that Jem was alternately licking and sucking her nipple made it particularly difficult to concentrate. But, as Jem had promised the previous night, the little spot close to the top of Olena's secret places seemed once again to be at the centre of the galvanising tremors that were beginning to ripple through her.

Jem had told her that the 'little spot' was called a clitoris, and that it was the tip of a large organ, devoted to giving pleasurable feelings, that was buried inside Olena's body and that responded to all the touches and caresses and smacks that Olena found enjoyable.

Olena writhed in embarrassed frustration as Jem's fingers seemed to wander all around her secret parts without quite touching the exposed tip of her clitoris. She had been amazed, and frankly disbelieving, that a woman's body could contain an organ that served no purpose other than to encourage sinful feelings. But as they spoke in whispers under the covers Jem had guided Olena's fingers between Jem's legs, and Jem had caught her breath as Olena had detected and touched the firm nodule at the apex of the opening into Jem's private places.

Olena could no longer think coherently. Her secret place was running with her juices, and she was grateful that the bedclothes were covering her and her shame. Jem's fingers were pressing into her gently but with a persistent rhythm that was causing waves of pleasure to roll over her. And there seemed to be a tingling line, drawing ever tighter, from her tongue-flicked nipple to the little bud that Jem refused to touch.

Olena had felt these sensations before, and she knew they were wicked in themselves as well as being proof of her uncleanliness. Here, in the dark, soft comfort of the bed, she felt for the first time able to bear the guilt. And she sensed that the feelings were gathering and building towards some sort of resolution. Each wave of pleasure seemed to be lifting her higher, and although she was frightened she couldn't help wanting to be propelled onwards.

Jem's lips pulled away from her nipple, which suddenly felt cold and very hard. 'Imagine that I'm spanking you,' Jem whispered, and resumed licking the nipple.

Yes, Olena thought, I'm thoroughly bad and I need to be punished. She imagined herself kneeling before Jem and asking for a spanking; another wave of pleasure engulfed her, and took her higher than ever. She managed to order her thoughts, and saw herself kneeling on a chair, exposing herself for Jem's inspection; then her concentration was shattered again as another wave broke over her, and Jem's fingers thrust deeply, and Jem's thumb touched her clitoris, and moved away, and then touched again, and pressed gently.

And Olena cried out, and clenched her hands into fists, and tossed her head from side to side on the pillows as the waves of pleasure combined to form a continuous fountain of ecstasy that lifted her up and up, transporting her on to a celestial plane that contained nothing but joy. And then, still filled with joy, she began to float down again, to where she was lying in bed, held tight in Jem's embrace.

Jem said nothing but, under the covers, she stroked Olena's shoulders and her stomach until Olena's tremblings ceased.

Olena knew that she had just committed a serious sin: she made a resolution that she would confess to Barat and ask for punishment at the first opportunity. This did nothing to lessen the wonderful elation that she felt.

She took several deep breaths and, when she felt able to speak, she peered under the covers to find Jem grinning at her.

'That was an orgasm,' Olena said. 'I've read about them, even though I know I should not have.'

'I guessed you hadn't had one yet,' Jem whispered, 'and it would have been wrong to waste the opportunity. Good, wasn't it?'

'It was – I can't describe it,' Olena said. 'Wonderful. The best feeling I've ever had. I'll have to be very soundly punished when I tell Barat.'

'And you'll enjoy telling him, won't you?' Jem said, her voice betraying an intellectual curiosity. 'And you'll enjoy being punished.'

'Yes,' Olena admitted, feeling suddenly wretched. 'I'm hopelessly wicked.'

'But the orgasm wasn't bad, was it?' Jem said. 'It was very good. Orgasms always are. We must talk some more about this. It's important. But now you'd better come down here under the covers and refasten my chains, before anyone gets suspicious.'

Olena slid further into the bed, until like Jem she was completely concealed beneath the covers. Each woman knew that the other faced a day of trials and ordeals, and they embraced and kissed with passionate intensity in the warm, soft darkness. Eventually Olena, at Jem's insistence, refastened Jem's wrist-cuffs to the chains that hung from the back of her collar, and the two women emerged from the bed.

'Let's use those luxurious bathroom fittings,' Jem suggested. 'Of course, you'll have to help me. I can't very well wash myself.' She shrugged her shoulders, and the chains rattled.

The two women were able to wash in a corner of the bathroom where jets of warm water issued from a bell-shaped rose that hung like a drooping flower from an upright pipe of chrome and gold. Jem told Olena to pull the faucet as far open as she could, so that the water fell in a steaming torrent. As they stood together, gasping in the needles of water and giggling when their nipples touched, Jem explained. 'We can talk now,' she said. 'Even if someone's listening, the noise of the water will obscure our words.'

'Of course,' Olena replied. 'How very clever.'

'And while we're talking, you can wash me. Use that sponge.'

Olena stepped from the curtain of water, picked up a large, irregularly shaped sponge, and re-entered the steaming waterfall that had Jem at its centre.

There was something indefinably enjoyable about sponging Jem's body. It was a very attractive body, of course, and Olena was full of gratitude and affection for Jem, but there was more to it than that. Finally Olena had to admit that it was the fact that Jem's hands were chained behind her that made washing her so exciting. Olena could use the sponge to caress Jem's neck, or to scrub her breasts, or to stroke her thighs, and Jem was powerless to prevent any of it.

169

Not that Jem appeared to mind. Olena was delighted with the squeals of pleasure that she was able to extract from Jem, and with the dreamy, eyes-closed expression that illuminated Jem's face when Olena used the sponge gently. Olena found that more and more she was concentrating on washing Jem's breasts, which were smaller than her own but very prettily shaped, with pink nipples that crinkled into hardness at a touch.

'Listen to me, Olena,' Jem said. 'While I'm still able to think properly. Come closer; let me kiss you while we talk.'

Olena pressed herself against Jem; she felt Jem's nipples sink into the softness of her own breasts. The water covered them like a sheet, but it was warm and moving and trickled between their bodies.

'Put the sponge between us,' Jem said, punctuating her words with hard kisses on Olena's lips. 'Hold it just there. Have you got it between your legs? Is it touching the right spot?'

Olena pulled back, nodded quickly, and returned Jem's kisses. She guessed what Jem intended them to do. The sinful feelings were returning, stronger than ever, and Olena found herself actually hoping that someone was watching them: it would be even more disgraceful, and she could depend on receiving punishment. Perhaps Nicole was about to rush into the bathroom and punish her and Jem immediately. The thought of being watched and of being whipped while kissing Jem made her thoughts fragment into shards of wonderful sensation. The sponge, with one end wedged into the gap at the top of her thighs, and the other held similarly by Jem, moved maddeningly as she and Jem embraced and pushed their hips against each other.

Jem was beginning to gasp as she writhed her hips, but she seemed determined to talk to Olena. She removed her lips from Olena's and pressed herself hard against the other woman. 'Remember, Olena,' she said, 'that you are blessed. You are lucky. You have a gift. Don't ever stop being ashamed. It's so valuable.'

Olena was beginning to feel the pulses of sensation that

she now knew could take her to an ecstatic climax. 'What do you mean?' she managed to gasp. She ground her hips against Jem's, and both women shuddered as the sponge between them pressed into their vulvas.

'Your shame adds to your pleasure,' Jem said into Olena's ear. 'Most people just have the physical feelings. You have them, certainly, but also the feelings that make you ashamed. And being ashamed adds to your pleasure. Which makes you even more ashamed. And so you want to be punished. But being punished is shameful, so just thinking about it makes you feel more excited.' She paused to take a breath.

'Yes,' Olena said, and felt her knees almost give way as another spark of sensation stoked the furnace of lust in her loins. 'And being punished makes me excited. I can't help it, I like to feel my bottom being smacked. But that's even more humiliating, particularly when people can see that I'm excited.'

'I think we're both close to coming,' Jem said quietly, so that Olena could hardly hear her above the jetting of the water. 'Let's see who can come first, shall we?'

Olena almost overbalanced as Jem pushed against her. But she was a little taller than Jem, and had the advantage that her hands were not chained behind her back. She pushed back, forcing Jem out of the tent of streaming water until Jem's back was against the ornately tiled wall. Gripped by desire and a desperate love for Jem, Olena crushed her breasts against Jem's and ground her lips on to Jem's gasping mouth. Olena, without thinking, was thrusting her hips against Jem's, driving the sodden sponge into Jem's secret place more and more rapidly as the pulses of pleasure accelerated in her own body.

'Olena,' Jem cried out in the brief gaps between kisses. 'Olena, Olena, you're so lovely. I'm coming, my love.' She began to pant; the movements of her hips matched Olena's. 'Remember: you're fortunate. Learn to enjoy your shame. Don't ever lose it. Olena –' Jem could say no more; as Olena's sensations blurred once again into a fountain that carried her upwards, she heard Jem's voice, as if from a great distance, crying out gutturally. And then Olena too had reached her summit, and was held breathless as exquisite stillness seemed to fill her and expand outwards from her. She gasped and gulped in air, crying hoarsely as wave after wave of pleasure swept over her, and then began to recede.

'I think you like your sexual climaxes,' Jem's voice said. Olena shook her head and opened her eyes. They were still pressed together against the wall, although they were now both beyond the reach of the cascading water. The sponge lay on the floor between their feet.

'Mm,' Olena said, and then was suddenly filled with dread: not at her own sinfulness, for once, but on behalf of her new friend. 'Jem! I mean, slave. If we are being watched, your climax will have been seen. And you're not permitted to do that.'

Jem kissed her. 'I just couldn't resist you. And it *was* lovely, wasn't it?'

'Oh yes,' Olena breathed. 'I think I'm going to enjoy being a bad girl from now on.'

By the beards of the elders, they were going to do it under the shower! Barat, crouching in the confined space of the tunnel that ran along the interior of the cell wall, could hardly believe his eyes. As he fumbled beneath his robe to grasp his hardening member he kept his face pressed against the eye-slit, one of many that cast narrow beams of light into the darkness and allowed him, by shuffling from one to another, to see every part of the cell and its attached bathroom.

He couldn't decide which of them to concentrate on.

Olena, of course, looked magnificent. Her long, dark hair, made sleek by the rushing water, clung to her shoulders and her back like a black silk shawl. Her coffee-coloured skin gleamed. The jetting water bounced from her jutting breasts and dripped from her nipples; as she moved, her shining buttocks rolled together and looked as though they had been oiled.

But the other woman also merited his attention. Although she was scarcely shorter than Olena, the delicacy of her elfin features, and the paleness of her skin, and the fact that Olena's breasts and bottom were so generously proportioned, made her look diminutive. The former Supreme Mistress, now the least of all the slaves, naked and bound in chains, was a sight to engender desire in anyone. Barat imagined squeezing her breasts in his hands; he pictured her chained to the foot of his bed, gazing up at him with those sea-green eyes as she was now gazing at Olena, anticipating the fall of his whip on her small, round buttocks.

And they were kissing as if they intended to devour each other. Barat had seen women kissing before, but never had he witnessed such a display of naked lust. He saw how Olena's breasts engulfed the slave's, and he tried to imagine how the meeting of nipples might feel. He saw their hips pressed urgently together, rocking back and forth as they excited each other with the long sponge. If only he could have them under his command; he would tie them together in this very position, and make them pleasure each other as he whipped their wriggling arses.

His eyes were drawn to Olena's face. She never looked less than pretty, with her large, dark eyes, her wide cheekbones, and her pouting lips, but now she was transfigured. Olena's eyes, with their lids half shut, were glowing with desire; her mouth was open, and her lips were twisted into an expression that was almost ugly but that was also more alluring than any he had seen. He suddenly realised that she was on the verge of a climax, and watched transfixed as she thrust herself repeatedly against the slave's pinioned form. He heard her cries above the sound of the rushing water. He watched her face recover its animation and register shocked delight, and then break into an unutterably winsome smile.

Only then did he stand upright. He had to struggle to suppress a shout of rage. This was not supposed to happen. Olena was not to be permitted to achieve ecstasy other than during her punishments, and not until Master Robert considered her ready. Above all, Olena was to be trained in Barat's presence; the Chatelaine had guaranteed it.

His manhood had already shrivelled. All thoughts of pleasure and excitement had been driven from his mind by an overwhelming sense of outrage that things were not going to plan. And he felt fear. In order to pursue and possess Olena he had long ago throttled his conscience and abandoned his holy principles; he had risked his standing in his community; and he had allowed himself to be humiliated here in the Chateau. He had perverted his life to obtain Olena, and now he sensed that she was slipping from his grasp.

He pressed his fists to his forehead. He wanted to scream, but knew he would be heard by the women in the bathroom. He set off along the dark tunnel, leaving behind the excited chatter of Olena and the slave. He would demand to see the Chatelaine. He would demand to be given Olena immediately.

As Jem and Robert made their way from the dungeons to the north range of the Chateau, Robert's right hand roamed continuously over the curves of Jem's bottom. She was naked but for her collar, matching leather cuffs around her wrists, the chains, and a tightly fitting leather helmet within which her hair was contained. From time to time Robert would pull on the leash and laugh when Jem stumbled. With the movement of her arms restricted by the chains, on occasion she almost fell; each time this happened Robert grabbed her roughly, pinching her nipples hard as he righted her, and gave her six lashes for being clumsy.

As he led her through the lamplit corridors he maintained a steady stream of muttered invective: 'Not so high and mighty now, are you, little whore?' he said, over and over again. 'My Mistress has got you, and she'll never let you go. She'll keep this pretty little arse so sore you'll never want to sit down again. And if she ever takes pity on you, you can be sure I won't.'

Jem succeeded in maintaining a subversive cheerfulness as she dutifully thanked Robert for his consideration, but she could not help feeling apprehensive. It was clear that

Robert had an ordeal prepared for her in the Chateau's kitchens, and that he expected her to be unable to remain subservient throughout it.

They had reached the wide passage that ran down the spine of the north range of rooms and separated the dining hall, with its tall, south-facing windows, from the cryptlike kitchens, sculleries and storerooms of the Chateau. This was one of the oldest parts of the building: the ceiling vaults rose from semicircular arches that were supported by thick, round, age-pitted pillars, and the flagstones had been worn by centuries of feet scurrying from hall to kitchen and back again.

Robert led Jem past the pair of vast swinging doors which led directly into the main kitchen. He stopped instead a little further down the corridor, in front of a single, plain door. Jem thought that behind the door was one of the smaller rooms devoted to food preparation: the bakery, perhaps. The main kitchen, of course, was so cavernous that the blackened ceiling was difficult to discern; the bakery, buttery and sculleries were therefore small only by comparison – each was much larger, for instance, than the spacious cell that Jem had shared with Olena the previous night.

Jem thought she could hear raised voices and laughter from behind the door. When Robert pushed the door open, the sound of voices abruptly ceased. The silence seemed ominous.

Robert propelled Jem through the doorway. She found herself standing indeed in the bakery, a large, square room of yellowed stone, its ceiling supported on squat pillars. The air smelled organic: yeast and hot bread, carried on currents of warm air. All the oven doors were open, the ovens were empty, and in the vast fireplace only a small pyramid of logs was burning. Nonetheless, the room seemed hot to Jem.

It also seemed crowded. Lounging on and around a sturdy wooden table were half a dozen kitchen slaves; all men, all young, and all staring at Jem with unconcealed interest.

Jem almost allowed her amusement to show on her face. Six strong, libidinous lads: was this supposed to be the ordeal that would break her will? She lowered her head and did her best to look demure; it would not do, she decided, to let Robert catch her eyeing the bulges at the fronts of the aprons that were the only garments the male kitchen slaves wore. She concentrated on absorbing the masculine atmosphere of the room: the heat; the earthy, arousing aromas; the penetrating gazes of hard-working, hard-bodied young men.

'Here she is, lads,' Robert announced. He unclipped the chains from her collar and cuffs, but left the leather helmet clasped around her head. 'She's all yours. The head chef's expecting her for lunch, and you'll be in trouble if he's kept waiting. But how you prepare the dish and cook her is up to you. Just remember a few things.' Robert hooked a finger through the metal ring at the top of her helmet and pulled her up on to her toes. 'This promiscuous little slut will do anything you tell her to. And she'll enjoy it. So don't be gentle with her. You like rough games, don't you, slut?'

'Yes, sir,' Jem said. She couldn't honestly deny it.

She felt Robert's free hand cup and squeeze her left breast and then thrust itself into the gap at the top of her thighs. 'She's already wet,' Robert said, 'and she doesn't know yet what you have planned for her.' He removed his hand and wiped a line of clear fluid on to Jem's stomach. 'Tell them the things you like, slut. You know what to say.'

'Yes, sir,' Jem said. She had a fairly clear idea of the words Robert wanted to hear her say. 'I like young men's cocks,' she said, shaking her head free from Robert's grasp. 'I like to touch cocks, and to lick them.'

The men had moved to form a semicircle in front of Jem. Several of them had their hands under their aprons. They passed sidelong comments to each other: 'Look at those tits,' 'She's a real whore,' 'I can't wait to get started.' Jem knew she was supposed to feel threatened, but instead she was excited, and anxious for the fun to begin. It occurred to her that perhaps, despite her efforts subtly to

176

disseminate the tales throughout the Private House organisation, Robert hadn't heard the rumours about the excesses of the Supreme Mistress. It was said, for instance, that during one night she had drained the energies of an entire fifteen-man sports team that had been brought to the House specifically for her purposes. And Jem had taken care to ensure that the rumours were always less remarkable than the real occurrences on which they were based.

'I like to take cocks in my mouth,' Jem went on, warming to her subject. 'And in my cunt. And in my arsehole. All at the same time,' she added, with a coquettish smile that drew a growl from the surrounding men.

'Tell them about the whip, slave,' Robert said.

Jem snatched a strap from his belt. She drew its tongue across the tops of her breasts. 'You can punish me, if you like,' she whispered. 'I'm your slave. You can do anything to me. You can whip me here. Or here.' She turned round, took one end of the strap in each hand, leaned forwards, and swung her bottom from side to side against the strip of leather. Then, as the young men roared their approval, she parted her legs, bent further forwards, and held the strap by its handle so that the tongue slapped between her buttocks and up against her sex.

'You lads just make sure she gets a thorough lashing,' Robert said, with a note of exasperation in his voice. Jem pirouetted and with a bow proffered the strap. He snatched it from her hand, raised it as if to strike her, and then, scowling, turned and left the room. 'Don't forget to have her ready for Chef's lunch,' he shouted as the door closed behind him.

The room was suddenly still and silent. Jem looked enquiringly along the line of lust-flushed faces surrounding her.

'We'd best make a start on preparing this little bird for cooking,' one of the young men eventually said.

'First step is to truss her,' another said. 'Hold her still while I fetch the rope.'

Two of the men stepped forward and grasped her arms with hands that had been strengthened by months of kneading dough. Jem felt suddenly vulnerable, and began to struggle even though she knew it was futile.

She felt a line of fire across her right buttock, and then another on her left. A man carrying loops of a rope, and swinging the loose end of it, emerged from behind her. 'Master Robert said you'd let us do anything,' he said. 'No struggling, no complaining. Said we've to tell him if you disobey, or even if you're just a bit unwilling. You're not unwilling, are you, you pretty cock-lover?'

Jem took a deep breath, and relaxed. 'I'd love to be tied up,' she said. 'Bondage is always a delight. Just make sure to tie me nice and tightly.'

She noted, with a managerial satisfaction that she realised was entirely inappropriate in her circumstances, that the men were using the correct type of rope. She had decreed that throughout the Private House, when rope was to be used for tight bondage it should be made of braided cotton. This material was soft to the touch, and of a light weight, and yet was quite strong enough to withstand any one person's attempts to break free.

The men had planned precisely how to bind her, and worked in silence. One stood on each side of her, holding her arms away from her sides. A third and fourth stood in front of her and behind her, passing the rope back and forth as they wound it around her.

A long loop was passed round the back of her neck. The two hanging ends were then pulled beneath her arms and crossed behind her back. The man in front of her pulled the two ends to the front, crossed them at the centre of her ribcage, and pulled them tight so that her breasts were resting on the rope. He then tied a knot, and left the long ends hanging to the floor.

'You'll need to work on her tits,' suggested one of the two men watching the operation.

'I know,' the man in front of Jem said. He placed his hand under her chin and lifted her head so that she was looking up into his eyes. 'Move your legs further apart, slut,' he said.

178

'Yes, sir,' Jem replied. The man had large hazel eyes and curly brown hair. His expression was carefully stern, as if he were concentrating on maintaining his masterly demeanour. Jem thought he looked lovely.

'Ask us to play with your tits,' he said. Jem widened her eyes and pretended to be shocked. 'And with your arsehole, too,' he added.

Jem understood the reasons behind the instruction. If her breasts were massaged, particularly while she was aroused, they would swell, and would look and feel heavier and larger. Once tightly bound with rope, they would remain enlarged, and would both look more prominent and feel more sensitive. She knew exactly what was required.

'Please play with my breasts, sir,' she said. 'And please don't be gentle. Pinch my nipples hard. And if one of you could insert a finger into my anus at the same time, that would be wonderful.'

She leaned forwards, and the man behind her slapped her bottom for a few moments before cupping his hand against her vulva. She felt his fingers press upwards, and couldn't prevent herself wriggling happily against the pressure.

'The little whore's got a cunt as hot as an oven,' the man behind her said. 'And she's sopping wet.'

He twirled a finger inside her vagina, and Jem, still holding the gaze of the brown-eyed man, smiled contentedly as she felt ripples of pleasure begin to expand within her.

The finger was withdrawn, and with a final smile Jem bent forwards a little more, so that her anus was exposed to the man behind her and her breasts were just swinging freely.

The brown-eyed man took one of her breasts in his left hand and began methodically to smack it with his right. At the same time Jem felt a finger, lubricated with her juices, begin to press against the tight ring of her anal sphincter. She relaxed the muscle, pushed back against the pressure, and gasped as she felt the familiar, yet always pleasurable sensations of intrusion and fullness. The finger began, very slowly but insistently, to creep into her; her breast was released, and the other was grasped and smacked. Jem surrendered to the sensations. She was in heaven.

As the brown-eyed man began to pinch her breasts, using the callused tips of his strong fingers and concentrating on her areolae and nipples, Jem was only dimly aware of tossing her head and moaning. Each shock of pain seemed to arc directly to her clitoris; she realised, vaguely, that if the two men continued to play with her she would start to rise towards a climax – and she had not been given permission to do so. She tried hard to clear her mind, but the feelings engendered by the men's persistent fingers could not be banished. A small part of her consciousness began to panic as she felt the pulsing of her climax gather pace: she was about to lose her wager with the Chatelaine.

'I think that'll do,' the man in front of her said. He gave her nipples a final pinch and twist, and took a pace back to look at her.

The finger was pulled from her anus, and with a gasp of mingled disappointment and relief Jem straightened her body. Her breasts felt hot and heavy, and they tingled all over and deep inside.

The man's brown eyes were fixed on the reddened, quivering cones of manhandled flesh. He seemed pleased, and Jem felt a strange sense of pride. His work on her breasts had clearly excited him: his member was so stiff that his apron was being held out in front of his stomach.

'Thank you, sir,' Jem said. On a whim she shook herself free of the men holding her arms, dropped to her knees, looked up at him and added, 'May I show my gratitude by kissing you?' She stared longingly at the front of his apron.

The men around her laughed and made lewd comments. The brown-eyed man stepped forwards and pulled on the ring at the top of her helmet. 'You really *are* a whore, aren't you?' he said.

'Yes, sir,' Jem said, and smiled up at him. She was happy to agree to the description. She wanted his cock in her mouth.

He released her hair, lifted his apron and draped it over her head and shoulders. Jem found herself in a tent that smelled of warm bread and male sex. His erect manhood was standing almost vertically, and almost touching her face. She pressed her lips to the veined base of the shaft and inhaled the musky odour of his testicles. She cupped her swollen breasts in her hands, and sighed with pleasure as she started to lick the wrinkled sac.

She heard a voice say, 'Show us your arse, slave,' and she obliged, making her back concave and thrusting her bottom up and back. She felt hands on her buttocks and between her thighs, and resulting tremors of delight, but they seemed distant: her world had been reduced to the dim, flour-powdery canopy beneath which she was lovingly licking her way towards the head of the proud member before her.

At last she reached the tip and, after tonguing with delicate flicks the slit of the urethra, she moved her head up and engulfed the entire helmet. It filled her mouth. It was warm, and as smooth as a polished plum. It pulsed against her tongue. The moment of taking a man's erection into her mouth never failed to give Jem a frisson of pleasure, and she let out an exclamation of distress when the velvet hardness was pulled suddenly from her mouth.

'That's enough,' the man's voice said from above her head. 'On your feet, slut. We've got to get you trussed up for cooking.'

He pulled his apron from Jem's head, and she blinked in the sudden light, even though the bakery was illuminated only by lamps hanging from the vaulted ceiling. She stood, and the men beside her grasped her arms once again in their unforgiving hands.

Once the brown-eyed man had assured himself that Jem's breasts were still engorged and sensitive, the business of tying them proceeded. He picked up the trailing ends of the rope and tied them together in a knot that was less than a finger's length from the one he had already made, thus creating a small loop. With the second knot resting above the first in the valley between Jem's breasts, the ends of the rope were passed beneath her arms, and the man behind her pulled the ends tight and knotted them together in the middle of her back. The ends, still long, hung to the floor. Each breast was now roped on three sides, although there was as yet no constriction.

'Cross her arms,' the brown-eyed man said to the man behind Jem. She put up no resistance as her arms were crossed behind her back. She glanced sideways and saw that two new lengths of rope were to be employed: each had one end tied to one of the cuffs that she had around her wrists.

The two ropes from Jem's wrists were passed to the brown-eyed man, who pulled tightly on them to ensure that Jem's crossed arms were pressed into her back, and that each of her hands was pulled up to tuck under the opposing upper arm. He passed the loose ends of both ropes through the loop between the knots that separated Jem's breasts, and then passed the ends over Jem's shoulders to the man behind her. He pulled them tight, so that the two knots were pulled upwards and the rope running beneath Jem's breasts embedded itself in the crease there; he tied the ropes together behind Jem's neck.

Still Jem's breasts were relatively unfettered. The man with brown eyes called for another length of rope, and carefully found its halfway point before tying the middle of it to the lower of the two knots nestling between Jem's breasts. There were now two long ends of rope hanging down the front of Jem's body, and two hanging at the back, from where the ends of the first length had been tied together.

'Legs wide apart, slave,' the man behind Jem said.

Jem obeyed. The man with brown eyes held the two ropes in front of her, one in each of his big hands. She assumed the man behind her was holding the two ropes there. The men who had been holding her arms were still at her sides, and all four of the men now worked together to bind Jem's body tightly with the ropes.

The ropes from her back were passed to the front, where they were slipped under the front ropes and then passed to the back again; both pairs of ropes were pulled against each other to create a tension that held the rope taut as it followed the contours of Jem's body. This procedure was followed once more, creating a rope lattice around Jem's torso, back and stomach.

Then, as Jem had expected, a pair of ropes was passed from her belly between her legs. It was quite usual in this school of bondage, Jem knew, for a pair of ropes to run between the labia and buttocks; often such ropes were tied particularly tightly, so that the bound woman was very aware of her bondage, and often large knots were tied in the ropes to put pressure on the clitoris or the anus. On this occasion, however, Jem noted with a slight pang of disappointment that the ropes were drawn into the creases at the tops of the insides of her thighs, so that her vulva was framed between them. The ropes came together between her buttocks and, once pulled very tight, were tied together to the lowest crossing-point of the ropes that zigzagged down her back.

The men stood back briefly to admire their handiwork. They tested the knots, and pulled on the ropes to ensure that all were tight. Now that Jem was attractively but very securely bound, with her arms tied behind her back, the men seemed more confident about touching her. Their hands strayed from the ropes to her breasts and bottom; within a few moments Jem found that all six of the men, jostling for space around her, had their hands on her. At least one man's fingers were puddling in the wetness of her vagina; other fingers were trying to infiltrate her anus; both of her breasts were being squeezed and pinched; fingers were inserted into her mouth; and at least one hand was slapping her buttocks. With her arms bound up Jem would have toppled over had it not been for the press of nearly naked strong young male bodies about her.

The brown-eyed man at last called his comrades to order. 'Let's get on,' he said. 'Chef won't be pleased if we're late. Let's tie her tits now.'

The knot behind Jem's neck was untied, and the loose ends were crossed and were passed back over her shoulders; at the front they were brought together and put through the loop between the two knots that separated her breasts. This loop, now anchored to the rope lattice around Jem's lower body, moved upwards hardly at all when the loose ends were pulled tightly up and to the left and right. They were passed under the ropes that ran from Jem's neck to under her arms, turned back over these ropes and pulled downwards, to the outer sides of Jem's breasts. Here they were looped under the ropes that ran under the breasts, and pulled upwards; the brown-eyed man used his big hands to adjust the tightness of the ropes and to prod and pull the flesh of Jem's breasts, so that they were entirely contained within the tightening network of bonds.

Jem's breasts were now constricted from underneath and from both sides, and were beginning to feel very swollen and tender. The two ends of rope went back up to and over the ropes lying diagonally across the upper part of Jem's chest, across to the central knot, and then, with a tug that Jem thought would snap the ropes, underneath Jem's arms to be tied at her back. Jem's breasts were now encircled with taut rope, and were held more tightly than by any corset or harness Jem had ever worn. Distended and almost spherical, their skin shining with tension, they jutted from her chest. He nipples stood out as large and hard as thimbles.

Jem was impressed. She had rarely been tied up as thoroughly. 'Thank you for binding me, sirs,' she said. 'I hope I'm adequately trussed now.'

'You'll do,' the brown-eyed man said, and rubbed his hands across her breasts. 'What's the next stage, lads? What do we do next before we cook our bird?'

'Tenderise her, tenderise her,' the other young men chanted. This made Jem apprehensive, and her fears were realised when one of the men went to a cupboard and produced various instruments of correction: four long, thin wooden dowels, and two leather straps.

Without further words, the men took one instrument each and arranged themselves in a formation that took up the entire length of the bakery. The two men swinging the leather straps stood facing each other at opposite ends of the room; between them, the four men with wooden switches stood at intervals.

It was clear to Jem that she was to run a gauntlet from one side of the room of the other. She had played games of this sort before, although she usually preferred watching to participating. At least, she thought, I'm not wearing high heels, and my legs and feet aren't tied.

'Come here, slave,' shouted one of the men holding a strap. 'Stand here in front of me, and turn to face the others. That's the way.'

Jem waited patiently for further instructions. She felt nervously excited, but she no longer believed that she was in danger of losing her wager with the Chatelaine – at least not here, this morning, in the bakery. All she had to do was to submit and show no resistance; in bondage, with her arms pinioned, and surrounded by six strong men, she would have little opportunity to rebel. They would carry out whatever plans they had made for her, and she would endure them. So far, she confessed to herself, it had been more a matter of enjoying than enduring.

'When I give you a smack, like this,' the man behind her said, whacking her bottom with the strap so hard that she almost fell forwards, 'you run straight ahead as fast as you can. Stop when you reach the other side of the bakery, turn round, and wait for another smack before you set off again. Understand, slave?'

'Yes, sir,' Jem said, looking over her shoulder and giving a smile to the serious-faced young man. 'And thank you for smacking me.'

The leather strap had been wielded with enthusiasm, and Jem's bottom felt afire.

'Get set, then,' the man said. 'Stick your arse out again.'

Jem did so, and was rewarded with another blazing stripe. She set off, running awkwardly because her arms were tied behind her back. As she passed the four men along her route she tried to duck and weave to avoid the hissing switches. Her breasts, held tight and prominent within their rope bindings, seemed alarmingly vulnerable, and most of the men tried to strike her bosom as she ran

185

towards them. They missed their target, but laughed as she bobbed and swerved, and shouted when one of them managed to imprint a glowing line on her right buttock as she raced past him.

She stopped in front of the other strap-wielding man, and drew in lungfuls of air. It was the young fellow with the hazel eyes, and she smiled at him as she tried to catch her breath.

'Turn around, you slut,' he said. 'You'll get no rest until we've finished this. We've got to make up time. Come on, turn round and stick your arse out.'

Jem had no sooner leaned forwards than the strap landed forcefully on her left buttock, making her gasp and propelling her at a run towards the men waiting with big grins on their faces and their switches raised. This time none of them aimed for her breasts; copying the example of the one who had succeeded in lashing her during her first run, they all waited until she had run past before swinging their thin wooden rods at her backside.

Jem's buttocks had four fresh stripes by the time she reached the end of the room.

'Turn!' the man shouted at her. 'Bend! Run!'

With a breathless sob, Jem started on her third run. The men wielding the switches had now learned the technique of swinging them in Jem's wake, adding a flick of the wrist to catch one or other of Jem's buttocks as she raced past. Jem could do nothing to avoid the blows except to try to outrun them. A rational part of her mind kept trying to remind her that the men would whip her as much or as little as they pleased, whether she ran through the gauntlet or strolled; the stinging lashes and the shouted instructions impelled her to run, however – and, in any case, she would lose her wager if she failed to obey the men's commands.

And so Jem ignored the voice of reason, and the jeering laughter, and the throbbing of her bound breasts, and the tightness of the ropes around her body and between her legs, and the increasing temperature of her bottom; she simply ran up and down the room, as fast as she could, until her legs felt weak and she was gasping for breath.

'Turn,' ordered the brown-eyed man as she staggered towards him for what, she thought, must have been the fifth or sixth time.

Panting, and proceeding at little more than a walking pace, she lifted her head and stared at him with what she hoped was her most winsome, wide-eyed expression of helplessness.

There was not a hint of pity in his face. 'Turn around, slut,' he shouted, 'and be quick about it.'

Sobbing with breathlessness and indignation, Jem presented her bottom to him. His leather strap swung upwards and landed with a loud report on the lower inside curves of both of Jem's buttocks; the tip went between her legs and caught her vulva. With a gasping cry, Jem set off again towards the other end of the room.

She could no longer sprint. Tears of frustration blinded her as, with her chest heaving, she trotted towards the line of young men with the wooden dowels. They were cheering her ironically, calling her vile names and making loud claims about which parts of her body they intended to aim for.

This time they concentrated on her breasts. Bound, distended and sensitised, the constricted bulbs of flesh were irresistible targets. With her arms tied behind her back, Jem could do nothing to protect them except to swing her torso from side to side, which seemed to make the young men even more excited.

The wooden dowels were very thin and smooth, and circular in section: they had no rough or sharp edges, and were obviously light and difficult to wield with much force. Nonetheless, each of the three that landed on one or other of Jem's breasts wrung a little shriek of pain from her, much to the amusement of the young men.

The fourth lash caught her stingingly on the right buttock, and then she was through the gauntlet and approaching the end of the room. She slowed to a walk, and veered from side to side as though she was having difficulty staying on her feet. If she exaggerated her exhaustion, she thought, the men might lose interest and move on to the next stage of this culinary ordeal.

At the last moment Jem stumbled, and fell against the man standing with his back to the wall. Her tight, sore breasts were pressed against his naked chest. She looked up at him imploringly.

He grinned. 'Turn around, slave,' he said. 'You're not ready for cooking yet. Turn and bend, my little chicken.'

The lash against her bottom was almost gentle this time, and Jem jogged forwards. As she approached the waiting line of men a voice behind her called out, 'Stop!', and she came to a halt in the centre of the room.

Grinning and joking, the four men with switches converged on her, surrounded her, and allowed her a moment to recover her breath before they began to whip her.

As she writhed and twisted within the circle of swishing laths, Jem felt stinging lines all over her body, catching her in such quick succession that she had no time to register them as individual stripes. She knew only that her buttocks, thighs and breasts were becoming incandescent. Her breasts, in particular, had never felt so hot and sore. Worse than the punishment was the sense of helplessness; she could not run away, she could not protect the vulnerable and tender parts of her body. The only way to escape from the torment was, she knew, to protest: to stand still, gather the tattered remnants of her dignity, and demand that they stop. And if she were to do that, the Chatelaine would have won.

As the switches continued to hiss and sting, and she found herself gasping with each lash so rapidly that, as the men laughingly commented, she sounded as if she was reaching a climax, she decided that she could bear it no longer. She would call a halt to this, and admit defeat. But then the whipping ceased.

It was the man with brown eyes who inspected her. He ran his hands over her breasts, and then her buttocks. He put a hand between her thighs, and pushed upwards so that Jem was lifted on to the tips of her toes.

'She'll do, I reckon,' he announced. 'Breasts and haunches feel nice and tender. And I tell you what, lads,' he added, 'she's still as wet as a lake down here. I think she enjoyed being tenderised. Did you, you little whore?'

Jem couldn't deny that she was aroused. Her whole body felt raw but alive, and the man's rough hand pressing into her vulva had shocked her by causing an almost climactic spasm of desire.

'Yes, thank you, sir,' she said, trying to control her panting voice. 'It was very exciting.'

The man laughed. 'We'd better hurry,' he said. 'Give me a hand to get her oiled.' With his hand still between her legs he lifted her from the ground, and with enthusiastic cries all of the other young men crowded around him, trying to grab Jem and to help carry her towards a corner of the room.

Jem had hardly had time to realise that she was being held aloft by six pairs of strong and intrusive hands before she was lowered into a shallow copper dish as wide as a bath. The vessel had a flat bottom, and apart from Jem contained only a few fingers' depth of warm cooking oil. She had been placed on her back, which she found uncomfortable because her arms were tied behind her. When she tried to sit up, however, she succeeded only in sliding across the floor of the pan: her bottom skidded sideways, and she toppled slowly on to her side.

'Let's turn her a few times,' the brown-eyed man said, 'and make sure she's coated all over.'

The young men formed a circle around the copper vessel. Some of them pushed Jem with their feet; others flicked her with the long switches. She wriggled and squirmed to avoid the stinging lashes, and was soon rolling over and over in the oil.

She was grateful, now, for the tightly fitting helmet, which was protecting her hair from becoming drenched in the viscous fluid. She presumed, as she tossed and writhed in the slippery vessel, that the helmet had been provided for precisely this reason. Rolling over and over in oil was, she decided, a pleasant interlude: her sore breasts and bottom, in particular, felt soothed by the emollient sweet-smelling oil.

189

The hissing switches fell silent, and the men stooped towards her. 'Get the oil worked well in,' she heard one of the men say, and suddenly hands were all over her body.

She was turned on to her back; her legs were lifted into the air; and two of the men started to massage oil into her bound breasts. Others began work between her raised legs, pushing oily fingers again and again into her vagina and anus. A rhythm started to develop, and Jem found herself gasping with pleasure as the insistent rubbing and pushing started to ignite sparks within her. She gave herself up to the sensations, and was disappointed when the brown-eyed man said, 'That's enough. She's ready. Let's get her on to the spit.'

With difficulty, slithering and ribald laughter the men took hold of her and pulled her from the copper dish. As they carried her towards the fireplace Jem began to worry that the conceit of preparing her as a bird is prepared for roasting was becoming too realistic; did they really intend to impale her on a spit and cook her on an open fire? She would have no choice but to object; the Chatelaine would have won; and she would have endured for nothing her rough treatment by the six young kitchen-slaves.

When she saw the cunningly wrought metal frame that was suspended between the two fire irons, however, she felt a wave of relief. The long, black structure, while it looked sinister and uncomfortable, was obviously not designed for cookery.

It was, she supposed, something like a spit, in that it was long, its core was a black iron rod, each end of which was resting on a soot-darkened support, and it was situated in front of a fire – although not close enough for roasting.

Welded on to the central rod, however, were a number of ornate curlicues of wrought iron, some of them padded with cushions of black leather. Hanging from the structure at various points along its length were leather straps. Jem recognised it as a framework to which a person could be secured, and she was in no doubt that she was destined imminently to be bound to it.

Jem's body was still slippery with oil, and the young men

190

took great care as they lowered her on to the spit. Her hips, stomach and ribcage rested in a shaped, upholstered cradle that was fixed horizontally and lengthways atop the central pole. Jem found it comfortable enough, although the men did nothing to loosen her bondage or to ease the strain in her shoulders caused by the tying of her arms behind her back. In fact, Jem soon found herself tied even more tightly: a broad strap was placed across the small of her back and tightened, to keep her in place in the cradle.

Like the arms of an armchair, two leather-upholstered spurs projected forwards and slightly upwards from the main part of the cradle to provide support for Jem's shoulders, and then curved towards each other to create a padded rest for her breastbone. Jem's tightly constricted breasts, still stinging and aching and feeling more sensitive than ever, hung unencumbered below her with the central bar of the spit running between them. When she lifted her head Jem found herself looking down the length of the spit to where one end was supported on a fire iron.

At first Jem had been allowed to keep her feet on the floor and bend forwards on to the padded leather in order to have her body secured to the spit. She had noted, however, that the cradle held her hips tilted up at the back, and that attached to the spit behind her were projections from which hung stirrups and straps; she knew that soon her legs and feet would be arranged in a much more revealing and uncomfortable position.

As soon as the strap was fastened across her back, the men turned their attention to her legs. Grasping the slippery limbs in many hands, they lifted her feet from the floor and bent her knees as they parted her thighs. They placed her feet in stirrups, which they then moved upwards and outwards, so that Jem's knees were lifted to the level of her torso. With her hips uplifted by the cradle, Jem's private parts were now exhibited for all to see, and her rounded buttocks were raised high.

Jem knew that her bottom must by now be cherry red and covered in stripes; her anus, she knew well, was delicately formed and its crinkled skin was dark pink; her shaven outer labia were prettily plump, while her inner labia, which she was sure must also be visible, were exquisite fronds over which several of her lovers had enthused. Headman, she recalled, had liked to whip her there because it was, he said, the prettiest part of his prettiest woman. With every part of her glistening with oil, Jem decided with satisfaction that from the rear she must be a most delectable sight.

Jem knew that she was positioned well for either penetration or more punishment, and she wondered which it would be: the sudden sting of a whip laid across her buttocks, or the thrilling insertion of a phallus.

The next words she heard, however, were, 'Let's get the skewers into her,' which filled her with dread. Were they going to pierce her flesh?

She was slightly reassured when she saw two of the men attaching something to the spit in front of her. They slid the contraption towards her along the metal bar, and fixed it in place in front of her face.

Suddenly she felt her head being tugged back, and she realised that one of the men had pulled her helmet. The tugging ceased, but she found she could no longer lower her head: it was being held up, presumably by a chain from the top of her helmet to a ring on the strap across her back, so that she was obliged to look straight ahead and could not lower her face.

The two men in front of her were once more at work on the complicated bracket they had fixed to the spit. They moved it back a little and adjusted its height, and then began turning a crank. Slowly, and pointing directly at Jem's mouth, a torpedo-shaped cylinder began to emerge. It was a carved phallus, and it was clear to Jem that she would have no choice but to take it into her mouth. She opened her lips and tried to remain calm as the cold, solid cylinder filled her mouth. At last it stopped, before it reached the back of her throat and could make her gag. She could not close her jaws, however, or move her head, and she reflected that she had indeed been very effectively skewered.

The men had referred to more than one skewer, and so Jem was not at all surprised to feel the rounded nose of something hard and cold insinuating itself between the delicate membranes of her inner labia. She assumed that a second device had been fixed to the spit behind her, between her splayed thighs. The phallus felt huge – much larger than the one in her mouth – but she felt no discomfort: even if she had not been aroused by the morning's events, the oil that had been massaged into her would on its own have eased the entrance of the giant cylinder.

'She's well skewered,' one of the kitchen-slaves said. 'Can we baste her now?'

'Just a moment,' another replied. 'Chef likes his rump-meat good and tender. Maybe we'd better just give her arse one more turn.'

'You're right,' a third said. 'And in that position, the little whore's just asking for it, I'd say.'

Jem could not have argued that her bottom was other than perfectly exposed for a flogging. And she was in no position to prevent the young men from inflicting one on her. As the switches hissed once more through the air, and a new network of thin lines was laid over the marks that had begun to fade on her taut and reddened buttocks, Jem clenched her teeth against the phallus in her mouth and consoled herself with two thoughts: the men were using the switches, which stung wickedly but only briefly and could not leave lasting marks; and in her current position, unable to move or speak, there was no danger that she might renounce her vow of submission.

Jem's bottom had become no more than a source of throbbing heat, and she was not immediately aware that the whipping had ended. It was only when something warm nudged her cheek that she realised that most of the kitchen-slaves had gathered around her head.

'Let's baste the bird,' one of the young men said. Jem heard another snigger. She could not turn her head but from the corners of her eyes she saw that four of the men were standing around her, and each of them had lifted aside his apron and was grasping in one or two hands his erect manhood. They began sliding their hands, still slick with oil from her body, up and down their shafts. They began to count the strokes; they masturbated in unison; the movements grew faster, the strokes shorter.

Jem heard their voices, and their increasingly loud cries of anticipation; she caught glimpses of pumping hands and glistening cock-heads. But she could do nothing except wait for the inevitable sticky climax.

With shouts and groans, they came. First one: Jem felt a splash of hot fluid on her forehead, and another next to her eye. Then another three reached their climaxes simultaneously, and Jem's face was deluged with spurts of hot, viscous semen. The musky smell was in her nostrils; the salty taste trickled over her lips and into her mouth, around the circumference of the phallus. She felt the cooling suspension begin to drip and slide down her face.

A moment later Jem heard more cries of ecstasy, and the two remaining kitchen-slaves shot their spurts of seed on to the pulsing, tender skin of Jem's buttocks. The hot fluid was soothing, and Jem was grateful when the two men used their hands to smear their semen all over the reddened, rounded surfaces.

Jem was confident that, when it came to tests of sexual endurance, she had as much stamina as anyone. But by now even she was beginning to feel tired, sore, used and uncomfortable. She was finding it difficult to keep at bay fantasies about hot baths full of scented bubbles. However, she reasoned, all six of the young men had now had their climaxes, and she knew that they would no longer be as diligent in their testing of her. Perhaps, she allowed herself to hope, she would shortly be released, and would be allowed a brief respite before she was obliged to submit herself to the next of the Chatelaine's ordeals.

She heard a door being flung open. A loud male voice filled the extensive space of the bakery.

'Is my bird ready, lads? Can I have her now?'

There were shouts of 'Yes, Chef,' and 'Here she is, Chef,' before the voice of one of the kitchen-slaves emerged from the concatenation. 'She's trussed and tenderised, Chef,' said the brown-eyed kitchen-slave, 'and oiled, and skewered on the spit, and basted. Just the way you said you wanted her. All she needs now is the stuffing.'

'Sauces and stuffings, those are my specialities,' the Chef said. 'That's a nicely done rump,' he added, and the shock of pain as a heavy hand landed on her backside revealed to Jem that the Chef had come to stand behind her. She felt strong but nimble fingers tracing the lattice of lines on her buttocks, and exploring the folds of her vulva under the stretched membranes of her penetrated vagina.

'This one's good and juicy, too,' the Chef commented. His fingers moved to Jem's anus, into which, thanks to the oil, he was very easily able to insert two fingers. 'She's ready for stuffing,' he announced, and without further ado he withdrew his fingers and instead presented to Jem's prettily and pinkly crinkled arsehole the head of his manhood.

As he buggered her he stroked her burning buttocks with one hand and used the other to vibrate the shaft of the phallus in Jem's vagina. As a result, Jem soon forgot her discomfort and was about to reach a deep and slow-building climax of her own when the Chef shouted, and jetted hot lava into Jem's bowels.

'A very tasty morsel,' the Chef commented as he withdrew his shrinking penis. Jem groaned with frustration. Around her, the kitchen-slaves began to untie her bonds.

The ormolu clock that sat on the rococo cabinet next to the Chatelaine's desk had a tick that was barely audible. It could be heard clearly now, however, counting the seconds of silence since Barat's last outburst.

The Chatelaine used long silences such as these to unsettle miscreants and, she told herself, both Barat and Robert certainly were in need of a reprimand. But on this occasion the Chatelaine's silence was unpremeditated; she was genuinely too outraged to speak.

She had instructed Nicole to continue with Olena's

training; Isabelle was sitting in Nicole's usual place, in the shadows beside the Chatelaine's desk. She had summoned Robert to attend her as soon as he had safely delivered Jem into the hands of the kitchen-slaves; he was kneeling, subserviently but with his habitual air of assurance, before the Chatelaine's desk in the circle of light cast by her lamp. Barat, still agitated and flushed, was kneeling beside him.

'Now that Robert has joined us,' the Chatelaine said at last, 'I will ask you once again, Barat, whether you observed anything significant in the behaviour of the new whipping-slave – the erstwhile Supreme Mistress – while you were entrusted with the task of observing her this morning.'

'Madame,' Barat replied, clearly making every effort to control his emotions, 'as I have already reported to you, the significant events I observed this morning relate to my ward, Olena.' His voice rose in tone and volume. 'I was given certain assurances about her. I was told that I would be present when she was allowed to have her first climax. I was told that I would be punishing her when she was brought to orgasm for the first time. I must protest. I feel I have been treated unfairly. I –'

'Be silent, Barat!' the Chatelaine shouted. 'I find it hard to discern whether you are obsessed more with Olena or with yourself. But you are in my Chateau and you must understand that neither you nor Olena can be my principle concern.' She took a deep breath. 'You will be punished shortly,' she said, and immediately felt a little calmer. 'I agree that it is significant that Olena has achieved her first orgasm other than under our supervision. However, the damage is not irreparable, and she remains the most promising recruit I have seen. Her training will continue, and you will be permitted to remain involved – if you can learn to restrain your outbursts of self-importance and self-pity. Do I make myself clear?'

'Yes, madame,' Barat muttered.

The Chatelaine sighed. 'Very good. Isabelle, go and prepare the water closet for Barat's punishment. I'll need a rubber suit for Barat, and a cane and a strap. Oh, and

I'd like you to wear the rubber incontinence pants – the large size, with the front opening.'

Isabelle raised her eyebrows, but made no comment before leaving the study. Barat, the Chatelaine noticed, was suddenly looking both worried and decidedly excited.

The Chatelaine turned to look down at her kneeling deputy. 'Now, Robert,' she said, 'have you had time to reach a more considered opinion?'

Robert frowned. 'With respect, madame,' he began, and the Chatelaine knew at once that Robert was going to prove as obstinate as Barat, 'with respect, I submit that we have enough evidence that the dirty little whore-slave is in breach of the terms of her wager. She is yours, madame. You have only to claim her. And the Private House will fall to you, by right of seniority and of victory.'

Sometimes, the Chatelaine thought, a servant can be too loyal and too dedicated.

'I disagree, Robert. And I am your mistress. Listen: we do not know that Jem – the whore-slave – defied our instructions in the matter of remaining chained throughout the night. Barat says he cannot be sure. We do not know that she reached a climax without permission; Barat is sure that Olena reached orgasm, but he was, apparently, unable to pay attention to both women. It is true that the whore-slave performed acts with Olena that she had not been instructed to perform and that we all would rather she had not performed. But the acts were not specifically forbidden, either. The High Council will not, I assure you, accept hearsay evidence and accusations of half-crimes. The former Supreme Mistress has many allies still on the Council, and if we are to succeed in keeping her here as my slave then we must have a conclusive case against her. Is that understood?'

Robert nodded. He seemed to the Chatelaine to be not at all contrite. 'Yes, madame,' he said. 'I'll make it my sole objective to break her. I'll give you the proof you need. I'll bring the filthy slut to you begging for mercy. I guarantee that she'll be unable to submit willingly to the torments I've devised for her.'

'Yes, Robert,' the Chatelaine said. 'Very good. I'm sure you're right. I suggest you leave her to the kitchen-slaves, however, for this morning. There will be other opportunities for you to supervise her tests personally, and you must not forget your other duties in the Chateau.'

Robert was about to protest but the Chatelaine raised a warning finger, and he nodded his acquiescence.

The Chatelaine sat back in her chair. She looked from Barat to Robert, and back again. They were both so enthusiastic and single-minded. Admirable qualities, no doubt, she thought, but of negligible value compared with discipline and obedience.

'You may go, Robert,' she said. 'Barat, you will come with me. You deserve punishment, and you are about to receive it.'

Olena was beginning to loathe her robe. Once again, Nicole had brought it and had insisted that Olena wear it while Nicole led her from her dungeon cell and through the labyrinthine corridors of the Chateau. The robe marked Olena out from everyone else; it should have ensured her modesty, but instead it made her feel conspicuous. Each person they met stared at her. They all know, she thought, that I'm failing every test I take, and that I'm on the way to receive the first of the chastisements that I will now receive daily.

And the worst of it was that Olena knew that her body, beneath the demure covering of the robe, was already betraying her. She couldn't erase from her mind the memories of the disgraceful things she had done with Jem, and the wonderful, overwhelming sensations that had swept through her, again and again, as they had embraced under the cascading water.

It was wrong; it was sinful. The more she thought about the pleasure she had experienced, the more she trembled and felt sick with guilt. And the more she wanted to experience again the transcendent delights of orgasm.

Looking ahead, to the future, was no more use than dwelling on memories. She was being led towards a punishment; she would display her body, and Barat and Nicole, and perhaps the sinister Master Robert, would pass comment on her lewdness as the smacking on her bottom made her more and more lubricious. The prospect made her heart sink, but she could feel that her body was already responding; just the thought of offering her bottom for inspection and a whipping was making her feel hot and moist. She wondered whether it would be possible for her to receive enough punishments to remedy her wickedness; she realised, with a shock that merely added to the cloud of shame that surrounded her, that the prospect of endless punishments was more attractive than that of returning to righteousness.

And concentrating strictly on the present brought no relief from lewd thoughts. The dimly lit, carpet-muffled corridors, with their closed doors and outlandishly clothed denizens, served only to remind Olena that she was in a realm where punishment and pleasure were intertwined; behind each closed door her imagination conjured scenes of such depravity that she was appalled at herself. The rough material of her robe rubbed against her breasts and her bottom as she walked. Nicole's costume seemed today to be skimpier than ever, and as Olena followed her she found herself watching for the moments when Nicole's movements caused the hem of her tiny, stiff skirt to lift at the back and reveal, between black skirt and black stocking-tops, the smooth, pert mounds of Nicole's bottom.

Nicole turned to the left and began to ascend a flight of stairs. Only a few steps up, however, she stopped, and cocked her head as if wondering whether she had taken the correct route. She clasped her hands in front of her as she thought, and the hem of her tiny skirt rose at the back. At the bottom of the staircase Olena was presented with a perfect view of Nicole's buttocks, and could see the delicate folds of skin between her legs. She wondered whether Nicole was as wet there as she was, and whether Nicole liked to feel hands smacking down on her bottom.

When at last she looked up to see whether Nicole had

made a decision about which direction to take, she found that Nicole was looking over her shoulder at Olena, and had a knowing smile on her face. Olena felt her face glowing as she blushed furiously.

'I don't mind you looking at me,' Nicole said. 'Although I suppose it's just more evidence that you're very naughty. I'll have to tell Robert. But you can touch, if you like.'

She returned to the foot of the stairs. 'That's the wrong way. We should continue along the corridor. And if you walk beside me you can touch my bottom as we go. Like this.' Nicole took Olena's hand and held it against her left buttock.

Olena was too shocked to withdraw her hand. Nicole's buttock was small, and fitted into Olena's palm. As Nicole walked it moved in Olena's grasp in a way that Olena found disturbingly delightful. Nicole and Jem were of a similar height and build, and holding Nicole's bottom reminded Olena yet again of the wonderful night she had just spent with Jem. She remembered her first sight of Jem's bottom, reddened and marked with stripes.

'Nicole,' she said, 'I hope you don't mind me asking you, but do you like to have your bottom smacked?'

Nicole laughed, and Olena felt the tremor in the warm, smooth globe pressed against her palm. 'But of course,' Nicole replied. 'I would not be here in the Chateau if it were otherwise. Of course, sometimes it gives more pleasure, sometimes less. It depends on my mood, and on who is smacking me. Perhaps you would like to spank me, one day, when your training is finished?'

Olena hardly dared to speak. 'Yes, I'd like to,' she breathed. 'Would we kiss and cuddle afterwards?'

Nicole leaned towards Olena and nuzzled her neck. 'Oh, yes,' she said, and kissed Olena. 'Now,' she added, briskly, 'we've arrived at the punishment room. Enter, and remove your robe.'

Olena stepped into the room. As she pulled the robe over her head she felt a sinful satisfaction that soon her shapely body would be on display again, and an even more wicked excitement at the thought of being smacked. She determined that she would try to make Barat understand that today she needed lengthy and severe punishment.

She couldn't estimate the size of the room, as the edges and corners were cloaked in darkness. The only illumination was a flickering light that could be seen in the gaps between several large panels that had been set up to create an enclosure within the room.

Nicole led Olena towards the circle of panels and through one of the gaps between them. The light came from dozens of candles, some on tall candelabra and others simply set on the floor, which surrounded the only item of furniture: a chaise longue, covered in red velvet.

The panels, Olena saw at once, were large mirrors, all facing inwards. The candlelight was reflected back and forth in them to create a soft, golden, shimmering illumination within the enclosed space. Olena saw herself reflected wherever she looked; her coffee-coloured skin seemed to glow in the light, and the curves of her hips and breasts and buttocks were gilded. Her eyes shone; her lips were slightly parted; her dark hair appeared to be threaded with gold. She knew that she was desirable; that men and women could not help but admire her and want her, simply because of the curves of her body, and the lustre of her hair, and the look of anticipation on her wide-eyed face. She knew it was wrong to engender such feelings in other people, but she could not help it. She felt perversely proud of her curvaceous, golden form, even though she knew that to feel such pride damned her.

There was another person standing within the circle of mirrors: a man, naked but for a leather harness. But it was not Barat or Master Robert.

Olena turned as Nicole entered the enclosure. 'Where's Barat?' she said. She feared that without his reassuring presence she would be unable to retain even the most tenuous grasp on the teachings of the community elders. And, she realised, she liked to feel his eyes on her body as she was being smacked.

'Barat has other duties to attend to this morning,' Nicole said. 'Don't worry: he's still here in the Chateau.' She gestured towards the harnessed man, who dropped to his knees and bowed his head towards Nicole. 'This slave will assist me to punish you. His name is Bernard. I think it will be instructive for you to be chastised in front of one of the slaves. Are you ready to begin?'

Olena tried to calm her racing heart. The slave Bernard was an attractive young man: his body was slim and looked hard, and Olena found herself comparing it with Barat's. He was tall, with dark hair. His face was lean, but his lips were surprisingly full, like a woman's. Like many of the slaves, both male and female, whom Olena had seen in the corridors, Bernard had metal attachments glinting on his chest; in fact, she realised, he had metal rings that appeared to pass through his nipples.

She pictured herself kneeling on the chaise longue, reflected from all angles in the mirrors, with Bernard's eyes on her. It was breathtakingly exciting.

'Yes, Nicole,' she said, 'I'm ready. Would you like me to kneel on the couch?'

'Not yet,' Nicole replied. 'Kneel here, on the floor in front of me. That's right. Now lower your head, like a slave. I think you should learn to ask politely for your daily punishments.'

Olena obeyed willingly. She deserved chastisement more severe than any she would receive at Nicole's hands, and it was only proper that she should be obliged to acknowledge the extent of her crimes.

'Please punish me, Nicole,' she said firmly. 'I know that there seems to be no end to my wickedness, but with sufficient punishment I hope to have instilled in me the discipline I need to resist temptations and impure thoughts. Please smack me hard, and for a long time.'

And then please touch me between my legs, she added in her thoughts, because I'm sure that I would experience another of those endless moments that feel so wonderful I think I'm dying.

'Very well,' Nicole said, 'and now you can kneel on the couch. At this end, please, so that you can lean against the back. Remember to open your legs very wide, and push out your chest. If I permit it, Bernard will be able to admire your breasts and see your genitalia.'

Yes, please, Olena thought; I'd like him to look at me. There should be witnesses to my shame and degradation.

It occurred to Olena, as she arched her back downwards so that her bottom was presented to Nicole, that something had changed since the previous day. It wasn't that she felt any less embarrassed: she was acutely aware that the position she had placed herself in was obscene, and that to be punished in front of a male slave would be almost unbearably humiliating. But she felt less troubled than she had when Barat and Master Robert had spanked her; in fact she felt happier than she had – well, for as long as she could remember. It was very strange. What had happened to bring about this alteration? The only thing she could think of was that she had spent the night with Jem – and Jem had given her the gift of reaching a climax, and had told her that she should embrace and nurture her shame as it would add to her pleasure.

She felt a hand stroking her cheek, and realised that she had closed her eyes and slipped into a reverie about Jem. She blinked, and found Nicole standing in front of her.

In Nicole's hands was an assortment of implements: a thin cane, two leather straps of different widths, and a strip of wood, thin but wide, which was set into a handle. 'I'm going to start on your bottom,' Nicole said. 'Which one of these would you like me to use first?'

Just looking at the implements caused a surge of longing to swell in Olena's insides. She felt the warm, trickling sensation in her loins that she now knew indicated that she was producing more of the shameful liquid evidence of her desire and sinfulness. She wanted urgently to feel the stinging fire of retribution and correction on her backside.

'What's this one?' she asked, pointing to the flat length of wood.

'I call it a paddle,' Nicole said, 'because it resembles something you might use in a boat. But a lot smaller.' She giggled. 'I'll start with that, shall I?'

Olena thought the paddle looked flimsy. 'Will it sting?' she asked.

'Let's see, shall we?' Nicole replied. She walked round the chaise longue, and with hardly a murmur of warning the paddle landed with a loud slap across Olena's bottom. Olena cried out and jerked upright: the pain stung like three cane-strokes all at once but, Olena realised, there was less residual smarting than with a cane, and a more diffuse warming sensation. She was becoming a connoisseur of spankings! The paddle, she thought, would give her the immediate, acute punishment she craved, and would efficiently bring to her bottom the heated glow to which she was becoming accustomed.

She hollowed her back again and rested the bottom of her ribcage against the back of the couch. 'Mmm, yes,' she said. 'Please use the paddle.'

But instead of a second searing stroke, Olena felt Nicole's fingers delicately probing her secret places. She trembled as the touches caused more pangs of desire in her loins.

'Keep still,' Nicole said. 'I'm only inspecting your little fleecy purse. I've inspected you here before, haven't I? So keep still.'

Olena hung her head. She was already blushing, because she knew what Nicole would find. She could feel the juices seeping from inside her, and cooling on her soft skin.

'Your little purse is leaking already,' Nicole said. 'All along the split. And when I open up the split a little, and put a finger inside – Aha! There is nothing but wetness inside. Olena, you really are a very naughty girl.'

'I know,' Olena sobbed. 'Please smack me hard.'

'In a minute,' Nicole said. 'First, we must get you clean. Bernard! Come here.'

As Olena looked towards the kneeling slave he lifted his head. Their eyes met. He smiled, and tentatively Olena smiled back. His gaze slid to her breasts, swelling magnificently over the back of the chaise longue. His smile widened, and he began to shuffle on his knees to join Nicole on the other side of the couch.

'Pay attention, Bernard,' Olena heard Nicole say. 'Olena needs to be punished thoroughly. She'll need to be smacked several times, so you will probably have an opportunity to use your strong right arm before the morning's out. Do you see how round and big and smooth her buttocks are?'

Olena felt Nicole's cool hands stroking the flesh that was about to be chastised.

'Yes, miss,' Bernard said.

'If you look closely, Bernard, you can just make out a few fading marks. You see – here, and here? She was given a good strapping yesterday. Olena is to be punished every day until she learns some self-control. It's easy to see how little self-discipline she has.'

Olena felt Nicole's fingers once again touching her most intimate parts. And the slave, Bernard, was watching closely.

'You will see, Bernard,' Nicole went on remorselessly, 'that there is quite a lot of Olena's natural lubrication visible between her labia, which are beginning to part. I have already ascertained that she is very wet inside, and it's clear that although she has not been stimulated in any way, and although she knows that she should not think lewd thoughts or allow herself to become excited, the wicked girl has once again proved to be a dirty tramp. But I can't whip her while she's in that condition. Bernard, use your tongue. Lick her clean.'

Olena squealed in protest, but Nicole pressed a hand into the small of Olena's back. For a moment Olena resisted, but she knew that she would not feel the paddle on her bottom until the slave had completed his task, and so she thrust out her bottom and tried to move her knees even further apart.

She felt warm breath on the delicate membranes between her thighs – around and inside her purse, as Nicole had called it. And then something touched her; something warm, and smooth, and probing. It was Bernard's tongue. Olena screwed up her eyes, expecting to be revolted, but she discovered that being licked was far from unpleasant. She had imagined that it would be like having her face licked by a dog, but even more slobbery and perhaps even painful. But it wasn't at all like that. It was like the touch of Jem's fingers, but somehow both gentler and more insistent.

She began to detect rhythm in Bernard's licking: he would slide his tongue along the left-hand side of the split of her purse, and then along the right, and then dart it inside her before starting again. Olena found herself moving her hips slightly to meet his licks, and she realised that only a few minutes of Bernard's attentions would be required to bring her to another of her recently discovered climaxes.

'That's enough,' Nicole said. 'She's clean enough to be smacked. Bernard, you may stand. Go to the other side of the couch and hold Olena's breasts while I whip her bottom with the paddle.'

Olena moaned and tossed her head. She understood that Nicole was merely doing her best to add to Olena's feelings of self-abasement and shame, but Olena knew that her breasts were sensitive, and were somehow connected – almost physically, as if by taut wire – to the place inside, near her secret places, where she most strongly felt her sinful desires and longings. The part that Jem had called her clitoris, perhaps.

Bernard was standing in front of her. She looked at his slim, hairless chest. She gazed in awe at the metal rings through his nipples. She realised, with a pang of guilt, that she had not thought about Barat since she had positioned herself for her punishment. She considered whether she missed him, and to her surprise decided that she didn't.

Bernard's hands were not large enough to hold Olena's breasts. With surprising gentleness he placed one palm underneath each breast and cupped them. Then, with great deliberation, he placed his thumbs on her nipples.

Olena looked up at him. Could he possibly understand the shivers of excitement that his touch was sending rippling through her body? 'Please,' she whispered. 'Please.'

He pressed his thumbs a little more firmly against the stiff peaks, and at that moment Nicole started to swing the paddle.

'Dirty. Wicked. Little. Girl.' Nicole spat out a word each time the paddle splatted on to one or other of Olena's buttocks. 'I'll. Whip. This. Naughty. Bottom. Until. It's. Red. All. Over.'

Olena gasped and started with each blow. Somehow the gentle, insistent touch of Bernard's hands seemed to subdue her urge to cry out and jump up.

Nicole was not restraining herself. The paddle came down again and again, hard and fast; Olena felt her bottom was on fire, and each new stroke added a searing line.

Olena soon began to appreciate the rhythm of Nicole's smacks, however, and with her bottom feeling as hot as a furnace, and its warmth spreading seductively into her body, Olena was soon drifting into what she had come to think of as her spanking dreamland: a state of mind in which the lightest touches on her body felt magnified; the pain of each smack lessened, while the comforting heat increased; and pulses of sheer pleasure began to ripple throughout her body – emanating, she now supposed, from the mysterious organ known as the clitoris.

In this floating euphoria she became gradually more conscious of her breasts. Like her bottom they felt warm, enlarged and sensitive. Bernard's thumbs were brushing their hard tips in time with Nicole's smacks, sending jolts of sensation to merge with the melting pleasure in her loins. Her gasps of pain had become little moans of pleasure; she was lifting her hips so that her bottom greeted each splat of the paddle; she could feel the waves of ecstasy gathering strength inside her, and she knew that if Nicole and Bernard continued they would soon take her to and over the brink of a climax. She was helpless to prevent her body shuddering each time she crested a wave.

As if in a dream, she heard Bernard's tentative voice. 'Miss,' he said, 'I believe she is becoming very excited.'

Nicole cursed. The smacking stopped.

Touch me, Olena pleaded soundlessly. Touch my secret place. Touch my clitoris, please.

'You're right, Bernard,' Nicole said. 'Come here and see

how wet she's made herself. You'll have to lick her clean again. Lick her buttocks, too. Then I'll try the narrow strap instead.'

Now Olena found the touch of Bernard's tongue as stimulating as his hands on her breasts. It was profoundly humiliating to think that he was cleaning up the evidence of her filthy thoughts, and to know that as he did so he could see all of her most private places – including, she realised with a rush of shame, her little back hole. When he began to run his tongue across her heated, sore buttocks the combination of the soothing touch with the degrading knowledge that she was being licked like a dinner plate was almost too much to bear, and in her confusion she started to sob silently. Her shoulders shook, and her eyes filled with tears.

And all the time she knew that if he were to push his tongue just a little further forward, to lick the place where all her sensation seemed to be concentrated, she would almost instantly experience the ecstatic explosion of an orgasm.

'Hold her breasts again,' Nicole said. 'Take her nipples between your fingers and hold them firmly. I want her kept still. Her bottom's sore now, and the strap's going to sting. It's hard to believe that a good girl would find anything arousing in what I'm going to do to this young woman's bottom. Let's see how good Olena is.'

The strap was certainly more painful than the paddle, and Olena's bottom was already very tender. Each lash, applied with merciless regularity and precision, blazed with vitriolic fire. As each stroke fell Olena would start, and Bernard would squeeze her nipples to ensure that she remained kneeling.

Drops of salt water fell from Olena's downcast eyes on to her breasts; she felt utterly wretched, and welcomed each blazing reminder of her iniquity that welted her backside. But no matter how hard she tried to concentrate on the purity of the pain, she could not ignore the treacherous feelings that swelled inside her. She remembered Jem's envious expression as Olena had explained to her that the merest pleasurable thought made her want to be punished, and that being punished only increased her desire and her shame.

Now the jolts of sensation from her bottom and her breasts began to echo each other, and once again Olena found herself drifting into her spanking dreamland. As the strap relentlessly laid down its dense grid of fine scarlet lines, Olena was lifted higher and higher.

Once again Bernard detected the imminence of her climax. Nicole threw down the strap. 'I despair of you, Olena,' she shouted. 'I begin to think you are an incorrigibly bad girl. I am trying so hard to give you discipline, and this is how you thank me. What do you have to say for yourself?'

Olena, emerging from her daze, could think of nothing to say. Nicole was right: Olena was thoroughly wicked. She was a disappointment to everyone: to her parents and the community, when they found out about her licentiousness; to Barat, her devoted guardian; and to the staff of the Chateau, who had gone out of their way to administer punishments. And still she could think of nothing but her own pleasure.

She began to cry again.

Nicole ignored her panting sobs, and summoned Bernard to her. 'You see?' Olena heard Nicole say. 'She's actually dripping now. I can't believe the extent of this woman's perversity. Being stripped naked excites her; being inspected by strangers excites her; being whipped excites her. And she's supposed to be pure and innocent! Is there no way we can punish her without stirring up her lascivious desires?'

Olena heard Bernard's voice; he seemed to be offering a suggestion. Nicole whispered a reply; they conversed in low voices for a while. At last Nicole announced, 'Very well; we might as well try it.'

She came to stand in front of Olena. 'Stop snivelling,' she said abruptly, but her tone was gentle, and she wiped the tears from Olena's face. 'We're going to try something new. Bernard will punish you in a manner that I think even

209

you will find difficult to enjoy, while I will instruct you to perform certain actions that even the most abandoned harlot would find distasteful. I promise that you won't enjoy the next ten minutes.'

'Thank you,' Olena said. 'I hope you're right.'

Olena was instructed to loosen her muscles by walking around within the mirror enclosure. For the forthcoming punishment she was to resume her position kneeling on the chaise longue, and Nicole wanted to prevent muscle cramps and fatigue.

Olena could not avoid seeing herself reflected in every mirror. Her tear-streaked face and trembling lips spoke of sorrow, but the light in her eyes and the languorous grace of her movements betrayed the simmering cauldron of desire within her. Her breasts appeared even larger than usual, with the nipples hard and very prominent. And her bottom was swollen and actually seemed to be glowing with its own heat, outdoing the flickering light of the candles. Nicole had applied the paddle with precise, overlapping strokes, so that both buttocks were evenly reddened; the lashes of the strap had been applied so close together that the individual lines were difficult to discern, and it was only by running her fingertips across the surface that Olena could detect the striations where the strap had fallen.

Olena admitted to herself that for all Nicole's effort she, Olena, had not lost one bit of her sinful pride: she still thought she looked desirable, and she was particularly pleased with her well-smacked bottom. She could hardly wait to show it off to Jem: that would be naughty, and embarrassing, and fun – all at the same time.

'Come back to the couch, Olena,' Nicole said. 'Adopt the same position. Place your left hand on the back of the seat, to give yourself some more support. Make sure your breasts are pushed well forward; Bernard is going to cane them.'

Olena sighed. It would do no good. As soon as Nicole had announced the punishment, Olena had felt the now-familiar lurch in her stomach that told her that she was about to enjoy something despicable. She remembered the illustration she had come across in the library: the servant girl, bare-breasted, tied to a post, awaiting the fall of the lash on her trembling bosom. The picture had intrigued and excited her; she had no reason to expect that the reality would do less.

'Move your legs as wide apart as you can,' Nicole went on. 'And put your right hand on your stomach. I'm going to make you touch yourself while Bernard whips you.'

Olena felt a hysterical urge to laugh. It was not that the punishment was lenient: the cane would sting her breasts, and the thought of touching her own secret parts with Nicole and Bernard watching her made her insides curl up with shame. But Olena knew that it wouldn't be enough to stop her enjoying the experience. She would disappoint Nicole again, and reveal even deeper pits of her sin.

'Are you ready?' Nicole said. Olena nodded and Bernard, standing beside her and flexing the thin wooden rod, said, 'Yes, miss.'

'Olena, start to move your right hand down towards your little purse. Don't lift your fingers from your skin. Stop when your fingers touch your hairs.'

Olena moved her hand. It was exciting just to imagine what she was about to do. Her fingers met the wiry curls of her hair; she played with the curls, as Jem had done, and enjoyed the tickling feelings. She pressed a little further, into the mat of hair, and realised that she was already close to the marvellous place that gave her such pleasure: the place where her clitoris peeked out from beneath tender folds of pink skin. She pressed with her fingertips: the place was close, but seemed to be inside her. She was being instructed to explore her own secret parts; it was supposed to be a punishment, but Olena suspected that she was going to find it delightful.

She looked up at Bernard to find him grinning at her. He must have been waiting for her to glance at him, because he immediately brought the cane whistling through the air to land on the undersides of Olena's breasts.

Olena let out a shrill shriek. She had expected the pain to be like that of a caning on her bottom, but it was different. The sting was the same, but there was also something that went deeper: something that sent a lurch of shock to her stomach, and made her want to curl her body inwards. It was a frighteningly intimate form of punishment; just the first stroke had made her feel vulnerable and helpless.

Bernard allowed plenty of time between his strokes. After three more Olena was beginning to absorb and appreciate the strange pleasures of having her breasts caned. The sick feeling in her stomach receded but remained in the background as a reminder of the peculiarly intrusive and perverse nature of the punishment; each lash seemed to sting a little more than the last, so that she was continually caught unawares; and, in time, a general feeling of heat and heaviness began to expand within her breasts, and she could sense that a few more strokes would carry her into her dreamland just as comfortingly as a bottom-smacking always would.

It was wrong to take satisfaction from such a thought but, nonetheless, she congratulated herself on discovering another source of shameful, painful pleasure. As soon as she had travelled away from her parents' community she had realised, without wanting to admit it, that people she met couldn't help staring at the promisingly large bumps concealed beneath her robe. She had discovered the shameful truth that her breasts inspired sinful thoughts in others; worse, when she touched them they caused feelings in her that were deceitfully enjoyable. With increasing guilt she had come to take pride and pleasure in her breasts; the shiver of embarrassment she felt when Barat, or anyone, stared at her body was increasingly difficult to disassociate from the tremor of desire that simultaneously ran through her. And now she knew that, like her bottom, her breasts could be smacked and whipped, and could transport her to the heights of ecstasy she had experienced with Jem.

The caning continued. The strokes caught her nipples and made her cry out. If Nicole would just instruct her to move her hand a little lower, to the exquisite point just inside the top of the split of her purse, she was sure she would have another climax immediately. She could imagine it: it would be like an explosion as soon as she touched the spot. A flash of light; she might scream with the beauty of it.

'I didn't tell you to move your hand,' Nicole said. 'You're not to touch your pleasure point. This is supposed to be a punishment. Put your hand further between your legs. Use your fingers to open your purse. Let me see inside.'

Olena moaned with frustration and remorse. Nicole was right: she was not supposed to be enjoying herself. As she tried to order her thoughts along righteous lines, the thin lath created another stinging line across the tops of her breasts. She concentrated on the flare of pain, and on the humiliation of being whipped, naked, by a slave, and did her best to ignore the heavy warmth that was building in the swollen globes and the vivid, jagged bolts of sensation that the lash sent shooting through her.

Now she was to use her own fingers to open her secret place for Nicole's inspection. It was impossible; it was too shameful. Nicole's fingers had, she was sure, performed the same operation, during the examinations Olena had been subjected to on previous days. But it was one thing to hold her body still and bear the degradation of being touched and exposed, and quite another to bring about the degradation herself. Perhaps, at last, she thought with a flicker of hope, Nicole has discovered a small kernel of cleanliness inside my impure body and mind. Perhaps, if I cannot bring myself to touch myself there, I will prove that I'm not completely wicked.

'Keep your bottom up, so I can see,' Nicole said. The cane sang through the air, and caressed Olena's breasts with a line of fire. And Olena knew that she was lost. Nicole's words had been enough to remind her of her exposed position; the sting of the cane had taken her one more step into her dreamworld of sheer sensation. She shuddered as she cupped her hand under the warm, fuzzy mound between her thighs, and felt on her fingers the stickiness of her escaping juices.

Jem's fingers had touched her here, and had explored inside her. It had felt wonderful.

Bernard's lashes with the wooden lath came faster now, but with less force; Olena was acutely conscious that the blushing globes were trembling and jiggling continuously under the onslaught of light flicks.

'Put your fingers inside, Olena,' Nicole urged. 'Feel for yourself what a wickedly wet girl you are.'

It was as if Nicole and Bernard were conspiring to direct Olena's thoughts away from the punishment she justly deserved and towards the tempting, sinful pleasures that her body craved.

Olena's fingers seemed to slip, almost without her willing it, between the parted lips of her secret place. Her fingers were enfolded in skin as delicate as silk and soaked in hot, sticky fluid. A wave of sensations flooded her body. She threw back her head and pushed her breasts towards the insistent beats of the cane.

'Are your fingers wet?' Nicole said.

Olena nodded.

'Take them out, then,' Nicole said. 'Putting your fingers in there isn't your punishment.'

As she reluctantly obeyed Nicole's instruction Olena was so frustrated that it took a few moments for her to appreciate the significance of the second sentence, with its stress on the word *there*.

Her horrified mind recoiled from the implication, and from the pictures that were only beginning to cohere in her mind, as Nicole gave the unthinkable command: 'Now put your wet fingers up your arsehole.'

It was impossible. It was dirty as well as sinful. No one had ever touched her there. She couldn't do it.

She hardly noticed that the caning had ceased. She hardly felt the throbbing soreness of her reddened buttocks and breasts.

'What's the matter, Olena?' Nicole said. 'Are you afraid that you'll like it? That it will make you even wetter?'

Olena had not even considered the possibility that she might like to touch herself there. But as soon as Nicole said the words, Olena was struck by the appalling, terrifying realisation that she would enjoy putting her fingers into the most intimate and shameful of her secret places.

She gave a sobbing cry of despair.

It was a despicable, disgusting thing to do. It would be horribly embarrassing in private, but to do it in front of the slave, Bernard, and with Nicole watching at such close quarters, would be the worst degradation imaginable.

And yet Olena knew she would have to do it. She had to know whether she was really so depraved that even such a monstrous act could give her pleasure. Only a few days previously she would not have believed such a thing possible in any person, and certainly not in her. But she had learned much in the Chateau. She knew now that, possessed of some demon of perversity, she took pleasure in the punishments that were designed to correct her licentiousness; performing the abominable act now required of her might hurt, and she had acquired an incorrigible liking for pain, particularly in the area of her bottom. She knew that the act was certainly the most shameful, disgusting thing she had ever been required to do, and she knew also that her treacherous body could therefore be relied on to fill her with lewd thoughts of yearning desire.

She lowered her blushing face, turned it away from Bernard's gaze, and allowed the tips of her fingers to creep from the warm, viscous security of her purse and along the furrowed ridge behind it.

All too soon her fingertips reached the lip of the crinkled crater.

'Just one finger, to start with,' Nicole said. 'Your index finger, please. Push it in.'

Olena sighed. Jem's words of encouragement seemed hollow now. What was the gist? That Olena was lucky, because she enjoyed the pleasures of being ashamed. Well, look at me now, Jem, Olena thought bitterly; what normal, good, decent person could take pleasure from what I'm about to do? If I find myself enjoying this, what kind of person am I?

'Come along,' Nicole said impatiently.

Olena placed the tip of her forefinger in the silky, wrinkled crater. She detected warmth, and a faint pulsing. At the centre was the tiniest of holes, surrounded by a ring of tightly furrowed tissue; it seemed unlikely that even one of her fingers could gain admittance.

She sighed again. She could hardly believe her own vileness. But she had felt an unmistakable thrill, of a kind with which she was becoming all too familiar, when her fingertip had circled the little hole.

'That's right,' Nicole said. 'Use your juices, on your fingers, to lubricate the entrance.'

The coarse words were enough to spark another thrill in Olena.

And then, when Olena pushed with her finger, and the back of her hand brushed the blazing, punished skin of her buttock, and she felt the ring of muscle expand slightly, she knew that this appalling, obnoxious act was going to give her a new, different, but exquisitely pleasurable experience.

Her finger slid easily into her anus as far as the first joint. Olena gasped in surprise. Experimentally she moved the end of her finger, and gasped again as a pleasure seemed to flow in tingling streams throughout her secret places and up to her hot breasts. The sensations were similar to those she had felt when Jem had caressed her secret places, under the bedclothes the previous night, but they seemed less acute: bass notes rather than treble. For some reason every slight movement of her finger in her little hole made her nipples tingle; in fact, touching her little hole seemed to make her more conscious of her breasts. And then, as she pushed her finger in a little more, she was overcome by a feeling of intrusion and fullness; it felt wrong, and sinful, and almost painfully uncomfortable – and breathtakingly wonderful. As she tried to analyse this remarkable new sensation, Olena wondered, in a moment of unguarded lewdness, what it would feel like to have a man's erect penis in her little hole; the fact that she

216

could conceive of such a notion was as appallingly shameful as the pulse of pleasure that suffused her as she thought of it.

'Now another finger,' Nicole said.

Olena needed no urging. She squeezed a second finger alongside the first, and pushed both further into the soft, warm interior. Her little hole felt stretched; her bottom felt full.

'Push them further in,' Nicole said.

Olena did so, and bit down gently on her lower lip to quieten a groan of pleasure.

'Now move your fingers back and forth, just a little way, while Bernard flicks your breasts with the rod.'

The thin lath struck Olena's sore breasts rapidly but lightly, making them jiggle. Olena closed her eyes, moved her fingers in the warm, soft space of her rectum, and surrendered to the sensations. Her body had become a conduit for delicious tremors and spasms; her nipples, her anus and her clitoris seemed to be communicating, urging each other upwards and upwards towards the clear, boundless joy of another climax.

She became aware of Nicole standing at her side. 'Does that feel nice?' Nicole whispered in her ear.

'Yes,' Olena gasped. 'Oh, yes.'

'Your breasts are getting as red as your bottom,' Nicole went on, 'and you've started to move your fingers in and out of your arsehole quite fast now, haven't you? Do you like to show me these things?'

'Yes, Nicole,' Olena said, recovering herself somewhat. 'It's good that others witness my punishments.'

'But you only enjoy it more when people are watching, don't you? It makes you more excited. You're getting very wet now, aren't you?'

It was true. Olena's wrist, which touched her purse every time she pushed her fingers into her anus, was covered in her own juice. Olena could think of almost nothing but the thrills running from her smarting breasts to her invaded backside, but it was beginning to dawn on her that something was amiss, that she had overlooked something important.

'Are you a pure woman, Olena?' Nicole's voice insinuated into her thoughts. 'How pure can you be, if you enjoy being caned on your breasts? If you like to put your fingers up your shit-hole? If you like people to watch?'

As Olena struggled through a lust-induced fog to perceive the meaning of Nicole's words, Nicole landed the final blow. 'What would Barat think of you if he could see you now?'

Nicole was right. Olena knew it. She was nothing but a slut. She could be relied on only to betray all the principles of the community that had raised her. She was filthy and worthless. And if Barat were there to witness the depth of her sin . . .

If Barat were there, watching her, she would feel utterly humiliated. She would feel so wicked, so naughty. She pressed her wrist against the wet warmth of her purse. Jem had been right: the more the shame, the more the pleasure.

If Barat were there, watching her push her fingers into her arsehole, watching her breasts dance and redden as the slave whipped them, she would be able to reach a climax almost immediately. She pressed her wrist harder into her secret place. She would be there very soon. She thrust her breasts forwards and pushed her fingers deeper into her rectum. Very soon . . .

'Stop!' Nicole cried.

Olena let out a howl of frustration as Bernard stepped back from her. Blushing, and feeling ridiculous, she withdrew her shaking fingers from her anus.

'Well,' Nicole said, 'now we know exactly what kind of girl you are, Olena. You really are proving a most difficult challenge. Is there any amount of punishment that will correct your behaviour? Is there any vile act from which you will recoil?'

'I don't know,' Olena said. 'I'm beginning to think that I'm just thoroughly bad.' And, she thought but dared not say, I'm beginning to hope so, too.

'Time will tell,' Nicole said. 'Time, regular punishments, and rigorous testing. You are indeed fortunate that you arrived at the Chateau.'

Yes, Olena thought. I'm beginning to realise that's true.

* * *

Barat, lying on his back, could move only his feet and his head. The rest of his body was tightly swaddled in a tube of sheer rubber that held his legs together and his arms pinioned at his sides. His genitalia protruded obscenely upwards through a hole in the rubber. The Chatelaine was holding his erect member firmly in one rubber-gloved hand.

The room, which the Chatelaine had called the water closet, was like a bathroom in that its floor and walls were covered in white tiles that glistened in the yellow lamplight. There were taps and basins, but no bath. Hanging from hooks on the walls were bottles, pumps, syringes and loops of hose whose functions Barat could only guess at. He was strapped on to a slim, rubber-covered dais, shaped to follow the contours of a human body. His head was resting on a padded circle which was attached by a metal rod to the main area of the dais.

The Chatelaine looked down at him and smiled in a way that he found both menacing and exciting. She lazily pulled on his manhood until he let out a groan of pain and desire. In her other hand she held a small strap made of rubber, its tongue divided into three. She let the tails play on his cocooned body.

'You must learn obedience, Barat,' she said. 'If you will not behave properly, you must learn through suffering. Isabelle, come closer.'

The tall brunette came into Barat's circle of vision. He looked up to see that she, like him, was clothed in black rubber. She was covered in skintight rubber from her neck to her fingertips to her waist; like his cock and balls, her breasts protruded through holes in the clinging material. She was wearing a short, flared, rubber skirt, and stockings of sheer rubber that gripped her thighs so tightly that the pale flesh swelled above the stocking-tops. And beneath the skirt, Barat could see as she approached, she was wearing a pair of baggy rubber knickers with strong elastic at the top of each thigh.

Without warning, the Chatelaine swung the strap in a slow arc that ended when the three tongues landed on

219

Barat's exposed scrotum. He yelped, and the Chatelaine smiled again.

'Isabelle,' she said, 'put his head in your knickers.'

Isabelle came to stand behind his head. With his neck bent back he watched in trepidation as she peeled down a flap of rubber that covered most of the front of the voluminous garment. He glimpsed the dark bush of her pubic hair. Then she stepped closer, her hands reached towards him, and he felt his head being supported by her hands. His crown was resting in the hollow of her stomach.

The Chatelaine released her hold on his member and came to join Isabelle at the top of the dais. She leaned forwards and adjusted something; he felt the headrest fall away.

Isabelle's upside-down face smiled down at him. 'Come inside,' she said, and lowered his head slightly as she moved forwards.

His face was pressed against Isabelle's pubic mound as his head was engulfed by her rubber knickers. She pushed forwards again, her legs widely parted, and his head was forced into the space between her thighs. His face was buried in her vulva, which was hot and damp. He fought for breath. He felt something solid under the back of his head: the headrest had been fixed back in its position, but now the gusset of Isabelle's knickers came between the back of his head and the padded circle.

With a giggle and a murmur of pleasure Isabelle settled her sex on to his face. His nose was lodged between her labia; he could hardly move his head, but when he tilted it back the slight distance it would travel he found that his nose slipped into her wet vagina.

Barat could see nothing but the smooth skin of Isabelle's buttocks, close enough for his eyelashes to touch when he blinked. His hearing was muffled. He felt very vulnerable and very excited; he was acutely aware that his manhood, standing rigidly upright, was at the Chatelaine's mercy.

And then she started to whip him. He knew she must be using short, gentle strokes, but the three tails of the strap stung the sensitive skin and made him writhe helplessly in his rubber cocoon. She let the strap play all over his penis and scrotum; sometimes she used it to lash him; at other times the three tails were used caressingly, to tease the most sensitive parts of his glans or to tickle the base of his tight ball-sac. She used her other hand to stroke him, sometimes gently and sometimes roughly, and to keep him hard.

Barat, breathing in the hot and mingled aromas of rubber and Isabelle's sex, gasped and moaned as the Chatelaine inflicted pleasure and pain unpredictably on him.

'You can do it at any time you wish,' the Chatelaine said. He heard her voice, dimly, and wondered whom she was addressing. Had a fourth person entered the room? He hoped that Master Robert had not arrived to see him in such a demeaning position.

But it was Isabelle who replied, 'Yes, madame.' And then nothing happened, except that the Chatelaine continued to torment his genitalia.

He had only a moment's warning. He sensed that Isabelle had tensed her muscles; he heard a strange hissing; and then his mouth was full of hot, bitter liquid, and his whole face was deluged with it. Streams of it ran through his hair and pooled under his head.

Isabelle was pissing on him. He gasped for breath, and took in another mouthful of the acrid stuff. He tried to jerk his limbs, but could move them not at all. He tried with all his strength to lift his head, but succeeded only in burying his face more deeply in Isabelle's sex, drawing from her an exclamation of surprise.

He had no choice but to swallow the mouthful of urine. But Isabelle seemed to have inexhaustible reserves of piss; the ammonia smell stung his nostrils, his head was lying in a warm pool that was now up to his ears, and still the stream hissed straight into his mouth. He was sure he would drown in Isabelle's piss.

As the stream at last reduced, in spurts, to a dribble, Barat realised that throughout his ordeal the Chatelaine had not ceased her attentions to his upright member. She was stroking it firmly, squeezing the glans at the end of each upward stroke, and he was very hard. In fact, he was getting close to a climax.

'Lick her, Barat,' the Chatelaine said. 'Lick her well, and I'll allow this poor, sore member a moment of relief.'

Barat was still gasping for breath. He was close to tears: he had never been subjected to such humiliating, frightening treatment, and he could not imagine how he would be able to face the Chatelaine again. And he was sure that Isabelle would tell everyone in the Chateau that she had made Barat drink her piss. His head was still lying in a pool of the foul liquid, and the acrid smell was all around him.

At the same time he could not deny that he was excited; in fact, the Chatelaine's hand around his shaft was making it more and more difficult for him to think of anything but the imminence of his climax. Now he was supposed to pleasure the woman who had just defiled him, and he had to admit that he did find it arousing to have his face in such intimate, helpless contact with Isabelle's sex.

He tilted his head back, and his nose burrowed into the entrance of Isabelle's vagina. She wriggled, smearing his urine-soaked face with her more viscous fluid. His mouth was now touching the forward part of the split of her sex, and he had only to open his mouth and extend his tongue.

He detected and licked into his mouth several drops of urine at the tiny hole that was the entrance of Isabelle's urethra. The stimulation produced a trickle of piss, which Barat swallowed. He extended his tongue again, a little further this time, and felt the tremor that ran through Isabelle's body as he licked close to the exposed tip of her clitoris.

Isabelle had clearly become very excited while she was pissing on Barat, and the movements of his tongue were increasing her arousal. Her sex fluid was now running almost as freely as her urine had, and was trickling into his mouth and down both sides of his face. He could breathe only through his mouth, and his hot panting breath seemed to stimulate Isabelle almost as much as the licking of his tongue.

Isabelle began to move her hips rhythmically, pushing

222

down to meet Barat's thrusting tongue. The Chatelaine was moving her hand up and down his shaft at the same pace.

'You see, Barat,' the Chatelaine said in a low, seductive voice. 'If you accept discipline, you receive a reward. Imagine how you will feel when Olena is fully trained and you have her at your disposal. You will be able to play any sort of game with her. Games like this, for instance. And to have her, you must merely obey me.'

The Chatelaine's words conjured images in Barat's mind. He imagined Olena on her knees before him, begging him to piss into her face. He added to the picture Nicole, standing behind Olena and encouraging her with flicks of a strap. He erased that image as one even better grew in his mind's eye: Olena wrapped in rubber, and lying on this dais, with her head inside Isabelle's knickers – and Barat, standing beside her, instructing her how to please Isabelle and punishing errors by using the three-tailed rubber strap on her breasts.

This second image was too seductive to bear. Barat lifted his head from the headrest and almost knocked Isabelle off her feet with the vigour of his thrusting tongue. The Chatelaine increased the tempo of her strokes, and with a muffled cry Barat felt the semen boil from his balls into his cock. He slumped back on to the headrest as he felt the seed pump from the tip of his straining erection.

As, with Isabelle's help, he disengaged his urine-soaked head from within her rubber knickers, he saw the Chatelaine flick his semen from her rubber gloves with a look of clinical neutrality. She snapped the gloves from her hands.

'Very good, Barat,' she said. 'It seems you have a talent for being obedient, when you're provided with the right incentives. I wonder if you know yourself as well as you think. You might prove to be an asset, after all. Now run along and clean yourself.'

As Nicole escorted her back to the dungeons, Olena promised herself that as soon as she was alone in the cell she would touch herself until she achieved the climax that had been denied her throughout the morning's punishments.

Once the door of the cell had been closed behind her, however, Olena found that she was not alone. She stepped hesitantly into the bathroom and found Jem, still wearing nothing but the collar, cuffs, and chains, trying to turn the tap that would produce the shower of water in the corner of the room. She ran to help her friend.

'You're sticky!' Olena squealed as she broke from the passionate embrace in which she had clasped Jem.

'It's cooking oil,' Jem said with a wry smile. 'And the copious emissions of six strapping kitchen-slaves. I'll tell you all about it in a moment. For now, just scrub me, please.'

As she used the sponge and plenty of soap to clean Jem's body, Olena found the marks of the punishments that Jem had been subjected to during the morning. She felt slightly aggrieved: her bottom and breasts were still glowing from the whippings inflicted by Nicole and Bernard, and when she had realised Jem was in their cell she had hoped to impress her friend with the evidence of her devotion to discipline. It was clear, however, that Jem had undergone chastisements at least as severe as those Olena had enjoyed.

Dripping with water, Olena turned off the shower, found a vast towel, and wrapped it around both herself and the bound Jem, so that their damp bodies were pressed together. Their lips met, and for several minutes there was silence as they kissed each other's mouth and face.

At last Olena drew away. A worrying thought had occurred to her, and she didn't know how to raise the subject.

'Jem,' she began, and then looked nervously over her shoulder as she remembered that she might be overheard. 'I mean, slave,' she went on, 'I hope I haven't misled you by kissing you so freely. What I mean to say is that I don't really prefer women, if you know what I mean. Or I don't think I do. It's been getting very confusing. So I hope I haven't disappointed you.'

Jem smiled. 'I like men and women,' she said. 'And I

224

particularly like you. But don't worry. It's all right for women to kiss and cuddle. Kiss me again.'

Olena pulled the towel more tightly around them and put her lips to Jem's. 'It's lovely kissing you,' she murmured. 'But it must be wrong, mustn't it? It makes me feel guilty and very naughty.'

'And that makes it even better, doesn't it? I wish I had half of your sense of shame. Did they punish you this morning?'

Olena knew that Jem had mentioned punishment as a way of reminding Olena that she took pleasure in being chastised for her sins. And it was true: she had enjoyed her punishments so much that several times she had almost reached one of the beautiful climaxes to which Jem had introduced her.

'Yes,' Olena said. 'Twice on my bottom and once on my breasts. And – something else, too.'

Jem looked into Olena's eyes. 'Let's compare bottoms,' she whispered, and burst into a fit of giggling.

'All right,' Olena said. She was thrilled at the prospect of showing Jem her striped bottom, although she told herself that she was merely doing so to demonstrate the strength of her zeal for discipline. She unwound the towel from around their bodies.

Laughing like schoolgirls they stood side by side, looking over their shoulders at their reflections in one of the bathroom's huge mirrors.

'Mine's redder than yours,' Olena said, proudly.

Jem wiggled her bottom. 'Yours is darker than mine to start with,' she said. 'And bigger. And you haven't got any of those wide strap-marks, like I have.'

'Yes, I have,' Olena protested. 'I had the paddle first, and then the strap. All over my bottom.'

'Let me see,' Jem said, and lowered herself to kneel behind Olena. Olena felt Jem's lips touch her smarting buttocks.

Jem gave an appreciative whistle. 'That's amazing,' she said. 'The marks are so close together I can hardly tell them apart. And you were paddled first?'

225

'Yes,' Olena said happily. 'All over.'

'I can see why the Chatelaine wants to keep you here,' Jem said. 'You're quite literally a glutton for punishment. Is this her handiwork?'

'No,' Olena replied. 'That was Nicole. She tries very hard to give me enough discipline.'

'I can see that,' Jem said. 'Nicole's obviously getting very practised with the strap. Your bottom must be very sore.'

'It feels very hot,' Olena said thoughtfully, 'and sensitive. It also feels bigger, in a way.'

'It's swollen,' Jem said. 'It's even bigger than usual, and bright red. Adorable.' She planted a kiss on the right buttock. 'Now help me to stand. I'm beginning to find these chains very tiresome.'

Olena pulled Jem up into another long embrace. 'Your breasts feel as hot as mine,' Jem said, and pulled away from Olena's kiss. 'Let me see.'

Unable to reach with her chained hands, Jem used her lips to explore the surface of Olena's tender globes. Olena, simultaneously proud that her round, punished breasts were worthy of such admiration and embarrassed that they were receiving such attention, could feel her secret place become wetter with each gentle touch of Jem's lips on her sensitised skin.

'You've been caned,' Jem said. 'A thin, light rod. The strokes varied in intensity; the earlier ones were harder. But I don't believe this was Nicole's work; the caning is thorough, certainly, but the stripes are positioned much less precisely than those on your bottom.'

'His name is Bernard,' Olena whispered, overcome with shame at the memory. 'He's a slave.'

'Bernard,' Jem exclaimed. 'Why, I know him. He's rather attractive, isn't he?'

Olena felt irrationally jealous. 'You seem to know everyone,' she snapped.

Jem merely laughed. 'That's not surprising,' she said, 'when you think about it. What kind of Supreme Mistress would I be if I didn't know my own people?'

'I suppose so,' Olena admitted. A wild, irresistible urge

came into her mind. 'Will you have to spank me now, for being grumpy?'

Jem merely twisted her lips and shrugged, making her chains jingle.

'I'd love to,' she said, 'but you see how it is. Tell me: what was Nicole doing to you while Bernard was caning your breasts?'

'Nothing,' Olena said, and lowered her eyes. She knew that she would have to tell Jem the things that Nicole had made her do, and she knew that telling Jem would make her feel miserably wicked and thrillingly trembly at the same time.

Jem said nothing. Her delectable pink lips were curved in a knowing smile. Her sea-blue eyes were fixed on Olena's face.

'She made me touch myself,' Olena whispered at last.

'Oh,' Jem said, innocently. 'Where?'

Olena was blushing intensely. Her face felt as red as her punished bottom. 'I can't say,' she whispered. Then she added slyly, 'Unless you make me.'

'I wouldn't be so cruel,' Jem said softly into Olena's ear, which she then kissed in a way that sent shivers down Olena's back. 'I'm afraid you'll have to show me.'

Olena sighed. Yes, she would have to show Jem what Nicole had made her do. 'It's disgusting,' she warned Jem. What if Jem found the act repulsive? What would she think of her? 'I had to do it,' she whispered, and felt tears sting her eyes. 'Nicole made me.'

'Hush,' Jem whispered. 'I know. It's all right. I love everything about you. I'll enjoy watching you.'

There was to be no escape from performing the deed. Olena wondered how she should position herself. She looked uncertainly about her. There was nothing in the bathroom that resembled the chaise longue on which she had knelt. 'I have to bend over,' she said, and looked imploringly at Jem.

'Then bend over,' Jem said. Her voice had an edge of impatience, and her eyes were glinting with desire. 'Lean towards me,' she said more gently. 'I can see your bottom in the mirror.'

227

Olena was sure that Jem had guessed what she was about to do. Slowly she bent forwards from the waist, and shuffled her legs wide apart.

'Very pretty,' Jem said, stroking Olena's hair. 'You have a most spankable bottom. Usually a big bottom is flabby, or unshapely. Your buttocks are so perfectly round.'

Olena felt a stab of pride and a wave of shame. Her secret place felt open; when she put her hand between her parted thighs, her juice streamed over her fingers.

'Leave that hand there,' Jem said, suddenly. 'Put your other hand behind your back, and use it to do what Nicole made you do.'

Olena was becoming accustomed to obeying instructions. This wasn't precisely the way in which she had performed the disgusting act for Nicole, but it was better: she could keep one hand pressed against the seeping wetness of her pulsing purse.

She closed her eyes and steeled herself to do the deed. She slid her hand down her back and into the valley between her sore buttocks. She remembered to collect some of her liquid on her fingers, and to rub it all round the crinkled crater. Jem whispered words of encouragement.

It happened almost without Olena willing it. Her longest finger slid into the little hole, and she gasped in surprise. To be able to perform so easily such a despicable act! She was becoming more and more dirty and sinful. And yet it felt good: wrong, and intrusive, but the finger in her little hole was sending tingling signals to her secret place, and to her pendant globes and their stiff nipples. A second finger slid in alongside the first, and Olena started to move them back and forth.

'Oh, Olena,' Jem breathed. 'You're such a beautifully naughty girl. And while you were doing that, Bernard caned your breasts?'

Olena nodded her head and nuzzled her lips against Jem's nipples.

'And did Nicole permit you to have a climax?' Jem asked, her words slow and careful.

228

'No,' Olena gasped, 'but I almost did.'

'You can now,' Jem whispered. 'If you keep your fingers inside you, and use your other hand to touch near the tip of your clitoris, as I showed you. I'll watch you.' She stepped back.

Jem was right. The full feeling in Olena's bottom, and the shudders of pleasure that emanated from there, would combine with the lightest of touches of her fingers at the top of the split in her purse to bring her quickly to the peak of sensation. The knowledge that Jem was watching Olena, and could see in the mirror every time her fingers pushed into her hole, only served to make the progress easier.

Olena heard the jangling of Jem's chains.

'It's no use,' Jem announced. 'I don't care who's watching us. I can't resist any longer.' Jem had unclipped the chains from her wrists; her arms were free.

'Keep playing with yourself,' Jem said. 'I'm going to smack you.'

Jem steadied Olena by cupping Olena's left breast in one hand. She began to bring down the other hand on Olena's tender buttocks, gently at first and then with increasing vigour. As the speed and severity of the spanks increased, she took Olena's nipple between her fingers and squeezed it in time to the smacking of her palm.

Olena cried out in pain with each slap. Her bottom was fiendishly sore and although Jem's hand was small it seemed to ignite a blaze wherever it struck.

Within seconds, however, Olena's cries had become exclamations of impending, inexorable ecstasy. Her body was a volcano on the point of eruption: nothing but heat, violent tremors and shocks. Her fingers, moving at an ever more frantic pace, found her secret place a cauldron of seething lava.

And then, as Jem's smacks rained down on her bottom, and with both her hands thrust shamelessly into her, Olena felt the quaking shocks run together into a shuddering, heaving, spouting explosion that seemed to go on and on indefinitely.

'Good girl,' Jem said, and stroked her face. 'Now clip

my chains on to my wrists, kiss me, and run and ask the guards for some food. I'm famished.'

'And then, madame,' Robert said, his voice rising with indignation, 'she released herself from her chains, and proceeded to spank the girl until she succeeded in reaching her climax. I saw it with my own eyes.'

Nicole looked from left to right: at Robert and then at the Chatelaine. Robert looked expectant; the Chatelaine concentrated on slicing into the *magret de canard* on her plate. Nicole glanced across the table at Isabelle, and caught her eye; Isabelle raised her eyebrows and looked upwards, silently communicating her disdain for Robert's manners.

Nicole felt slightly nervous: the Chatelaine seldom took lunch in the small private salon, and when she did Nicole and Isabelle might be called on to serve at table but very rarely to eat with madame. However, the Chatelaine seemed to want to be informal today, and as the business to be discussed over lunch included both the new whipping-slave and Olena, it had been deemed appropriate that both Nicole and Isabelle should join the Chatelaine and Master Robert.

Nicole ventured to break the silence. 'But madame,' she said, 'it seems to me that the new slave has done nothing that cuts against the grain of our programme for Olena. She was in a humiliating position, fingering herself in ways that she finds embarrassing, and she was being spanked. These are ideal circumstances for her climaxes.'

The Chatelaine, to Nicole's relief, smiled. She took a sip from her glass of the local *cabernet franc* and, Nicole thought, was about to reply when Robert's voice once again rang out across the table.

'That's not the point,' he said, with an exasperation that Nicole and Isabelle noted with another exchanged glance. 'The whore-slave was free. She released her own chains. This she has been expressly forbidden to do. She is in breach of the terms of her wager. She is yours, madame. The Private House is yours.'

The Chatelaine sighed. She carefully placed her knife and fork on the side of her plate, rested her elbows on the table, and put her fingers to her chin as she stared, deep in thought, at her deputy.

'No, Robert,' she said. 'It is not enough. You must understand that we need verifiable evidence. To be absolutely sure of keeping my new slave I must be able to demonstrate, to a gathering of the High Council if necessary, that she is consistently incapable of submitting to discipline. We have to find the point at which she rebels against our regime of punishments, and then exploit it over and over again until her wilfulness is clear to everyone, including the slave herself. Is that understood?'

'Yes, madame,' Robert said.

'It seems to me,' the Chatelaine went on, 'that after a day and a half in the Chateau the whore-slave is finding few difficulties in submitting to the programme we devised for her. Her behaviour with Olena, only a few moments after both of them had been severely chastised, suggests that her spirited personality is undimmed. Hers is hardly the behaviour of a slave in dread of the next torment and in fear of remaining a slave for ever. After today we have three more days in which to secure her. This particular slave is resourceful; remember, I know her well. I did not expect this wager to be easy to win. We have to acknowledge the possibility that the slave will subject herself entirely to our discipline, and that she will therefore win her freedom.'

There was another silence. Nicole, who had met the new slave when she had been the Supreme Mistress and had been charmed by her vivacity and beauty, found herself hoping that the slave could endure her ordeals. She wondered whether such thoughts were disloyal to the Chatelaine.

The Chatelaine had brought to the table, and had left lying incongruously among the silver cutlery on the white damask tablecloth, a short whip of plaited leather. Nicole suspected that the Chatelaine intended to take a siesta after lunch, and that Nicole, or Isabelle, or perhaps one of the

231

slaves who were serving the meal, would be taken to the
Chatelaine's bedchamber to keep her amused. Nicole
hoped she would be chosen; training Olena was fascinating
and enjoyable, but it seemed to Nicole a long time since
her own bottom had felt the lash, and she began to think
about the pleasure of demonstrating her devotion to her
mistress by submitting to a thorough whipping.

She looked at the Chatelaine until she caught her eye,
and then allowed her gaze to slide to the coiled whip. She
let the Chatelaine see that she was squirming on her chair;
she rested a hand on her left breast; she looked again into
the Chatelaine's face, and was rewarded with a smile.
Nicole felt momentarily dizzy with desire. She was
trembling inside, and her sex was getting wet. She would
offer her bottom to the Chatelaine; she would beg to be
flogged until the Chatelaine was too tired to continue; she
would bury her face in the Chatelaine's vulva and drink its
elixir; and then they would sleep together, with Nicole's
face still nestling between her mistress's thighs.

Nicole's reverie was interrupted by an explosion of anger
from Robert.

'I will not countenance defeat,' he stormed. 'Madame,
we have an opportunity to ensure that you achieve your
rightful place. We must not even think of wasting it. Only
the whore-slave stands in our way. We must break her. We
will break her. There must be a way.'

The Chatelaine waved a hand to summon the slaves to
clear the *entrées*. 'What do you propose?' she asked.

'We have been too lenient, madame,' Robert replied.
'We should not have permitted her to share a cell with
anyone.' He paused, as if suddenly remembering that it
had been the Chatelaine's idea to imprison the slave with
Olena. When the Chatelaine remained calm, he continued.
'Tomorrow, I will arrange for the slave to be subjected to
a session of intensive obedience training. As you know,
madame, Max and Ilsa can be extremely strict. I will
ensure they devise a programme that is so degrading that
even the most submissive would baulk at it. I guarantee
that the whore-slave will not be able to submit willingly.

And I suggest that we summon the High Council here to witness the slave's downfall and to appoint a new Supreme Mistress. Madame, your destiny awaits. Tomorrow, you will win.'

The Chatelaine sat in thought. A frown furrowed her high forehead. At length she looked up. 'Very well,' she said. 'Robert, I will entrust to you the arrangements for the obedience training. Nicole, after lunch we must immediately dispatch the invitations to the councillors.' She smiled at Nicole. 'And after our work is done, we'll retire to my room.' Her fingertips touched the handle of the whip.

Nicole was elated. She blushed, as she thought the others might be able to see her trembling. 'Yes, madame,' she said.

Six

For the first time in months, Nicole had that morning
ventured outside the walls of the Chateau. She had risen
early, before dawn, and, wearing a fur coat and a pair of
long boots, she had crossed the rear courtyard and found
her way through the stables and outbuildings to the east
postern gate. With her breath pluming white, by the
growing light of the sky she had discerned the path across
the walled kitchen garden. Once through a tiny gate in the
wall, she had been outside.

Here the park was less carefully tended than it was at the
front of the Chateau. The grass had stood in dew-jewelled
clumps; the trunk of a chestnut had lain where it had fallen
in a storm the previous autumn, its labyrinthine roots
reaching skywards. Nicole had been able to make out the
edges of clouds racing across the sky, which had been
lightening perceptibly – from opaque black, to foggy grey,
to a pink-tinged, watery blue. A blazing sliver of orange
fire had crept into view above the tree-lined horizon;
impulsively Nicole had unbuttoned her coat and spread
wide her arms, welcoming the rising sun with her naked
body.

She had remained still. A herd of small deer had trotted
from between the trees and begun unconcernedly to browse
the sparkling grass. There had as yet been no bright green
leaves sprouting on the branches; the air had been cold,
and the tracks that led away from the Chateau into the
park had been no more than churned mud. But the
sunlight had been warm on Nicole's skin, and the blind,

featureless shoots of spring plants had been visible, thrusting through the sodden grass and from the neglected borders and planters.

Now, as one of the Chatelaine's most trusted retainers, Nicole was standing in her maidservant uniform, ready to serve, at her post on the right-hand side of the ornate fireplace in the grand salon. As she listened to the councillors wrangling and did her best to keep her face expressionless, she was glad she had gone outside to watch the sun rise. Here the shutters and curtains were still closed across the tall windows; lamps provided pools of illumination, and a log fire heated the dusty air.

The one to watch, Nicole had decided, was the chief of the guards. Her name was Julia, and every movement of her slim, black-clad body spoke of controlled passion. Even the Chatelaine addressed her with a respect that she extended only grudgingly to the other councillors.

'The guards will adjudicate,' Julia stated, 'under my supervision. I really can't see why this should present a problem.'

The Chatelaine, along with most of the other councillors, nodded. But Nicole saw that Robert was incensed.

'The problem, Chief Julia,' he almost shouted, 'is that we all know whose side you're on. Perhaps you'd like to remind us how many times you shared the whore-slave's bed when she was Supreme Mistress?'

Julia thrust the tip of her riding-crop into Robert's face. 'I make no secret of my personal preference, Master Robert. But in this matter I am required by my office and my duties to remain strictly neutral. I do hope you're not impugning my integrity.'

Robert, quivering with rage, was about to launch into a reply when the Chatelaine's voice rang out.

'Robert! Stop squabbling. Once again, your enthusiasm has overwhelmed both your manners and your sense. I will speak with you. Wait by the fireplace. Julia,' she said in emollient tones, 'I apologise for my hot-headed deputy. I'm sure I speak for the whole council in assuring you that

235

I have no doubts whatsoever about your professionalism. It is entirely appropriate that you and your guards should act as the council's eyes and ears in a matter of such importance. As soon as the meeting is concluded I shall have someone take you directly to the room in which the slave is to be tested. We shall remain here and await your report.'

'Thank you, Chatelaine,' Julia said. She smiled politely, but Nicole saw that as she turned to speak with her guards she cast a vitriolic glance towards Robert.

All the councillors look worried, Nicole thought, but Julia is as tense as a wound spring. She can't keep still. Nicole understood Julia's predicament, and had to blink back tears of sympathy. It was, as Robert had pointed out, well known that Julia and the former Supreme Mistress were devoted lovers. Now Julia was going to have to watch as her dearest friend underwent a test of submissiveness that Robert had pledged she could only fail. Nicole knew Robert to be entirely ruthless; it seemed certain that Julia would have to report to the High Council of the Private House that the former Supreme Mistress had been reduced to slavery in perpetuity, and would henceforth be at the Chatelaine's disposal.

Several of the councillors, as aware of Julia's cruel plight as Nicole, had come up to her and tried to offer words of comfort. Julia had shrugged them off, casually or with a snarl. She seemed to be able to relax a little, only in the company of the half-dozen guards she had brought with her. In their carapaces of gleaming black leather they formed a sinister group in the corner of the salon.

The Chatelaine, having chatted to several other councillors, made her way to join Robert who was waiting impatiently by the fireplace. They spoke urgently in low voices; Nicole was the only servant within earshot and they contrived to appear to all other onlookers as though they were conversing normally.

'Robert, you're a fool,' the Chatelaine said. 'Julia is the one witness whom the entire council will believe. The fact that she is known to be close to Jem – to the slave – will simply add credence to her report.'

'Yes, madame, but –'

'Furthermore,' the Chatelaine went on, 'if I am to be effective as the new Supreme Mistress I will need to be able to rely on Julia and her guards. You must think politically, Robert.'

'Yes, madame,' he replied. 'Of course. I understand that Julia will be necessary. At least for a while. Until, perhaps, you see fit to appoint a new chief of guards.'

Nicole saw that Robert failed to notice the puzzled frown that appeared briefly on the Chatelaine's flawless face.

'And it occurs to me, madame,' he pressed on, 'that it can only serve our purposes if Julia is present during the whore-slave's ordeal. They are lovers; it will be impossible for the slave to submit willingly to the degradation she is about to face, knowing that her friend is watching every cruel humiliation.'

He smiled contentedly. Nicole turned away and shuddered.

Jem had been confined alone, in a small dungeon cell, since she had been separated from Olena the previous day. She had been provided with several excellent meals, and had eaten well. She had lain on the bed for much of the time, lazily daydreaming in the gaps between deep sleep. Her chains and cuffs had been removed, and she was naked but for the collar. With her hands free she had been able to bathe in comfort, to pamper herself with the oils, perfumes and cosmetics with which the cell was plentifully supplied, and to relive – with her fingers exploring the damp folds between her legs – the pleasures and pains she had experienced in the Chateau.

Now she felt refreshed, and almost keen to discover what new trials and tribulations the Chateau had in store for her. She felt more confident than she had since entering the Chatelaine's domain that she could meet whatever challenges she had to face. She had submitted for two days, and considered that she had enjoyed almost everything. She had to submit for only another three days. It would be a pleasure, she thought.

She estimated that it was now late in the morning. She was becoming bored. She wondered why she had not already been summoned to some dim chamber in the bowels of the Chateau, there to suffer indignities and punishments. The stripes on her buttocks and breasts had faded almost completely, and she was looking forward to the bitter thrill of feeling the lash on her body again. It would be more interesting than sitting on a bed in a cell and staring at a wall.

At last she heard footsteps beyond the door. A key was turned; bolts were pulled back; and the door opened.

A man and a woman walked into the cell, filling it with their combined presence. Jem cast a quick glance at them as she scrambled off the bed to adopt a kneeling position in the confined space between the bed and the wall.

Both were tall and imposing, and dressed in buckskin, with short whips hanging at their waists. Jem did not recognise them, nor could she tell from their costume what function they performed in the Chateau. They were clearly not slaves; she guessed, from their whips and stern demeanour, that they were trainers of some sort.

'I am Ilsa,' the woman said. 'My partner is Max. You will not address either of us. You will not speak. Do you understand?'

Jem nodded, and kept her head lowered. It was already clear that this dour couple would accept no nonsense, and she decided to bide her time before making any attempt to flirt with them.

'We are obedience trainers,' Max stated. 'Today you will be trained to be obedient. Wear these.' He tossed a number of small articles on to the floor in front of Jem.

None of the items was familiar to Jem. She picked up two that appeared identical, and realised that they were mittens. She pulled them on. The tips of her fingers and thumbs appeared through holes at the ends of the tight-fitting envelopes of material. The mittens were of tough leather on one side, against the palms of her hands; on the other, on the backs of her hands, they were covered with soft fur. The fur was long and reddish-brown; Jem

238

realised that it had been chosen to match exactly the colour of her hair.

'Dainty paws,' Max said to Ilsa. 'I think she might show well.'

'We'll see,' Ilsa replied. 'Looks aren't everything. We need obedience and character, too.'

Jem was beginning to understand how she could expect to be trained. She was to take the part of some animal. Well, she thought, there can be nothing very challenging in that. But in the pit of her stomach she felt a stirring of anxiety.

There was, of course, another pair of paws, longer than the first, that covered her feet, ankles and shins and, at the front of her legs, projected over her knees. They slipped over her feet like moccasins and were held in place with straps that buckled across her calves and behind her knees. The leather pad on each extended along the sole of her foot and over the tips of her toes; there was a second leather pad covering each knee. The rest was covered in fur that matched that on the mittens.

That makes sense, Jem thought; if I'm to be an animal I'm certain to spend a lot of time on my hands and knees.

There was one more part of the costume: a mask that covered the upper half of Jem's face. It was a beautifully crafted item. The internal surface was soft, and moulded itself precisely to the contours of Jem's face and forehead; she wondered whether it had been made specifically for her. With the mask fitting comfortably against her skin, Jem found that the eyeholes were in exactly the right position: she could see, and blink, without obstruction.

The trainers adjusted the straps and buckles at the back of Jem's head to ensure that the mask was secure. Then Max clipped a leash to the ring on Jem's collar.

'Come along,' he said, and tugged on the leash. 'Walk on all four paws.'

As Jem crawled on her hands and knees behind Max and Ilsa she found herself becoming both nervous and excited. Once the trainers had led her up from the dungeons, she was aware of being the subject of some interest from the servants and slaves running errands through the Chateau's corridors. Jem always enjoyed dressing up in outlandish costumes, and being on her hands and knees drew attention to her – and particularly to her raised bottom, which she suspected looked rather attractive as she crawled behind her trainers.

It was only when their route took them along a corridor lined with full-length mirrors, however, that Jem discovered what sort of animal she was supposed to be.

Jem had always thought of herself as feline, and she had assumed, for no better reason, that the face of the mask would make her resemble a cat. But when she turned her face and found herself looking in a mirror, she recognised the half-woman, half-beast as herself, and could not at first decide what animal she had been dressed up to be.

She thought she certainly looked desirable. The fur of her paws and mask complemented the paleness of her skin and the sea-blue of her eyes, and was so similar in colour to the titian curls on her head that it could have been her own hair. Just a couple of days in the Chateau had made her body look thinner while accentuating her breasts, which swayed beneath her ribs, and her buttocks, which were presented upwards by the curve of her spine. And her collar, with the leather leash being held taut from above her, implied both her bondage and her debasement.

But if she was not a cat, what was she? The outside of the mask was not a literal depiction of any creature. Its design had large eyes, so that her pale irises glinted at the centre of inhumanly large, dark orbs. A short snout covered her nose and ended in a shining, black button. And there were ears: long, fur-covered flaps that appeared to be sprouting from the midst of her auburn hair.

She was a dog. A young dog, she realised, with floppy ears and big paws.

Max and Ilsa stopped in front of a door. Max squatted next to Jem and held her by the chin.

'Now then, slave,' he said. 'We're at the training room. You've probably realised that today you're a little puppy. You're going to be taught how to behave and be obedient.

We'll turn you from an unruly puppy into a well-disciplined bitch.' He allowed himself a thin smile.

'Therefore,' Ilsa continued, 'from the moment we lead you through that door we want to see you acting like a puppy. You will be boisterous. You will run and jump aimlessly – until such behaviour is beaten out of you, of course. You will be pathetically eager to please. The slightest failure to act in a puppyish manner will be regarded as a breach of your promise to remain submissive and obedient. And, as you are about to discover, today your adherence to your vow will be particularly closely monitored.'

A heavy, cold dread constricted Jem's heart. This was going to be a difficult day. Until now she had been able to find distractions in each of the ordeals she had endured: the taste of a man's penis in her mouth, the exhilaration of a whip lashing her flesh, the shivers and warmth of sexual arousal.

But today, it seemed, there would be nothing to take her mind from the constant humiliation of being required to obey instructions. Worse, she would have to concentrate on colluding in her own debasement: if for even a moment she behaved other than as a puppy, she would forfeit her freedom for ever.

Jem gathered her resolve. Her imagination had already shown her a gallery of the degrading acts she might be obliged to perform during the course of being trained as a puppy; if she could imagine them, she could endure them. It was only play-acting, after all, and she knew she was capable of throwing herself into a part. She had the measure of what was to come; there would be no surprises.

She became a puppy. She opened her eyes wide and stared at Max; she licked his hand, and then lifted her front paws from the floor and began to scrabble at his hands and the leash until he almost lost his balance, and hurriedly rose from his squatting position.

'Down, girl,' he said. 'I can see that obedience training is just what you require.'

Jem felt a booted foot touch her left buttock. 'A puppy

wags her tail,' Ilsa said. 'Nearly all the time, and certainly when being paid attention by her trainers. Let us see how enthusiastically you can wag your tail, puppy.'

Jem wiggled her hips from side to side, slowly at first but faster as Max and Ilsa moved behind her to watch her bottom jump about. She lowered her head to the floor so that her twitching hindquarters were thrust upwards and her anus and vulva were in full view. She could never resist showing off, and she could feel the trainers' eyes on her shaven sex, making her warm and wet.

'She's one of those disgusting puppies that likes everyone to see its backside,' Ilsa said in an offended tone.

'We'll tie her down and flog the parts she's so keen to display,' Max said. 'It's cruel, but it inhibits this sort of disgraceful behaviour.'

Jem wagged her tail faster. In the eyeholes of the mask her eyes sparkled. Perhaps, she thought, obedience training would have its consolations.

'Keep wagging, little puppy,' Ilsa said. 'It's time to go into the training room.'

Jem, immersed in her role, trotted on hands and knees to the door and began to scratch at it with her right paw. Max pushed the door open and Jem raced through it, pulling taut the leash as Max followed her. She felt her collar being released from the pull of the leash, and wiggling her bottom excitedly she darted from side to side and ran in circles.

The room was large and high-ceilinged. Dusty light came in shafts through tall, half-closed shutters, leaving the corners of the room in darkness. The furniture – chairs, sofas and screens – had been pushed towards the walls, although there were a few less readily identifiable objects placed more centrally. Rugs covered only patches of the wooden floor, and Jem was glad of the leather pads covering her knees, toes and hands. And, she realised, the room was not empty of people.

Around the shadowy perimeter of the room, almost invisible against the dark panelling, figures stood silent and still. Men and women, Jem saw, dressed in familiar uniforms of gleaming black.

They were guards. Her guards, from the main House.

Don't forget to wag your tail, she told herself, even as her circling run brought into view the one person she most wanted to see – and who she least wanted to witness her present humiliation.

Julia.

Unsmiling, standing rigid, her face showing no expression, no sign of recognition or greeting.

Jem wanted to run to her and hold her in her arms. Instead she pretended that a scent on the floor had attracted her puppy attention, and as she sniffed, with her bottom in the air, she gave herself time to think.

Julia's here, she told herself, with a squad of guards. They're here to watch me perform. Julia is the only councillor that the others would trust to give a fair and accurate report of my behaviour. The Chatelaine wouldn't have summoned Julia unless she was confident that there would be something to show her. So the Chatelaine knows I'm going to fail.

And she's right, Jem thought. I can't do this. Not with Julia watching.

She ran in a circle and used a paw to scratch her ears.

But I'll do my best, she vowed. This might be the last time that Julia and I see each other. I'll put on a good show.

Nicole helped Olena to remove her robe. When Olena was naked, she felt Nicole's lips brush her ear.

'Remember,' Nicole whispered, 'we must be very quiet. Not a sound.'

They were in a dark, tiny space, behind a black lacquered screen in the corner of a room. There was room only for the two women and one high-backed armchair; not enough room, Olena noted with a twinge of disappointment, for anyone else to stand and watch while Olena was tested, or for Nicole to swing a cane or a strap.

'Kneel on the seat of the chair,' Nicole whispered, 'so that you're facing the screen.'

Olena did as she was told, placing her knees as far apart

as she could and curving her back inwards so that her bottom was pushed out. The position came naturally to her now.

She leaned her head against Nicole's, so that they could communicate in soft voices.

'I'm already wet,' she said, blushing. 'Are you going to spank me?'

Nicole giggled. 'Not yet,' she replied. 'It would make too much noise. I'll just stroke your bottom, like this, to remind you that you'll be punished later.'

Olena shivered as she felt Nicole's fingertips brushing the most sensitive part of her left buttock, where it curved inwards near her little hole and her secret parts. 'That's lovely,' she said, and kissed the lock of dark hair that Nicole always had carefully curled on her cheek. It felt naughty and exciting to be pressed close to Nicole in this confined space; it reminded her of cuddling Jem under the covers in the cell that they had shared.

'I've brought you here to watch something,' Nicole said, her fingers gently twining the hairs of Olena's secret parts. 'If you put your face against the screen, just there, you can see through it.'

'What will I see?' Olena said.

'You'll find out,' Nicole replied. 'I think you might find it instructive. Perhaps you'd like to do it yourself, one day soon.'

Olena was intrigued. She found the opening in the screen and stared through it. She was grateful that Nicole, so as not to distract her, had stopped playing between her legs and was instead using the palm of her hand to caress her bottom.

'You're so lovely,' Nicole whispered. 'You have so many round curves,' she giggled, 'and your skin is so smooth. I could stroke you for ever.'

'You can,' Olena said, but her attention was already fixed on the strange scene that she could see in the room beyond the screen.

She realised instantly that the woman kneeling in the centre of the room was dressed – if that was the expression for someone who was almost entirely naked – as an animal. It took her only another moment to recognise the woman's mane of auburn hair and petite figure. It was Jem, wearing paws, a mask and a collar.

Standing beside Jem were two tall, menacing figures wearing tightly fitting leather clothes and carrying short whips. The male figure was holding a leash that was attached to Jem's collar. Their voices, echoing in the room, carried easily to Olena kneeling behind the screen.

'That's not how a puppy sits,' the man said. The woman casually flicked the tail of her whip against Jem's bottom.

'Front paws close together,' the man said, 'and keep your back legs apart so that your front paws fit neatly between your knees. Lift your backside so that you can wag your tail.'

Olena, fascinated, saw Jem arrange her body as instructed and begin to wag her bottom from side to side. The long furry ears flopped ludicrously. Jem looked just like an overgrown, soppy puppy.

'Good girl,' the man said, and delivered three stinging slaps to Jem's wiggling buttocks. 'Now let's see if you can remember how to do it. Run and play.' He unclipped the leash from Jem's collar.

Jem began to trot forwards on her hands and knees, keeping her face close to the ground so that it looked as though she was following a scent with the black-button nose on her mask. Her floppy ears trailed on the floor. Her pale body seemed luminescent in the shadowy room, and it was impossible not to stare at her rounded, upthrust bottom. The man followed her, touching her with the tip of his whip sometimes to guide her and sometimes, it seemed, simply because it entertained him to remind Jem that her buttocks and private parts were accessible to him.

'Sit!' the woman shouted, and Jem stopped, straightened her body, and brought her hands together between her knees. She remembered to wiggle her bottom.

'Very good little puppy,' the man said, emphasising each word with a hefty smack on Jem's bottom. 'Now we'll teach you something else.'

Olena pulled her face from the slit in the screen and exchanged a wide-eyed look with Nicole.

'The trainers are Max and Ilsa,' Nicole whispered. 'They're new to the Chateau.'

While watching Jem, Olena had thought of little but how it would feel to be trained as a puppy. The thoughts had made her very wet indeed. Perhaps this was just the sort of training she needed, with plenty of simple instructions to obey and frequent smacks. She looked imploringly at Nicole. 'Please?' she murmured.

'It will probably be necessary,' Nicole sighed. 'Ordinary punishments seem to have little effect on your bad behaviour. But we should take the present regime to its limit before we start to try new methods.' She began stroking Olena's bottom again with brisk brushes of her hand that reminded Olena of the chastisements that were in store for her. Between each stroke Nicole's hand dipped between Olena's parted thighs, making Olena squirm and gasp.

'Now let's watch more of the puppy training,' Nicole said. 'I wonder what the guards are making of it?'

'The guards?' Olena said, but as soon as she put her eyes to the screen she saw them: half a dozen dark, sinister figures, standing still in the shadows around the edge of the room. She had not noticed them previously because they were as motionless as statues.

A shiver of fearful excitement rippled through Olena's body. She imagined herself in Jem's place, suffering not merely the trials and punishments of being trained to behave like an animal but also the humiliation of being observed by such a sombre audience. Olena decided that she would like both to be trained and to be watched; if the training was necessary, which in the case of her sinfulness it most certainly was, then she deserved also to be compelled to let others see her shame. And, she admitted to herself, she was sure that if she were in Jem's place she would already be starting to feel the mounting sensations that she now knew could become a plume of inexpressible, body-racking joy.

As she watched the trainers harrying Jem, standing beside her, shouting instructions, and flicking her prostrate body with their whips, Olena bit her lip. She was sure she would like to be trained, and in front of an audience, but she was less confident that Jem was enjoying it.

'Lie down!' Max shouted. 'Come on, girl. Lie down.'

Olena thought she detected unfeigned uncertainty in Jem's movements as, with much flopping of ears and waving of paws, she tried to put herself in the position that a dog would adopt when resting. She ended curled on her side, with her knees pulled up to her chest. Olena thought she looked pathetically helpless.

'That's not how a puppy bitch lies down,' Ilsa cried, and slashed her whip three times across Jem's defenceless bottom. Olena saw a movement from the corner of her eye: the black-uniformed guards were as stationary as ever, but one of them, a woman, had raised a hand to her mouth.

'Puppy, sit,' Max said.

Jem knelt in the correct position.

'Now bend your front legs, and stretch your front paws out on the ground in front of you. Keep them neatly together. That's right. Now your body is horizontal. Keep your back legs well apart. That's it. That's how a puppy must lie down, when instructed to. Now you're being an obedient little puppy. Good girl. Wag your tail.'

Jem was on her knees and elbows, with her masked face buried between her outstretched arms and her breasts touching the floor. With her legs apart her buttocks were widely parted and lifted upwards; the position, Olena saw, was degrading and uncomfortable to maintain. When Jem, instructed to wag her tail, began to move her prominently presented bottom from side to side Olena stared wide-eyed at the blatant obscenity of the display.

Even as she sympathised with Jem, however, she was visualising herself in the same position, pressing her large, round breasts against the floor and opening to her trainers and to her audience the generous curves of her bottom and the depths of her secret places.

It occurred to her that she imagined Max and Ilsa, tall

and severe in their tight leather costumes, training her. Why, she wondered, had she not imagined herself being trained by Barat? She had hardly thought of him for days.

That's naughty of me, she thought. Later, I'll tell Nicole about it. I'll probably be given another punishment.

She smiled happily, allowed the guilty feelings about Barat to dissipate like morning mist, and returned to observing the training of Jem.

Barat was on his way to report to Master Robert when he saw a familiar figure.

He was permitted to wear his robe only when attending Olena's training sessions, and he still felt embarrassed at walking alone through the corridors of the Chateau wearing only a pair of leather briefs. Therefore he crept circumspectly through the narrower passages and the back stairways, keeping to the shadows. He had in this way explored a large part of the four main ranges of buildings that surrounded the Chateau's central courtyard, as well as many of the outbuildings.

He was taking a circuitous route to Master Robert's office when he saw a tall, slim figure disappearing through a doorway. He recognised Isabelle instantly, and felt an immediate pang of longing so intense that it was almost a physical pain. She was wearing a dark red corset and black stockings; her long dark hair was tied back in a ponytail. Without pausing for thought he tiptoed to the door, now closed, through which she had gone.

He put his ear to the ancient, carved wood, and heard voices from the room beyond. He needed to know what Isabelle was doing in there, but he did not dare to open the door and announce his presence. He ransacked his memory for the mental maps of the Chateau's interior that he had been constructing during his explorations. He remembered that there was another passageway, so narrow that it was no more than a gap between two walls, that ran parallel to the one he was in. Perhaps from there he could find another way secretly to enter, or at least to look into, the room into which Isabelle had gone.

Within a few minutes he was edging through the narrow passage, trying to prevent the dusty walls and hanging cobwebs from coming into contact with his naked skin. He had climbed a short stairway and therefore felt that, while he was now approximately opposite the door through which Isabelle had gone, he must also be on a slightly higher level.

The only illumination came from shafts of dim light that pierced the darkness of the passage. Each shaft of light indicated a fissure in the stonework, but most of them were high above Barat's head and he could not use them to see into the rooms beyond. There were doorways, too, with doors of crumbling wood that appeared not to have opened for centuries. Most of these also allowed light to seep into the passage, as the wooden panels fitted badly in their frames. Barat was able to peer through these, and several times he almost forgot his urgent desire for Isabelle as he found himself spying on scenes of debauchery and discipline that astonished even his fertile imagination.

Each time, however, he dragged himself away from the peephole and onwards, until he arrived at a sagging door beyond which he could hear Isabelle's voice.

It was easy to see into the room; pressing his face against the door frame he found himself looking down on a scene that made his stomach tighten and his eyes widen.

The room was small, at least compared with many in the Chateau. Its walls were hung with dark red silk that shimmered in the light of four lamps. Most of the polished wooden floor was covered with a carpet that matched the colour of the hangings; a large four-poster bed took up most of one side of the room. Its woodwork, and that of the other furniture, was almost black with gleaming polish. It was a crowded, sensual room. A boudoir. Isabelle's boudoir, Barat suspected. The thought made his penis harden and push uncomfortably against the restriction of his briefs.

Isabelle was still wearing the scarlet corset and black stockings. Now she had equipped herself with a short, slender cane that she was flexing between her hands as she

249

lounged in an armchair and gave instructions to the two men standing in front of her. The men were naked but for collars and cuffs around their necks, wrists and ankles.

Both men, Barat saw at once with a twinge of envy, were young, slim and muscular. One was blond and tall, with tattoos on his bulging arms; he was staring at Isabelle with defiance as well as lust in his eyes. The other was darker and a little shorter; his head was lowered, and he was shuffling from side to side. Barat noticed that the darker man was not entirely naked; he was wearing a belt with an arrangement of thin, tightly fastened straps between his buttocks and around his genitalia.

'It's your turn now, Grant,' Isabelle said to the blond giant. 'Place yourself over the box so that Gustave can chain you.'

Grant looked agitated, but remained where he was. 'This is not right, miss,' he said. 'This is not as I requested. We had agreed that we would be alone together. I am not a mere slave, to be pressed into use for the amusement of others.'

Isabelle smiled lazily and opened wide her bright blue eyes. She parted her legs and drew one of them up so that her foot was resting on the seat of the chair. Barat, peering from a distance through a dusty crack, found the gesture arousing; he could guess the effect it must have had on the blond man.

'But Grant,' Isabelle said, 'you told me that you wanted to worship me. That you would do anything I asked. And what I'm asking you to do is to play a few games with Gustave. Are you going to do as you're asked? You know,' she added, in a low voice, 'that I'll make it worthwhile in the end.'

'Oh, very well,' Grant said, and without another word he turned and strode to a large padded box in the centre of the room. The box resembled a vaulting horse with a solid base; unlike most gym equipment, however, all four sides of the box had leather straps and metal chains attached to them.

Grant pressed his rippling muscled stomach against one

edge of the padded top of the box and bent forwards until he was lying face down on it.

'Put the chains on his wrists first, Gustave,' Isabelle said. 'I want him to know he can't escape.'

As Barat watched in amazement, the blond giant submitted to being chained and strapped into a most unmanly position, with his hands near the floor, his face pressed into the soft top of the box, his knees pulled up alongside his torso and his arse uplifted beyond the end of the box.

'Is he getting hard, Gustave?' Isabelle asked.

Gustave, who was red in the face from the exertion of binding Grant, was lost for words. He stared at Isabelle, opened and closed his mouth, and then bent, gingerly, to look at Grant's cock and balls hanging beneath his protruding arse.

'It's quite big, miss,' he said.

'But Gustave,' Isabelle said sweetly, 'I asked whether it was hard. Come here. Turn round. Bend over.'

The lithe rod whistled shrilly in the air and landed across both of Gustave's buttocks. He squealed.

'Now, go and look properly,' Isabelle said. 'Hold Grant's penis in your hand and tell me whether or not it's hard.'

Barat was aware that his own penis had become very stiff. Isabelle, playing games in her own little domain, was more alluring than ever, and he couldn't help wishing that he, instead of the two other men, were with her in her boudoir.

Grant writhed and cursed in his bonds as he heard Gustave approach. Gustave seemed wary of the big blond, even though he himself had secured the straps and chains. He positioned himself next to the back of the box, where Grant's pale buttocks stuck out. He turned to face Isabelle, his eyes full of mute appeals for a reprieve. Isabelle merely smiled and gestured for him to continue.

Barat saw Gustave grimace as he placed his left hand on the small of Grant's back. Grant shouted an oath. Gustave leaned forwards and, with an expression of loathing on his face, slowly extended his hand under the bound man's buttocks.

Grant roared and bellowed. Gustave had obviously found his target. He remained unmoving until Grant's protests died away.

'It's big, miss,' he said, 'but it's not very hard. Although I think it's getting harder.'

Grant roared again, and eventually subsided into silence.

'And now?' Isabelle asked Gustave.

Gustave took a deep breath. 'It's definitely harder, miss,' he said. 'May I let go now?'

'Certainly not,' Isabelle said. 'Not when we're getting such a positive result.' She uncurled her body from the armchair and, swaying her slim hips in a manner that made Barat's erection threaten to burst from his briefs, she sauntered to the box. She stroked Grant's right buttock and drew her fingertips along his spine until she reached his head, where she stroked his cheek.

'Well, Grant,' she said, 'you're obviously getting excited. Do you like having your penis held by a man? Is that it? Or are you looking forward to having the wooden phallus embedded in your anus? Or perhaps you have already suspected that while you're tied up and helpless I'm going to take the opportunity to tame you a little. My whip collection is in the cabinet in the corner. I thought I might test a few of them. Would you like that?'

Grant mumbled a reply that Barat was unable to hear.

'He's getting harder, miss,' Gustave said. 'I can hardly get my fingers round the shaft. Can I let go now, please?'

'No, Gustave,' Isabelle said. She looked over her shoulder at Gustave, and laughed. Barat thought she looked magnificent. 'Try to make him harder. And use your other hand to squeeze his balls.' She turned back to address Grant. 'I like a slave with a big cock,' she said. 'If you're very good, and do exactly as I say, I may let you choose where you put that big cock of yours.'

Barat could stand it no longer. If he could not have Isabelle, then at least he would take the edge off his appetite for her by masturbating while he watched her. He moved his hands to the front of his body and started to undo the buttons of his briefs.

It was difficult to move in the confined space, and it was difficult to concentrate with Isabelle's voice describing the many humiliations she had in store for Grant and Gustave before she would let either one of them so much as touch her.

And then the third button seemed to become caught in the buttonhole. Barat pulled; he tugged desperately, eager to free his confined erection.

The button came free, and Barat's fist, suddenly released and still holding the button, smashed through the wormholed wood of the door. He staggered forwards, blinking in the cloud of dust, and found himself standing on a landing accessible by an open flight of stairs from the room into which he had been looking down.

Isabelle and Gustave stared up at him. Grant, tied face down, shouted questions that everyone ignored.

'Barat,' Isabelle said. 'What a pleasant surprise. I see you were getting ready to join us.' She looked pointedly at his crotch; at that moment his erection finally broke free of its restraint and, swaying, pointed upwards.

'No, no,' Barat said, blushing. 'I was just passing. On my way, you know. I must go.'

'What a shame,' Isabelle said, and placed her hand between her legs. 'And I thought you liked me, Barat. Well, go if you must. If you stay I'll only set these two muscular chaps on to you. I'll tell them to play roughly with you, and then tie you up, and then put something up your arse to make you feel full and stretched open. And then I might whip you. And then, if you've been good, I might let you lick me. So, if you go, you won't be missing much.'

Barat licked his lips. He couldn't decide what to do. He couldn't bear the thought of being touched by the two men; but he wanted more than anything to be held again between Isabelle's slim thighs, and to adore her female parts and her delicate arsehole.

The choice was to submit to Isabelle, or to spend the

morning assisting Master Robert. Barat took a step down the stairway. Isabelle smiled, and flexed her cane provocatively.

'Turn left,' she said, 'and you'll find a bathroom where you can wash off all that dust. Don't dry yourself; I'll have finished with Grant shortly, and I'd like to see him and Gustave drying you.'

'Come here, puppy!'

Jem took a deep breath, renewed for the hundredth time her vow to submit, and set off on her hands and knees across the wooden floor towards Max.

Every position she was obliged to adopt was uncomfortable. She was sure she would have had an attack of cramp by now, were it not for the fact that Max and Ilsa were so thorough in their training that they sped her through exercises that had her sitting, lying, crawling and jumping. Each exercise seemed designed to cause discomfort but gave a little relief from the one that had preceded it.

'Come to heel!' Max shouted as Jem approached.

She knew what she had to do. This was, after all, about the tenth time she had been called to heel. She was beginning to think that Max and Ilsa were trying to make her rebel simply by ordering her to do the same uncomfortable things over and over again. And Jem was not at all sure that they wouldn't succeed.

Jem positioned herself, still 'standing' on her hands and knees, next to Max's right leg. She remembered to rock her bottom from side to side.

'Good girl,' Max said, reaching down to ruffle her hair. He ran his hand along her back, adjusting her posture slightly so that her spine curved downwards a little more. He reached under her torso and ran his hands roughly over her pendant breasts. 'Good little puppy,' he exclaimed, slapping his hand upwards against Jem's breasts with each word. He stroked her back again. 'Good little puppy,' he repeated, this time stressing each word with a smack on Jem's wiggling bottom.

Jem had lost count of the number of slaps and

whip-strokes she had received. The trainers used their whips to guide Jem through the exercises, and to punish her for minor shortcomings in her performance; they administered hefty smacks as encouragement and reward for good behaviour; and, it seemed, they were also happy to deliver slaps and whip-flicks whenever they considered that Jem's raised bottom and displayed vulva were targets too tempting to resist.

As a result Jem's bottom felt as hot as a furnace, and very sore. She knew the skin of her buttocks must be criss-crossed with irregular stripes. Usually Jem could be persuaded to enjoy the sensitivity of a well-whipped backside; in fact, simply being bound ready for punishment, or held naked across someone's lap, was normally enough to ignite her arousal. After the first few spanks the stinging pain was subsumed into less specific feelings of warmth and well-being.

But being trained by Max and Ilsa was very different. There was no rhythm to the punishments they administered. Jem was given no time to touch herself, and when the trainers handled her breasts or her vulva they did so roughly, and without any attempt to excite.

However, the frequent slaps and lashes and the growing heat of her bottom were a constant reminder to Jem of the more pleasurable punishments she had received. In particular she remembered the many long, thorough sessions of mutual spanking and lovemaking she had enjoyed with her beloved Julia. But thinking of Julia only served to bring Jem back to reality, because Julia was here, watching her cavort and exhibit herself, watching her wag her bottom playfully as the trainers' whips and hands striped and reddened it.

Julia was here to watch Jem fail. And Jem knew that she would fail. She could find no pleasure in being trained as a puppy; it was hard, demeaning, uncomfortable work, and the trainers made sure that she understood that her education had only just begun. There would be hours more to endure. In fact, Jem suspected that they would continue until she could bear it no longer. Her stamina would be

eroded by continuous repetition of exercises; her will would
be softened by the whippings, and by the endless necessity
of appearing boisterously puppy-like. Eventually she would
fail; she would baulk at the instruction to perform some
degrading act, or she would simply lose the spirit to keep
wagging her tail and running around on her hands and
knees. However it were to come about, it was inevitable;
and it would be Julia who would have to report to the
Chatelaine that the Chatelaine had been right: Jem had
been incapable of submitting to the discipline of the
Chateau, and had no right to retain the leadership of the
Private House, an organisation dedicated to obedience. Jem
would be deemed fit only to be a slave, and she would be the
Chatelaine's plaything until the Chatelaine tired of her.

I might as well give up now, Jem thought. They'll have
me running around in this puppy costume until I can't
stand it any longer. They'll make me do more and more
disgusting things. They'll whip me harder and harder.
What's the point of putting myself through this ordeal any
longer? And of putting poor Julia through it, too. I should
stop now for her sake. It must be unbearable for her to see
me like this. Being the Chatelaine's personal slave won't be
insupportable. It can't be worse than this. I should simply
stand up now and announce that the Chatelaine has won
her wager.

'Walk to heel,' Max said, and strode away. Jem padded
after him, hurrying to keep pace with him and remain at
his side. 'Good girl,' he said, and flicked her bottom with
his whip. 'Now run and fetch.' He threw a ball across the
room; it bounced twice, and rolled towards a black
lacquered screen at the edge of the room.

Jem scampered away to retrieve the ball.

I'll put up with it a little longer, she told herself. Just in
case they stop soon, or at least start to let me enjoy myself.

But she knew that it was only the stubborn, contrary
streak in her character that prevented her from admitting
defeat. And the streak was wearing very thin.

Jem saw that the ball had rolled to a stop beside the
screen; she saw that Ilsa was approaching her and intended

to walk alongside her as she retrieved the ball. And then she saw a figure emerge from behind the screen and pick up the ball.

It was the Chatelaine's servant Nicole, as pert and darkly pretty as ever, dressed as usual in one of her delightfully revealing costumes that made her resemble a flirtatious maid. In one hand she held the ball; the other was extended behind the screen, and she seemed to be trying to pull someone out and into the room.

'Come along,' Jem heard Nicole say. 'Come and say hello to the little puppy. Give the puppy her ball.'

Jem watched as Olena allowed herself to be pulled from behind the screen. Olena was naked; she needed no costume or accessories to emphasise the lush desirability of her slim, curvaceous body and the innocent beauty of her wide face.

How many more people are being allowed to see me like this, Jem wondered. Her pace faltered as she remembered the night she had spent with Olena; the trust and care the young woman had devoted to her.

'Come along,' Ilsa said. She was beside Jem now, and encouraged her progress with a flick of her whip that caught Jem between the buttocks.

Jem yelped and looked up to see Olena's face, wide-eyed with shock and confusion. Jem looked away, and felt tears well in her eyes.

Nicole pressed the ball into Olena's hands. 'Give the ball to the puppy,' she said.

Olena leaned forwards as Jem approached, but Ilsa intervened.

'A well-trained puppy knows how to ask for her ball,' she said. 'Come on, puppy. Sit up and beg.'

I can't go through with this, Jem cried internally. But she stopped in front of Olena, adopted the sitting position, and then raised her hands so that they looked like the paws of a pleading puppy. She even remembered to start moving her bottom like a puppy wagging its tail.

'Good girl,' Ilsa said. 'Now beg properly. Get up on your hind legs. Beg!'

Jem rocked back on to the balls of her feet and lifted her knees from the floor. She was squatting now, with her legs wide apart and her forearms waving in the air in front of her face. She had never felt so humiliated and vulnerable.

Ilsa knew precisely how to accentuate those feelings. Jem felt the tip of Ilsa's whip touch the parted lips of her sex. 'Now be an eager little puppy,' Ilsa said. 'Bounce up to ask for the ball. That's right.'

The whip flicked upwards, stinging the delicate folds of skin. Jem lifted her body and flailed her hands; it was difficult to keep her balance.

'Isn't she a pretty little bitch?' Ilsa said, with a flick of her whip to Jem's anus.

Jem gasped each time the tip of the whip licked her sensitive skin. She felt her breasts bobbing in front of her. But, above all, she could not drive from her mind the realisation of how absurd she must look.

In her misery she glanced up at Olena's face – and stared in amazement at her young friend. Jem had expected to see in Olena's expression pity and contempt, and perhaps even disgust and horror. Instead she found Olena gazing down at her with eyes that sparkled with blatant desire.

'Take the ball now,' Ilsa said, and Jem stretched up to use her mouth to take the ball from Olena's hand.

Olena finds it exciting to see me like this, Jem thought. But that couldn't be right; Olena had no desire to control or punish others.

With a gasp, Jem understood. Olena was envious. She had watched Jem being trained, and she wanted to experience it for herself. Simply watching Jem as she was exercised and instructed and disciplined had aroused Olena, because she could imagine it was happening to her.

Olena looked down at Jem, holding the ball like a gag in her mouth. Olena smiled, and the smile broadened into a grin of sheer delight. She was happy: happy to watch a training regime that she knew she herself would enjoy, and happy for her friend Jem who had the good fortune to be enjoying it.

Jem saw the hand in which Olena had been holding the

ball move to rest on the young woman's hip; then it slid towards the triangle of dark curls and into the gap between the tops of her thighs.

'This is making me so wet,' she said. 'Nicole, I can't help it. I'll have to be punished soon, please. Make me beg like a puppy, and whip my secret places. Please.'

But as she said the words she was looking into Jem's eyes. Jem stared back. She remembered how even the slightest hint of shameful behaviour caused Olena to become aroused. She thought of all the eyes watching her – those of Julia and her guards, Max and Ilsa, Nicole and Olena – as she knelt with her striped bottom thrust out and wiggling, and with a rubber ball stretching open her mouth. She felt the hot throbbing of her sore buttocks. And she experienced, faintly but unmistakably, the warm tingle of arousal in her sex.

If it had not been for the ball in her mouth she would have laughed aloud with relief and joy.

Thank you, Olena, she thought; thank you for showing me the way. Now I know that I can withstand anything they do to me. In fact, the more they humiliate and punish me, the more I'll like it.

She wagged her tail excitedly and looked up at Ilsa, and over her shoulder at Max.

I bet they think they've trained some very submissive young puppies in their career, Jem thought; they've seen nothing yet.

'Would you like to stay and watch?' Ilsa said to Nicole and Olena.

'We'd like to,' Nicole replied, 'but Olena needs her discipline, and she hasn't had so much as a single smack today. And then I have to attend the Chatelaine. But please do tell us what you intend. The little puppy seems well trained. Is there much more for her to learn?'

'The puppy has learned all the basic positions. But as she's a young bitch, she needs to learn how to behave when she's on heat. We'll soon have her in rather more revealing positions. We'll teach her to use her paws to display her sexual organs. We'll teach her about pushing her nose into

259

people's crotches, and trying to lick them and so on, and rubbing her bottom against people's legs. Young bitches are quite disgustingly exhibitionist when they're on heat. And then, of course, we'll have to discipline her until she learns that she must not behave in such a disgusting manner unless we tell her to.'

'Yes,' said Max, who had joined the group at the edge of the room. 'Once we've seen how she behaves while she's on heat we'll probably have to tie her down and whip the affected area, between her hind legs. One flogging is usually enough, but this particular puppy is very wayward.'

'Then we move on to training her how to eat and drink daintily,' Ilsa said, 'from bowls on the floor. And she's not house-trained yet, of course. Once she's had her face rubbed a few times in her own piss, though, she'll probably learn.'

'Finally,' Max said, 'she'll be made to beg for her proper tail. You've probably noticed that at the moment she doesn't have one. The one we've designed for her has a double fixing, in that it penetrates both her anus and her vagina. Both prongs are very large, so we'll have to insert them carefully and slowly. But the tail is magnificent, so it will be worth the discomfort she'll feel while wearing it. And then we'll bathe her, whip her hindquarters soundly to remind her to be well behaved, and she'll be ready for display at the Chatelaine's dinner party. I understand the entire High Council is here. I expect they'll be delighted with the Chatelaine's well-trained new pet.'

Jem and Olena exchanged a long look of mutual understanding. Olena's hand had not moved from between her thighs while Max and Ilsa had explained Jem's training programme. Olena's face was flushed, and her luscious lips were half open. It was clear that she wanted more than anything to undergo the humiliations of puppy training.

While Jem listened to the activities that were in store for her she had been watching Olena's face. Max's and Ilsa's words conjured up a series of images that Jem would have found daunting had she not been able to imagine seeing them through Olena's eyes. Now she couldn't wait to act

260

as disgracefully as a young bitch on heat – and to be punished for it. Jem imagined Ilsa's whip flicking relentlessly into the soft flesh between her legs, and felt the trickle of juices inside her begin to seep from between her labia.

She was going to have fun.

Nothing seemed to have changed in the grand salon. The logs still blazed in the depths of the vast fireplace; the shuttered windows still admitted only thin shafts of pale light; the lamps still cast unsteady pools of yellow illumination. And the councillors were still there, ill at ease, standing in small groups with glasses in their hands or seated individually in chairs and on sofas, trying to concentrate on reading a book or simply staring into the flames of the fire.

The Chatelaine, resplendent in a tight-fitting gown of purple silk, was chatting to her guests, moving from group to group, flattering and charming them. Robert stood by the fireplace, his eyes darting expectantly to the main doors whenever he heard a sound.

The servants and slaves had little to do. The councillors were drinking abstemiously, and few called for their glasses to be refilled. A gathering of the High Council might usually be expected to provide a pretext for an orgy of licentiousness; on this occasion, however, few of the servants and slaves had been summoned to satisfy the councillors' whims. Here and there a naked body was to be seen kneeling in front of a seated male councillor, or half concealed under a female councillor's skirts; their movements were desultory, as if the councillors had simply forgotten to urge them on.

All this Nicole saw at a glance as she slipped through the gap between the tall doors. She beckoned Olena to follow her, and Olena, awed by the size of the salon and the number of richly dressed guests in it, crept nervously into the room.

'Take off your robe,' Nicole said.

Olena's hands hesitated on the fastenings. She glanced

261

from side to side, as if to make sure that no one was looking at her.

'Come, Olena,' Nicole said. She really didn't understand what had come over the girl. 'You know you must be naked except when walking in the corridors. Remove your robe at once. Don't you want to show all these fine people how well your bottom has been punished? I've quite worn out my arm with smacking you, and I wouldn't want all that effort to be wasted.'

Nicole watched, entranced, as a dark blush spread rapidly across Olena's face and a light began to burn deep in her mahogany eyes. It was enough merely to mention to her a spanking, or showing off her body, and Olena's lickerishness overwhelmed her natural modesty. She was as wanton as she was beautiful, and she was ashamed of both characteristics, for neither of which she could be held responsible. It had occurred to Nicole that it might be unfair – perhaps even cruel – to play on Olena's sense of her own sinfulness in order to encourage her to believe that she needed discipline. But Olena took such illicit, shameful pleasure in being punished that it seemed crueller to deny her.

Now Olena was naked, and although she and Nicole had taken only a few steps into the room she had already attracted the attention of several of the councillors, who turned in their chairs or broke off desultory conversations in order to look at her.

'Nicole!' The Chatelaine's crystal voice rang across the room. 'You have brought our dear guest. Bring her to me, and I will show her to my colleagues on the council.'

Nicole gave Olena a reassuring smile, took her hand, and led her towards the Chatelaine who was with a group in the centre of the room.

'She's perfectly lovely,' the Chatelaine was saying as Nicole approached. 'So young and slender, and yet so generously endowed with feminine charms. I believe she defies the laws of gravity!'

There was polite laughter, which died quickly as Nicole pulled Olena into the circle of councillors. Nicole felt strangely proud, as if Olena were her protégée. The councillors could see for themselves that the Chatelaine had not exaggerated.

'Her name is Olena,' the Chatelaine said. 'She is from an isolated community that observes strict laws and morals. She has an acute sense of sin, and since we started to plumb the depths of her desires it has become very clear that she is thoroughly steeped in wickedness. We have undertaken to provide the discipline that she so sorely lacks, but so far we find that we merely uncover further layers of wilful lewdness. Olena, my dear, have you been punished today?'

Olena's head had sunk lower and lower as the Chatelaine had described her sins. Now she blinked back a tear and bravely looked up at the Chatelaine.

'Yes, thank you, madame,' she said. 'Nicole used a cane and then her hand on my bottom. I asked her to cane my breasts, too, but she told me to wait until later.' She glanced resentfully at Nicole.

'She was quite right,' the Chatelaine said. 'You will appreciate your punishments more if they are administered separately. Perhaps my guests would like to see you being caned; some of them might like to participate. We'll see if there's time for that, later. Now let us see your bottom.'

Olena's blush deepened. She stifled a sob, and turned to face away from the councillors. Nicole, who was by now very familiar with Olena's reactions, guessed that Olena was distressed because the thought of showing off her sore bottom had caused a surge of lewd arousal. She went to stand in front of Olena.

'You've only just been punished,' Nicole said, stroking Olena's face, 'and you're already having wicked thoughts again, aren't you?'

Olena's eyes were full of tears, but Nicole thought she detected in them a mischievous glint, as if she were aware of the role she was supposed to play. 'I'm so bad,' Olena said. She smiled slyly. 'I don't think you punished me hard enough, Nicole.'

'Well, Olena,' Nicole said, 'you are in a room full of

disciplinarians. If we announce that you want a spanking I imagine it will be difficult to organise an orderly queue. Perhaps it would be better if we simply bring forward my caning of these.' She pressed her palms against Olena's perfect breast globes; she noticed that the nipples were already as hard as pebbles.

Olena smiled happily. 'I knew you'd see things my way,' she said. 'Please do it soon. I can hardly wait.'

'Lean forwards, please, Olena,' the Chatelaine said. Olena obeyed. Nicole moved to stand beside the Chatelaine, who was tracing with a fingertip the lines on Olena's buttocks. Nicole was pleased to note that her caning had left parallel, regularly spaced stripes; she knew the Chatelaine would approve.

'Good work, Nicole,' the Chatelaine said. 'I assume this is ten on each cheek horizontally, followed by ten vertically?'

'Yes, madame,' Nicole said. 'And then half a dozen more into the valley between. The marks aren't easy to differentiate, but I assure you they were hard enough.'

'Followed by a spanking,' the Chatelaine said. 'Very thorough.'

Several of the guests followed the Chatelaine's example and let their hands caress or pinch the reddened skin of Olena's bottom. Nicole noticed that Olena couldn't help squeezing her thighs together and squirming her hips.

'She is quite remarkable,' one of the councillors said. 'As you say, Chatelaine, she is young and slim and beautiful. And her arse is perfect: large, but high, round and resilient. Her skin is a lovely colour, and without blemish. And she has such a sweet nature. A eunuch would be tempted to spank her. She is irresistible.'

'You may spank her later,' the Chatelaine said. 'I still have to catechise her a little more. Tell me, Olena: while she was caning and spanking you, did Nicole touch you?'

Nicole heard Olena sigh. 'Yes, madame,' she said.

'Well, then,' the Chatelaine said, 'use your fingers to show us where Nicole touched you.'

Olena shuffled her feet apart and bent further forwards.

Nicole – and the Chatelaine and the councillors – could see the pendant, fleecy bulge of her sex, its split seam glistening with moisture. Olena's hand appeared, and cupped the bulge. Two fingers ventured to press against the seam, and seemed to draw back in surprise when they found the wetness and no barrier to entry. They slipped inside, and emerged slick with juice. The hand moved forwards slightly, and the fingers insinuated themselves into the seam at a higher point. Olena's hips started to writhe gently as her fingers moved.

'I see,' the Chatelaine said. 'Stop now, girl. Aren't you ashamed of yourself?'

Olena stood straight and turned round with her hand to her mouth. It was clear that she was very ashamed: her face was scarlet, and her eyes were bright. 'I'm sorry, madame,' she said. 'I just can't seem to help it. I'm so wicked. I need lots and lots of discipline.'

The Chatelaine seemed delighted with Olena's tearful confessions, but Nicole found that once again she was suspicious. There could be no doubting Olena's enthusiasm for punishment, or the physical evidence of her intense arousal when smacked or made to feel ashamed in almost any way. But Nicole had thought that the Chatelaine and Robert were exploiting Olena, for their own amusement and to increase the prestige of the Chateau; now she was beginning to suspect that Olena was the one in control of the game.

'And what happened when Nicole touched you there?' the Chatelaine said.

Olena opened her mouth to reply, but she, like everyone in the salon, had become aware that the quiet hubbub of voices in the room was being replaced by a silence. It was as though a plain white sheet was being drawn across a colourful canvas. Soon the silence had covered everything, and Nicole's eyes, like those of everyone in the salon, were drawn to the seven uniformed figures standing as still as statues in front of the fireplace.

The Chatelaine was the first to recover from the shock of seeing the guards. She stepped forwards to greet them, but remained sufficiently distant from the leader that she had to raise her voice to speak to her. Nicole knew that this was to be the Chatelaine's moment of triumph; she wanted everyone to hear.

'Julia,' the Chatelaine said, 'I assume you have come to make your report?'

The chief of the guards paused before replying. Nicole knew – everyone knew – that she and the former Supreme Mistress had been close friends. The announcement would be difficult to make.

'Yes,' Julia said, her voice strong but curt. 'The former Supreme Mistress has failed willingly to submit for five days to the disciplinary regime of the Chateau. She has conceded that she can no longer be the Supreme Mistress and that her fate shall be at the discretion of the Chatelaine. She has been removed to her cell in the dungeon of the Chateau.'

Julia took a deep breath. 'No doubt you would all like to know the point at which her resolve gave way,' she said, looking around at the councillors with undisguised disdain. 'She was being put through obedience training,' Julia said with a sneer in her voice. 'Obedience training for dogs.' There was a catch in her voice now; Nicole hoped she would stop before she broke down in tears.

Nicole glanced around at the councillors; several of them were looking away in embarrassment; a few had tears in their eyes.

'She took the house-training.' Julia ploughed on, her voice loud and angry. 'She took the pointless, repetitive, cruel whippings. But when she was required to beg for the insertion of a tail – a tail that would have been difficult for a horse to accommodate . . . Well, it's over now.'

Nicole heard a quiet voice beside her. It was Olena, who looked shocked and puzzled. 'No,' she was saying, over and over again. 'No, it's not possible. Jem wouldn't give up. Not Jem.'

Julia took three steps into the centre of the room. Her booted feet crashed on the wooden floor. 'As interim Mistress of the Private House,' she declared, 'I hereby accept the chair of this meeting of the High Council.'

266

'By whose authority?' a male voice queried. Nicole recognised Robert's voice.

'For goodness' sake,' Julia almost screamed at him in frustration. 'We will have to appoint a new Supreme Mistress or Master. That decision will need to be carefully made, after some time for thought and discussion. I'm sure you don't need reminding that there is no mechanism for appointing a new leader of the Private House. In the past the process has been, shall we say, unofficial. Therefore we need an interim leader – to chair this meeting, to set up the system for appointing a new leader, and to ensure the smooth running of the Private House until the new leader is in place. I'm the chief of the guards; it makes sense for me to be the interim leader. Do you want to dispute that, or would you rather be humiliated with a show of hands, which will indicate clearly that your fellow councillors are entirely happy with me?'

Robert emerged from the throng of councillors to stand in front of Julia. His face was red with indignation.

'I'm not suggesting that we should have a different interim leader,' he shouted. 'I'm saying that we don't need an interim leader at all.' He turned to face the crowded room. 'We are the High Council. We can be in session within seconds. We don't need an interim leader. We can choose our new Supreme Mistress today.'

'No, Robert,' Julia said. 'You're going too fast. We all know that there are precious few constitutional rules in the Private House, but one clear tenet is that in the temporary absence of the Supreme Master or Mistress the chief of the guards has the authority to govern. It is my duty to do so.'

Robert waved his arms in exasperation. 'That may be so,' he roared, 'but it's irrelevant. This is not a temporary absence. The former Supreme Mistress is now a slave in the dungeons of the Chateau. Permanently. We need a new leader now. I propose my mistress, the Chatelaine. Who will second her?'

As the salon was overwhelmed by a wave of shouts and urgent conversation, Nicole saw Julia standing in the centre of the room, alone and very still.

* * *

267

The councillors, gathered in hectic groups to debate the gravity of the situation, had forgotten about the slaves and servants. Even Olena, naked and displaying the stripes of her recent punishment, found that she was able to move from group to group without being noticed.

She was fascinated by the politicking. She could not understand how Jem could have failed to win the wager; it was, after all, Jem who had explained to her the pleasures to be found in accepting shame and punishment. And Jem had been entirely correct: since she had embraced her shame, and nurtured embarrassment and humiliation, Olena had started to enjoy her life – for the first time ever, it seemed.

None of the councillors, however, as far as Olena could tell as she overheard their urgent conversations, had any doubt that Jem was now no more than a slave of the Chateau. Nearly all of them spoke of her with affection; they regretted the passing of her rule. But, as they repeated again and again, as if to absolve each other of blame, the former Supreme Mistress had, after all, chosen to make the foolhardy wager with the Chatelaine, and her downfall was her own fault.

None of the councillors could understand why Julia refused to allow herself to be nominated as the new Supreme Mistress. They talked of little else, as she was the preferred candidate of – well, of all the councillors, as far as Olena could tell.

In the end, when Robert had managed to bring the discussions to a close and restore some order to the proceedings, it emerged that the Chatelaine was the only candidate: nominated by Robert and seconded by a councillor named Terence Headman, whom Olena gathered had once been the Supreme Master of the mysterious organisation known as the Private House.

'There is, then,' Robert announced, 'no need for a vote. I declare that the Chatelaine is the Supreme Mistress of the Private House.'

Robert paused, his hands aloft, as if expecting the room to ring with applause and cheers. Instead there was an awkward silence, broken at last by the Chatelaine's laughter.

'Well, Robert,' she said. 'It would seem that your enthusiasm has taken everyone by surprise. However –'

The Chatelaine stopped in mid-sentence; she had seen that the tall double doors were opening.

Olena's heart leaped. She stifled an inappropriate giggle. She had recognised instantly the figure standing in the doorway. The councillors, who must have been accustomed to seeing Jem Darke in her ornate guard's uniform, seemed unable to believe the evidence of their own eyes.

'Don't be too hasty,' drawled Jem.

Julia punched the air with her fist. 'I propose Jem,' she shouted in a snarling voice as the figure walked into the salon.

'Seconded!' The unison shout came from all corners of the room.

'It's too late!' Robert yelled, but his voice was drowned in the sea of excited shouts and questions.

It seemed to Olena that the shouting went on for hours. Why did they need to talk so much, she wondered; it was all so simple.

At last the nominations were approved. The Chatelaine was proposed by Robert and seconded by Headman; Jem was proposed by Julia and seconded by so many people that Julia was obliged to cut the list to three – a tall, thin man named Sebastian, a short, red-haired woman named Rhoda, and the Chatelaine.

The vote was a formality. The Chatelaine's candidacy received two votes – Robert's and Headman's. Everyone else, including the Chatelaine herself, voted for Jem.

After the cheering subsided, Robert was still shouting that the vote was invalid, and that the whore-slave had reneged on her agreement with his mistress. The Chatelaine walked over to him and slapped his face. 'Shut up, Robert,' she said. He looked at her in amazement, and burst into tears.

'Jem has submitted willingly to every single requirement that the Chateau has imposed on her,' Julia announced to the councillors. 'Including every element of the obedience training that I and my guards witnessed today. She has kept her side of the wager. And therefore the attempt to replace her as Supreme Mistress is without foundation.'

Olena heard these words with a smile. She had never believed that Jem could fail.

'I went through the charade of pretending that Jem had forfeited the leadership,' Julia continued, 'as I thought it would be interesting to discover which councillors would be prepared to rush to replace her. Would the Chatelaine please come forward.'

The Chatelaine stepped from the crowd. There was silence in the room as she made her way to stand before Jem. The two women stood face to face for a moment, and then the Chatelaine dropped to her knees.

'Mistress,' she said, 'I hope I can persuade you that my error was simply to want you too much. The prospect of making you my slave blinded me to the ambitions of my deputy. I can only pledge myself to you again, throw myself on your mercy, and offer to take the place in your House that I wanted for you here in my Chateau – take me as your slave.'

Olena heard a collective gasp from the councillors.

Jem reached out her hand to touch the Chatelaine's face. 'Now that's a very tempting proposition,' she said. 'And I would accept, but for the fact that there is no one who can run the Chateau with your energy and efficiency. Therefore you will be my slave only for one day each month; you will come to the main House and you will present yourself naked at my feet. I'll make sure that your visits are varied and entertaining, Chatelaine. And painful.'

'Thank you, Mistress,' the Chatelaine said. 'May I plead on behalf of my impetuous deputy, Robert? His crime was only that he loved me too much; his ambition was all for me, and not for himself.'

Jem helped the Chatelaine to her feet and kissed her. 'You may plead, Chatelaine,' she said, 'but to no effect. You are too forgiving. Both Robert and Terence are banished from the Private House.'

Another gasp came from every part of the salon. Olena

270

presumed that banishment was an unusual and severe punishment; as she considered it, she realised that the worst thing that could happen to her would be to have to abandon the company and discipline of these people, who understood her wickedness so well.

'The Chatelaine has recently acquired two visitors,' Jem went on. 'The man named Barat will be permitted to remain here. His training is to be at the Chatelaine's discretion. I owe a special debt to Olena, however, and I will take her with me to the main House. To the victor, the spoils,' she added, with a smile to the Chatelaine. 'I will also take with me, for a short time, the trainers Max and Ilsa. Not for myself, you understand; I have had enough of their brand of instruction. However, I think that Olena would make an excellent puppy, and I'll hand her over to Max and Ilsa for a week or so, as the next stage in what promises to be Olena's long and interesting education. Olena, are you happy with that?'

Jem searched for Olena in the crowd. Olena shyly raised her hand. She was too nervous to shout, but she nodded and smiled. Was she happy? She was overjoyed. She hoped that Jem would come to watch her being trained; she hoped that she could be a difficult, naughty puppy, so that Max and Ilsa would have to use their whips frequently.

'I have one final announcement,' Jem called out. 'I would not be surprised if some of you still had doubts about whether I was able to submit to the entirety of the obedience training course. I hope this dispels those doubts.'

She turned round and leaned forwards. The short, stiff skirt at the back of her tunic lifted into the air, to reveal her pert bottom, angrily red and marked with a myriad stripes. From between her buttocks sprouted a magnificent tail, its luxuriant fur matching exactly the red-brown of her hair.

She turned to acknowledge the applause of her councillors. 'Thank you,' she said. 'I thought it was so pretty that I'd keep it. It's held in place with two really big plugs, you know,' she added, with a mischievous smile.

* * *

271

'It's just as well that I was able to submit to that ridiculous puppy training business,' Jem said as she undid the last buckle of Julia's tunic and pulled it from her friend's body. 'There. That's better. Now I can play with your nipples. But perhaps I'd better chain your hands first. You do wriggle so.'

Jem stretched on the bed and watched Julia as she sauntered to the bondage cupboard. She had been back at the main House for only a day, and already the events at the Chateau seemed like a dream. She knew that her few days at the Chatelaine's mercy had changed her a little, however; she no longer felt languid and bored. Perhaps, she thought, she needed to submit to a severe regime of discipline every once in a while. She had certainly discovered a capacity for enjoying punishments and degradations that she had previously only suspected.

'Why?' Julia asked as she returned to Jem with an assortment of silver chains.

Jem sorted through the chains, and found what she was looking for: two lengths of chain, joined in their middles. She clipped two of the ends to the cuffs around Julia's wrists, and the other two to the cuffs at Julia's ankles. Then she pulled the central join up to the back of Julia's neck, and clipped it to Julia's collar. Now Julia could take only short steps, and could move her hands only a little way to the front of her body.

'Very pretty,' Jem said. 'Why what?'

'Why was it just as well that you managed to submit to all of the puppy training?' Julia said, sitting on the bed next to Jem and presenting her nipples to be played with.

'Because,' Jem said, rolling Julia's right nipple between her fingers, 'if I'd failed, obviously you wouldn't have been able to make your trick announcement. I mean, that worked only because I succeeded, and was able to make my triumphant entrance wearing the uniform you so far-sightedly brought for me.'

Julia stared at her friend in amazement, and then started to laugh.

'What's so funny?' Jem demanded, and pinched the nipple she was playing with.

272

'Ow!' Julia said. 'You are. You're so naive. Do you really think I would have left you to be a slave in the Chatelaine's dungeons? I'm surprised at your lack of trust. No, my dear; you were coming back with me, and as Supreme Mistress, whether you won or lost your wager with the Chatelaine.'

'Julia!' Jem exclaimed. She was genuinely shocked. 'That's dishonourable. It would have been cheating. I mean, I'm moved by your devotion, but –'

'Don't mention it,' Julia said. 'I just love you too much, that's all. I can't hug you in these chains. Come here and kiss me.'

They kissed for a long time. Julia, in chains, was helpless to prevent Jem pinching her nipples and then toying with the bar that pierced the hood of her clitoris.

'Stop it, darling,' she said. 'You'll make me come. And, anyway,' she added, 'I didn't need to cheat. It looked to me as though you were rather enjoying the things those trainers were doing to you. I didn't know you could be quite that submissive.'

'Neither did I,' Jem said, remembering the punishments she had endured and the acts she had been made to perform in the Chateau. 'But I'm glad I found out. However, I'm not feeling submissive today. So go and fetch me a cane. I imagine your bottom hasn't had a smacking for days. And I'm just in the mood to watch you wriggling in your chains while I turn your pretty bottom bright red.'

The Author's Afterword

I'm writing this in July 1999; It's almost exactly ten years since, as a part-time and very junior editor of what was then a small science fiction imprint, I took on the additional job of managing the Nexus line.

In those days Nexus books had twee covers, with tiny photographs of cheesecake models wearing Victorian dresses. The stories were genuine or pastiche erotica with Victorian, Edwardian or 'Jazz Age' settings: lots of dastardly gents and jolly romps.

One Week In The Private House was written, in part, to demonstrate a new direction for the imprint and to delineate the limits of what was permissible in modern erotica. I had also laid down comprehensive guidelines for prospective Nexus authors, and I wanted to know how easy – or otherwise – it would be to write a story according to those guidelines.

One Week went on to become the imprint's best-selling title of the 1990s, so I suppose I must have been thinking along the right lines.

During the past decade I and the remarkably talented staff who came to join me have launched Black Lace, the imprint for erotica written by and for women, whose success has eclipsed that of Nexus; Idol, homoerotic fiction for men; and, most recently, Sapphire, the imprint for lesbian erotica. Each imprint was the first of its kind in the UK, and strengthened the position of Nexus's parent company as the pre-eminent publisher of erotica.

So that's who Esme is. And as I'm no longer the Nexus

publisher, and as I'm proud of the Private House books, I'm happy for Esme to come out of the closet at last.

Whither the Private House?

The Private House is the rather amorphous setting for the three Nexus books I've written: *One Week*, *Amanda*, and this one, *Discipline*. It's also a state of mind that, given the number of copies of these books that have been sold, I presumably share with a reasonably numerous readership.

I'd like to enlarge and diversify the world of the Private House: more books; a website; illustrations; who knows what else? The problem is that I've written three books in ten years; at this rate I'll be in my dotage before there's a reasonable corpus of Private House merchandise.

Therefore I intend, first of all, to set up a Private House website. On it I hope to feature extracts from the books, and from works that have influenced me, and a gallery of photographs by the photographers whose pictures have illustrated the covers of the Private House books. The site would welcome links to and from other like-minded sites, as well as to the Nexus site. It could become a forum for erotic stories and their authors, and for fetish art and photography. It would, I hope, be the focus for creative people who want to participate in the Private House project, through writing, illustration, photography, or other media.

All this is very ambitious, and I've hardly even begun to think about how to go about doing it. However, I have at least set up a Private House e-mail address and so, if you would like to comment on the Private House or, even better, if you can contribute in any way – with website advice, or stories, or links, or marketing ideas – to the Private House project, please write to me at:

esmeo@postmaster.co.uk

I hope you have enjoyed this book; I enjoyed writing it, and I feel privileged to have been at least partly responsible for making Nexus and its sibling imprints the best in British erotica.

NEXUS NEW BOOKS

To be published in August

SATAN'S SLUT
Aishling Morgan

Aishling Morgan returns to the sleepy, mysterious environment of seaside Devon, explored in *Deep Blue*. Someone has been performing the Black Mass in an old, abandoned chapel at Stanton Rocks. The local priest, Tom Pridough, is convinced it was Nich Mordaunt, local high-profile pagan, and his friend, the stunning brunette Juliana. Tired of the churchman's confusion of diabolism with his own nature-worship, Nich too sets out to find out who is responsible, and all three become embroiled in a weird and perverse world of sex-magick beyond their darkest imagination.

ISBN 0 352 33720 6

BARE BEHIND
Penny Birch

Penny Birch is currently the filthiest little minx on the Nexus list, with thirteen titles already published by Nexus. All are equally full of messy, kinky fun and, frankly, no other erotic writer has ever captured the internal thrills afforded by the perverse and shameful humiliations her characters undergo! In *Bare Behind*, Penny discovers that a friend of her family, also on the fetish scene, may know more about her private passions than is good! In the search for him, she encounters the pop band Madman Klien, and she must submit to their most perverse desires if she is to find her quarry!

ISBN 0 352 33721 4

MEMOIRS OF A CORNISH GOVERNESS
Yolanda Celbridge

Accepting a position as Governess in the household of the eccentric, port-loving Lord and Lady Whimble, the young and ripely formed Miss Constance soon finds her niche giving special lessons to the local gentlemen, including the vicar! Administering unique attention to their unusual requests, she performs her duties with glee. Employing all manner of Victorian instruments of correction, not least Mr Izzard's box of hygienic but curious bathroom accessories, Constance is destined to have a very rewarding career. A Nexus Classic.

ISBN 0 352 33722 2

To be published in September

BELLE SUBMISSION
Yolanda Celbridge

Domineering Trina Guelph is intrigued at her new corporate mission – to run the quaint Louisiana island of New Arras, a female academy with a code of flagellant eighteenth-century French discipline, to train submissive, sultry southern belles. She suffers serial misunderstandings as she is imprisoned as a spy, then the subject of court intrigues and battles for domination, waged with the lash and the tawse. Throughout her ordeal, Trina quivers under strict discipline until she accepts her true nature, as a submissive belle. As long as Trina is around, the dominant men of the South are sure to rise again and again.

ISBN 0 352 33728 1

NEW EROTICA 6
Various

The sixth volume of the very best of erotic writing from Nexus. *New Erotica 6* is a selection of ten of the horniest and most bizarre scenes from Nexus novels published over the last two years. Also included are two brand new, previously unpublished stories from Penny Birch and Aishling Morgan. All in all, that's twelve reasons why Nexus remains the market leader in fetish fiction.

ISBN 0 352 337 51 6

THE GOVERNESS AT ST AGATHA'S
Yolanda Celbridge

Having taken up residence as the principal of St Agatha's Academy for Young Ladies, the elegant and perverse Miss Constance de Comynge is determined to make her establishment the envy of all others. The most beautiful and lascivious of her students join the select 'swish' club where they learn the art of administering and receiving a variety of invigorating punishments. Their passion for discipline soon finds favour with a number of gentlemen in the locale. A Nexus Classic.

ISBN 0 352 33729 X

If you would like more information about Nexus titles, please visit our website at www.nexus-books.co.uk, or send a stamped addressed envelope to:

Nexus, Thames Wharf Studios,
Rainville Road, London W6 9HA

NEXUS BACKLIST

This information is correct at time of printing. For up-to-date information, please visit our website at www.nexus-books.co.uk

All books are priced at £5.99 unless another price is given.

Nexus books with a contemporary setting

Period

CONFESSION OF AN ENGLISH SLAVE	Yolanda Celbridge ISBN 0 352 33433 9	☐
THE MASTER OF CASTLELEIGH	Jacqueline Bellevois ISBN 0 352 32644 7	☐
PURITY	Aishling Morgan ISBN 0 352 33510 6	☐

Samplers and collections

NEW EROTICA 3	Various ISBN 0 352 33142 9	☐
NEW EROTICA 5	Various ISBN 0 352 33540 8	☐
EROTICON 1	Various ISBN 0 352 33593 9	☐
EROTICON 2	Various ISBN 0 352 33594 7	☐
EROTICON 3	Various ISBN 0 352 33597 1	☐
EROTICON 4	Various ISBN 0 352 33602 1	☐
THE NEXUS LETTERS	Various ISBN 0 352 33621 8	☐

Nexus Classics

A new imprint dedicated to putting the finest works of erotic fiction back in print.

AGONY AUNT	G.C. Scott ISBN 0 352 33353 7	☐
BAD PENNY	Penny Birch ISBN 0 352 33661 7	☐
BRAT £6.99	Penny Birch ISBN 0 352 33674 9	☐
DARK DELIGHTS £6.99	Maria del Rey ISBN 0 352 33667 6	☐
DARK DESIRES	Maria del Rey ISBN 0 352 33648 X	☐
DIFFERENT STROKES	Sarah Veitch ISBN 0 352 33531 9	☐

------ ✂ --------------------------------

Please send me the books I have ticked above.

Name   ....

Address   ....

            ....

            ....

            .... Post code....................

Send to: **Cash Sales, Nexus Books, Thames Wharf Studios, Rainville Road, London W6 9HA**

US customers: for prices and details of how to order books for delivery by mail, call 1-800-343-4499.

Please enclose a cheque or postal order, made payable to **Nexus Books Ltd**, to the value of the books you have ordered plus postage and packing costs as follows:

UK and BFPO – £1.00 for the first book, 50p for each subsequent book.

Overseas (including Republic of Ireland) – £2.00 for the first book, £1.00 for each subsequent book.

If you would prefer to pay by VISA, ACCESS/MASTERCARD, AMEX, DINERS CLUB or SWITCH, please write your card number and expiry date here:

....

Please allow up to 28 days for delivery.

Signature ....

Our privacy policy.

We will not disclose information you supply us to any other parties. We will not disclose any information which identifies you personally to any person without your express consent.

From time to time we may send out information about Nexus books and special offers. Please tick here if you do *not* wish to receive Nexus information.   ☐

------ ✂ --------------------------------